MW01118746

Sons of the Rumour

By the same author

Novels

The Pure Land
The Empathy Experiment (with D. K. Lyall)
Moonlite
Plumbum
The Adventures of Christian Rosy Cross
Dog Rock: A Postal Pastoral
Testostero
The Pale Blue Crochet Coathanger Cover: Dog Rock 2
Mates of Mars
The Glade Within the Grove
In the New Country
The Land Where Stories End

Sons of the Rumour

DAVID FOSTER

PICADOR
Pan Macmillan Australia

This project has been assisted by the Australian Government through the Australia Council, its arts funding and advisory body.

First published 2009 in Picador by Pan Macmillan Australia Pty Limited
1 Market Street, Sydney

National Library of Australia Cataloguing-in-Publication data:

Foster, David
Sons of the rumour/David Foster

ISBN 978 1 4050 3958 1 (hbk.)

Image of the Jinni from Richard Burton's *Alf Laylah Wa Laylah* (1885), artist unknown, courtesy National Library of Australia
Calligraphy by Lexie Arlington
Typeset in 12/17 Adobe Jensen Pro by Midland Typesetters, Australia
Printed in Australia by McPherson's Printing Group

Papers used by Pan Macmillan Australia Pty Ltd are natural, recyclable products made from wood grown in sustainable forests. The manufacturing processes conform to the environmental regulations of the country of origin.

CONTENTS

For Gerda

Uxor tanto virtuosa quanto bella

Nature always goes too far

Turba Philosophorum

Drive Nature out with a pitchfork, always she comes back in

Horace

The human soul has a tendency to divest itself of its nature in order to assume the nature of the angels and to become an angel, in reality, but for a moment. This moment comes and goes in the time it takes a human eye to blink. The soul then resumes human form, having received in the world of the angels a message it must transmit.

Ibn Khaldun of Tunis

Why, all the Saints and Sages who discuss'd
Of the Two Worlds so wisely – they are thrust
Like foolish Prophets forth; their Words to Scorn
Are scatter'd, and their Mouths are stopt with Dust

'Umar-i-Khayyam of Khurasan / Edward Fitzgerald of Suffolk

Arabian Nights

And so on the seven-hundred-and-eighty-sixth night, Shahrazad resumed her *Tale of Abu Niyyatayn and Abu Niyyah*, and the Shah, staring at the carpet, listened as she picked up the tale precisely where, the night before, she had broken off . . .

'And so Abu Niyyatayn left Abu Niyyah to die in that well, and when night fell, two Jinn came down to the well to converse the one with the other, and Abu Niyyah, from where he sat forlornly at the bottom of the well, overheard them. And the first Jinni said, "What is to do with thee, O my brother, and how is thy case at present?" and his fellow replied, "By Allah, my brother, to be sure I am well satisfied for that I never leave the Sultan's daughter at all." And the first Jinni asked, "And what would forbid thee from her?" and the second answered, "I should be driven away by somewhat of wormwood powder scattered beneath the soles of her feet during the congregational prayers of Friday." Then said the other, "I also, by Allah, am joyful at present in the possession of a Hoard of jewels buried without the town near the Azure Column which serveth the town as bench-mark." "And what," asked the other to his friend, "would expel thee therefrom and expose these jewels to the gaze of man?" Whereto the second answered, "A white cock in his tenth month slaughtered upon the Azure Column would surely drive me from that Hoard and break the Talisman whereby the gems would become visible.'"

☾

And so we who listen to the *Hakawati* as we sip a coffee and smoke a *Narghile*; do we want Abu Niyyah to perish? Are we patiently awaiting his emergence? Why will this victim of injustice not stride from the wellhead, as we might, intent upon revenge? And given that we may expect further misadventure to befall a solitary traveller – escapades that will so exhaust him he may scarcely recall what has happened here tonight – shall we not observe the *Hakawati* observe Shahrazad observe Abu Niyyah observe an oasis that contains a mansion in which Abu Niyyatayn is bound to be found, living it up, and rumoured to be ruled by a Sultan in utter despair at the conduct of his daughter? And do you not see how that Azure Column that arises from the dust by the roadside is gleaming like a needle of gold as it captures the last light of the setting sun?

Iranian Days

And so on the thirty-second night, Shahrazad resumed her *Tale of How Abu Hasan Brake Wind,* and the Shah is not staring at the carpet tonight. Bemused that she might think his attentions captivated by her wearisome tales, he seldom listens to Shahrazad, instead revering her cumbrous breasts. Belly imperceptibly swelling as a foetus suckles on an overdue mense, Shahrazad speaks from a winding sheet draped upon a Martabah and brown with congealed blood, through her hands and her lips, non-stop, cross-legged, bare-breasted, by the light of a huge waxen taper, while Dinazad, scarcely more than a child, sprawls fully clothed upon a crimson Kelim, twirling a filigreed frontlet studded with carnelian and dripping in silver bells as she absorbs her sister's narrative.

In the course of his ordeal – the result of a dereliction by a Sufi – the Shah finds that should he weary of counting the veins in Shahrazad's breasts – the massivest yet seen in the realm of Samanid

Khurasan and, through congenital malformation, boasting an aureole around each nipple so vast as to encompass half the entire breast, producing two hemispheres of mucous membrane that a Jinni could not cover with his outstretched palms nor grasp in his vulture's talons; and the white skin over the firm residual meat so pale as to be translucent, exhibiting therein a plexus of vessels never before witnessed, no, not twice among the one thousand one hundred virgins the Shah has heretofore betrothed, all as they were newsreaders or full moons a-rising – Khazars, Nubians, Tibetans, Oghuz, Alans, Franks, Huns – and having deflowered next morning beheaded, each wrapped in her maidenhead stain – then his eyes may happen upon Dinazad, whom he regards with paternal complacency, observing with a smile her sidelong glancing, the anticipatory sparkle in her almond eyes that presage her attempt to restrain her embarrassed mirth at yet another fart joke from Shahrazad.

Donkeys bray; false dawn, the wolf's tail, Dum-i-Gurg, the first brush of light – Alhamdolillah! Shahrban al-Mutliq, Shahrban the Divorcer, marzban of metropolitan Merv, may now take leave of his Wazir's daughters to prepare for the dawn prayer. He enters the water closet with a ewer, does there his need and, having emitted no semen since last Friday's bath nor had his blood cupped, he takes clean water, pours it over his hands and washes his hands twice, then rinses his mouth and sniffs water into his nose thrice, then washes his face thrice, then washes his arms up to the elbows twice, then wipes his head with both of his hands, from the forehead to the neck, and also his two ears, the internal parts with his two forefingers, the back parts with his two thumbs, then washes his two feet, in full Wuzu-ablution, beginning as always from the right side but not before Shahrazad assures him, with a grin, that his torture must resume upon the sunset.

'Don't you find farts funny?' she complains as he leaves. 'Gee, all the others did.'

Leaving the palace as buzzards begin to alight on the marble balustrade, the Shah pauses before the brilliant latticework of the ornamental brick. From the wall of an empty Zenana depends, in a basket, the skull of the wife of his youth surprised – in flagrante delicto – with a slobbering blackamoor. The fleshed head originally held the blackamoor's member in its teeth but the boneless member has rotted to leave the skull jaws agape. Underpassing, the Shah salutes.

'Don't choke up there,' he cautions.

Shortly thereafter, modestly dressed and after a cheerful cup of wine – Sahba, the red wine preferred throughout Iran for the morning draught – and supplicating the veiling of the Veiler, the Shah leaves the garden using a postern opening on a lane behind an illegal offal souk. Assailed by the stench and the heat, though diverted by the clamour and colourful spectacle, he recalls what he must presently recite; the last observation conveyed him by a Son of the Rumour the previous day.

It was, in fact, an ejaculation, for in fury the old man had shouted, 'And do you suppose that we Sons of the Rumour cannot authenticate our Rumour? Among us are many enlightened saints who can aver that Happiness *is* possible. Regrettably, most of us, less advanced, merely *pursue* such Happiness, and the saint will always feel obliged to set aside his own bliss in order to assist a fellow like yourself, merely intent upon becoming Happy.

'The result is that Happiness cannot prevail here till no one pursues it. And while Rumour remains more powerful than Truth, we are Sons of the Rumour.'

☾

Having completed Salat as-Subh, the first of his five daily prayers, the Shah walks on, a parasang and more. Leaving the ark, ancient fortified citadel, through the mud rampart, he enters the Shahristan, walled city, beyond whose walls extends the suburb, or Rabad, to the west. He passes the observatory where by night an astrolabe moves over a marble quadrant in search of unknown stars. He passes the Greek gymnasium. He passes the Christian cathedral. He passes the former residence of al-Ma'mun, Caliph of al-Musawwida, the Wearers of Black Raiments. Further and further he walks. He enters the Rabad, home to bazaars and caravanserais. He passes the western silk-mart, a Bazistan the vaulted lanes of which are closed by night with heavy doors. He passes the Bimaristan, a private hospital for Jinn-mad lunatics. He passes the perfumers' bazaar. He enters an alley. To his left an unbroken wall constitutes a housing tenement. He counts the doors in the wall as he passes – twenty-five, thirty-four, sixty-six and counting. Some are open, revealing women stirring pots and geese disturbing dirt. A bare-bummed brat, squatting, throws a stone at the Shah who, smiling, returns it.

The sun now strikes the alley and the Shah turns past a woman selling pigeon poults towards a particular door; alerted, perhaps, by the creaking of the brass hinge, stirring, yawning, brewing up the tea, drifting to and from the privy and its neighbouring ablution-bath, murmuring in Dari – Sons of the Rumour, al-Mubayyida, the Wearers of White Raiments, men in white tunics and Phrygian caps who, on the evidence thus far, know two questions: 'Are you Happy?' and 'Would you like to be?'

As if a king can be happy, whose wife betrayed him with a blackamoor! While simultaneously, within her view, ten concubines betrayed him with ten mamalik.

The Shah approaches the Shaykh hand on heart then straightens and exchanges a handslap, palm to palm.

Sons of the Rumour

'Tea, Comrade?' The first to address the Shah is ever the Pir, the Shaykh – 'Ali Zindiq Ibn al-Waqt 'Abd al-Kimiya.

'Don't seem very 'appy this mornin', mate,' says the Pir. 'Feelin' a bit weary on it?'

'Always.'

'Wanta try workin' for a livin'. Hey, could you refresh our memories, buddy?'

The Shah, a diminutive man in his early forties, rubs his kohl-daubed eyes. He rubs them with his beard which is somewhat longer than can be grasped in his fist. There are times, at this hour of day, when he doesn't understand why he subjects himself to this, but thirty-two days back the knife in beheading a wife had chipped on a cervical bone and the Shah, in the mood that day for a stroll, was sent by the Wazir to see a swordsmith and the swordsmith happened to be a Sufi who sleeps in this very Khangah to which the Shah returns daily as he finds it keeps his mind off a certain pair of boobs.

'Happiness. We spoke, as always, of happiness and the pursuit of happiness. We spoke of what we always speak of; how no one person can possibly retain it, though all, despite themselves, pursue it; and many here have known it, if only briefly, given the state of the world.'

'Attaboy and on you be The Peace. Kurban-at basham – may I be your sacrifice, O Shadow of Allah? Have you topped that blonde, Shahrban?'

'Not as yet. I'm waiting on a certain person here present to sharpen a certain knife until it can cut bones before flesh. I want that blade as sharp as Samsam, sword of the Himyarite Tobba, Amru bin Ma'ad Kurb.'

'Sorry, Cob, see, it needs a reinforce? Wants another ferrule on the handle. And I'm still awaiting that steel from the crucible I ordered be tempered by plunging it into a slave. I will then anoint it with an egromantic unguent that it may not rust until the Day of Resurrection.'

'I think we'll move on,' says the Pir. 'I think we've wasted enough time on Happiness. Let's just pretend we're all Happy and see how we feel towards those who aren't. Allah save and favour the king! Praised be Allah, to Whom belong Might and Majesty, Who raised us into existence from non-existence and Who favours His servants with kings that observe equity and justice in that wherewith He has invested them of rule and dominion, and who act righteously with that which He appoints at their hands of provision for their lieges; and most especially, our sovereign Shahrban through whom He has quickened the deadness of our oasis with that which He has conferred upon us of bounties, and has blessed us of His protection with ease of life and tranquillity and fair dealing.'

At this, a man with a silver artificial nose, badge of an escaped Chinese toll-barrier guard, exclaims, 'Kurban-at basham – may I be your sacrifice, O Shadow of Allah? I could speak of Mercy, indeed, I've a tale to tell anent ... *The Fire Lamb*.'

The Fire Lamb

Like every Son of the Rumour I was born restless, full of discontent. Some contend all nomads are born like this but, if so, we are dissuaded from it young. The nomad, of all men, must learn to conserve strength. He can afford to waste nothing.

As a child, I recall discovering my parents were not as I had wished them. This, I suppose, is a common finding, but mine were Sand People – desert-wandering shepherds. Is this my mother, I asked myself, this moon-faced creature missing her front teeth? And this old man, with his forked beard and hooked nose; can he be really my father? Am I some day to smell like *that*? Isn't he hot, in his cope and trowsers, goatskin boots and sheepskin cap? And that little troop of bare-bummed brats with the salt lake under each nostril; is it true they're as like to me as a pebble of dung to a pebble of dung? If so, I need to *escape*.

At first I didn't know *how*. Then one day father presented me a tortoise that slept for ten months of the year. Each spring, when the tulips flowered, he would wake, eat, drink, mate, relieve himself, then return to sleep.

'Study this creature,' my father advised, 'that you may be rightly guided.'

I kept the tortoise, warm as a prayer and dry as a curse, in a sandbag I had fashioned from the skin of a giant monitor lizard, the kind who would crunch a tortoise as you or I might a sunflower seed. Once in a while I removed him, dusted off the sand and sniffed beneath his carapace to ensure he was still alive. One autumn he woke for a whole week and wandered around the yurt at pace; but as a rule he was no trouble, an excellent companion.

One dusk, as I sat in a shittim tree watching a fox and a jackal fighting over a long-toed marmot, I heard a scream from my youngest brother who'd not long been parted from his catheter and swaddle. I ran down to the camel-thorn stockade where I found him by a gate, clutching a newborn karakul to his breast.

Father, concealing a knife behind his back, was down on one knee. 'Lambs must die,' he said, 'at fourteen days of age – no more – in order we procure these pelts that earn you frankincense.'

Unpersuaded, my brother, convulsively sobbing, would not let go the lamb.

'Hand him over!' ordered Father. 'It won't hurt if I cut his throat. Hand him over, there's a good lad, and I'll do it quick as I can. Happen you see the legs twitchin' a bit, it won't mean he's not dead.'

My brother thrust out his little chin, compressed mouth down-turned at the edges like that on a coarse woman reminded of a man's fundament.

Father reacted as though his own throat had been cut. His shoulders slumped under his red cope. He took off his hat and shook his head. Then he turned on me. 'Why are you here at *all?*' he said.

Being eldest I felt, with pride, I understood that face, but never had I seen it quite so pale.

He looked down at his hands. He stared down at his knife. He scrutinised the blade. Then he rose, hurled the knife into the sky and roared, 'Ulcers to your Soul!'

He cursed himself. He cursed his mother, he cursed his father, he cursed his brothers. He cursed Iskander Rumi, Lord of the Two Horns. He cursed the Prophet Luqman who could dig a well with his nails. He cursed me, he cursed my mother, he cursed the camels, he cursed the kufans, he cursed the gazelles. He cursed the gepards. He cursed the goats. He spat at the sheep. He cursed the sand, he cursed the wells. He cursed the moon. He cursed the Iron Peg, a star the name of which he knew. Then, having paused to collect his breath and his knife, he walked to a grove of black saxaul trees, cursed them, fell among their leafless branches and covered himself in sand.

'And are you pleased you've upset Father?' I asked my brother who was sucking his thumb while clutching the doomed lamb in his free arm. He removed from his mouth this only clean digit he possessed and jerked it towards me.

The whole wretched scene made me sorry I'd been born. I returned to the yurt, took my tortoise from his sack and held him to my breast. We drifted off to sleep together.

Father was crouching over me shaking me awake. Looking about, I saw I was lying on grass in a grove of pistachio.

'Time to make felt,' said Father. 'Put the tortoise back in his sack.'

We made our felt in autumn. It seemed I had slept all summer and yet I felt still so weary. One of our auburn camels had a swag between her humps and pointing at it, Father said, 'That's where you've been sleeping.'

The mother felt lay all prepared under the layers of wool. A troop of boys, some unfamiliar to me, was fetching water. We had twenty thousand wells, all fed from the Oxus, to maintain. When the boys stood over the felt they emptied their vessels on it.

'New brothers,' explained Father. 'I had to marry uncle's wife. He fell off that wall-eyed mule while you were asleep. Now we need a new yurt.'

We dragged the sodden daughter felt between two camels to mature. It wasn't just for yurts; we sat on felt, we slept in felt, we rode on felt, we dressed in it. We made our felt of adult wool; fleece from newborn Persian lambs was sold for frankincense. Father had an avidity for frankincense.

'Tell us what you dreamed,' he said, wrapping the mother felt in hide. 'That's what I've been longing to hear all this time you've slept.' He fastened the straps about the hide and hooked the felt to a rope. A gepard, our local cheetah, ran by, chasing a goitered gazelle.

'Naked women,' I told him, 'in a red room, prancing in a circle – blondes.'

'To think that's the best you could come up with.'

'Wait! You haven't heard what comes next.'

'I don't want to hear what comes next as I suspect I know. Furthermore, I know what comes next after that – strife and servitude! How you disappoint! I'd hoped you might have something of the *prophet* in you. Here, grab hold of this rope and get on that camel and do a bit of *work*.'

That day and after we'd made our felt and cut wood for a new yurt frame, we had a bit of wood left over, so made a fire and stared at it. I asked Father what had become of uncle's wall-eyed mule.

'Thinkin' of runnin' to town to chase them blondes?' he said. 'Forget it. You'll marry a girl of my choosing, a houri with a bindi and bound to be a blackhead. Can you imagine you owe me a *thing*? Where would you be without me?'

'Unborn?'

'*Dead* more like, which is pretty much the same. See, by rights, I should have killed you. Should have drowned you at birth. Should have sprinkled your blood on an altar, fourteen days, no more. Cut your throat, then burned your rump, kidneys, and the caul above your liver as a Sweet Savour unto the Lord of this Flame, which is our nomad way. Eases the conscience and justifies the murders. Those who open their mother's matrix are meant for a mercy seat, ah well – that's why things have not gone smoothly here and never could.'

He muttered a prayer at the flames.

I took the tortoise out of his sack and went back to sleep on the pile of fresh felt.

Next thing I knew, it was winter and I awoke shivering. There above me stood Father, this time shouting in joy.

'Absolution!' he cried. 'Wake up! Bestir yourself and follow me.'

I put the tortoise back in his sack and ran through the snow to the lambing hut. All my brothers and mothers were there and in a corner, on hay, lay a lamb, still wet, with a skin that *glowed*. The frightened ewe, attempting to escape, refused to look at this lamb while Father, shouting and lifting the air with a fist, held her by his knees.

'First born, too!' he roared. 'Well done! The fire lamb opened the matrix.'

We'd heard tell of fire lambs though only old men had seen one; Father's father once met a man who'd seen one in these very Black Sands.

After a bit, the glow faded and someone went to fetch a lamp and in the light of the lamp we could see that the lamb, whose mother was black, was golden-haired.

'Fetch me the knife,' said Father to me with a wink. 'This fleece is worth a fortune, Prophet. We can't have it getting dirty.'

But when I returned with the knife he slashed up his face with the blade, Uighur-style.

'Ah, that's better,' he said. 'Now, fetch me a black sheep, Prophet, I've had a change of heart. While you're about it, fetch *all* the black sheep. We'll murder them, every last one.'

All our sheep being black, the women muttered in disapproval. What were we to live on? A fight broke out, with various brothers contending in various factions. Part of the stockade fence fell down and the sheep ran out among the wolves. Father chased after them, clutching his ewe and fire lamb, knife between teeth. The camels began breaking hobbles.

I took my tortoise and returned to sleep.

Spring. We woke in the same instant. The wall-eyed mule stood nearby grazing tulip, hyacinth and iris. While my little pal went off to eat, drink, mate and relieve himself, I explored the camp, of which now only the lambing hut remained and in that hut, stroking his golden fleece, I found my father. But the fleece was still attached to the lamb and the lamb had grown quite friendly.

'Ah,' said Father, 'you'd be hungry. Care for some ... well, there's nothing much to eat.'

'Where are the others?'

'Wouldn't know and wouldn't care. Took the frankincense and stock. Took the rice and watermelons. Watch that mule, he's wall-eyed. On reflection, the only things stupider than sheep are the people who keep them. Mind you, this fire lamb can *speak*. He has been moved to prophesy. The fire lamb I give to you as well as the wall-eyed mule.'

'But I can't leave you here alone!'

'Why not? All you ever do is sleep! Mind you, if you could tell me what frankincense is and where it hails from, then I should be most warmly obliged, but if not, I can live without. I'm actually feeling quite close to Ahuramazda so it's best I keep myself to myself as nothing could be more easy than to persuade a holy man he's mad. I've done it myself. Off you go, convert the world with this fleece. I'll look after the tortoise.'

'But what's the use of this fleece,' I said, 'when the lamb it's attached to is still alive?'

'The same use as a prayer,' he replied, 'when the god it's addressed to has yet to appear.'

Iranian Days (continued)

The Desert-born Son of the Rumour takes grain from a trowser pocket and clucks, whereupon an ancient wether the Shah had not noticed struggles to its feet. This wether boasts a golden fleece or, more precisely, what has been one.

'Sons of the Rumour would never consider adjuring God's Mercy,' says the Turkmen. 'God must smile at our prayers when His Greatest Medicine lies in His Poisonous Dragon. Seeking only to assist in His work I had no way to convert the world. Nor has this lamb ever spoken to me, so my prayer, originally the Nazarene's prayer – "Thy will be done on earth as it is in Heaven" – has become the word "Islam", which means, in Tajik, "I surrender to God's will."'

'And how would you know God's will,' says the Shah, 'if, as the Nazarene taught, His will is not here to be seen?'

'Because it is realisable. Because through His Mercy I visited Paradise and while there was given to understand that in this Work we have need of two things: Heat and Timing. Off you go now, back to your griddle.'

But first, a spiritual exercise, a Wird – Duty and Repetition.

The Pir sits calmly on a stool counting off rosary beads as the imam cantilates from al-Qu'ran – shouting in a hoarse field holla would send shivers up your spine – while the brothers, now wearing white skullcaps and kneeling on prayer mats close-ranked, work themselves into ecstatic trance by rhythmically jerking side to side as they recite, antiphonally, 'a-la bi-dhikri-'Llahi tatma 'innu-l-qulub!' They are accompanied by three drummers striking at three big Dervish drums of tinned copper with parchment faces.

Sons of the Rumour got a beat goin' down.

Shortly thereafter the Shah falls asleep and Glory be to He who sleepeth not! His head rests on the withers of the wether. He wakens to the bells of a caravan making ready to depart Merv. It could be heading north towards Khwarazm, Urganj and the Volga Delta, or west towards Baghdad via Nishapur and the Caspian Gates, or south-east across the Black Sands to Balkh then down into the Sindh, or north-east to Numijkat and by the Warm Lake onto Bilad-al-Turk, or east to the Realm of the Celestials or south to the pines of Herat. The contents of the saddlebags, textiles in the main – Merv being the centre of the textile trade – could be headed almost anywhere but typically, Sur or Ma'rib. The Shah is alone, his colleagues having gone off to their work as road-builders and elephant-keepers, while the door to their Khangah, or cloister, swings idly in the desert wind.

The wether, pulsating with every breath, sleeps.

Outside, the sun is gone from the alley. Soon it will be dark again. The Shah feels his member masculine stiffen as he foolishly envisages

Shahrazad's boobs whereupon the spittle runs from his mouth to moisten his moustachios – so he backtracks, fast as he is able, to the palace, terrified at what she might be getting up to in his absence and puzzled by a dream he just had in which he foresaw the sack of Merv.

Before he retires to his bedchamber to spend a thirty-third night with Shahrazad – and Dinazad, because Shahrazad cannot bear to be parted from her sister – the Shah must confer with their father, Abu Bakr, his Grand Wazir. The responsibility of a Padishah's Wazir is to know everything. Should action be needed on some matter it would not be undertaken by the Shah – a responsibility of whom is to appear so composed as to spurn the interrogative – but by a ghulam. Ghulams are military mamalik, Turanian nomads from the Low Steppe, seized in raids by rival Turks to be sold in the markets of Binkat in the Land of Shash. For years many have gone on to Baghdad to serve the 'Abbasid Caliph as Slavs, captured by Franks, now serve in Cordoba 'Abd ar-Rahman. The Wearers of Black Raiments are also known as 'Abbasids; the Caliph in Cordoba is Emir of the Ummayads.

Training barbarous men as dogs to control their human cattle is an inspiration of the nomad horde but Shahrban, a sedentary Iranian, having bought five ghulams for his guard, is so impressed by their steadfast energy, their fascination with the workings of his city, their fierce, instinctive loyalty to a master, their promiscuous willingness to learn, that acting against his Wazir's advice he goes on to purchase several thousand, insisting they all possess penes and testes and now, by way of gratitude, Turks control not only Merv, but the whole oasis of Margiana, extending for almost two thousand square miles and, according to the Hindu Puranas, the birthplace of the Aryan Nation. If successful in impressing the Wazir during a gradated probation ghulams may, but not before the age of thirty-five, supervise irrigation works, serve as provincial governors, undertake breeding of bloodstock, enforce both law and order, check the accounts of bookkeepers, deputise all tax collection, manage all dam maintenance, superintend the royal mint, oversee the granaries – of wheat, millet, barley and rice, all grown within the oasis – inspect and tax all caravans and approve, or disapprove, charitable works.

Nor are they content, these yurt-born slaves, to act as functionaries, but insist on spending hours each night in tedious adult education, cramped onto rugs designed for boys, struggling to repeat a teacher's phrase in Sanskrit, learning to solve equations with many a glance towards the next rug from primers belonging to little Mervis, boys no taller than these men's ruined knees, who during daylight hours strive to fulfil parental dreams of careers in jurisprudence or admission to the School of Hellenic Philosophy and Medicine at Jund-i-Shapur. The complete works of Aristotle are held in a Mervi library where a scholar whose name concludes in 'al-Marwazi' ('the Mervi'), translates them into Arabic. In which language they read as well as they would in any other for they appeal to the intellect. Al-Qu'ran, in contrast, has the force of an untranslatable poem. The song of the Surat in cantilation, the visual beauty of the vowel-less Kufic script – al-Qu'ran, a work of poetry, of music and of visual art, the content of which could only bemuse a reader familiar with the Torah.

Al-Qu'ran, The Recital, a list of the Prophet's vatic injunctions, the first of them (tacit) – 'Speak thou Arabic'.

Unbelievers, seeking to acquire a sympathetic understanding, will achieve the contrary by reading, in silence and in solitude, a book presented them as 'the Koran'. Al-Qu'ran does not translate. It cannot become 'the Koran'. It does not comport with solitude and silence. First committed to memory by professional remembrancers, its verses were transcribed onto stones and palm leaves in no particular sequence.

Meantime, the Arabs, or Tajiks, of Merv – Tayy from Al-Iraq, Kalbites and Khayyamites from Al-Yemen, Qaysites from the Jordan – are wearing trowsers and drinking wine, dwell miles out into the countryside, prefer to marry Khurasani women and celebrate the festivals of Mihrigan and Nawruz, the equinoctial fêtes of Fire Worship.

Arabian Nights in Khurasan, which is Dari for 'Land of the Rising Sun.'

'I'm dirty on you, Shahrban,' says the Wazir. 'I'm absolutely filthy. You took a whole month off. Took a month off with several thousand maidenheads awaiting your attention and they keep coming. Inshallah, what is wrong with using a new blade to clear the backlog?'

'Wouldn't feel right. In years to come, Abu Bakr, Dhu'l-Fiqar will become a relic, Inshallah, an object of veneration. The ghulam using just any old knife would show disrespect to posterity.'

'You're not tiring of your deed of kind? Can I fetch you a coffee with ambergris?'

'Shahrazad being your own daughter I thought you'd delight in delay.'

'Rather you get on with it. Never mind that with Shahrazad you've yet to consummate the deed but no more nights off.'

'Not Dinazad.'

'What?'

'Not Dinazad!'

'No, not Dinazad. Bismillah, I procured you a houri, Ghazalah hight, a slender, black-eyed, long-legged piece of the type we know you prefer to get you back into the mood and she'll be up there now and if she must await that old knife, we've an empty Zenana. We'll store them there, Inshallah, till Dhu'l-Fiqar is ready. When will that be?'

'Ah, pretty soon. Tell me again, Abu Bakr, why Shahrazad wished to be mine.'

Each night the Shah must pose this question to receive each night the same answer.

'Because, seeing you riding by on horseback, she falls into a swoon, striking out with her hands and feet and when she comes to, inquires of me, "And who was the uppermost of those two creatures?"'

'When was this?'

'She would have been Dinazad's age.'

'Did I still have the wife of my youth?'

'Away'llahi! You did.'

'Where was I going on that horse?'

'You were off to sit, as you did back then, on the horse in the snow all night.'

'Then she would have known it was me, Shahrban the marzban of Merv.'

'No, because she lives wrapped up in books. She's an utter bookworm. Where do you suppose she gets those stories? Saw you through a lattice in the library, peering through the Mashrabiyya. "Father," she says, "Alhamdolillah! I saw today a man so just and upright."'

'Handsome and attractive?'

'Just and upright were the words she used. Women like a stranger's face. "The son of the quarter filleth not the eye" and yours, I believe, was the first Samanid face she had ever beheld. See, I keep my daughters close. "Father," she says, "my eye today was filled by this man so just and upright, I feel that he is the one man to whom we could entrust these … norks."'

'Go on. You told her then who I was.'

'No, because you weren't then what you have become. I merely described you to her as a man in love with his wife. Arab influence, I blamed. "Well," she says, "I can't be his concubine", and stuck her head back in a book.'

'Tell me of her mother.'

'Don't recall her.'

'Does Shahrazad understand why I find it … difficult to trust women?'

'Ask her yourself. I well recall those days, Shahrban, when you first came to power, it must be thirty years ago – how in the depth of winter when snow was falling you'd ride alone to the scaffold you had erected in the square of the Shahristan and there you would sit on your horse quite motionless until the dawn Shahada and when I once asked why you did so, you replied, "There is no power nor strength save in Allah, the Glorious, the Great, but it might well be that some oppressed victim of injustice could come into my court and he might have neither money to cover his expenses nor roof to shelter him. Now, if I am to remain in my palace with its doors, curtains, vestibules and corridors, then certain perverse or ill-intentioned folk could well obstruct the petition. But out there at night, alone on my scaffold in the square, I am available to all."'

'And when did I stop doing this?'

'The day you caught your wife with that blackamoor kitchenhand and lost your senses.'

'Because I loved her so.'

'More fool you.'

'I don't feel like going to work now.'

'Yes you do! Off you go! Ajal! Justice must be done! You may not rest until you have saved this oasis from the perfidy of women.'

'They all do it.'

'Of course they do. Now, I've written up this marriage contract, given her the dower and her money down, witnessed her silence as acceptance and all you need do is recite a quick Fatihah. Off you go.'

'Is she slender of waist and heavy of hip, the way I like 'em?'

'She has aquiline nose and ruby-red lips, eyebrows arched as for archery, black eyes of Babili gramarye, and very delicate skin, as of the full moon, having been raised on a bed of satin, clad in silk and fed on marrow and cream and the honey of virgin bees.'

The Shah shakes a kerchief of dismissal.

Abu Bakr has ways of procuring silence in young women.

Ghazalah – white-skinned but thin as a foot-rasp, a basil stalk in contrast with Shahrazad, who is built along the buxom lines of Yang Guifei, 'Fat Concubine', with whom Xuanzong, Son of Heaven, Tang Faghfur, was famously besotted and who, through intrigue with a Sogdian rebel, An Lushan, all but destroyed the Tang Empire, forcing the Faghfur to flee Chang'an and this within living memory – converses with the pubescent, red-haired Dinazad.

'Blondes and redheads out,' says the Shah. 'I've a job of work to do upon the carpet-bed. Dhukul – the night of going in, of seeing the bride unveiled. Walk to the end of the corridor and back. Inshallah, I should be finished by then.'

'Can't I watch?' says Shahrazad, pouting. 'Please? I like to watch.'

'Oh, very well then you can stay, but your sister must leave. Dinazad!'

'Why?' demands Shahrazad. '*Why* must she leave? She was here when you did me!'

'Only because you insisted!'

'We are not sisters german but we have been through a great deal. We may not be parted.'

'Well, you may have to be at some stage because according to Surah al-Nisa, a man may not marry two or more sisters at one and the same time.'

'Ha! Deed of kind then butchery! That's your idea of marriage.'

'Oh, what have they been saying about me now? It's clear that if I'm to father a son, the lamp of my dark house, as I must, Inshallah, I should have to marry someone, but all the women I seem to meet are not the kind you would trust. As things stand, I've no one to sit at my deathbed and weep as I die. My cousin-wife was inconceivable.'

'But you'd concubines!'

'They were unbearable.'

'Oh, tears for the dead form a river in hell,' spits the houri, black eyes aflash.

'You're a Tabari,' says Shahrazad. 'That's a quote from the Avesta. I *so* enjoyed the Avesta. You're a Magian, a Fire Worshipper, a Mazdayasnian, a Zoroastrian, a Parsee, a Zarathushthrian. Indeed, you *do* resemble Hur from Asavahisht. You're so beautiful. I wish *I* were beautiful! As things stand, I was born an elephant – a big, fat, ugly elephant. Prssht!' Shahrazad gives her comic rendition of an elephant, rocking side to side. She has many such comic stock routines, most of them featuring elephants.

'If Dinazad is to remain,' says the Shah, 'she must move to the corner of the room, she must face the wall, shut her eyes tightly and stick her fingers in her ears and she may not sing.'

'Will it be painful?' whispers the houri, clad in a winding sheet.

'Nah,' replies Shahrazad, 'lucky for you he's not that well-endowed. Eyebrows, have you a four-eyed dog for the Sagdid, the dog-sight ceremony? Under the religious authority of Zarathushtra the Spitamid, the girl's corpse will need to be scrutinised by a four-eyed dog. It's the least you can do.'

Shahrban laughs, showing the backs of his molars, a thing an Arab never does. 'All that reading you've done has led you astray in the matter, Shahrazad. The fact is, there is no such thing as a four-eyed dog and you have it wrong. I am *well*-endowed – the richest man in Khurasan – and the deed of kind, with me, can take a long time and be very painful. You were lucky. I once had a Sudanese blackamoor wife who'd had the member feminine sewn with a packneedle using a thread of sheepskin. She made her water through a metal tube. That was perhaps the most serious challenge I have yet to face, yet I pride myself that with the aid of Dhu'l-Fiqar, I was equal to the task.

'Well, I see Dinazad has retired so we may as well commence. First, a quick Fatihah: In the name of God, the Pitiful, the Compassionate, praise to God, Lord of the Worlds, The Pitiful, the Compassionate, King of the Day of Judgement, You alone we worship, You alone we beseech, Lead us in the straight path, The path of those upon whom is your grace, Not of those upon whom is your wrath, nor of those who have gone astray, Amen. Right, we're married. Shahrazad, take off the wife's sheet, please, and place it under her hips to catch the blood. Do you intend to keep telling tales?'

'Haven't I a right to speak? Aren't I your wife as well? You've *two* wives.'

'Oh. So I have. This is the first time I've had two wives. Mind you, I can have up to four.'

'I want you to know how the Badawi – who had his hair in ringlets only undone to be washed in the urine of she-camels – lived with the shame of having farted at his own wedding.'

'Oh Shahrazad!'

But she will persist and the Shah, for the first time, fails in the defilement. At one point, Shahrazad shouts encouragement, but when the Shah looks up towards her face as it were a moon, observing on the way to her pale blue eyes that her pale pink nipples are flaccid and he sees her glance towards Dinazad, then he feels compelled to withdraw; foolish, for as he should have known he is now incapable of repenetration. Dinazad has a song she sings in a tongue that kills the member masculine, which is why she may not sing; but the Shah cannot see her, having lost with the years some flexibility in the neck, and the thought of her young ears not being properly blocked or back not properly turned and face averted, reduces his member masculine to a filbert he can barely see.

'Must I endure *that* again?' says the houri, as donkeys begin to bray.

'Where's all the blood?' inquires Shahrazad, scrutinising the sheet.

'I seem to have muffed it,' says the Shah, 'so I'm very dirty on myself. I must seek the Wazir's advice.'

'Try holdin' your bum a bit higher and tighter,' says Shahrazad, 'as all the others do.'

'Oh, you and your stories,' protests the Shah. 'I blame that Abu Hasan! And I see you're prepared to look in my bum where you won't look in my face. I didn't want Dinazad in the room but you would insist she remain.'

Leaving the sisters to ply a depilatory of quicklime and yellow arsenic on Ghazalah's veil of nature, Shahrazad, who has no pubic hairs, needs to have the procedure explained. Because it is sometimes hard enough knocking down a levee without bashing through a jungle first, the Shah heads off towards the Khangah fully determined to retrieve Dhu'l-Fiqar, the blade he blooded in personally slicing the scrotum from that screaming blackamoor. He feels he simply cannot endure another of Shahrazad's tales – Shahrazad the Sammar, Teller of Nocturnal Tales. Two wives is anyway a bad idea as they tend to get jealous and fight. A wise man prefers abundance of concubines with just the one wife and this wife, ideally, will be his first cousin, the daughter of his father's brother.

If only the Shah knew how Mervis, who once so loved him, detest him, he might feel less inclined to wander the city unescorted for all that the Veiler may veil him; but few, in fact, would recognise the Shah, such has been the change in his appearance since the day he caught the daughter of his father's brother with a blackamoor.

A blackamoor! A kitchenhand with a face like a cobbler's apron, a dish pig!

The Shah's natural reserve has become reclusion. A willingness to delegate authority has seen him shrug off all official duties to the point where he has not gone forth from Merv to receive a foreign dignitary, posed with a disabled veteran, opened a convention, given a speech, laid a wreath, turned a sod or pinned a medal to a juvenile champion of chess in over three years. Mervi perverts of a uranist persuasion who cackle at the spoliation of the women are nonetheless apprehensive that the ghulams are merely biding their time, abetted by the cunning Wazir who encourages the Shah in his nightly debauch.

The woman who sells the pigeon poults accosts the Shah as he passes. 'You from the palace?' she asks.

'What's it to you?' retorts the Shah.

'Ooh, charmer, little charmer. Someone up there ordered some poults. I supply poults to the palace. I thought you was the new Farrash, albeit a bit hairy-arsed.'

To be thus taken for a 'useful' puts the Shah in a frightful sulk. That blackamoor worked in the palace kitchen, stuffing poults and polishing the pots when he wasn't mounting the queen's bosom and so, upon entering the Khangah to be confronted by the Pir, the Shah gives him a good spray. But first, he must put his right hand to his heart before high-fiveing (Musafahah).

'Don't speak to me of Mercy! I'm here for me knife! Where is he? Where's that swordsmith?'

'Wouldn't appear to be about. Oh yes, that's right, he's off. Probably went to fix yer knife. Inshallah bukra! – may it please God, tomorrow. I wouldn't be overly concerned.'

'If I was you I'd be overly concerned as you're nothing but a pack of frauds. As if a man can become happy by listening to other men speak!'

'That's only the first part,' explains the Pir, 'and what else would you suggest? Allah save and favour the king.'

'Action!' avers the Shah, slamming down his fist. 'Personal effort! Striving for the good, comforting the weak, donating alms to the poor and ...'

'Wrong wrong wrong.' The words issue, with a lacerating contempt, from a stocky Tartar, a breed that figures, oddly enough, in the Shah's nightmare of the sack of Merv. 'Real Teaching begins with the Lords of Knowledge,' continues the Tartar. 'Real Happiness, sad to say, is *not* got through Faith, Hope and Charity because Real Love is rendered possible only through Genuine Know-How. Now listen carefully, Deed-of-Kindwit, and learn how Truth could lead a man astray. Kurban-at basham, O Shadow of Allah. May I be your sacrifice? My tale concerns ... *The Mine in the Moon*.'

The Mine in the Moon

'And where do babies come from?'

Seven babies had overnight appeared and the question was posed of Four Qutlugh by one of my brothers, Five Olot. He and I were about four years – old enough to pose questions.

'Come from the mine, same as you. We get the babies from the mine.'

'And where is this mine?'

'Out there. Far off.' Four Qutlugh pointed and we followed his finger east.

East was the gap where the ice fell. Strictly forbidden to do so, we often crept out amid crevasses to peer down at the ice-fall. Fifteen thousand feet below was a lake a little bluer than the sky. We used to stage mock battles at the fall, using icicles we'd pull from crevasses, hitting and poking each other about the head with pieces of sharp ice.

Our monastery perched on the side of a cliff hollowed out by the flank of a glacier, a cliff too sheer to hold dust and at times barely clearing the ice. Built of stone with open windows, it cantilevered over the moraine. A staircase had been cut into the stone just above the surface of the cirque. There were forty-nine monks.

Far to the west, beyond a ridge where our glacier flowed round a corner, a dusty plain was littered with boulders and cut in half with a ravine in which some said you could hear water, though no one had seen any.

To our north were smooth, bare hills all covered in icy scree that we used to throw at each other. To our south, where no living soul had ventured, we could hear another glacier which must have had a runny nose and a dirty snout because, in spring, it would snuffle and sneeze while ours merely groaned and crackled.

We'd never seen a plant or an animal. We'd never even seen a bird. We knew of no people other than ourselves, no habitation but our monastery. High above us, higher than you might think possible, a plume blew off a peak, but down where we lived, the world was composed of dust, rock, sand and ice. We lived on tea and butter and flour, all warmed by fires of dung, all made by spells put on sacks. We went barefoot, wore open gowns, ate a single meal a day and slept on the floor in a smoke-filled loft.

We knew of no way out. We'd never been anywhere else. We spoke a language that no one else speaks and when the wind dropped, all we could hear, aside from the groaning and crackling, was chanting that went on day and night in our meditation hall. Some of the voices were so low that you felt them rather than heard them and if that chant were ever to stop, the sun would no longer rise.

Would this be a problem? Not to us, as we seldom saw the sun. We usually played in the dark, for we played when the mood suited. Our one daily duty was to collect ice. The rest of our time was our own. We used it to scamper about in, mostly, waging war upon each other. We weren't yet men but one of our seniors, at only eight years, was a man. His brother Oirat remained boys but they no longer played with the Olot.

Men don't laugh. That's how you tell. They may smile but they don't laugh.

One of our boys, Four Juchi, was forty-two years old. He played and laughed by himself.

Seven Olot, seven Oirat, seven Juchi, seven baby boys. I had a wonderful childhood though as you see, it was based on a deception.

We didn't know what a woman was. We'd never heard tell of women.

Yes, it was a genuine monastery and I believe it survives. Why? Because the sun keeps rising here, in the Land of the Rising Sun. We liked it best when a full moon rose over the ice-fall – Full Ice Moon, we called that. We looked forward every spring to that night and the following night.

On the second night of Full Ice Moon when I was four years old, the glow had faded from the cliff face and the moon was rising on the ice and we were dividing ourselves into hordes, preparing to commence hostilities, when one of us observed that there was no one out but Olot. Normally at Full Ice Moon all but chanters emerged, but this night, not even one Oirat – only Olot on the ice.

They turned the lamps off in the hall. We'd never seen the monastery in darkness. If all of us felt a mounting concern we tried hard not to show it, but then the chant – which followed a cycle that took a full day and night and never varied – stopped, only to recommence as something we'd not before heard.

Little by little the moon rose till it filled the whole horizon. All we could do was stare at it. We'd lost the desire to fight.

'There's a man,' said Four Olot, over the chattering of his teeth.

'Where?'

Straining our eyes in the dim light we watched a man crawl from a crevasse.

'Where am I, lads?' he shouted.

We'd have run but our legs were frozen and not merely with terror; you need to keep moving about in a place like that or your limbs go numb.

'Don't be afeared of me, boys,' he went on, 'I'm as frightened as you are. Live round here then, do you, lads?'

One of us must have nodded. I guess we felt relief he meant no harm as we'd never seen a stranger.

He was four foot tall, twenty stone and could run the hundred in ten seconds – built like Imam 'Ali, whose face Allah honour, with a neck like an elephant's throat. He'd only one good eye and a squint and he wore a leopard pelt. Having never seen a snow leopard, we thought it part of his body. His face was as round as the face of the moon in front of which he was standing and marked the same, too, with nine blue birthmarks taking the place of the seas. The rest of his face was as white as the moon with wens for the bright craters – one on his chin, one below his good eye. He had no hair.

'Where are you from?' he asked us.

We pointed to the monastery. 'And where are you from?' we asked him in return.

He pointed at the moon. 'I'm from up there,' he said, 'and I work in that big mine near the mountain. See that bright spot down to the south? That's a mountain like this.'

'And what's it look like up on the moon?'

'Looks a lot like here. *Just* like here, without the ice. Mountains and deserts, the same flat light, the same big boulders. I feel quite at home.'

'Come here often?'

'This is my first time. I've been kept busy.'

'What do you do to keep busy up there? Chant?'

'Work in the mine. Work for the great Khan Tengri. Know what a mine is, do you, lads?'

We didn't but were keen to learn.

'Hole in the ground, like this crevasse, in which you could find treasure. Know what treasure is? I brought some down to show you.' Glancing about to see that no one was looking on, he fossicked in the fur between his legs and came up with a clenched fist and something in it shining. 'What do you think there is in that mine on the moon?'

'Babies?'

'Yes. And?'

'Treasure?'

'Yes. What kind? Do you know what treasure is? Treasure can make you both Happy and Wise. Are you Happy and Wise down here?'

We didn't know, which proved, as he said, that either we were or we weren't.

'Draw near,' he went on. 'I've a stone in my hand from the mine in the moon. Draw near!' Slowly, finger by finger, he opened his fist till light shone out. It came from a faceted gemstone, most likely moonstone or mutton-fat jade.

'How would that make you happy?' asked Seven Olat. 'What can it do?'

'Makes you a man, if you rub a bit off and throw it. So. Now.' Turning his back he raised his hand to produce a sparkling in the air. Showers of a crystalline dust flew up, every colour of the rainbow. 'Stand back, lads!' he warned. 'You're not yet ready to become men!'

Then he said, pointing to the moon, 'Can you see my caravan up there? Do you see where the dust is rising?'

Two of us could see it. Then three of us could see it then all of us could see it.

'That will be laden with stones like this, which Tengri uses to make men. When Khan Tengri looks down here and sees a boy He thinks should be a man, He grabs some dust and throws it but the boy won't see or feel it.'

'Why not?'

'Because he's asleep. He'll wake from sleep all sticky between the legs. Hey! It's late! The moon is getting smaller. I best be going back.' White skin gleaming in the moonlight, he ran and jumped back down the crevasse.

He hadn't told us not to tell anyone and so we told everyone. The men just smiled but Oirat annoyed us by claiming that they had met him, too.

'You can't have done,' said Four Olot. 'He's never been here before!'

'That's what he told us.'

'Describe him!'

Six Oirat described him: four foot tall, twenty stone, could run the hundred in ten seconds. It was him, all right.

Years passed and in keeping as we did so busy we forgot the little man except, of course, at Full Ice Moon. We always thought of him then.

We didn't like him anymore. We thought he was a cretin.

The babies had grown into little boys, one of them a cretin. The Guyuk preferred to play by themselves and so we seldom spoke to them.

We didn't like the Guyuk, either.

At new moon which was destined to become Full Ice Moon when the Guyuk was four, the abbot asked to see the Olot. We met him at the ice-bend.

'Lads,' he said, 'I'm here to tell you what's to happen shortly. At Full Ice Moon you will stay indoors and the lamps in the hall will go out.'

'Is Guyuk to meet the man from the moon?' said Four Olot. 'Does he come here when you tell him?'

'He comes when he has a mind to come. He won't come if he sees us all outdoors and the lamps on. He comes when he sees little boys alone on the ice. It's then he comes down.'

'But he said he hadn't been here before!'

'I don't know why he says that. I think he must forget.'

Some of our memories are unlike others in that they never fade. It pays us to examine them. That Full Ice Moon we stayed indoors and the abbot covered the windows in sacks so we couldn't see out when the lamps went off.

The lamps went off and a chant went up that was yet another we hadn't heard.

As I curled up to sleep that night, I wondered what I might dream. In the event, I don't think I dreamed anything. But when I woke, in the middle of the night, with sacks off the windows and moon shining in, I lay a long time looking at it, filled with a Happiness I still recall. I'd woken unsure of what was happening to me, my body in convulsion. And then I was sticky between the legs; I'd felt the touch of Tengri.

When I see that icy place in my mind's eye, it is on that night. It is on that very mat. It is in that very instant.

I see the limbs of my brother Olot sprawled about me. I see the smoke mark on the stone ceiling of the loft above me. I see the full moon through the stone window peering down upon me. I smell the smouldering dung smoke. I hear above the groaning and crackling of the glaciers the chanting from the hall. It's the new chant that I, too, must learn. I begin that night to learn it. No one has to tell me to learn the chant. I do so instinctively.

'Thank you, Tengri,' I whispered to myself, over and again. 'You've made me a man. I'd no idea my own body could contain such bliss. What a wonderful world.'

I found, eventually, the path out.

It was downhill all the way.

Years later, a trader in jade with a shop in the Kashgar market, I saw that man from the moon again. He was one of a dwarf juggler troupe entertaining a caravan. Wearing a fur-lined bonnet with earflaps he made no attempt to hide but then, you couldn't really hide a face like that. No hiding those birthmarks.

I suppose I smiled but even so I wanted to be alone, so leaving my wives and children in the care of an associate, I walked to the edge of the Kashgar oasis where, staring up at the High Pamir, I gathered a handful of gravel washed down by the Kizil River. Like me, those stones were glacial. They too had been worn smooth.

I hurled them, cursing, at the waning moon.

One felt a little different. Scrutinising it, I saw its face was all white and spherical. Turning it over I saw it was marked, on its obverse, with the face of the moon and there were the same nine seas, the same bright craters, as on the little man.

The door between Two Worlds had opened briefly yet again.

'Thank you, Tengri,' I whispered through my tears. 'It's more than I deserve. I confirm that You exist.'

And He might well have responded, 'And you'll forget again.'

Iranian Days (continued)

After the tale the Khutbah. After each tale, a sermon.

'If Tengri wants to speak to us He always finds a way. The way we speak to Him is how we act when He is silent. Amen.'

'And who is this Khan Tengri?'

'The Sky, but does it matter? Can it really matter when all religions are attempts, more or less unsuccessful, to describe One Truth?'

'And what is it? What is this Truth?'

'It has to do with the Two Worlds though perhaps such attempts are misguided. They seem to work in practice but not in theory, resulting in the imposition of *Rules* where in fact, it is not a case of, "Do this, that or the other and you will achieve Happiness" but rather "Achieve Happiness and you will find yourself doing, instinctively, this, that or the other."'

'I had a nightmare featured a man like you. He was cutting my throat.'

The Shah of Marw al-Shahijan falls asleep, head supported by the wether. Slumped beside him, also sleeping, is the Tartar, who owns a nearby foundry.

In the Shah's dream he becomes a swarm of lice-pitted, vermin-ridden, pony-riding archers who, picking at their noses while scratching at their buboes, are darkening the heavens with their bow-spawn. They are smashing the dam, burning the cathedral, torching the library and looting the mint.

'Ahh!'

Shahrban wakes to find Olot staring. Also staring quietly at the Shah is the wether with the golden fleece.

'Your knife,' says Olot, reaching in his groin to produce the Shah's Wondrous Blade. He draws it, grinning, across his own throat before handing it over.

'Good!' says Abu Bakr. 'Your mood may improve now you have back Dhu'l-Fiqar. A knife is the bravest of arms. I'll organise for Shahrazad to be put to death first thing.'

'Ahh ...'

'Bismillah, have you a particular ghulam in mind?'

'Ahh ...'

'If you don't, may I suggest ...'

'Abu Bakr! Let us not ah let us um ah ...'

'What's the matter, Shahrban? You've gone as pale as Shahrazad's throat. I thought you'd be delighted by the prospect of consummation. Hamdillah, they all do it.'

'They do indeed and even if they never actually did it they were tempted. The problem is I'm plagued with this nightmare in which Merv is sacked and the population butchered.'

'Razing Merv would be a mistake – far better tax the inhabitants. Think of your dream as an instance of where bad advice could lead. Now, we've a real problem: the cotton growers tell me there is insufficient water in the river. But all that time you spend with the riff-raff in the Rabad, I'm not surprised you've nightmares. Give anyone the nightmares, that lot. Any joy with the houri? Do her tomorrow with Shahrazad?'

'I cannot consummate my love for women in my present condition. I blame that nightmare. I see the people being led into the desert on camel halters, Abu Bakr, there in strings of ten or twenty to have their throats cut. Their blood drains into the desert sands like the waters of the Murghab beyond the dam. Here, give me back my Wondrous Blade, I should hide it under the throne.'

'My word, he's done a lovely job. I told you he was a master.'

'You didn't tell me that he was a Son of the Rumour.'

'Do what?'

'I say, you didn't ...'

'Shh, boy, have you no idea what you're saying? If I'd known what you just said I could not have commended him. Let's go outdoors. The curtains here have ears.'

So the two walk down to the orangutan enclosure.

'Tell me, Shahrban, what does the name "Hashim ibn Hakim" mean to you?'

'Al-Muqanna?'

'He who wore the Qina, our veiled prophet of Khurasan. Correct. What do you know of him?'

'Not much. Only that Arabs trapped him in his tashkurgan near Kesh with his hundred concubines and single slave whereupon he disappeared. Some say he translated to heaven using basil and butter; others that he threw himself into his furnace and burned himself to a crisp; others that he underwent occultation and is still about, sure to return in glory with 'Isa to judge the quick and the dead. Mind you, this is before my time, in the reign of Caliph al-Mahdi. Al-Muqanna led that revolt against Arabs which nearly succeeded. Being a bald, one-eyed dwarf he couldn't show his face in public so he wore a gold mask or, for casual occasions, a green Qina. Turks worshipped him.'

'Yes, because he claimed to be the equal of 'Isa and Bih-Afarid! Said he had the soul of Abu Muslim! Claimed, that like Mani and Mohammed – on whom be The Peace! – he was the Seal of the Prophets! He could summon up a moon from a well, though, Shahrban, as I've seen him do it – good sorcerer. Put a second moon in the night sky for a time. Complete rogue, had the notion that women and property should be held in common – as if! Mazdakite. Communist. Carpocratic lecher. Still has satellites in Merv, though, Shahrban, satellites in Mawarannahr. They practise dissimulation, al-Taqiyyah, as authorised in Surah al-Nahl: "Those who are forced to recant while their hearts remain loyal to the faith shall be absolved". Outwardly, I'm told, these Sons of the Rumour profess Islam while inwardly they await the return from the dead of al-Muqanna. It wouldn't do for a Shah to frequent their lodge.'

'Oh. You mean ...'

'I do. These Sons of the Rumour, al-Mubayyida, Safid-jamagan, these Wearers of White Raiments, await the return, from the Land of No Return, of al-Muqanna. Now, they may have told you they await the return of some other Once and Future King – the Prophet Ilyas perhaps, or 'Isa ibn Maryam, on the twain be peace.'

'I can't recall them telling me they await the return of any dead man.'

'Good. Because they're worse than Nazarenes and worse than Jews. Fancy worshipping a bald local, an ugly, one-eyed dwarf, a fuller who worked in the clothing factory over the road! I could show it to you. Now then, what say we line the river channels with concrete to reduce percolation? I can't have the mirabs on my back. They've been here since the Bronze Age.'

The Shah must now return to work. Let a ghulam deal with the mirabs. The Shah's work consists in chatting by moonlight (Musamarah), chatting over the cup (Munadamah), deflowering virgins while throwing the odd general-invitation feast (al-Jafala), and making toothpicks. He has forty nights in which to consummate a marriage, which means another night with the blackhead, yet when he enters his chamber, he finds Ghazalah has gone missing.

'Where's my second wife?' he demands.

Dinazad runs to a corner of the room, lifts a carpet and returns with a sheet, spilling in the process the cowry-shell dowry. 'Look,' she says. 'See all the blood? You *did* it, Shahrban! Mashallah! Well done! Proof positive of pucelage. This is the houri's sheet. Alhamdolillah, you did it. You did deflower that houri.'

'But Shahrazad said there was no blood.'

'Oh, Shahrazad, as we know, has red eyes through all her reading. She's a Qarmat.'

'How do we know that's blood?' says the Shah. 'It could be anything. It could be pomegranate juice. And if blood, it could be menstrual blood, or perhaps she cut her toe. Where is she?'

'Gone.'

The Shah laughs from a heart full of wrath, showing the backs of his molars again. 'Dinazad, there's a ghulam on guard in the corridor!'

'She knows nothing of that,' snaps Shahrazad, 'as we're in here! The girl was gone when we woke. That's all we know about the matter. She could have bribed that ghulam with a deed of kind. You've set her on the road.'

'I'm not so sure I have. I'd have noticed a stain this size. I let myself down with that houri and I'm very dirty on myself. This is what comes from doing things out of sequence. I should have killed you first. I wasn't meant to have two wives and how I wish you hadn't watched me doing the business as it put me off.'

'The others, it always turns them on, and don't say you let yourself down. All things considered, we thought you went well. It's just the flow came late; the hymeneal discharge was delayed.'

'Your father, Inshallah, must convoke three crones to adjudge this stain. I have my suspicions. Shahrazad, you may keep your head in order to bear witness, but no more tales, I beseech you. Please! I need some sleep!'

'I'm telling you a tale and it's a good one. You don't have to listen. It's called *The Lady and her Five Suitors*.'

But the Shah doesn't listen to the tale. He knows the minute he shuts his eyes he'll dream again of the sack of Merv which can't be right. Tartars ride horses like donkeys and carry spears like spindles. Furthermore, they are disorganised.

Come false dawn, having done his need and performed ablution and said his prayers, he trudges back to the Khangah of Hashim ibn Hakim. It's become a daily ritual and serves to reacquaint him with his city or, at least, the dogs and babies, as he daren't lift his eyes to make eye contact with adults through fear of 'Ayn, the Evil Eye. Because of the Shah there is scarcely a virgin left in Khurasan and he stands out from the mob as his eyebrow is distinctive. Highly desirable, well-nigh unique, inherited from a Tocharian grandfather, it is thick, black, with just a splash of white and perfectly conjoined in the middle with wiry tufts the length of long lashes – a great mark of Arabic beauty. God willing, the Shah knows he can sleep on the withers of that wether – sleep on that pulsating fire lamb that was moved to prophesy.

But he wakes at dawn, appalled by dim recollection of yet another nightmare. Not as bad, perhaps, as the sack of Merv, but bad enough. He never consciously thinks of his cousin-wife anymore, though he dreams of her and in these dreams he still desires her, wretch that she became. Walking back to the ark, he thinks again of the death of his mother, who was not the daughter of his father's brother but a concubine captured in war – a valuable Kabbazah able, astraddle, to milk the member masculine through constriction of the muscles of her privities.

'Don't cry, son,' his father is saying, 'as the whore only gets what she deserves. We belong to God and to God we must return – Inna li-Llah wa inna ilayhi raji'un. I mean to put her head in a cage as a lesson to the rest for they all do it and it makes me absolutely filthy. I don't want you looking up from your Recital as you walk about the grounds for I know you were fond of your mother and you won't be certain where her head will next appear as I shall have it moved. Just when they've grown accustomed to seeing it here they shall see it there. And when they've grown accustomed to seeing it there, I shall move it again. One morning they might see it, Inshallah, in a kitchen by the stove. The next, up a chimney in the smoke. The next, perhaps, in a basket in the hammam bath among the petals and if you could think of any other place might be a good place, let me know.'

'Don't talk to a Shahzada like that!' says Abu Bakr, who's standing nearby – Abu Bakr having been the Shah's father's Wazir as well as the Shah's.

The Shah instructs Abu Bakr to convoke three crones to assay the stain. He then informs his Grand Wazir his second wife has gone missing.

'What? Not possible! I'll fetch the chamberlain! The vinegar worm is of and in the vinegar here, let me just check the roster, would have been … Satuq. Now then, wife for tonight? You can have up to four.'

'Call me when those crones arrive. I'll be down with the orangutan. Another thing, that cage with the daughter of the first wife's skull in. Have it removed.'

'Whither?'

'Whithersoever! Bury it! I take refuge in Allah from Satan the Stoned! I'm sick of the sight of the wretched thing every day as I go off to the Khangah.'

'You're not still going back to that Khangah after what was said?'

'Where else am I supposed to sleep? I can't sleep in my own chambers, thanks to that daughter of yours. Yap yap yap, she never lets up.'

'Won't be for much longer. Soon as you're up to it, off comes that head and up dry those lovely norks. Then you'll have time to catch up on your toothpicks.'

Dinazad, entering the throne room, duly and meekly prostrates herself.

'*Look* how your sister shows respect,' says Shahrban to Shahrazad. 'Why can't *you* do that? Why, you won't even look me in the face or call me Shadow of Allah!'

'I can't kiss the floor,' says Shahrazad, 'not with the size of my rusty dusty.' She then gives a comic impression of an elephant trying to kiss the floor.

All but the Shah must suppress a smirk at this blasphemous allusion to the Sujud in the Salat but the Shah is a stranger to humour. In consequence, he makes the perfect butt for Shahrazad's wit. A man of the world might feel unease at such a coarse wit in such a great beauty but the Shah is merely bewildered.

Three crones from a neighbouring household, all wearing Chadors, inspect the sheet.

Abu Bakr, after kissing his daughters' eyes, confronts a sullen Satuq. 'Now then,' he says, 'your tongue is beneath our feet, you scumbag. You were charged to suffer that none of the creatures of Almighty Allah would enter or leave that chamber. You will now swear by Allah, All-Knower of All Hidden Things, that you will speak the Truth, the whole Truth and nothing but the Truth – unless, of course, you have planned for someone present a surprise birthday party.'

Satuq, however, has set his jaw and bent his head and refuses to swear; a bad sign, too, for no amount of torture can make them speak, even plied with wine.

As Abu Bakr attempts to educe a plea from the sullen ghulam, the Shah summons one of the crones to hear the decision on the stain.

'Ya fulan, O certain person! Well then, would you say it's blood?'

'Yes.'

'Maidenhead?'

'That or pigeon poult. Hard to distinguish the two. Patience is an adornment and God is gracious, Sabrun jamilun wa-Llahu karim.'

The Shah resolves to visit the woman who sells the pigeon poults but before he can move, Abu Bakr drags Shahrazad before the crones.

'This stain here,' says Abu Bakr, 'on this sheet on this girl. Well?'

'Older than t'other.'

'Well, of course it is older. It is older by a lunar month but maidenhead?'

'More likely poult. See that patch of yeller? That, I'd say, is from a giblet.'

The Shah rewards each crone with a dinar engraved with his own handsome face and on the obverse a legend acknowledging al-Ma'mun as his suzerain.

'Alhamdolillah, I know that woman who sells those poults,' he proclaims. 'God willing, I shall have a word with her. In the meantime, let's be fair to Shahrazad. A woman's virtue is like skim milk, the least dust fouls it; or like glass, which, if it be cracked, may not be mended.

We have no proof of deception. Where be her guilt upon the heads of witnesses? Did four credible witnesses see the Kohl-needle in the Kohl-etui?'

'If *I* had menstrual blood and one more dinar,' says the tallest crone, '*I'd* have proof. I'd have proof of systematic deception goes all the way to the top.'

'And Allah ya'tik,' declares the Wazir, 'and may Allah (not me) give it you.'

'Shahrazad's friend hasn't come this month,' says Dinazad.

'O Dear my Daughters, then 'Iddah becomes three months,' says Abu Bakr. 'La baas ba-zalik – no harm in that.'

'Bullshit. Pimp! Pander! Procurer! Ponce, look at these boobs! Think I don't know when I'm *pregnant*? My *knockers* swell! I mean, *look* at them! Talk about choke a mule and as if they weren't big enough. Satuq, what do you think, mate? Bigger than before?'

'Take no notice of a thing she says,' says Abu Bakr, with a wink. 'A woman about to lose her head will often say silly things.'

'They'll always let you down,' commiserates the Pir, 'if not after, then before you meet them, and even if they never actually did it, they were tempted. It's in the Design. What we will need to do soon, though, is separate Dinazad from Shahrazad. In the meantime, as we await that woman who sells the poults, Allah save and favour the king! Mawdudus will speak to us. All hail the linguist. Kurban-at basham – may I be your sacrifice, O Shadow of Allah?'

Mawdudus al-Marwazi – stooped, auburn-haired, green-eyed and freckle-faced – tells a tale which, were it graven with needle-gravers upon the eye-corners were a warning to be heeded by whoso would be warned, anent ... the curious effects of *The Tears of the Fish*.

The Tears of the Fish

My complexion betrays my ancestry but, unlike most Khurasani Greeks, I am not of Macedonian descent. No, I am Thracian and owe, indirectly, my presence in this city to the breeding achievements of Parthians on the pastures of Media. There they bred an equine monster, a horse so big, so fast and so strong, it could gallop under the weight of armour. So was born the cataphract who defeated the Roman legions at Carrhae, as Romans call Harran. The Battle of Carrhae in 54 BC was a great defeat for Rome and ten thousand men, a full legion, were brought back here as slaves to Merv when Merv was a Parthian city. The Roman commander, Crassus Dives, was killed by having molten gold poured down his throat.

Parthians were Philhellenes who used Roman currency. In my belief it was this currency inspired the art of the Mahayana which spread across the Nanlu Basin from Balkh for Kushans, like Parthians, were content with the dregs of Greek art.

Thirty-four years after Carrhae there was a detente with Rome and Augustus gave up threatening Parthia in exchange for the captured standards and any surviving prisoners.

My own forebear, now a *mawla* if still a Roman citizen, chose to remain in Merv with his Bactrian wives and his Sindhi concubines.

It was an age of *muluk al-tawa' if* – shahs of shreds and patches with over all the 'Padishah' or 'foot-shah', his foot on his vassals' necks. I note that on our coinage, Sahib, you style yourself 'the Padishah' and yet you say a ghulam and an odalisque deceived you. And then on the obverse of those coins you become an emir of Caliph al-Ma'mun.

Aristotle, tutor of Alexander, wrote a series of works in which he expounds every subject known to man. This is my obsession. Aristotle speaks of the danger in men becoming either beasts or gods. Between these extremes is the 'Gate of the God' or 'Babylon' to use an Akkadian word and the god is Hermes Trismegistus.

As men we need to move between the world of the flesh and the world of the spirit. This is seldom easy. We need a god to facilitate our passage and the god is Thrice-Great Hermes. Return to the flesh from the world of the spirit can be particularly awkward, as we learn from the number of myths that speak of the danger in looking back.

Nazarenes, as you may know, prefer to funk the return journey. We let the dead bury the dead.

Parthians could not govern Babylonia from their capital Hecatompylos. Nor could Sassanids, who followed the Parthians, govern from Fars. Either established a capital in Ctesiphon, a suburb on the Iranian bank of Seleucia-on-Tigris. By the time of the birth of our Lord Jesus Christ, Suffering Son of a Sorrowing Mother, Babylon, gate of the god Marduk between the Desert and the Sown, had gone.

Not so Babylonian culture, which survives in Harran.

The last Babylonian Emperor Nabonidus was a son of the high

priestess of Harran and some believe he intended to move his capital there from Babylon. He certainly favoured Sin over Marduk, patron god of the capital. Seleucids, the Parthians who supplanted them and Umayyad Caliphs in general were religious latitudinarians. Indeed, Seleucid Harran became a centre for the worship of Hermes Trismegistus, Hellenised Thoth and Father of our Rumour. My Harrani colleague Jabir ibn Hayyan 'Geber' uses the alchemical language 'Gibberish' which he has developed to address the Rumour deploying his concept of the *Philosopher's Stone*. The first Sassanid, Ardashir, organised the Zoroastrian Church and yet Harranis were not converted to this Reformed Church of Mazdayasnians but, like the Athenian professors who found sanctuary in Ctesiphon having been expelled from Athens by the Nazarene Emperor Justinian, found their paganism winked at.

Despite the best efforts of Sassanids, Khurasanis felt no great allegiance to Zoroaster of Balkh. Following Arab conquest, most were keen to convert to Islam and not for spiritual reasons – to avoid *jizyah* and *kharaj*, taxes imposed upon *dhimmis*, People of the Book, taken to include Magians. Your own Tokharian grandfather Saman Khuda, in converting to Islam, made you and your brothers in Samarkand, Shash, Fergana and Herat, marzbans of the marches and now, no doubt to your embarrassment, Shahrban, you find yourself in the vanguard of Islam so that Mervis today would know of Harran as the city where their Father Abram – reckoned by Mohammed as superior to Jesus and second only to Mohammed – lived until he was seventy-five years old, according to the Jewish Torah, which is our Nazarene Old Testament.

When Abraham, as he'd become, with his elder son Ishmael left Harran to organise in Mecca the adoration of a black fetish, I think we glean a clue as to the tolerance of Islam toward Harran and the continued status of pagan Harranis in *dhimmitude* to this day, for something momentous happened in Harran – something to persuade Abram, a man from the dying culture of Akkad – Ibrahim al-Harrani – to reconfigure God.

Abraham, *pace* Aristotle, makes a *friend* of God – Ibrahim, Friend of Allah. As Aristotle says in his *Ethica Nichomachea:*

> *'where there is a wide discrepancy in virtue, evil, wealth or what not, then that discrepancy excludes not only the possibility of friendship, but even pretension to it; and this is evident in the case of shahs, but even more so in the case of gods, who enjoy crushing superiority over men in advantages of every kind. Friendship cannot survive the gulf that separates a man from a god, which raises the puzzling question as to whether a friend can really desire for his friend superlative advantage; for being a god is an advantage that is assuredly superlative, and yet, when your friend has become a god, you can no longer be a friend to him, and therefore no longer an asset, which is what a friend is. If, therefore, we are correct in supposing that a friend's motive in desiring advantage for his friend is altruistic, he is bound to want his friend to remain a human being, rather than become a god, or a shah.'*

Male circumcision becomes Abraham's covenant with his new Unseen Friend.

> *'Every man-child among you shall be circumcised. And ye shall circumcise the flesh of your foreskin; and it shall be a token of the covenant betwixt me and you.'*

In defence of the Muslim practice of infant clitoridectomy, Muslims believe that Sarah mutilated Hagar and was then ordered by Allah to circumcise herself.

☾

Harran has an Umayyad mosque. Renowned for scholarship, it has the first university in Islam. The high priest of the Temple of Sin is a noted astronomer. I am informed that Caliph al-Ma'mun, since moving from Merv to Baghdad, grows increasingly restless with these pagans on his doorstep and will shortly insist that Harranis convert to Islam or at least become 'People of the Book' – Jews, Christians, Sabians or Magians. I suspect they will become Sabians – Mandaean Jews like John the Baptist – because Icthys, fish-symbol of Christendom, is the son of Atargatis, the goddess worshipped today in Harran.

I went to Harran in part through curiosity to see the battlefield of Carrhae but forgot to ask where it was. I went to attend a conference. With Merv and Jund-i-Shapur, Harran hosts every three years the Seminar in Hellenic Studies. To me, it remains a bit of a blur. The papers were given in Latin. John of Damascus gave a plenary address – strangely off-key as I thought, it had to do with the perpetual virginity of the Blessed Virgin Mother's parents – and was thanked by Geber, whom I've recently read may not even be an historical figure. I presume I gave a paper on Aristotle.

Oh, you say, your typical convention. No, you must hear my tale.

It's a four-month journey from Merv to Harran through the Caspian Gates. The Gates themselves are long gone but the gatehouses remain. From Merv to Babylon you're on the principal highway of the Achaemenidae, the Great North-East Road, which is still in pretty good shape, considering Alexander used it.

I chose to ride my Argamak horse rather than my camel, feeling I could always sell an Argamak horse. I took my wife's ox-blood Mervi rug – an heirloom – as saddlecloth, then set off, tagging along with a caravan laden in silks. The seminar being scheduled for Nawruz I had to leave in winter but we had no snow.

We went south of the Dry Mountains through the land of the

great chenar trees, climbing onto the plateau at Tus, Geber's birthplace, through valleys filled with woods of walnut and mulberry, ash and white sycamore, with orchards, watered by rills, rising one above each other on the slopes. It was here Caliph al-Mam'un poisoned Imam Riza.

A few miles from Tus is Mashad-i-riza, a village which now houses a shrine to this eighth Imam of the Shi'ites – enemies of yours, too, Shahrban. Deplore Sunni rule of Khurasan.

We went past the turquoise mine north of Nishapur towards Damaghan and through the Caspian Gates. Then, on leaving Khurasan, the caravan made on to Trebizond while I followed the highway that turns south at a *Nawus*, a Tower of Silence. Mazdayasnians do not bury and cannot cremate their dead, and the cameleers said that if I climbed that tower I would find laid out upon the roof sixty-one corpses, variously decomposed, although the smell suggested more.

Ecbatana, where the highway drops back down to the plateau, must be a pleasant place in summer; each year the Achaemenian court spent two summer months in Ecbatana, three spring months in Susa and seven winter months in Babylon. I found a church of *Nasturi*, Nestorian Christians, in which I was made welcome – oh yes, I'm a Nazarene, a *Tarsa*, a funker, I teach Sunday school in the cathedral. I have to pay *jizyah*, the poll tax. I follow the teachings, best I can, of Isaac of Ninevah, who said, 'A merciful heart is a heart on fire for the whole of creation, for humanity, for the birds, for animals, for demons, for all that exists. The eyes of the merciful pour forth tears in abundance – for beasts, for the enemies of God, for the people who do harm, for the family of reptiles – that all should be protected and receive mercy.'

I told the priest I wanted to spend at least a week in Behistun as the inscription there contains the first known mention of the word 'Merv', but I'd heard reports of brigands in the area. The priest assured me that there are no brigands in the Zagros Range.

Two weeks later I'd made camp by the famous limestone crag that Darius, first Achaemenian emperor, had chiselled smooth and inscribed in cuneiform with everything he had to say concerning the year 522 BC. It's interesting to a scholar as it's written in three languages – Old Persian, Elamite and late Akkadian. Brushing off the snow and ice I set about copying the inscription. I learned that Darius, 'favourite of the great god Ahuramazda', always spoke the truth. His rivals, by contrast, were inveterate liars. This was unpromising but even so I spent a week up there. Time seemed to whiz by but one afternoon as feared, brigands appeared at the foot of the cliff. They carried bows and daggers.

'Tax please,' they shouted up. I had no choice but to comply.

I tried to annex them the notes I'd taken but these they had no use for. Eventually we settled on my horse and saddlecloth as tax. They had their eye on that horse as she was dapple-grey. So I walked all the way down to the plain burdened by my notes but I didn't go on to Baghdad as I can't stand modern cities. I took the North-West Road from Susa where it intersects the North-East Road, tracking across the Diyalah and Lower Zab rivers on to Arbil, then crossed the Upper Zab at the site of ancient Ninevah, crossed the Tigris and went on to Nisibin the Roman frontier fortress, subsisting, all this while, on frumenty of green barley and dates. The willows by the river banks all had a tinge of green and there was traffic aplenty once I got down to the plain. The Muslim, give him his due, will always help a traveller. From Nisibin I continued to Mardin on the Armenian border, seat of the Jacobite Metropolitan, but also home to Sunnis and Shi'ites, Melchite and Paulician Armenians, Manichees, Nestorians, Chaldaeans, and Sun-, Fire-, Calf- and Devil-worshippers. How they could all live together on the same small hill you wouldn't know, but from Mardin I could see a road stretching south-west to Harran where I arrived in good time for the Seminar.

☾

'I hope you'll be comfortable up here,' said the rector. 'As you're first in, I've upgraded you, Mawdudus.'

The great mosque of Ulu Cami to which is attached the university sits on the north slope of Harran. Opening my door on a small terrace, I could see the venerable city spread out below me the colour of mud. There's a city wall and within it hundreds of conical houses that date back to the days of Ur, with a huge temple in the shape of a ziggurat next to the university. I could see a ramp leading to the sanctuary and a dome over the entrance. The ziggurat was of mud brick but the dome was of Lebanese cedar. So this, I thought, is the Temple to Sin where the Emperor Julian worshipped.

Sometime that night I was awoken by a scream coming from the temple. It sounded like the scream of a man. Gradually it weakened, subsided, there was a sound of sloshing water, then more screaming from another voice. Straining my eyes, for the night was dark, I could see a line of men moving up the ramp.

'Bit of noise coming from the temple last night,' I remarked to the rector at breakfast.

'Oh, just a few local men preparing for the Battle of the Waters. Would you like to be moved, Mawdudus? I can find you a quieter room. You have the place to yourself at present. There'll be more noise tonight, I fear. The festival is in ten days and the men need time to heal. Have you been yet to the temple?'

After I'd finished my coffee – wonderful coffee in Harran, plenty of cardamom, properly made in a proper copper coffee pot – I walked to the temple. A few priests were sitting on the ramp mending musical instruments. They smiled as I walked by them and made no attempt to detain me.

Inside the entrance was a courtyard and in this courtyard two huge tanks. Everything was on a massive scale but especially these tanks. They were filled as I saw with water. A set of steps led down into the larger of the two and I could make out a trail of water there that hadn't properly dried. As I ventured onto the top step to see what the larger tank might contain, a priest shouted out. He ran over and something moving in the water caught my eye. It was a fish, orange and red and black, of the size of a Nile pike.

'Come back tonight,' said the priest, speaking in Aramaic. 'You can feed the fish then.'

'And how many fish would you have?' I asked.

'Twelve.'

Later that day a pine tree was pushed up the ramp. It was dressed in a woollen skirt and decked out in red roses.

I found it hard to concentrate on my Aristotle. When night fell I sat on the terrace drinking wine and coffee. Around midnight a queue of men began again to form and I joined them.

On approaching the larger tank the men removed their skirts. One by one they entered the water, filing slowly down the steps. A couple of burly priests supported each man, one on either side, and when the water was up to their waists there came a flurry from the tank. That's when the scream went up, if a scream went up though some men didn't scream. I couldn't see what was going on until I got to the steps and seeing the men emerging all clutching their groins I decided to funk it.

'Where are you off to?' said the man behind me in the queue.

'Second thoughts.'

'Get it off!' he demurred. 'For Ichthys' sake, give yourself a *chance*.'

As I mingled among the men who were now being dried and dressed I caught a glimpse of a ragged, bleeding frenulum between a pair of legs. Two priests conferred and advised the man concerned that he must go back in the tank.

Ha! Those fish had been trained to prune a prepuce from the meatus to the sulcus. They were making children to Abraham.

They were circumcising those men.

I asked the rector at breakfast next day where all the students had gone.

'There'll be an influx of pilgrims soon so anyone with a room to sublet makes a tidy profit. Will you be participating in the festival, Mawdudus?'

'How can I? I'm a Nazarene.'

'It doesn't matter what you are, provided you're a stranger. You cannot attend a festival twice. We get a lot of Christians – Monophysites, Arians, Dyophysites, Docetists, Melchites, Monotheletes, Paulicians, Marcionites. Conference won't take all your time; why not have a bit of fun and help revive our crops?'

'You say the festival is in ten days?'

'Depends on Ha. Generally speaking, the equinox, yes. The night Ha emerges is the Battle of the Waters and the day after the Battle becomes the Day of Blood. Mind you, there's always some woman up there. Have you been yet to the temple?'

'Only got as far as the tanks.'

'You want to get past those. Come here to this window. Now, back of that area there – see where I mean? – there's a dormitory. That's where the women sleep.'

'Women?'

'Yes, the women. The young women of Harran. The young mothers, the young married women. The breeders.'

'Why would they sleep in the temple?'

'Ah, look, best talk to a woman. Why not talk to Uzza? She's been up there ... two festivals? Maybe you're the man for her.'

'I have a wife in Merv!'

'Give her my regards. Uzza is a girl with a wen on her nose. She'll be there alone. Look, I'll give you your money now, Mawdudus. I'll give you your full travel allowance and per diem and I'll start the per diem from the day you arrived. How's that?'

After finishing my breakfast I went to find this dormitory. It was a spiral ramp like the one in Hagia Sophia but lined with chairs and cushions and stools and couches and priests everywhere rigging up slings from the roof and plumping cushions on the floor. I found a woman there with a wen on her nose. Eating fruit which had lodged in her crooked teeth she couldn't speak at first and started to choke.

'Uzza?'

'Oh, is it that time of year again?' she said. 'Yes, I see it is. Needn't waste time on me, my friend. There'll be some beauties here soon.'

Her eyes began to moisten above her sharpened tusks. *My* eyes began to moisten. Fancy looking like her in a city renowned for beautiful women.

A priest appeared. 'Don't cry,' he said. 'You can have her cheap. Any silver coin.'

'Shut your mouth!' I said, but he hadn't heard. He turned and left us.

Uzza had a hunch and a belly as well as the wen on her nose. One leg was thicker than the other, too, and she dribbled when she spoke but she was perspicacious.

'I can see you're no man of the world,' she said, 'so I'll give you the drum on this festival. All fertile women of Harran must do a deed of kind here with a stranger. The money we get for doing the deed we give to Atargatis and until I have given money to Atargatis I can't go home and my little boys are growing up without me and my husband seldom sees me.'

'Don't fret, Uzza,' I said, impulsively, 'for I shall do the deed of kind on you. By the Truth of the Messiah and the Faith that is no Liar, you'll be home again with your family before I leave Harran.'

'Thanks,' she said, I thought, without conviction. 'Would you like to see my veil of nature?'

'Ah no, there'd be no need for that. No need for that at all. You stay here and I'll be back as soon as the sun is set.'

'Do it *now*! We should do it *now*. Why, if one of these wretched ...'

'I'd prefer to wait till dark.'

'It's never dark here. Swear to me you will do as you say. Swear by the blade and the book! Swear by the great god Sin!'

So I swore by the great god Sin and returned to my rooms.

Surah al-Mu'minun defines the Blessed as '*believers who are humble in their prayers, who avoid profane talk, give alms to the destitute, are true to their trusts and promises, diligent in their prayers, and restrained in their carnal desires, except with their wives and slave girls.*'

This I believe is sound prophecy. Monogamy in a monotheistic society is quite dangerous for it tends towards Romantic Love which confuses God with His creature.

The Prophet, on whom be The Peace, was accorded dispensation to have eight wives and two slave girls, his favourite being 'A'ishah, the daughter of Abu Bakr.

In His Sermon on the Mount, the Christ – Who had no wives and no slave girls – equates lust with adultery and goes on to propose emasculation as a sovereign remedy. I believe Christ, a funker in regards the deed of kind himself, well understood the impossibility, even the undesirability, of marriage. Mind you, his Kingdom is not of this world, but like Mohammed – on whom be The Peace – Christ is very harsh towards adulterers because no adulterer ever felt, in his heart of hearts, that he was doing wrong. He may concede it, grudgingly, on suffering the consequence – he may be trained through public shaming, beatings, torture and nagging – but this is not the same as to admit wrong in one's heart of hearts.

We have here a problem.

In any case, I funked it. I didn't return to Uzza that night as I'd promised the moon god.

Over the next few days the college filled with strangers and it wasn't easy to tell pilgrims from scholars as everyone made for the temple as soon as they'd finished coffee. Priests were now giving hand-ink tattoos to prospective pilgrims. First up, they scrutinised the back of a man's hand for a pre-existing tatt. Once accepted, the new pilgrim received that year's model as it varies year to year to ensure that no one makes a pilgrimage twice. Mine's almost faded. There's Icthys – just the two strokes.

I hear from pilgrims that someone in Mardin does a good job removing these tattoos.

The mood in the city had now become uncongenial to scholarship. I believe they made a mistake, scheduling the seminar for Nawruz.

So I'd made this promise I hadn't kept and my conscience was troubling me. But the kind of help Uzza needed from me was not in my power to provide, not with the temple decked in lights. They'd lit the ziggurat with fires and *noise*, you never heard such noise – cymbals, trumpets, drums, horns, a terrible cacophony – sleep was out of the question. The 'music' went on day and night.

Pilgrims sat on their terraces drinking wine and coffee. 'One for me!' they'd shout if they saw a young lady walk by.

Often as not she'd shout back up, 'I hope you bought yer money wit' ya? Hope you're a big spender! I don't come cheap!'

Laughter, all good fun I dare say but I wasn't in the mood. I thought of visiting the mosque which appeared to be deserted. I gave up on my Behistun inscription, just sat there on the terrace drinking wine and coffee and wishing I could go home, but having come all that way I was dreading the return journey.

On the third night of the bonfires the women began to arrive. I realised then why the college was in demand. It overlooked the ramp to the temple.

'Phwoar, check that out, mate, there on the left. Like a slice o' that?' This was the kind of remark I had to endure all night from the next terrace.

Before the women were ushered into the temple by the priests, they said goodbye to their husbands, some of them men with whom I had queued. Holding the children by the hand the men walked off into the night.

Poor Uzza. She now shared a dormitory with all these sultry beauties and I knew exactly how many there were because we kept a tally.

'Hundred and twenty-three last night, makes – what? Four hundred and fourteen?'

'Four hundred 'n seventeen.'

'Pass the coffee. Hey, piece with the big shnoz, wooo ... get a glimpse of that? Like big noses.'

'Hittite. Carchemish.'

'Phoenician. Ugarit.'

'Armenian! Erivan.'

'Jew! Gadara!'

'Settle down, settle down!'

'Syrian. Mambij.'

Connoisseurs of female flesh. The temple was now off-limits. The priests I'd learned were eunuchs. Now you'd think, you'd hope, that a man dependent on his powers of observation for his living might have noticed this but I hadn't – wasn't getting any sleep through drinking too much coffee.

A notice appeared on the noticeboard to announce the Seminar in Hellenic Studies would begin in two days sharp.

Nawruz, night of the Battle of the Waters, the Temple was darkened and the fires extinguished. The musical instruments fell silent. The mood on the terraces was sombre. As the moon rose, thinking I saw the gate to the Temple opening, I ran up the ramp. This is not me, I thought as I ran and in fact, I was early, but some other men came, too.

The gate opened as we reached it. Admitted, having flashed our tatts, I saw a sight I shan't forget. The smaller tank, lit now by the moon, was giving birth to a *monster*. Clambering up a ramp I hadn't noticed on previous visits, a water creature was struggling to ascend, dragging itself on fins or legs. I thought at first it was a dolphin or perhaps a Nile crocodile but no, it was a fish – vast, blue, ancient, venerable and covered in carbuncles. It settled itself at the top of the ramp on an altar placed there for the purpose and as it rested, gasping and dripping, the priests prostrated themselves.

I turned to the man next to me.

'Ha,' he explained, 'it's their god Ha. He's six thousand years old. They brought him here from Eridu. He's the father of Nabu and Marduk. He comes out this night every year to feast on the Day of Blood and when he starts to weep, which he will do, stand back as I was here first.'

'Why does he weep?'

'He weeps because he sees us keen to forfeit immortality. He weeps for mankind. Stand back please, as I was here first. I was first up that ramp.'

Then the great fish began to weep – pinguid tears that ran down its cheeks to be collected in chalices and, smelling these, you soon realised why the priests were eunuchs.

Music – barbarous, I should call it – beat an African rhythm. There was one instrument pitched so low that you *felt* it rather than heard it. The atrium shook. The noise was visceral. The temple reverberated. The bonfires were relit and in the red light of the flames we could see strangers hastening towards the temple from every quarter of Harran.

A shocking thought occurred to me.

'Oh no, you didn't forget your *money*?' my friend asked. 'You want to go back and get it quick.'

I struggled down the ramp towards the massive mob ascending. Hundreds and hundreds of pilgrims, men of every breed, pushing and shoving and yes, there were blackamoors, Shahrban – Habashis and Takruris. I fought my way back as best I could against this uprushing tide and ran to my now-deserted lodgings to grab my alms-pouch. One more sniff of the tears of that fish and I'd *do* the deed of kind on Uzza, so I would.

Limping and now impeded as well by a grossly tumescent member – the effect of the tears – I re-ascended the ramp. The courtyard where sat the venerable Ha was deserted. Beast that I'd become, I ran to the dormitory to find the women had been gagged and bound and dressed in silver-studded leather undergarments and trussed in camel halters and tied to benches and walls. A queue of pilgrims had formed behind each breeder in the silhouette formed by the torches in the cressets. Fights were common. Most of the pilgrims had thrown off their skirts and roamed the precinct naked. Because of the fires it was quite warm and sweat was pouring off us.

A eunuch priest took charge of each queue, maintaining order as best he could and wiping the sweat from our brows with a towel while collecting money in a goat-horn. The firelights flared, the drums and cymbals beat their incessant rhythm, the money tinkled into the coffers, but nothing could stifle our curses and our groans. There was no joy in us. Each man's face was grim.

As soon as a pilgrim had completed a deed of kind and supposing he still had cash, he ran back up to the courtyard to purchase a fresh vial of tears which a priest, chanting in praise of Atargatis, duly applied to his nostrils. He then hobbled back to rejoin the queue he'd just left or join another.

Let no man here pass judgement on us who never smelled the Tears of that Fish!

First up, I searched for Uzza. Get her out of the way, I thought, salve the conscience. I knew the night would be long but it couldn't be long enough for me, as I meant to do a deed of kind on every woman in the place, but I felt I should begin with Uzza.

I found her where I'd left her. The priests had dressed her in what looked to me like a legionary's metal corselet. She had her hair quite nicely combed over and there was no queue behind her.

'Quick!' she whispered to me. '*Quick!*'

Oh, it was going to be quick. I fumbled round in my skirt eager to commence a deed, when the priest appeared.

'On your way,' he said.

'*Tawakkul ala 'llah!*' I replied, using language I didn't think I knew. '*Fuck off! Here's* me tatt, *there's* me coin. I suppose you could watch.'

'Sorry, Cob, strangers only.'

'Ah, but I'm a scholar, see, come all the way from Merv.'

'Yes, but you were seen talking to this lady so you're no stranger to her. On your way.'

I went straight to the nearest queue. I wasn't about to argue. It wasn't till dawn when slouched more dead than alive against a wall that I started reflecting on how very harsh it had been, that call, and how unfair to Uzza. The music by now had ceased. The tears of the fish had dried. We sat sprawled against a wall.

Happy? I should say not.

The married men returned through a side door to reclaim their women. We watched listlessly as they rasped away, breaking up then clearing out our soft plugs. Staring defiantly at us the while, they then deposited their own.

The women were released – all, I suppose, but Uzza – the cash conveyed to the treasury, the bonfires extinguished. The Battle of the Waters was over and the Day of Blood had begun.

First up, a priest came strolling among us, slashing up his arms, Uighur-style. He read our mood pretty well. 'Filthy, sleazy perverts,' he said. 'You filthy, wicked, beastly creatures. Does any among you feel he deserves to be *Happy* after what he just did?'

No hand went up.

'But who among us would *like* to be Happy? Who's ready to change his behaviour *now*? Who wants to tie a knot in it?'

I think most hands went up. We'd lost something of value, possibly our souls, and we all knew it. How could I return to my marriage bed having done what I'd just done? I'd be guilty and I'd be bored.

So more music, but this time soft and sweet and the priests began to dance. They understood Happiness whereas we had been mistaken.

A bucket of knives appeared to act as Babylon. And still that great fish sat out on his altar, water being poured upon him now as he felt the heat.

The breeders reappeared dressed in white and smelling of frankincense. We'd hoped they might look our way but they didn't, which hurt our feelings. Indeed, mightily miffed, an Arab from among us, a pilgrim from the tribe of Banu Udhra, leapt up and facing off these breeders, seized a knife in his right hand, and clutching in his left his massive genitalia, sliced them off in a stroke, shouting as he did, 'For the Kingdom of Heaven's Sake!'

He had the women's attention now. He had the attention of all Harran. A *roar* went up the likes of which you never heard and the fresh eunuch, fortified by the adulation and holding high his genitalia, entered the temple, hastened to the altar and hurled them straight into the mouth of Ha. They were gone in one gulp. Then another pilgrim did the same. Then another and another and the ramp was soon slippery with darkening blood. I was going to say that before I knew quite what I was doing, but I think I knew what I was doing and there are times I wish I'd done it, I ripped off my own skirt and, wanting to share in the adulation of the Whole Wide World, reached for my Babylon, when a voice called out to me, or so I fancied, 'Mawdudus!'

It was the voice of reason. It was the voice of my wife, or so I fancied.

I funked it.

When Ha had eaten his fill he went back in his tank and the temple now had its funds and some new priests and the earth its blood and the merchants of Harran their profits and the next day was the Day of Rest, much needed, on which began the Seminar.

Uzza, for all I know, is still there. The rector showed me a cemetery next to the mosque in which are buried women who enter that temple never to emerge.

Iranian Days (continued)

'In regard to the one confirmed bodily resurrection and ascension,' says Mawdudus, a Nestorian, 'the synoptic Gospels inform us that the resurrected body of Christ Jesus, who left no offspring, was, if difficult to recognise at first, the same as the body crucified. This suggests that Jesus was born perfect with no amelioration to be attempted through a deed of kind. He was, it seems, the perfect carnal specimen of God's chosen race.

'Had that body a virile member? Of necessity; we know it drank wine. And had that member a foreskin? He was a Jew so, as we've just heard, the Whore of Babylon was in his very Covenant. In fact, he was an ethnic Galilean, descended from a gentile people forcibly circumcised in 104 BC in the first historical instance of a forced religious conversion – and as no fuss attends his circumcision, which is not mentioned in the Gospels, we infer that he possessed a sulcus, that indispensable ridge of tissue where the glans, which is the head of the penis, emerges from its shaft, a feature designed to remove a soft plug of semen for, Mary excepted, they all do it. 'Indispensable, because women who simulate a deed of kind on other women report that a sulcus is a non-negotiable component of any dildo they may use.

'Did the resurrected body of Christ Jesus boast a sulcus? Inasmuch as he hadn't been dead long enough to have decomposed, it must have, but it served no purpose. When Paul, who knew only the risen Christ, determines that a Christian may be gentile, which is to say, need not attempt to sharpen and improve, through circumcision, the sulcus, he is positing, *pace* Peter, the New Jerusalem as a spiritual place. Peter, like most of the Jews of his day, thought the Messianic Kingdom would be earthly.

'The Nazarene, indeed the Islamic, position remains, that we can expect to be resurrected bodily before the Last Judgement – a Zoroastrian concept picked up by the Jews during their Babylonian captivity. To be resurrected as the world's most beautiful Jew, though, is one thing. Are the rest of us really so fond of this body we cannot bear to be parted? Look at my round shoulders and freckles.

'Yet even though I pray to be reborn as Jesus, in the body of the risen Christ, Jesus, like Adam, is *not* perfect, for in perfection is solitude. Adam fell away from what Jesus strives towards. Plotinus speaks of the spiritual quest as "the flight of the alone to the alone". The impulse towards solitude is expressed, paradoxically, in the deed of kind, which proclaims, "I am dissatisfied with this body and wish to improve upon it. Thus, I lust after such women as may rectify my perceived deficiencies."

'Paradoxically, because Paradise is a place of beauty, light, pleasant scents and bliss, while Hell is a place of horror, misery, darkness, evil smells and suffering, both may be found between the same pair of legs in the same individual, where a dual-purpose organ is designed to evoke a full gamut of response.

'When God in the company of Mary and all those men taken bodily to paradise – Jesus and Moses and Mazdak, Abu Muslim and al-Muqanna, Enoch, Elijah and Ezra, Baruch, Zoroaster and Melchizedek – inspects, at the eschaton, the resurrected dead, He will seek out Adam without a sulcus. He will seek out the First Man. The rest He must repudiate.

'"My own Beloved Self," He will say, "it is *good* that the man should be alone. Sorry."

'Our longed-for body of resurrection is not, then, the body of Christ Jesus but a body more perfect still. We eat his flesh and drink his blood in order to become more beautiful than he was – *truly* beautiful, sulcus-free, possessed of a round tower pointed towards heaven, the original Adam, who was male and female both. And in this fallen world, Shahrban, for all its ghastly failings, we can still make a Mystical Marriage and liberate ourselves from the deed of kind. Amen.'

'Poor misguided creatures,' says the Shah, still thinking of the Day of Blood. 'I don't know where I'd be without my own fine penis with its glans and sulcus. You were lucky, Mawdudus, and so in truth were we, for we need your work in our College of Knowledge. You have explained to us, through Aristotle, why we have no friends. There is, of course, that brother in Samarkand but he's just family. We can't be sure he likes us. And literary men may be the least of men – ugly, duplicitous, lazy, cowardly, innumerate, prone to vice and gossip, overweight – but your translations of Aristotle will educate the world and you say you saw no perky boob?'

'Eunuchs are released from death to become, if not gods, at least philosophers. Follow things through, Shahrban! Make an effort. You may taste Eternity as I, too, have done. By the virtue of the

Virgin, it tastes so sweet. Meantime, do you realise you're the most miserable man in Merv? Not to mention the richest. Have you any conception of *sin*? Now there's an interesting word – etymology unknown. You've a long way to go yet, Shahrban, a long way to go but stick with it. In the words of Isaac of Ninevah, "There is no torment more keenly felt than the sin against love. It is absurd to assume that sinners in hell are deprived of God's love. Love is offered impartially. Love gives joy to those who have been faithful but torments sinners. Those who are tormented in hell have sinned against love, for the torment of hell is compunction." What do you want, Thabit?'

'Woman who owns them poults is back. Pir thought yez should know.'

There follows Duty and Repetition: Sons of the Rumour get a beat goin' down.

The Shah examines the cage of poults as he plucks up courage to speak. 'Records?' he inquires.

'And why would I keep records? I'm just a small concern.'

'Taxes.'

'Oh, you're a publican! More money for the Beast o' Merv, as if he ain't got enough and he was such a lovely boy. Shockin' thing what he become, butcherin' all them women. The world having dazzled him with delights has seduced him with its snares and taken him in its toils. He takes no thought to the condition of his subjects nor looks to the administration of justice. One of them Darwayshs next door was tellin' me the spell can be broken only if he does one of them twice or lets two of them go but that won't happen, knowin' his form. I'm speakin' of them concubines of his, for the day after workin' his will on 'em he shortens their highest part by a span.'

'He is only trying to defend your city to make sure you don't get another dud queen. By the virtue of Him who created His servants and computeth their numbers, fain would the Shah lay up merit for the world to come by taking his wreak of wicked women. Sell any poults lately?'

'Might have.'

'No crime, sellin' a poult.'

'Glad you think so! Wouldn't care if it was. What's crime in this place, where the criminals run the show? Sold some up the palace, if you must know. Sell a lot of poults up there.'

'Do you indeed. And would you be selling a poult to the palace, say, thirty-five days back? Or three or four days back? It's vitally important.'

'I can't keep records in this game and I have no recollection.'

'I suppose you knew that the blood of a poult can resemble the blood of a maidenhead?'

'Naaw! Get away with you. Look, a bloke took a box of twenty off me at the side gate just now. Satisfied? One o' them Turks. Tell you what, the Beast o' Merv, his balls are bigger'n his brains. Fancy lettin' Turks run Merv.'

'Well, they don't actually run it.'

'Oh yes they do.'

It is mid-afternoon and the Beast of Merv cannot find his Grand Wazir. When he ventures to his chambers he finds the bedroom empty. No ghulam on guard in the corridor. Dhu'l-Fiqar, the Wondrous Blade, is gone from under the throne. The Shah ventures to the scaffold in the courtyard to find it smeared in blood. Abu Bakr discovers him down on his knees looking for feathers.

'Shahrazad? Is she dead? I wasn't even here to watch! I hope it was done with the correct Nimchah. Where is it, by the way?'

'You may reign, Shahrban, but you no longer govern Merv so I shall retain Dhu'l-Fiqar. It was mine to begin with.'

'I hope you haven't deprived me of my consummation with your daughter. I'd be filthy if you have. As you said yourself, 'Iddah was three months and I hadn't divorced her. She might have been pregnant with my son and heir!'

'Only if you lost control before a morning execution could any woman ever become pregnant to you, O King of the Age, and you tell me you never lose control during deflorations. Did you lose control the morning of the night you deflowered Shahrazad? Think hard.'

'I never lose control before a morning execution.'

'I was speaking to the doc. He says that even if you didn't lose control deflowering Shahrazad, if you'd attended an execution that morning which certainly you had – because that was the very execution in which Satuq damaged the blade – then you didn't need to lose control if you didn't bathe yourself properly. Now, did you bathe yourself properly? Did you perform thorough Ghusl? Did you go underwater? Do you scrub your entire body with lot tree leaves?'

'I always ablute correctly! I am scrupulous with Ghusl. I never leave a spot of my skin unscrubbed and I find it hard to conceive that I actually deflowered Shahrazad, I mean – I have no recollection of having abated her maidenhead. Still, Allah createth whatso He willeth. Caliph 'Ali, whose face Allah honour, got three sons off the Virgin Fatimah. It's odd, though, I don't seem to recall entering your daughter's member feminine to weave for her and full her yarn, though what with the stress of losing Dhu'l-Fiqar to repairs after Satuq botched the execution, and then your insistence that I should take up that very evening with your own daughter, even though you must have realised that, what with the blade being chipped ...'

'I told you why at the time! I could no longer deny her. She would not let the matter rest. She had been badgering me. "Let me be his next victim," she'd say. "Oh, just let me be his next victim, Father, because I so admire the man." And don't forget, Shahrban, I have many daughters.'

'None with a body to compare with hers but how I envy you. As it says in the Recital, wealth and children are the ornaments of life and I have not fathered one single child. Even a daughter would be better than nothing. No one will remember me, Abu Bakr. I shall pass from existence as though I had never existed. The sweetness of life is in little children. Alhamdolillah, how I love them! How I adore the sweet, innocent creatures and how my heart bleeds that I have no son to be a slice of my liver and a sight to cool my eyes, for while peradventure an heir may squander my wealth in lewd living, whoso leaveth issue dieth not. Why, I might as well be a mule. It makes me absolutely filthy. Is some foreign magnifico, Abu Bakr, some Adfonsh or Aguetid, to seize my lands and palaces and hoards? And has Shahrazad gone to the mercy of Almighty Allah, be He exalted and extolled? Has Shahrazad found mercy? No soul may depart but by leave of Allah according to the writ which affirmeth the appointed term, so it wouldn't be my fault.'

'No indeed. In Allah is compensation for every decease, Shahrban, but she didn't seem to have found mercy when I seen her just now going up to the library. Can we change the subject? Aside from women, you have other problems to address – a shortage of regal toothpicks, for one thing, and dissent among the mirabs. Now they're grizzling over the cotton. When are you going to get back to your toothpicks? Regarding women, more bad news: Satuq, under bastinado to the point where the nails fell from his toes, admitted he did a deed of kind on your second wife. Committed adultery with that blackhead. Released her in exchange for a knee-trembler in the corridor so she'll be back in the Elburz making jokes about the size of your … turband.'

'Then what's to do with Satuq? That's *two* mistakes he's made! First up, he damages Dhu'l-Fiqar, now he deflowers my blackhead. As my head lives, the man's a knave. Nail him up!'

'Too late. But as to his fate, the scaffold gives a clue.'

'Does it. What kind of fool do you take me for? I put it to you that this is poult blood, Abu Bakr, intended to deceive, and that Satuq is making his way to Mawarannahr as we speak. I further put it to you that you are complicit with Satuq and Shahrazad and that Satuq, given his form, is likely the father of Shahrazad's son. Now what do you say to that?'

'Enough of your theories, say I. Wife for tonight?'

'Shahrazad. Tell her I want to hear the rest of that tale that she was telling me.'

'And what tale was that?'

'Oh, I don't know. It's bound to feature a Jinni and a palace with a trapdoor. As you would know, there's only one tale ever interested me.'

'Oh, God damn everything an inch high, are we back to that bloody blackamoor?'

'You look 'appy this evening, Shahrban,' says Shaykh 'Ali Zindiq. 'If I didn't know better I'd say that blackamoor who mounted your wife's bosom has died. Kurban-at basham – may I be your sacrifice, O Shadow of Allah?'

'Well, that shows how little you know, good Pir, as I killed him the evening of the day he did the deed.'

'Did you. Your mistake was in falling in love with a woman like a god and then behaving like a beast. In order to discover Real Love we should never speak to an apparent one. I've a Uighur here could tell us more about that. Marquis Singqu, you awake? Tell the Shah about the Uighur Khan and his gilt felt yurt. Now then, Shahrban, have you murdered that blonde?'

'There's a complication. She claims she's pregnant. I can't see how that could be but I need to wait another two months in order to ensure she's not. As you would appreciate, I can't risk losing an heir.'

'Of course not. So we have another two months. Allah save and advance the king.'

The Gilt Felt Yurt

It was a close call. I nearly died when I was two. I'd like to claim I was saved from death by a wolf but it was a tarpan.

I've not seen a tarpan in Merv. In Margiana they're interbred with Arabs and Argamaks but the wild tarpan is the native horse of the High Steppe, a shaggy little brute in winter, big-headed creature in summer, mane that sits right up like that on a Margiana *kyang*, the wild ass, and no forelock – good horse for an archer, sure-footed, easily controlled with the knees. There may be years as when Tibetans have raided his pastures, the *Faghfur* needs mounts; at other times he'd have tarpans to burn. There'd be some tarpans in Cathay! They can't breed horses themselves, Chinese, being too stupid or too tired, but they like to refer to the tarpans they're forced to buy as 'barbarian tribute'.

Barbarian tribute – how would you be? I was born before the Uighurs ruled the High Steppe. It may have been about the time the *Faghfur* banned the Manichees. I recall being hidden by a mother among the sheep in the fold during our war against the Sons of the Wolf, who fought under a Gold Wolf's Head. I was the only member of my family to escape, thanks to the presence of mind of one mother who placed me on my pony among the sheep in the fold. When that pony, spooked by the flames and the screams took off, I held on. He was no taller than a sheep that horse, no more than seven hands, and I still recall the roars of delight from the Sons of the Wolf as they watched us disappearing across the grass like a rat in a dust storm. Being on dragon horses themselves, sixteen hands, they could have run us down but preferred to enjoy the mothers and sisters while they were still warm, fathers and brothers having had their eyelids removed, being forced to observe.

Nowdays even the *Faghfur* owns a stable full of dragon horses – uses them to play polo – but he buys a great many Uighur tarpans at forty bolts of silk a head. I've seen them on sale in Shash for two so he pays top price if he'd pay, which he won't. At the present time the *Faghfur* owes the Uighur khan – Kuclug Bliga Chongde – millions of strings in copper cash because we provide him annually with thousands of our tarpans, whether he wants them or not.

The Chinese claim that they are the first, the best, the sedentaries par excellence, but the *Faghfur*'s a Turk – a *Hsia* – that's the joke of it. He calls the Turks barbarians, this Son of a Turk, but *he's* a Turk. The Hsia were Turks. Why else would the Son of Heaven have the eyes of a Slope? If you were to dress me up like a *Faghfur* or dress him down like me then cut our throats and wait a week, you'd have two snow peas in a pod. In life it's a different story.

A Turk walks unlike a sedentary Chinese. A Turk has no home but his horse. He walks *tall*. He's bandy. He stands different, he squats different. He spits harder. He pisses further. He drinks only fermented mare's milk. He looks you square in the eye and doesn't feel a need to smile. He knows, too, the compulsion to pull down your cities but he can build cities.

Karabalghasun, Black City, first nomad city unless your notion of a city is a semi-circle of stone men eyes set too close together reviewing a few tent pegs, which is all you'd see in the so-called Turghiz cities of Suyab and Talas.

Talas is on the Talas River, ancestral home of the walnut; while Suyab is on the Chu, ancestral home of the opium poppy. Chu flows north-west of *Issyk Kul*, the Warm Lake, the Mirror in the Sky, the Navel of the Earth, the Garden of Eden to sedentaries, the ancestral home of their apple.

I could be civilised. Mostly, it's step aside when I come to town or I might just make big trouble. During the Heavenly Riches reign the *Faghfur* passed a law that orders non-Chinese while visiting his Tang Empire to wear national dress. He did it through fear of his allies. He did it through fear of his tarpan supplier. He did it through fear of the Uighurs.

A Turk doesn't like to return from a campaign empty-handed, so if he hasn't been able to sack his foe he sacks his ally.

I don't think I was born a Uighur though I'm certainly a Turk. I couldn't properly walk or talk when I left home so I can't be sure. I haven't the green eyes of a Uighur though I'm certainly a Slope. I may have been born a Shatou but I was raised a Uighur.

Confused? There are hundreds of species. We are like the flowers on the steppe. Tartars are Turks, Xiongnu are Turks, Avars, Kazakhs, Oghuz, Kipchaks, Gepids, Tanguts, Uzbeks, Bulghars, Azas, Azeris, Karakalpaks, Chigils, Yagmas – all Turks, all Slopes.

Turks inhabit the regions with the purest air, the loftier locations. There we are distinguished by high cheekbones, friendliness, good taste, filial piety, loyalty, simplicity, frugality, modesty, dignity, intelligence and courage.

He'd snap his head back to nip me, that horse – he was a vicious little creature. I sang him a *gingo* to encourage him: the hideous battle cry of a horde is each rider singing a *gingo* as each horse has his own *gingo*: the first thing you must do, when breaking a pony, is compose a *gingo* for him. Once that pony rolled on his back and kicked his legs but I wouldn't let him go. I had the wit to realise I wouldn't survive on all fours.

I don't know where we were but I've worked it out. I think it was the Ili Valley that drains into the Jetisu where Sogdians dry farm the delta under a Turkic suzerain because the forest, when we met with forest, was spruce and spruce is the only tree that grows on the north slopes of the Tien Shan. I'd say we were moving west through the Ili Valley.

We fell in with some wild tarpans. One of them took a shine to me, even let me drink from her. A Turk must not drink water. I've had but the one drink of water and I still have nightmares about it. I'd been scratching a bit of blood off my pony here and there, nibbling his ears. I could mount and dismount although I could barely walk. He'd given up trying to kill me.

The tarpans were headed somewhere west so we tagged along. You'd reason they were making for the Naryn Valley, ancestral home of lucerne. We drifted for months at four thousand feet, resting in stands of fir, licking snow and chomping on edelweiss, dandelion and fescue, till we made our way into a little valley not far from Issyk Kul. Nothing flows out of that Warm Lake yet forty-four rivers flow in and each one of those river valleys is the ancestral home of some important plant, because while Turks were domesticating animals, oasis dwellers were domesticating plants and they all come from Issyk Kul. One valley is the ancestral home of ephedra. Another, the ancestral home of pear. Another, the ancestral home of raspberry. Turks, I might add, don't eat plants, though shamans drink piss from the captives we force to eat the magic mushrooms before we cut their throats that haply our idols may look lovingly upon us.

We were, I suppose, east of that lake, the west of it being desert. They say it never rains on the lake itself. The constant westerly wind makes all the snow fall on the Alatau. Issyk Kul is one hundred and twenty miles long and forty miles wide and full of the world's best fish – chebachok, chebak, sazam, sig – any big fish you might fancy, and the northern banks were the winter camp of the Turghiz khan, his summer camp being Shash. He kept the Arabs out of Binkat for a bit.

The Sogdian citizens of Shash may not have realised they were part of the Turghiz Empire; the Turghiz khan was in no doubt of it.

Rascals' grass – from one end to the other, that valley was full of great bhang plants, thirty-six hands in full flower drooping their resinous heads, this being the ancestral home of bhang. The tarpans fell into it greedily. Actually, it was a convention. There were big black eighteen-hand *dong*, *kyang*, mountain goats, gazelle, antelope, blue sheep, Siberian ibex, bears, boars, silvery field voles, red wolves, badgers, camels, foxes, porcupines, otters, weasels, ermines, martens, I even saw a snow leopard. And birds! You never saw more birds. Hissing swans, grey geese, pink pelicans, bearded vultures, black storks, partridge, golden eagle, bustard, crane, bullfinch, woodcock, alpine jackdaw, every bird and animal in the whole blessed Tien Shan was there, tucking into each other or feeding on the bhang. Some I couldn't identify as they hung upside down in the bhang plants. I saw no men. Issyk Kul is Uighur and back then it was Turghiz but there were no Sakyas. I was the only human being, drinking from a tarpan's bag.

Issyk Kul, the Mirror in the Sky because Khan Tengri put it there so his *Shakti* could admire her reflection. Eventually the bhang was gone. After a week what hadn't been eaten was trampled flat and the valley was a mess of dung and bones and seeds and hooves and massive sheep horns too big for a man to lift, in which foxes bred.

No creature seemed keen to move.

No creature seemed capable of movement.

The Warm Lake never freezes so we lay in a mild torpor. It was dusk and I was enjoying the beautiful sunset from under the tarpan's belly when the silence, hitherto broken only by the ruminant belching of cuds, was suddenly shattered with a horrible shrieking, coming from over the west ridge.

'Reeyaaaaaark! Reeeeeyaaaaark! Ip. Cree-eeeurrrk! Ruck.'

It curdled the blood as it wasn't the cry of a man. It wasn't the cry of a beast. It wasn't the cry of a Tien Shan bird. It seemed the cry of a hungry ghost but then it made some human words, forsworn by hungry ghosts.

'Dong jie zhi qi suowu ze wu tong yi. Yaark!'

The effect was a stampede into the valley north-east, ancestral home of the apricot. Most of the beasts in the Mountains of Heaven make horrible noises but none speak.

'Raaaooww. Rup. Eeeearrrrk! Rep. Eeearrrk, eeearrrk! Dong jie zhi qi suowu ze wu tong yi, yaaark. Yaaaraaark! Yaaaraaaaaaarrrk! Herp.'

I was alone. The tarpans were among the first out. The darkening sky to the west became black with birds and then it emptied.

The noise over the ridge had stopped. I started crawling towards the ridge to see what had made the noise. I could crawl better than I could walk. Turkic babies lie tightly swaddled and immobilised in their cribs with a catheter so when we are finally freed to move we never take movement for granted and we can freeze. An army of Turks can remain on horseback for weeks at a time, dismounting not even to sleep or to answer the calls of nature and bear in mind that a horse to a Turk is not just a locomotive, it is food and drink – meat, alcoholic kumis, blood, dairy products. We were the people who first tamed the horse and the first horse tamed was a tarpan.

And some do say that with our feet nearly touching the ground, we look silly on them. But we do say that we can wipe the smile off any face.

When I cleared the ridge I looked to see what was making the noise. Surely, it couldn't be that little white bird with the yellow pigtail wandering round like a duck, poking the ground with its grey-blue beak?

'Yeer. Rrwa.'

He'd quietened down. Next day I took a closer look at him. He was digging up onion bulbs with his beak, this being the ancestral home of the spring onion. I started crawling towards him. We were in the Tiup Valley. There were men on donkeys and yaks. I wanted to befriend the bird. When my hand went out to touch him, he dipped his head and his pigtail expanded into a great yellow crest.

'Dong jie zhi qi suowu ze wu tong yi!'

Then he bit me, taking my little finger at the top joint. See?

A white cockatoo – all the princesses have one. A breeder in Luoyang breeds both fighting crickets and white cockatoos and while no one knows where they come from they can be taught to speak which makes them excellent companions for imperial concubines' daughters.

I sucked the stump till the bleeding stopped and the bird started waddling back down the ridge, happy to find so many tasty onion bulbs to worry.

We like sucking blood. We suck the blood of men we kill. We drink from horses' jugular veins.

Eventually the bird accepted me. I was permitted to stroke him provided I didn't interfere with his onion hunt. He had wonderful feathers – smooth, glossy, well preened.

'Dong jie zhi qi suowu ze wu tong yi,' he would say quietly from time to time.

At first I replied using the two words of Turkic that I knew

– 'horse' and 'no'. But by day's end when that cameleer from the Bright Camel Envoy appeared over the pass, I could say '*dong jie zhi qi suowu ze wu tong yi*', as well as any cockatoo and I can still say it. It's the only Chinese I know.

I don't think Chinbat wanted to return to his cage but, come dusk, he felt a need to screech. '*Erraaaaaaaarrrrrk! Erraaaaaaaarrrrrk! Riyowa! Rup.*'

They'd have heard him in Aksu. It was worse than the crowing of all the roosters you hear in Karabalghasun. The cameleer sent to scour that valley came racing up to grab the escapee. He was wearing a leather gauntlet like the goshawk handlers wear so he had some experience of Chinbat or knew what to expect. Chinbat, in two minds about being caught, waddled off digging onions as he went and I think it was actually the camel found me.

I'd have liked to have seen her up on the snow-covered saddle of the Bedal Pass. Have you seen a white camel? They moult in long streamers. So as not to lose their precious white hair the cameleers gift-wrap them.

A Bright Camel Envoy usually travels at a gallop and the cameleers ride. They serve as dispatch riders bringing news from the front to the *Faghfur* but here they'd been sent in a friendly gesture to accompany a Tibetan princess.

Big animals hate toddlers. That bright camel drenched me in sputum then kicked me, reducing me to tears. The bright cameleer, a tall young man, came over, Chinbat on his arm, to pick me up. I recall the last rays of the sun shining on Chinbat's pigtail.

'*Dong jie zhi qi suowu ze wu tong yi*,' I said to the cameleer.

He doubled up – couldn't wait to get back for his mates to share in the fun because it means 'if action occurs so it always comes to nothing then things will go smoothly' which is from the Tao-te-ching. What a thing to teach a cockatoo. Still, if you live your life out in a cage …

Sons of the Rumour

☾

I'd have to say my own life has gone rather smoothly.

As you see I'm an old man now. The time of which we speak was ninety years back. We were in the Tiup Valley where the road comes up between the Tien Shan glaciers from Aksu. There are four passes along that road and we were between the second and the third. The first and biggest is the Bedal. The Chinese and Tibetans weren't at war for once, having allied themselves with the Turghiz to give the Arabs a bloody nose, so it was a time of comparative peace on the passes. Alliances in those parts are always sealed with marriage and Chinbat belonged to Lghags sgrog ma, a Qiang princess from Tibet who was on her way to Issyk Kul to marry I-jan, Khan of the Ten Arrows, and her party was under escort from Wuwei by the Bright Camel Envoy. Those foolhardy cameleers, Blue Turks from Chang'an, had taken their camels over the Bedal Pass which at fourteen thousand feet is a dangerous place to a camel. Should a camel get caught short of feed she can't scratch holes in the snow like a horse. The princess had a black yak caravan loaded with salt and furs and each yak dragged a stalactite furbelow where they'd just forded the river. As well as yaks, there was a guard of surly, one-armed Tibetan veterans, a few Tibetan mastiffs and Chinbat's cage with its broken door and reinforced swings and playtoys.

Those cockatoos all come from the same shop in Luoyang and the second time we sacked Luoyang I made it my business to find it. It was in a gate by the Pien Canal till someone torched it, but I mustn't get ahead of myself except to say that Princess Gold Immortal, when she came up to Karabalghasun, had a cockatoo that said, 'Those who speak don't know,' which Bogu thought quite witty, seeing as how Transcendent Treasure had a silent cockatoo, but back to the Tien Shan.

Better yet, on to the Turghiz winter camp: hundreds of white felt tents sprawled over the Kungey Alatau from Suyab on the Chu to the shores of Issyk Kul.

Princess Lghags sgrog ma grabbed hold of me and wouldn't let go. She didn't want to marry the Turghiz khan. Mind you, I don't expect he was overjoyed to see her as she stank of rancid butter and wore a filthy witch's hat and a felt overcoat that made her look twice her size. She was no Chinese courtesan force-fed from infancy on perfumes and she took my screaming when she pressed me to her as rejection which made her cry the more. I was just a bit sunburnt, always a danger round Issyk Kul.

When we got among the thousands of brown and white fat-tailed sheep grazing the shores, each with his tail on his truck, making for the tent of the khan, a tutuk came up and snatched me away, appalled that a princess would dare turn up for a wedding with a babe in arms. The Bright Camel Envoy had gone, anxious to get back over the passes before winter, none of the Turghiz spoke Tibetan, the Tibetans couldn't understand the Turks and while there were some Sogdian merchants, trading silk for last year's wool, they wouldn't involve themselves in any matter of polity.

So the tutuk didn't know quite what to do. He was determined to hide me from the khan but he didn't want to kill me as the princess had gotten herself in such a state they had to subdue her with clubs. Tibetans regard a foundling as a reincarnated saint.

In the end I was sent off to the Irtysh River and consigned to the care of the tutuk of the Irtysh, where things continued to go smoothly. There are twenty tutuks among the Turghiz, each of whom must muster five thousand mounted men because the Turk is a fighter. Any brawl will suit him nicely. Issyk Kul had only been just been wrested from the Western Blues and the Turghiz were soon to lose it to the Uighurs because not content with fighting the Oghuz, Chinese,

Tibetans and Arabs, they were given to fighting among themselves, tutuk versus tutuk.

But what of the last man standing, you ask. Who's he going to fight?

Good question. I shall now tell the tale of the mighty Uighur who destroyed first Uighur culture and second his own human nature. His name was Bogu Khan and I was his best friend.

The valley of the Irtysh was the westernmost pasture of the Turghiz horde. Further west was the territory of the Eastern Blues and, in particular, three vassals of the Eastern Blue, one Uighur, one Uduyut, one Buriat. The Utikien Uighur were camped along the Selenga, a tributary of the Orkhon River which flows north into Lake Baikal, a sea with a population of seals. The Orkhon being the choicest pasture and paramount valley in the whole High Steppe, it seemed hard to the tutuk of the Irtysh that a vassal tribe should occupy it. Yet every time he'd set out to put matters aright with a punitive excursion, meaning to drive the Uighurs to where they'd have to trade tarpan for reindeer and build themselves tents of birch bark and hunt hare on snowshoes, he'd receive, often that morning, intelligence from his khan requesting that he and his men repair forthwith to the walls of Numijkat or Baykand or Kesh or Nasaf or some other Transoxanian city there to discomfit Arabs, or else relieve the Chinese garrison in Kashgar or Kucha or Aksu or some other Nanlu city, because a nomad empire is not like that of a sedentary. It doesn't last long as it has an inbuilt fuse. The nomad has no liking for administrative chores and while he can trade wool or fur or sell his tarpans for silk, he much prefers to raid cities, even those under his aegis, while should he defend them it's only to stop some other thief from stealing what he intends to steal.

Metal for arrow heads; gold and lapis lazuli for superfluity.

The Selenga is a journey from the Irtysh of some weeks if you intend a leisurely campaign. We had camels pulling yurts on carts but when we got among the Uighurs we found to our consternation that we couldn't tell Uighur from Turghiz. Our tarpans wheeled in stupefaction. Not one arrow left a quiver. The Uighur dressed the same way we did, rode the same horses, spoke the same language, lived in the same yurts, had the same faces – Slopes with slits for eyes and leathery skin just like us – owned the same livestock, drank the same kumis, worshipped the same gods – the white, hare-skin puppet *Chandaghatu*, god of the chase, outside the yurts; the two sheep fleece bolsters, *Ongot* and his wife, under the smoke hole; at the door, the rawhide *Emelgelji*, god of the herds – and in the confusion I got left behind along with quite a few others, including the tutuk, who soon became a vassal of the Uighur.

So he was given to eat a red mushroom and when he'd stopped spewing up his ring, made to piss.

Surely the power of a Uighur shaman showed itself that day but it made no difference in my life where things continued to go smoothly. I remained churning the kumis, standing over a smoked goatskin, bashing with my kumis staff the ewe-milk starter in the mare's milk – such being the life of a Turkic orphan. That's how I met Bogu, though he wasn't then Uighur khan, he was just a little chap like me but he would insist on taking a turn at the churn the day we got a visit from his father, Mo-yen Cur *Iltirish*, Utikien tutuk. And so we became good friends. Indeed, we used to wrestle every afternoon.

It was a time of ferment on the steppes and not just in the kumis churns. One day, resting from our wrestling, Bogu and I received a Sogdian. There were Sogdians from Samarkand fighting among the Turghiz – refugees from various rebellions against the Arabs – and the Sogdian tutuk appeared one day seeking the support of Mo-yen.

'You want my help against the Oghuz or the Turghiz or the Kyrghyz or the Arabs?' asked Mo-yen.

'*All* of them *and* Algorithms and Bukhariots and Chinese and Tibetans.'

'Sit down. Bogu! Singqu! Fetch this gentleman a drink. He's been through hard times.'

Mo-yen offered our Uighur support in the annual Samarkand rebellion.

'Can we come, too?' said Bogu, putting an arm around my shoulder. 'Let us come or we will slay ourselves.'

'How old are you?'

'Seven.'

'Can you ride seventy miles in a day?'

'We can.'

'Could you shoot an arrow three hundred yards behind you through the eye of a wolf riding at full gallop?'

'Yes.'

'Can you stay on your horse ten days and ten nights never once dismounting?'

'Yes.'

'Would you eat the meat of a lynx? Could you cut up a woman great with child and cleave the fruit of her womb? Can you tie a knot? Do you know how to flay mice? Can you sew?'

'Yes.'

'Do you need a saddle or bridle or reins?'

'No.'

'Would sleet bother you?'

'Probably not.'

'Very well, you can come. I'll have you each fitted with a cuirbouly.'

So we were each fitted with a cuirbouly. A yak was killed, the leather boiled till soft then fitted to our chests and left to harden in the sun. At first it was hard to breathe or move. We fashioned two leather bottles for our kumis, sharpened the larch arrows in our quivers – thirty light, thirty heavy, all armed with steel tips – mounted our ponies and went off under the *tuk*, the horsetail standard of the horde.

It's a forty-day ride from Selenga to the Chu riding three stages a day. The journey is over grass and there was ice, so there was milk. Each Uighur had fifteen tarpans for his meat and milk as well as locomotion, and our riding mounts had been carefully selected for thick hides, long hair and pot bellies.

Two hundred men kept two days in advance of the horde as forward scouts; two hundred were two days in arrear as rearguards; a further two hundred men rode a day away on either flank.

Now and then we'd take a day off to play *buzkachi* with a headless foal or go hunting gazelles. Mo-yen explained to us that these days off were not *sport*; they were *nerge*.

Nerge is Turkic military training. In the course of the hunt we practised the technique of the battlefield. We were broken into decimal divisions with an officer to each ten men and to each hundred men and to each thousand men and to each ten thousand men, so that no officer ever needed to speak to more than ten subordinates. Mistakes of any kind were punished with blows from a studded cudgel, the number received being always odd and never to exceed seventy-seven. We watched Mo-yen receive twenty-nine blows for a dangerous tackle in *buzkachi*. Each blow was delivered from a separate cudgel, each held by a different man. As boys we never got more than nine blows as thirteen might have killed us.

We learned to shout in unison. We learned to show no sign of pain. We learned to gallop at a wheel perpetually doubling back and forth in close rank so as to appear to a hapless gazelle half the number we were. We'd gallop in retreat from the terrified creatures then fire back over our shoulders at them before wheeling to mount yet another attack, breaking rank in all directions. We learned to sit quiet as Mo-yen dismounted and, putting hand on heart, swore by Allah, be He exalted and extolled, that he would never harm gazelles. Then, killing the gazelles, we learned to do it quickly with a nick of an arrow to the neck, so that by the time we got to Issyk Kul we could each of us kill four hundred creatures in one hour.

It takes another forty days to get to Samarakand from Issyk Kul travelling down the Talas Valley into the Land of Shash, through stands of walnut and juniper trailing honeysuckle and wild roses and glades of poppies and tulips and iris and daisies, for it was spring by this time – our numbers all the while increasing with Sogdian rebels, Tibetan mosstroopers, Turghiz and Oghuz with nothing much on – brawlers who'd come running to any brawl along with some strange blond-haired round-eyes who couldn't stop laughing.

Mo-yen Cur scowled a bit when he saw these laughing cavaliers. '*Hauma* drinkers,' he muttered. 'Saka haumavarga. They're not Slopes, they're Sakyas. Sakyas like the Buddha, Sage among the Scythians – *hauma* drinkers.'

'What's *hauma?*'

'Ferment of opium, ephedra and bhang, infused with raisins, cucumber seed and toasted betel leaf. You ask too many questions, Bogu.'

We kept to the foothills of the Chatkal Range at seven thousand feet. Our tarpans, moulting, would feel the heat once we got down on the Red Sandy Waste, that scrubby desert that lies beyond the Land of Shash on the far bank of the Sayhun. This great stream which Turks call Syr Darya and Greeks Jaxartes is the border between Mawarannahr – Transoxiana, Bilad-al-Sughd, the Land beyond the River – and Bilad-al-Turk, which more or less begins at the Syr Darya.

Coming round a bend we suddenly saw beneath us the city of Binkat, but we hardly noticed, focused as we were on the river we could see in the distance. If we meant to fight in Samarkand we had to ford that river and it was two miles wide, the colour of mud and roaring along in great whitecaps. A thousand-year-old juniper tree trunk, travelling at speed, went by – then an orchard, walls and all.

Back went Tibetan cavalrymen who, like their horses, wear chainmail. *Saka haumavarga* said they could not risk losing their precious *hauma*. There was no spoil, they said, no adventure, more precious to them than *hauma*.

Iskander's army had crossed the Oxus on rafts of inflated skins so we thought we'd give that a try. We soon had the skins but we couldn't work out how to inflate the rafts.

'Let's not delay,' said Mo-yen. 'The Arabs won't be expecting us. They wouldn't expect an army to be crossing this river in spate.'

In the end we did what we always do; each man sewed a skin sufficient to hold his quiver and bow, his kumis bottles and curds, and with the bundle tied to his horse's tail he wrestled his tarpan into the stream and held on; but there's not much mane on a tarpan and it was spring and they were moulting.

I drank a deal of water. Ninety years on I still dream I'm drowning in that river but I survived, as did Bogu and Mo-yen, but no Sogdian and none of the Turghiz or Oghuz and only eighty-seven Uighur. It took us a full day and night to get over, those of us who did, and another week to reassemble on the shores of Bilad-al-Sughd.

'All fathers should have such sons,' said Mo-yen as he mustered us.

☾

Once we got in the Red Sandy Waste, we'd pick so we'd blood. We'd fire an arrow into our pony's neck till blood gushed then press our mouth to the wound which always heals up pretty quick.

Wadi-al-Sughd, Zarafshan River, Stream of the Gold-strewer: why does everything round this place have to have ten names? The Sogdians of Panjikent who'd smelled us before they'd seen us were so terrified by the sight of us and so appalled at the stench of us, that Mo-yen ordered us not to dismount on learning that Samarkand was only forty miles downstream.

'The Arabs won't be expecting us,' he said to Bogu as we trotted through the night. 'This will be a great victory. People will wonder why we're here. To think we're only eighty-seven men.'

And indeed, the Arabs addressed themselves to flight, perhaps inferring the eighty-five men they could see were the forward scouts of some great force.

But that force by now was a bloat of inflatable rafts in the frigid Aral Sea.

Samarkand, like Binkat and Panjikent, is a walled city on a low hill. With Ghutah, Basrah and Shiraz, it is one of the four earthly paradises. The walls are eight miles round and fifty foot high with many a barbican, but approaching from the south-east, we saw no sign of the Arab garrison.

'They must be on the other side of that hill,' said Mo-yen. 'You boys wait here.'

Just from the way Bogu had been staring at the walls it came as no surprise when as soon as his father was out of sight, he said we should go take a look.

'You're Uighur Tegin,' I said. 'I suppose you can do as you like. I'll stay here.'

'Don't you want to see what's inside? Have you no curiosity?

This is the third walled city we've seen and we haven't been inside one gate!'

'You think they're going to let in a pair of Turks with cuirboullies on?'

'We have our bows and arrows and I still have my knife.'

'I'll stay here.'

'No! You'll come with me! I *command* you to come with me, Singqu! Otherwise, I'll have no one to share my memories with.'

So we went into Samarkand that day and Mo-yen, when emperor, used to complain that if only we'd done as we'd been bidden, Karabalghasun would not exist because it was built by Bogu.

I guess the ordeal we'd just been through had sharpened our perceptions but oh what a memorable day we had, that day in Samarkand.

We had no trouble getting in a gate. No one took the least notice of us even though we had fitted arrows to our bows and were wearing stern expressions. The first thing we saw was an elephant doing tricks for coins. They had it painted pink and white. We'd never heard tell of an elephant and this was a great big bull.

'*Look* at that thing,' said Bogu, 'it's alive! It has no neck at all! It must have internal testes like a bird. The tail is a camel's tail. Is that a sleeve hangs from its face? I want one of those in my city.'

Then a vendor went by, selling rhubarb and spring onions. Bogu became interested in a bareheaded boy our age who, buying a bunch of these onions, put them on his head. He was a beauty, too, such as serves the True-Believer in Paradise.

'*I* should have such a cap,' said Bogu and going up to the vendor, he offered to cut his throat.

I don't know what might have happened next had the boy not come to our rescue. We were in filthy cuirboullies while he wore pink damask trowsers, crocodile-skin buskins with a yellow and mauve silk jacket patterned with paired facing geese in red roundels intercalated with Moline crosses and flared at the waist with a mandarin collar. Buying the onions Bogu had his eye on, he braided them and handed them to Bogu as a gift. Then he smiled, as though he thought he was better than we were and perhaps he was: he spoke a kind of Turkic – *Muwalla'*, or piebald.

'Wall you frim?' he asked us. 'Hongra? Ball you vent zim shagery kik?'

'Sugary cake sounds mighty fine,' said Bogu, adjusting his new headwear.

'Don't go eating sugary cake,' I warned. 'You'll make yourself sick!'

But he was bent on eating anything and everything we came upon that day. Cakes of millet flour with plums and pistachios all paid for by our *cicerone* – we'd never seen money – candies of almond and mutton fat, hard-boiled eggs dyed red and blue with pancakes and raisins and peaches and honey, conserve of pomegranate grains with sugar and pepper, cherries with crushed ice and grape syrup, pillows of tamarind and honeycomb, mock-date pies stuffed with rice, gugglets of sherbet flavoured with rosewater scented with musk and cooled with snow – ooh, it makes me sick just to think of it. I had to force the rhubarb down him in the end, get him to eat his own hat.

And would you believe he was our only Uighur casualty that day?

Our new friend, Anahitaivandak, decided to take the day off school – a school in which he studied the thirty-six languages together with mathematics – in order to show his two new pals around the city of Samarkand, a gesture perhaps formulated on some mercantile gut instinct and amply rewarded in later years when Bogu decided he needed Sogdian help in building Samarkand-on-Steppe. It was

Anahitaivandak, by then a wealthy shroff, to whom Bogu turned to procure him the sculptors, blacksmiths, masons, faience artists, potters, builders, landscape architects, milliners and pastry cooks to help him realise his dream – a dream, no doubt, begotten the day of which I speak, beneath a fringe of spring onions.

First, we went to a warehouse owned by Anahitaivandak's father in which were stored all goods in transit, with black-bearded agents organising backloads. We spent a couple of interesting hours there marvelling at the many and varied goods, which included a box of bezoar stones from the fourth stomach of a Bhutanese yak as used in treating aconite poisoning, bound for the court of the Byzantine king; gum guggul, the frankincense adulterant, consigned to an address in Ba'allak; cakes of Kyrghyz asafoetida as used to treat itchy bums in China; snail kohl from the Atlas Mountains for inscribing moth eyebrows on courtesans; and stained glass pounded in a menstruum of onion juice for treating intestinal vermicules in lap-dogs. We saw cast-iron stoves made in Yangchou on consignment to Syracuse and glass carriage windows from Syracuse on consignment to Yangchou. We saw Japanese walrus tusks transshipping to Trebizon on the Black Sea and camphor and dried proboscis monkeys from Borneo bound for Chang'an; there was Khotanese jade, red Idrisid coral, pods of musk, Lettish amber for Fars and Venice treacle, an antivenene, bound for Hum in exchange for muslin. We smelled cloves and turmeric from Cholas, and satin pillow sachets stuffed with Merovingian lavender. We tasted salt from a Tibetan salt lake, wine from a cellar in Shiraz. We sniffed ottars and applied plasters while eating tamarinds and sparrow-olives. We tried on rose-coloured headbands from Tabiristan made of satin and corduroy and woollen striped stuffs from Sana'a, the ancient capital of Al-Yemen. Dressed in Mauretanian burnouses and hauberks of scented goats' leather from Taif, we staged a mock battle, two against one, wielding Maqasiri sandalwood candlestick holders and kettles of Andalusian copper. We fanned ourselves with ostrich feathers; taunted each other with elephant goads; chewed betel nut till our spit went red; hid in three lead containers used to transport mares' teat grapes in ice; tickled each other's ears with falcon jesses of clouded brocade; cleared our nostrils with alum from Lop Nor as used by Bukhariot Jews in setting dyes; played chess on a chessboard from Zabulistan with ivory and ebony pieces made in Bam; rolled each other up in Yemeni kimcobs; mixed firework ingredients from a saltpan in Taklamakan; felt the skin of a Barbary panther; lay on some Khazarian miniver furs; tied each other's feet up with skeins of raw silk, then pelted one another with storax and borax, bladders of ambergris and lacquered tortoiseshells, and bashed each other's noses' bridges with logs of Malagasy cinnamon, until ordered out.

Anything you might want, it was in this warehouse. If not, it could be ordered.

'Any *hauma* here?' inquired Bogu as we left.

'No ware kin git,' replied Anahitaivandak.

Next, we visited a bazaar that specialised in sweetmeats for the warehouse workers, all of whom, unlike a Slope, had bushy black eyebrows and beards. Bogu wanted more cake while I preferred to bask in the polyglot. I heard Sogdian, Turkic, Chinese, Latin, Arabic, Dari, Kuchean, Aramaic, Brahmi, Burushaski, Toyuk and Hibernian, all outside one stall.

Next, we took in some temples. We saw the *mihrab* in the Mahummery, the *menorah* in the synagogue, the eternal flame in the Zoroastrian temple, the crucifix in the Christian temple, the empty tribune in the Manichean temple and a giant reclining Buddha. And at every temple we visited we were given handouts in Turkic.

Our heads were spinning. It was hot and we were laden with

handouts as well as our bows and arrows. The streets of the city were dark, steamy, narrow and crowded, and filthy with dung and bones and rinds and beggars – for the most part, Turks like us.

The merchants by contrast – *Sarts* as they're called – wore golden earrings with a drop pearl and multicoloured jackets of ikat-weave silk but we stumbled over monks in *kalats*. We got pushed by matrons in *kaftans*.

We watched an execution. The victim, said Anahitaivandak, was Korean. He wore a black skullcap and a quilt of padded cotton and they halved him at the waist.

Near the slave market we passed a park with a single battered maple tree and some Sand People squatting in the dusty grass round a little fire they had built. One of them, a woman with a black eye, was swigging at a bottle that was being passed about.

Anahitaivandak sprang into action. 'Homer!' he shouted at Bogu then ran to this woman, threw her a dirham and snatched the bottle from her. She tried to protest but fell. The bottle, a filthy brown goat-gut, was still half full of some liquid.

Bogu initially held back. That fetid bottle sloshed round with us most of the rest of the day.

After lunch – don't ask – we went back to Anahitaivandak's house, a bagged mud-brick mansion cheek and jowl with the one next door. All the Sarts of Samarkand live in these multi-storey mansions that cantilever over the lanes so the lanes are very dingy. The ground floor was leased to a man who bought a lot of metalworking flux. No one was home at that hour, but a slave girl showed us up and we saw the ballroom where they do the Sogdian whirling dance and the reception area which was Chinese style, all low lacquered tables, but time was getting on and Bogu was turning green so we thought we'd best get back to that orchard where we'd hobbled our tarpans.

'Wrist, din go. No fogit frind!' Anahitaivandak pointed to himself.

'Read these,' said Bogu, sweating and gasping. He handed over the temple handouts then drank his *hauma*. Skolled it straight down.

When we got back, there they were, all eighty-five of them awaiting us. Been there most of the day.

Mo-yen was livid. We each received seven blows of the cudgel but he couldn't be too upset with us, he said, because we just weren't worth it and he'd won a great victory. The Arab garrison of twenty thousand men had taken to its heels. They just went down to Balkh and then came back, but that wasn't the point. This was the beginning of the Uighur Empire, the greatest empire in all the world and no one even noticed.

'Look at that beautiful pattern the moonlight makes on those ... those ... those things with leaves there,' said Bogu, as we rode towards Panjikent.

'You mean trees?' I said.

'That's it! Trees! Now what was I saying?'

Over the next five years Uighurs seized control of the High Steppe. There was warfare all this time between the Chinese and Tibetans but most of the fighting took place round the Gansu corridor and in the Pamir passes, and while various hordes, including the Turghiz, fought on both sides, the Uighurs sat it out.

There'd never been a war, I explained to Mo-yen, in which Turks were not involved, but if we'd half a brain we'd realise what it meant that we were always in the front lines. We could rule the High Steppe, certainly Shash, perhaps Sogdiana and possibly Tibet if we'd show a little *discipline*.

We were no longer fit to be vassals. No more tithe to the Eastern Blues.

☾

We sacked the Turghiz on our way home. Laden with their silks and gold, I noticed as we passed through Issyk Kul that my Qiang princess benefactrix had gone. Back at the Orkhon we found the Eastern Blues squabbling among themselves so we didn't actually have to fight anyone. Indeed, as I pointed out to Mo-yen, if we simply *refrained* from fighting – which, I suppose, is the hardest thing in the world for a Turk to do – if we became the first horde in history to turn our arses on a brawl, we would inherit the steppe. So that's what we did. For five whole years we did nothing. And things went smoothly.

We had to tie ourselves up, at times, break arrows over our knees, slaughter tarpans, stuff wool in our ears, drink kumis till we couldn't move, but we did it. We showed discipline. Then, when our neighbours had fought themselves to exhaustion, we knocked them over, just as the Arabs crushed the East Romans and Sassanids when they'd bled themselves white. We pushed the Turghiz out of all the lands east of Issyk Kul and what was left of the Eastern Blues we drove through the land of the Khitans and who knows where they ended up and who cares. I mean, no one down here knows or cares what happens up on the steppe. You only notice us when we arrive on your doorstep in a bad mood. You laugh at our empires. Bogu, like his father, felt we had a point to prove. This time, things would be *different*. We'd show you what a Turk can do and if you would come with me to Karabalghasun, Shahrban, I'll show you a city to rival Merv – well, Tahirid Nishapur. I can show you a Prophet's garden watered by running streams set in a grassy plain where the Orkhon debouches from the gorge in the Khantai Mountains and it's warm. Well, it's comparatively mild. Everyone down here has the notion it would be cold up there, but it's comparatively mild. Warm enough to grow apples and barley; warm enough for a civilised life.

Gates! You speak of gates! You should see the twelve iron gates of Karabalghasun.

The city went through several phases. First up, we built a mud-brick wall six foot thick. We wanted to use slaves and vassals for this but they were too slow so we did it ourselves. We made the wall rectangular, fifty foot high, five miles wide and two miles deep. And we left openings for gates as we wanted the best gates money could buy and we had no money, back in 744. All we had was slaves and vassals and livestock and gold and silk and felt, but we had mud and we had willing hands.

Inside the walls we built a second, smaller wall for our ark. This was to be in the north-eastern corner for Mo-yen Cur's palace. The first Karabalghasun which was built in consultation with the tutuks was just yurts, which proved impractical. The biggest yurt was meant for a palace but Mo-yen, now emperor, said he wouldn't live there, he wouldn't feel safe. He wouldn't feel safe inside two sets of fifty-foot high walls because, as I say, we needed gates, though they have proven less useful than hoped, being too heavy to open and close. Beautiful, decorative Chinese cast, though, best quality. In retrospect they didn't need to be both fifty foot high *and* six foot thick but you learn some things through experience.

We'd trouble getting people to settle. We had, in fact, to mount guards to stop them escaping because Uighurs who didn't reside in that city were always raiding Uighurs who did, breaking into the yurts by night to plunder and rape and thieve. Looking back on it, the yurts were too close together. Livestock had to be kept indoors. And no matter how many blows of the cudgel a malefactor received, he would always insist he had done no wrong and would quickly re-offend; and the stock was starving.

When winter came and the Orkhon iced over, there was no pasture outside the walls for stock because what hadn't been eaten was used as mud in the walls and we had no hay or grain in storage; indeed, we had no stores of any kind and people inside the city were not free to move to pasture.

'Cultivation,' conceded Bogu. 'We need farms and barns. I hadn't thought of that. We need villages and orchards and irrigation canals and silos and waterwheels. It might be better, as well, if the camels, at least, were kept outside because they make a terrible mess of the yurts. They've ruined the teahouse. People spend their days taking sheep up and down to the river and now the river has frozen the streets are very muddy. I nearly broke a leg.'

'Camels outside the walls,' I observed, 'will be easier to steal.'

'Yes, we need temples,' admitted Bogu. 'Uighurs don't know how to conduct themselves. They're not god-fearing.'

'Shamans say our gods will never live inside those walls.'

'Good. We don't want Shamans' gods. We need some sedentary gods. Did we keep those handouts, Singqu? Let's sit down and choose ourselves some proper gods.'

Luckily, we had kept the handouts. And Bogu had meantime learned to read and write so that when Mo-yen, visiting from the winter pasture, threatened to pull the city down, Bogu could reply: 'Your people may leave, but just for one year. Let them disassemble the yurts and move in the customary fashion, and when they return they'll find a *real* city awaits them, with housing and temples. I never wanted yurts inside the walls.'

Now, just as a sedentary wishes at times that he could fight like a Turk, so a Turk wants to feel that he can build a city with a teahouse.

'I've money coming in,' confided Mo-yen. 'I formed an alliance with the *Faghfur*. I will help him against the Tibetans in exchange for silk, which I shall barter for cash. I know you want to build a city, son, but you don't know what you're doing. You're making a meal of it. We'll get the Chinese and Sogdians in to build Karabalghasun. You watch how it's done. Then you can build other, better cities all over the steppe.'

'Good, but we still need temples,' advised Bogu. He withdrew the handouts. 'Listen to this. "Abel was a keeper of sheep but Cain was a tiller of the ground and in process of time it came to pass that Cain brought of the fruit of the ground an offering unto the Lord. And Abel, he also brought of the firstlings of his flock and of the fat thereof. And the Lord had respect unto Abel and his offering. But unto Cain and his offering He had not respect." And this: "Samuel said unto Jesse, Are here all thy children? And he said, There remaineth yet the youngest, and, behold, he keepeth the sheep." And this: "And there were in the same country shepherds in the field, keeping watch over their flocks by night. And lo, the angel of the Lord came upon them, and the glory of the Lord shone round them; and they were sore afraid. And the angel said unto them, Fear not, for, behold, I bring you good tidings of great joy, which shall be to all people." And the shepherds were first to hear it. This tract here is Christian while that one there is Jewish, no, wait a bit ... wait a minute ...'

'I've heard of Turks becoming Jews but I never heard of any Christian Turk.'

'We could be the first. It would be a further feather in our bow.'

'If I were to build a city, son, I should have a temple in it of each kind.'

'Noted.'

At this point I felt I owed it to my Qiang princess benefactrix to speak up. 'God of the moon and god of the sun,' I said, genuflecting to Mo-yen. 'I dare say you will now marry a princess of the Tang?'

'I dare say so, Singqu.'

'Then be advised that no Tang princess would want to live in a Uighur yurt.'

'Who cares what women want?'

'No, no, no,' said Bogu. 'Singqu is absolutely right. Have the good sense to listen to him. And since we are shepherds, would it make sense for us to be Jews?'

'I never heard of any Jewish shepherd. Why, every Jew that …'

'Ah! Don't go on! Don't complain to me about the Jews. You see, if we're to live in our city then we need to be tolerant of Jews. And if we're to retain our alliances then we need to respect our womenfolk. That's where the Turghiz came unstuck.'

These were concepts Mo-yen Cur could never get his head around but over the next ten years he didn't have time to think.

Four topics are avoided by Confucius whose thought I hold in high regard – extraordinary phenomena, arbitrary acts of violence, revolutionary upheavals and apparitions of transcendent beings – because these, in not conforming to ordinary law, afford the student fewer, if any, lessons worth the learning.

So Confucius would advise silence, concerning events of the years in which we built Karabalghasun.

We had to get our palace right, to tempt Mo-yen. We built it like a caravanserai with a courtyard for stock and cloistered walls, but its main feature was the flat roof, designed to accommodate a yurt. We'd heard the Tibetan emperor has a tent atop his palace and we were determined to have the world's biggest yurt on top of ours.

So now we have a big felt yurt dominating the skyline and – well, it looks pretty ordinary.

'What can we *do* with the bloody thing, Singqu? No Tang princess would want to live *there*!' said Bogu in his usual despair before the day's first *hauma*. He drank his *hauma* from a porcelain cup. He affected silk trowsers and waistcoats. He let his moustachios fall to his hips.

Karabalghasun, all but complete, lacked a finishing touch. Bogu wanted something outrageous, but at the same time, distinctively Uighur. We had two streets. We had a Nestorian cathedral, twelve idol temples for our Sogdians and Chinese, Mahummeries for our Arabs – one Shi'ite, one Sunni. Our Chinese citizens, all craftsmen jewellers, had workshops down one entire street. We had a gold market and a bazaar. We had a teahouse serving sparrow's tongue tea in Chinese blue and white. There were buildings for our architects and court secretaries, and each of our twelve gates had an individual purpose. At one was sold millet and corn, at another rams and goats, at another oxen and camels, at another, tarpans and wagons.

Bowing to pressure from those wretched tutuks, we still had yurts inside the walls – not as many as they'd have liked, but this was a problem with that palace yurt – it needed *differentiation*.

At first, we thought to solve the problem by having Arab builders fairly go to town, so that here one saw a *Tiraf* of leather, there a *Khabaa* of black wool; here stood a *Nakhad* of goat's hair, there a *Khaymah* of cotton cloth; here a *Fustat* of horsehair, there a *Wabar* of camel undercoat, but nothing seemed to improve the look of that wretched palace yurt, which remained an eyesore.

Tang Dynasty had a new emperor. The Chinese civil war raged on with the sons replacing the fathers.

An embassy from this new Son of Heaven, Suzong, came begging for our help. After they'd duly learned and performed our ritual submission dance, Mo-yen, who lived alone in a tent by the river, nursing wounds, declared Bogu would lead an army to relieve both Tang capitals.

'I've not been on a horse in *years,*' laughed Bogu. 'Can't someone else do it?'

'You'd better do it if you want to rule. Take nothing for granted, boy. Tutuks complain they never see you fight, reckon you're a *hauma* drinker, first to a feast and last to the fray. I give you four thousand battle-hardened men, you go down and liberate Chang'an. And remember; the Uighur reserves the right to plunder every city that he liberates.'

Bogu was concerned as to what might happen if he went away. Not all Uighurs were keen farmers and once in a while they would drink too much, ride into the city and do their Uighur thing.

The night before Bogu was due to leave, we walked the ramparts together. Drunk on kumis and high on *hauma*, he was sucking at a bottle of piss.

I recall it was a windy night.

The moon appeared from behind a cloud.

'Ah!' he said and I saw him blink. 'Izthathyurt ... covrin ... *Gold?*'

So Khan Tengri solved the problem. When Bogu left, I sent for the Syndic of the goldsmiths and we gilded the felt on the palace yurt from the smoke hole down to the floor so now we have a gilt felt yurt which can be seen from miles out on the steppe. Mo-yen was so overcome by the concept he moved straight in and that gilt felt yurt, with resident khan, was safe from Uighur assault.

When Bogu returned from Cathay, his hair and moustachios had gone white. He'd driven the rebels from both Tang capitals, Chang'an and Luoyang, but the *Faghfur* had prevailed upon him to loot the smaller of the two, so for three whole days while Bogu was scratching through the hardware markets of Luoyang looking for left-hand thread tap fittings, his Uighurs were smashing temples, looting liquor stores, raping women, torturing men, and tying firecrackers to the tails of all the cats. Nonetheless, it cheered him a treat to see Mo-yen in the palace.

'I've two Tang princesses on the way to marry you, Father. Is it warm up here? I fancy it would be jolly warm.'

'No, it's actually rather cold. I'm just minding the place, Bogu. Never mind about those princesses. I can't get the arrowhead out. I'm not long for this world. But I hear you did pretty well. I must say you surprise me. You'll be next Uighur Emperor. Did you organise a consideration?'

'Ah … consideration?'

'Bride price! Have you seen their faces? I don't like it how they won't let us see their faces until it's too late.'

Mo-yen married the elder of two sisters, as they proved to be – Gold Immortal. She was no spring chicken, either; she'd been widowed three times. When the next month she'd been widowed again, we let her return to Luoyang as Bogu didn't want her and she was too old to be buried with Mo-yen.

We buried him under his favourite tree in the Khantai Mountains and hundreds of Uighurs, men and women both, we killed, to attend him in his death. These, we buried alive in the Chinese method of vivisepulture. At the graveside, we slashed our faces up as Uighur custom demands while Bogu, to show filial grief, cut off both his ears. This did him no harm in the eyes of the tutuks.

When ready to marry Transcendent Treasure, Mo-yen Cur, on seeing her face, just laughed and said, 'Leave her for Bogu.'

And when she turned to us – modest, eyes downcast, pallid yet so refined, brave yet so composed, compliant yet so well-bred, with such tiny little feet and her glorious complexion, with those long gold earrings held in milky lobes and lustrous hair under a gold and lapis crown in the wide loops of her scarf – well, we could understand Mo-yen's decision. Here was a ravishing, civilised creature of no more than thirteen years and it would have been a shocking thing entirely had wrinkled old Mo-yen seen fit to paw her about.

When Bogu married he could never bring himself to touch her, or so he said, and as he had no other wives and wouldn't take a concubine he remained a bare branch, the last Utikien khan.

He'd hand picked fifty fighting knights to guard Transcendent Treasure. We were his court. None of us, of course, was to enter the Gilt Felt Yurt. We convened daily in the palace which as a rule meant the courtyard. There sat Bogu on his ivory throne while we sprawled before him. He'd let his hair grow long and rank so it spilled down over his belt. His silk gown had the same pattern as the one Anahitaivandak had worn – paired facing geese within decorative roundels interspersed with Moline crosses. A dagger attached to his belt was meant to dangle at his side.

The counts, the dukes, the earls – I think I was the only marquis – lazed about sipping sherbets and nibbling camel tripes. We had no work but every day began with a ceremony where we'd gather in the eastern gate mounted on dragon horses, wearing chainmail and standing in shovel-stirrups, holding battleaxes.

As dawn broke Transcendent Treasure would leave the yurt in which she lived with her silent cockatoo, holding high a crystal chalice from which she drank a daily jade suspension. Her hair was mounted in a high bun and she wore a plain silk gown and I can't imagine that she could see us as we could barely see her.

For a time things went smoothly but then came a second Tang envoy seeking our help against the rebels and among them was the heir apparent who refused to dance our submission dance!

So we gave him a good few blows of the cudgel, indeed, a few too many.

Bogu now felt he had no option but to lead a second army to relieve Chang'an. The knights of the Gilt Felt Yurt were to stay behind to guard Transcendent Treasure but he had to lead his army so I went to keep him company. I had the inspiration to have a little idol of the gilt felt yurt made up.

All the tutuks insisted on coming which meant we had fifty thousand mounted men, each of whom had brought along a camel to be loaded with loot.

'Wouldn't be so bad if they'd pillage items of *use*,' complained Bogu from his camp chair. 'Hoes, braziers, crossbows, scales, deodorant, soap – that kind of thing – but no, they much prefer zithers, jujubes, goldfish and lapis lazuli.'

Our route took us through the Gobi Desert. We crossed Yin hills at Piti Springs. We continued south along the southern bend of the Hwang-ho skirting the Ordos. We found the Great Wall deserted. Tibetans were using the muddy Ordos to mount armed raids upon us but any measure we took to weaken Tibet would strengthen the Tang and Bogu preferred his southern neighbour in a state of civil war. When previously driving rebels from Chang'an he'd taken great care not to harm them. He wanted them to return to Chang'an as soon as he'd gone which they had. But now we had an army ten times stronger than the one back then.

At dawn each day I held up the idol of the gilt felt yurt for him to worship. And if I were to tell you that Transcendent Treasure was now about fourteen years of age, I'd be telling you more than you need know because the less you know about any Transcendent Treasure the more potent her effect.

Finally, in the distance of the Lower Wei amid the persimmon groves appeared Chang'an, the world's biggest city.

We engaged the rebels in the Eastern Market, a venue that nullified our horsemanship but Bogu couldn't prevent his archers rushing in the Tonghua Gate. There's a price to be paid for fighting, as Bogu did, in the front lines – communication.

The rebels had armour-piercing longbows which meant we had to grapple them. Bear in mind we're in cuirboulies and tunics and they're in suits of chainmail. Then catapults, hidden in the garden of the villa of the Chief Ceremonialist, lob a volley of smoke bombs – earthenware pots filled with realgar and lime. Talk about cough and sneeze! Then loyalists, hiding in the five-star hotel, reply with incendiary arrows so the market catches fire. Talk about sneeze and cough! Camels and tarpans running about upsetting all the stalls, hail of sandals and prunes and goose feathers, toothpicks, cotton bolts – but no one can see, no one can breathe.

We lost five thousand of our archers, most drowning in the duck pond. So, heading for Luoyang, we were pretty filthy on the Chinese. We stopped outside the walls by the steps of the White Horse Temple which commemorates the entry, on white horses, of the first two Indian Grass Eaters. Do you know their *Sutra in Forty-Two articles?*

'He who abandons his family to follow the law, is called sramana (renunciant).

'He observes two hundred and fifty rules and must rid himself of the lust for fame, wealth, the deed of kind and hauma.

'The greatest law is universal compassion.

'This, says the Buddha, is how to be Happy. Regard the heaven and earth and say, these will pass. Regard the mountains and rivers and say, these will pass. Regard the ten thousand beings and say, these will pass.

'The affection which ties a man to his wife, his children and his

property, enslaves him worse than prison, manacles and fetters because the prisoner has a chance of being released in an amnesty.

'The worst of all afflictions is carnal love, the deed of kind being the root of all evil. The Buddha says, try not to look at women and girls but say to yourself, I, sramana, ought to be in this world as a lotus which grows in the mud but is uncontaminated by it. If, for some reason, you must regard a woman, do not consider her tits, arse, face and hair, but think of what is inside her, all that guts and shit and piss.

'In this world of the six, where every being is doomed to suffer – whether or not he strives to eat grass – birth, senility, sickness and death are doomed to succeed each other, so long as this longing for women – and all that accompanies this longing – persists.

'The Buddha says, what exertions are necessary, to extricate oneself from the hells, the beast world and the world of the hungry ghosts, to be reborn in a human body!

'What further exertions are necessary, to be born as a man and not a woman!

'What further exertions are necessary, to be born in Central India!

'What further exertions are necessary, to observe law, to maintain the faith, and to become a bodhisattva, that is, one who realises that he cannot remain Happy until the ten thousand beings are Happy.

'As for me, says the Buddha, I regard all times as past, all gold and jade as smashed, all carpets and brocades as worn through.'

I was given the task of addressing the troops as Bogu had his mind set on going to the city alone.

'Fellow barbarians,' I bawled, 'scarcely human fellow Turks! God of the sun and god of the moon has asked me to address you but I have a problem – loyalist or rebel, how can I decide? Celestials all look the same to me, so I suggest we kill every man in Luoyang and that way, no rebel will escape.'

They liked my wit but I hadn't reckoned on theirs; *they* couldn't tell men from women so men were to be raped along with women – by applying a sharpened tent peg to the male crupper-bone and knocking till the sphincter opened – and women butchered along with men. Nor could they spare, in their haste, Tangut, Tibetan, Korean or Turk, but every Slope we encountered was to die and only Sogdians spared – Sogdians, Tokharians, Khwarazmians, Arabs, Hibernians – all the round-eyes, because whenever a horde massacres a sedentary people it spares a few, as a point of honour.

So the Sogdians were spared and when, after a week, they realised we meant them no harm, they asked if we'd like to borrow money from their shroffs and we said yes, because we knew they bankroll the Arabs.

It takes no more than three days to load any camel. A camel should carry no more than two hundred and fifty pound weight for a longhaul so by rights we should have been out of there in a week, but Uighurs were so reluctant to return to their new sedentary lifestyle, that they set up camp outside Luoyang and maintained there a six-month siege for the sole purpose of consuming anything and everything in Luoyang. By spring, surviving citizens were eating the bark off trees while plump Uighurs dined from the silos at the San Men portage gates.

God-botherers sought refuge in the temples. Luoyang was famous for temples. There was a temple of the Doctrine of Fire Worship; three temples of the Doctrine of Light – that's the Doctrine of the Babylonian Grass Eater, Mani; two temples of the Doctrine of Yesu Jidu, Cannibal King; thirty-five temples of the Doctrine of the Way and fully one hundred and sixteen temples of the Doctrine of the Indian Grass Eater, Buddha. Hiding in these temples didn't do them any good as we barred the doors and burned them to the ground. Oh, you'd have laughed to have heard it, Shahrban – some of them screaming, some of them praying, the roaring of the painted wood.

Eventually, there were just three temples left: the temples of the Buddha of Light, Mani's guise in Cathay. The *Faghfur* in the year I was born banned the teaching of this Doctrine on the ground that Mani, in presenting himself as a Buddha, had misled the Chinese people. That said, he also presented himself as avatar of Lao-tzu and apostle of Yesu Jidu. Resident Sogdians were exempt from the edict provided they didn't proselytise – no doubt because the Fat Concubine, Xuanzong's favourite, had a Sogdian squeeze. In any event, all the Sogdians of Luoyang had gathered in these Manichee temples and there, clutching his idol of the gilt felt yurt, I happened on Bogu. I'd like to say I'd been looking for him but I'd been having too much fun to go chasing after anyone.

He was sitting on the temple steps, head in hands, rocking to and fro – seemed to be upset about something. I made a mental note of where he sat and ran on – chasing some Slopes.

Next time I saw him, he was talking with the priests. By this stage the temple was crowded and seeing him smiling, apparently at ease, I didn't stop, just waved and ran on – chasing some more Slopes.

The next time I saw him he saw me first.

'Singqu!' he said. 'Come over here, mate! Slow down! What's your hurry? Come and meet a wise man.' He introduced me to the Chief Grass Eater, the bishop of the temple. Like all Manichee priests, he had a big black beard and little red eyes.

Have you seen their writing? They have the smallest writing in the world.

'*Mahistag* are in at their desks,' said Bogu, 'making translations. Did you know that our Turkic alphabet is based on the Syriac script? That's handy for us.'

'And why is that handy for us?' I asked.

Sure enough, the arm went round my shoulder, a gesture I dreaded. 'Singqu,' he said, 'our Uighur nation is to become a Friend of the Light. Let our nation, with its barbarous customs and reeking, as we do, of blood and gore, transform itself into a nation where people abstain from eating meat. Let our nation where men shed blood and delight in deeds of kind, transform itself into a nation where vegetables are eaten and compassion shown to beasts. Let the calamity of birth be discountenanced that the population decline, but in the meantime, let the people refrain from idolatry and magic and stop drinking kumis and blood and *hauma* and urine and tea.'

I couldn't contain myself. 'It's not enough you bury us in your wretched city,' I cried. 'It's not enough you have us all shitting in the same hole, now you want us to eat grass!'

'Read this,' he said, thrusting a book at me. 'Oh, that's right, you can't read. Singqu, I have found my Divine Self! Be happy for me, Singqu. Singqu, you could be happy, too.'

I said I was happy enough. He said that being happy enough was *not* being happy. Being happy enough is *never* being happy enough. He wanted me to be *truly* happy, as he was. He insisted I be baptised alongside him. It was to be my camel loaded up with all the Grass Eater texts, now transcribed into Turkic, to be taken back to the University of Karabalghasun – Erh-zung-jing, the Sutra of the Two Principles, the Grand Confessional, Hymn to the Moon, Portrait of the Buddha Yesu Jidu, Sutra of the Light-Particle Paradox, Sutra of the Descent and Birth of the Crown Prince, Portrait of the Four Kings of Heaven, Gatha of the Sun and so forth.

Most of the Sogdian Grass Eater priests of Luoyang came home with us. On return, we beat the drums of rejoicing and released the prisoners in the jail. It was a coup for the Manichees – first convert emperor! What price now, Asoka, Vishtaspa and Constantine? The Manichee priests were to burn yurt idols and instruct Uighurs on how to eat grass. Bogu appointed one in every ten Uighurs to instruct the other nine. Monasteries were built on the steppe in which to this day live *Electi*, the wandering monks of the Manichee Faith. No more cities were built as the silk had now to pay for the monasteries. Most Uighurs, of course, remain *Auditors*, mere laymen. There are no grass-eating nuns, the First Man having been seduced by a woman. Not many Uighurs became *Electi* but Bogu, of course, was first. He couldn't do things by halves, our Bogu! So now we have an emperor with no property, no ears, no fixed address, no wife, no children, no concubines and no worldly ambition, who won't eat meat or drink kumis or *hauma* or urine or tea or attend a séance or take up arms – about as much use as two Turks short. You can't have your wife and your shakti as well, so he sent Transcendent Treasure home on condition she enter a Taoist nunnery, saying that having caught the fish he had no further use for the net. Her cockatoo went with her. The gilt felt yurt remains to this day the glory of the High Steppe but Bogu took to wearing the idol of the gilt felt yurt for his crown. He tied it to his head with a red silk ribbon fastened under his chin. The university – which, I concede, is nothing but half-a-dozen caravanserais interspersed with lawn because we'd absolutely no idea of how to build a university – became the first Manichee monastery. The knights of the Court were disbanded.

Uighurs, of course, still eat meat and drink kumis and conjure up spirits, but aspects of the Grass Eater faith have proven sufficiently congenial to guarantee respect for the Manichees among the Uighurs.

Grass Eaters don't pray for outcomes and Uighurs don't pray for outcomes. Prayer, to a Turk, is never supplicatory; prayer, to a Turk, is always laudatory. We can say, with the Turghiz Muslim, 'Islam' meaning 'I submit to the will of God' and we don't mind praying to the sun and the moon because that's what we've always done. Mind you, even a Tang rebel respects Celestial genii – urinating while facing the sun or the moon – three demerits.

Iranian Days (continued)

Marquis Singqu then gives a sermon.

'Even as the Karluq horde, fighting in the van of the Battle of Talas River, crossed from the Chinese to the Arab camp midway through the battle, so Bogu Khan, three years into his reign on the High Steppe, went from the Camp of Life to the Camp of Death and he took us along.

'Uighurs always do as their Khan instructs – such is our proclivity. And so Uighurs within my lifetime have ceased to be nomadic Turks to become a nation of city dwellers and sedentary farmers and it can only be a matter of time before we are driven from the steppe by the Kyrghyz horde.

'What, then, of this counterintuitive impulse to die before one's time? For that is what it amounts to, the urge to eat grass. I submit it is the saving grace, the counter-vice of the sedentary. I see it in the Doctrine of the Zoroastrian heterodox renunciant, Mani. I see it in the Doctrine of the Aryan heterodox renunciants, Buddha the

Awakened One and Vardhamana the Fordmaker. I see it – polluted – in the Doctrine of the Jewish heterodox renunciant, Yesu Jidu. So there must be something to it.

'I believe it arises from a child's consideration of the most palpable of human mysteries; the obscene mystery of conception, the product of man's desire to penetrate a woman's member feminine, which is an excretory orifice, using for his purpose an organ which is also an excretory orifice, structured to factor in that woman's preconceived deceit, because they all do it.

'This is unacceptable. One cannot respect any woman prepared to engage in such activities. There follows a nine-month period pressed against a gurgling bag of shit before we are flung into this world, blood-covered, through a series of obscene convulsions. This, too, is unacceptable. One cannot respect any man prepared to be born in such a fashion. Little wonder that we look about us in disgust, nausea and terror. For those who survive childhood there awaits years of pain or ennui before the inevitable drift into old age and dementia.

'The warm bosom of our mother with its comforting solutions, how greedily we drink from it. Yet the milk we imbibe has come at the expense of the death of other creatures – unacceptable again.

'For we eat to live and we must kill to eat and we must do the deed of kind to procreate, yet something in a sedentary rebels against all this. The grass eater says, I will not inflict the curse of life and death on other creatures and so as not to have to kill to eat, I eat only fruits and nuts and grains.

'This, to a nomad, is madness. Show us, grass eater, the untended orchard not full of insects, bats and birds! Show us the silo without the vermin! Show us the flock unravaged by wolves! Show us the gatherer bothering to gather unless the hunter has failed in the hunt.

'And speaking of flocks unravaged by wolves, Yahwe, tempestuous

Lord of the Jews, comes closest to the god of the Life Force. Here is a god who demands blood sacrifice, punishes men for the fact of their existence, orders exterminations of whole hordes and forces his people into sin through issuing commandments that no man could obey. Driven into exile, dispersed throughout the sedentary world, the Jews must now bear the indignity of seeing this Arab, who's gotten it all wrong, claiming, asquat upon their Temple mount, that he has the Keys to their Kingdom and that they have falsified their own Scriptures! Was ever a horde of donkey-riding shepherds off a steppe more harshly dealt with by a god?

'Yesu Jidu, whether god or man, or apparition, or man-god, or seal of the prophets, with one nature, or two, or three – and whether possessed of a round tower or a normal human penis – you cannot endorse monogamy as sacramental! That is to place too heavy a burden on human law and sufferance.

'The deed of kind remains the ultimate carnal pleasure. It sanctifies matter. We all know it to be the most unspeakably filthy act with the most dire of consequences, yet we cannot be prevented from engaging upon it, not by Mani nor Sakyamuni nor Mahavira nor Yesu Jidu – not by reason nor poverty nor childish revulsion – not by god nor man nor Khan nor *Faghfur*.

'Supposing we were to give it up, as we all, in our more refined moments, might prefer – why, even Iblis (whom Allah Almighty accurse!), with his hooves and horns, is likely vegetarian – suppose, in particular, that every Uighur were to become celibate and consequently, peaceful, and not just every Uighur but every Turk, and every hunter, so that there were no more men. Why then, the Chinese and the Babylonians, the Indians and the Sogdians, from their filthy fields and cities, will offer to fill the entire world. They will become as a herd of gazelles with no predator to cleanse them. For while the sedentary feels this urge to eat grass, as a rule he resists it. "O True-Believers, forbid not yourselves the good things which Allah has allowed you" – al-Qu'ran. The Talmud declares that man is destined to give account to his Maker for all the good things his eyes beheld of which he did not partake. The Christians study the Torah as well as the Gospel – two bob each way. "Are we insanely to countenance the foolish error of the Manichees?" says Augustine. "When we say 'thou shalt not kill' we do not understand this of the plants, since they have no sensation, nor of the irrational animals that fly, swim, walk or creep, since they are dissociated from us by their want of reason and are therefore, by the just appointment of the Creator, subjected to us to kill or to keep alive for our own uses." Asceticism is a Zoroastrian sin equivalent to theft. Celibacy, says Confucius, is the worst of all possible crimes, for not to provide posterity for one's ancestors, in depriving them of offerings, condemns them to a premature extinction. Under the Constitution of the Chou, bachelors and widowers – even men of seventy years! – were married or remarried officially if they failed to do so voluntarily.

'And let us not speak of the Bhagavad Gita, in which a man reluctant to slaughter others is divinely chided.

'I say the urge to eat grass arises from premonition of a future in which the sedentaries have overrun the earth, annihilating all life else. Amen.'

Walking back to his ark, the Shah takes in, at last, what Shahrazad said. *Think I don't know when I'm* pregnant? *My* boobs *swell!* The horrid recollection breaks the Shah out in cold sweat. Was she, perhaps, no virgin? He must speak with Abu Bakr.

'Away 'llahi! Abu Bakr, Thou Councillor to my Kingdom and Keeper of my Secrets, I feel you may have been less than candid with me. For if Shahrazad has been pregnant before, would that not imply she's no virgin?'

'You're calling me a liar. Get a grip. And just as I was musing this morning how long we'd been together as a team and how well it's working out. Why, it must be thirty-five years.'

'Thirty-four. I was nine and you still treat me as if I were.'

'Thirty-four years, eh? That's a long time. La aba lak – you have no mother or father, still, if you feel you can do better without me …'

'I didn't say that! I'd be lost without you, as well you know. I reign but I do not govern Merv.'

'So what did you want?'

'Why did you lie to me regarding Shahrazad?'

'In what sense?'

'Well, she claims she has been pregnant before.'

'If so, it's news to me. Mind you, I must have up to fifty daughters. I can't be monitoring their every move and running this city as well. She's up there now, by the way.'

'Up where?'

'Up in your chambers! Up in your bedchambers, all by herself. Well, you said you wanted to hear more of that story. Should have seen her lovely eyes light up when I told her that and you know what else? I think you may have scored with her, Shahrban, I really do. I feel you may have impregnated her. Her breasts have certainly swollen. Alhamdolillah, they must be a *fearful* weight for the poor girl to be heaving about. I'm only glad it's her and not me.'

As he leaps up the stairs, the Shah thinks back to his first night with Shahrazad, which remains a technical mystery. It was as fast as ever Mawdudus would have done the deed with Uzza, but Shahrazad was as dry as the soil under a lined irrigation canal. Shahrban would have had to have pushed quite hard and as a result lose control, so he didn't enter her member feminine, as he recalls, which makes it hard to see how she could be pregnant. Still, these things happen. Allah is bountiful. The Shah was surprised, next morning, to see blood all over the sheet but the sight of it had its usual effect of making him want to see more. He was actually rather surprised to see the blood red and not some pastel shade, given Shahrazad's colour. Well, it was likely only poult blood. He'll need to purchase a pair of poults, decapitate them and see if that excites him.

Shahrazad is sitting alone. Her hands and feet are henna-red. She wears a suit of diaphanous silk with nothing beneath it. She seems to favour these suits of silk with nothing beneath them. Oh well, that's all right inside a Harem. Over her suit she wears a loose robe, diapered in red gold with figures of birds whose beaks are of beryl and claws are of red rubies. Around her neck is a necklace of Yemeni work with bezels of diamonds. Her shoes are of green pebbled donkey leather. Her trowsers have a drawstring off which hang glittering beads, and her blonde locks are fastened over her mouth to resemble moustachios.

A ghulam opens the door for the Shah. Shahrazad pats the bed beside her with her long, exquisite fingers, each boasting a ring of ruby, amethyst and sapphire. Then, with a smirk, she starts back into her *Tale of the Lady and her Five Suitors*.

'So when this Kazi sees this lady, he, too, falls in love with her, Eyebrows, and begins to drool and sleaze on. "Come on, dear," he says – slurp, drool – "rest up here with my slave girls. You must be hot" – get it? He doesn't mean hot, he means *hot*. "I'll send for the Wali. Now if only I knew the sum he wants to bail this brother of yours I'd pay it from my own purse, provided you give me a root" – wink, sleaze.

'"Fair enough," says the lady. "Allah preserve our lord the Kazi! Mind you, it better be a *good* root. Not the kind of thing I normally do, you understand, but if it brings my brother's release ..."

'"And where do you live?" says the Kazi, so she tells him and makes an assignation for the same time and day as she made for the Wali. Then she goes to the Wazir in the hope that he will release her lover before her husband gets home. And the Wazir, equally smitten with love for the lady, says, "And let me give you just the one root, I'll get your brother out, no sweat. Your place or mine?" "Mine," she says. "Allah keep our lord the Wazir! I wouldn't want you to get a bad reputation" – get it? He already has one. "And it better be a *good* root. That's the one thing I hanker for." "No worries," says the Wazir – slurp, drool – "where and when?"

'So she tells him and makes an assignation for the same time and day as the Kazi and the Wali then she goes to the Shah and ...'

'Shahrazad ...'

'Yes, Eyebrows?'

'Sorry to interrupt but I have a question.'

'Fire away.'

'Where's Dinazad?'

Well! Shahrazad stamps her feet, making the bells on her anklets ring. She jumps up and, frowning, storms from the chamber – she looks so lovely when she's angry, thinks the Shah. As she stalks off to the library to resume her study of a Vendidad, she shouts back over her shoulder, 'It would be nice, wouldn't it, if you could stop thinking of other *women* when we meet!'

He won't ask that question again. It's actually rather reassuring that she's capable of jealousy, for what could be more human than jealousy? What could be more human than looking through the cortex at other people's crocodile brain behaviour?

Little by little, the Shah is slipping back into a bad old habit. He wants a woman with whom to grow old. He wants to find something that will last forever.

There are many endowed libraries in Merv as well as a street of booksellers. Attached to the observatory is a mathematical library. The Katuniya, or Queen's Library, where Mawdudus holds the chair in 'Falsafah', has thousands of medical and philosophical holdings, chiefly in Sanskrit. A library in the Madrasa specialises in Islamic jurisprudence; the Chief Confectioner's Library holds a thousand Persian love poems; the Great Mosque Library has but one holding of twenty thousand copies while the Shah's library, the smallish Samaniya, endowed by an uncle of his father, has a fine collection of comparative theology and Chinese and Indian pornography. The catalogue is lost. The librarians are two mute eunuchs, either of whom holds a ladder. No one may borrow from the Samaniya Library in view of the rarity of its contents but Shahrazad, among others, is free to rummage through the boxes. When Shahrban next day enters, he finds her kneeling on the floor.

'Care for a coffee?' he whispers at her nape. He'd like to bite that nape. The lush blonde locks are resting on the floor, skirting a smutty tome.

'Cool,' she says. 'Oh mate, the weight of these *tits*! I have to lift them by hand. So where's this coffee?'

'In the alley of the coffee-makers near a Funduk is a great coffee house tale-teller who plays a mean Rababah.'

'Awesome. I wish I was allowed to go to other libraries. I've read everything here.'

'You can't come dressed like that. You're wearing transparent silk.'

'So?'

'Well, you may as well be naked! Look at your cleavage!'

'But what about the Chinese girls and all *their* cleavage?'

'They've yet to hear the Word of God and they haven't as much as you to cleave. Surah al-Nur tells us that a modest woman draws a veil over her bosom and may not display her finery except to her husband, her father, her husband's father, her sons, her step-sons, her brothers, her brothers' fathers, her sisters' ...'

'Oh, don't go on. I'm wearing a veil over my bosom.'

'Yes, but it's immodest, being made of transparent silk.'

'I've read al-Qu'ran. While I don't know it by heart, unclean women are for unclean men and unclean men for unclean women, so don't go on about it.'

'And if I sanctify blood and piss and shit with mumbo jumbo, would that make it clean? Hmm? Grass eaters aren't complete fools. Look, I don't want to argue, Shahrazad; I just thought you might like a coffee. You looked so lovely last night and I want to thank you for cheering me up. I must say silk becomes you.'

'I wear silk for a reason, Eyebrows. Don't ask me to change.'

'If you intend to walk through Merv dressed like that with your charms discovered I shall have to organise a guard and then we can't enjoy privacy. What would the people of Merv say if they see a woman dressed like that? Why, they will say, what kind of place this Merv is?'

'The guard can wait outside. Why won't *you* dress up?'

'Beg yours?'

'Well, *look* at you! You always wear that filthy foreigner's robe! Properly dressed, with shagreen slippers, you'd scrub up a treat if it weren't for that eyebrow. I wish you'd let me pluck it.'

'I have reason for dressing as I do. It appears we are indeed similar. You see, Shahrazad, if I were to dress like a shah, people might kill me. The Shah, from what I hear, is misunderstood. No man returns his "Salaam"; when he leaves the camp by night they light the Fire of Rejection. I even heard him referred to as "The Beast of Merv", can you beat that? The Beast of Merv. But whatever lies they have been telling about me, no ghulam can guarantee the safety of a tyrant so I must come in my foreigner's robe – my hufu – if you intend to wear silk.'

'Silk ensures my safety, Eyebrows. I guess it's like your hufu. It *does* appear we have things in common, apart from blue eyes. You do have blue eyes, don't you?'

'If only you would look me in the face, Shahrazad, you wouldn't have to ask. Why, you won't even give me a side-glance, an Ilhaz, which looks so nice from a woman in a Niqab.'

'I can't look at that eyebrow. Eeek! It makes my blood run.'

There's a Kahwah, or coffee house, by a Funduk, which is a Wakalah, or caravanserai, on the road that leads to the Khangah. The streets of the Rabad are daily sprinkled in summer with water against the heat and the royal party wends its way along a dry line left for camels, which are prone to slippage. The market outside the shop is crowded with itinerant cameleers and despite the ghulams, the cameleers, on seeing Shahrazad, go berserk. If Shahrban hoped to be anonymous he's now completely invisible. He shakes a kerchief of dismissal but no one pays him any heed. The Nakkal with his one-stringed viol is asked to leave the shop so the Shah and his good ladywife can drink their coffee in peace. The Shah insists this coffee be served in a proper copper coffee pot and by the time one is found, the lane outside the shop is in tumult.

'Welcome to my world. I must say, Eyebrows, none of the others ever asked me out for coffee.'

'Speaking of that, may I ask you about your past, Shahrazad?'

'Feel free.'

'Well, tell me of your maternal uncle and your maternal nephews ...'

'You want to hear about my mother.'

'Only if it won't upset you.'

'The man is like, going to totally cut off my head but he doesn't want to upset me.'

'As your head lives, Shahrazad, it must remain between your shoulders, at least until our child is weaned.'

News of the buxom blonde, so scantily clad, has spread rapidly. The ghulams are hard-pressed to keep cameleers from entering the shop. They must link arms against a sea of leering Turkish low-lifes.

Shahrazad smiles her crooked smile, discovering her teeth. 'Oh, those guys are getting to me. I'd forgotten what this was like. Can't you do something to stop them?'

'Sshh! We'll hear about my problems after we've heard about yours.'

'That's my problem, right there. I can't go anywhere or do anything without being *perved* on and I'm so over it.'

'Had you thought of wearing a Chador with a Niqab, you know, the black tent the good women wear with the veil that covers the face? You see, Shahrazad, you are as lovely as the Jinniyahs who guard ensorcelled hoards, what with your brow as bright as the crescent moon, Hilal, of the Feast of Ramazan, and your hair so lush and long and blonde and your mole as it were a crumb of ambergris, an ant creeping to the honey of your mouth wherein are your teeth as moist as hailstones, with lips of carnelian and gums of pomegranate; and your skin so white and your waist as it were a roll of fine Coptic linen with creases like scrolls of pure white musk-paper and your hind-cheeks so huge, like hillocks of blown sand over the well of lavender, and privities like hare with ears lain back, the very throne of the Caliphate; and fore-buttocks so heavy and unusual, with nipples like the noses of albino muskrats, and your navel would hold at least an ounce of benzoin ointment, perhaps two, while the rhythmical motion of your wonderful calves, like bolsters stuffed with ostrich down, makes mute the tinkling music of your ankle-ringlets.'

'Oh yeah. What do you want, Slobodan? Sleaze on! I've come to expect being perved on, Eyebrows, but can't they do it with *decorum*? I mean, I wouldn't want to be *ignored* – Heavens, I know I would hate that! – but this is supposed to be a civilised city. Why can't a woman wear what she wants to wear in a civilised city? Guys wear what *they* want to wear. Why can't a woman do the same?'

'Because Allah has made the man superior to the woman. The blood money for a woman is half that for a man. Shahrazad, my goodness me, your eyes become so lovely when you're angry.'

'Wonderful! I'm over the moon I'm not just a great rack of perky boob.'

Pieces of pavement now rain down on the ghulams. They can't hold out. And suddenly a group of mirabs appears – the last righteous men in the oasis.

'Let me go sort those guys out, Eyebrows. They want a tit show, I'll give 'em one.'

'Shahrazad, please! Let us make our way back to the palace. We should leave now. It was a mistake, us coming here. As usual, I failed to think things through. Put this tea towel over your head and this tablecloth round your shoulders.'

'No. I haven't finished my coffee yet. So you want to hear about my background? Well, I never knew my mother, Eyebrows, and Abu Bakr is not my father: he bought me at the Slav market in Cordoba last year. I'd been living in Cordoba with Ziryab, the Andalusian 'ud master, but Ziryab, ever the big spender from his alms-pouch, had to put me up for auction even though I was a present to him from 'Abd ar-Rahman and he credits me with inspiring the shape of the modern 'ud. He calls his 'ud "Shahrazad". When he lays it in his lap it gives him a hard-on. Okay, I'm finished my coffee.'

'Put this tablecloth ...'

'No! Why should I? You won't cut my head off, Eyebrows, I'll tell you why. 'Cause you don't want these *titties* cold and dry and no man does but you're the biggest pervert of them all and that's a fact. You have a serious problem with women, do you realise? I think you should *talk* to someone.'

'I'm talking to you. So you're the one with the problem. I wish I hadn't asked you out for coffee now.'

'Yeah, me too. Oh well, none of the others ever asked me out for coffee.'

'Must you be *constantly* referring to these others? I'm Padishah of Merv, King of the Age, Sahib az-Zaman! I rule over Jann, Cohens, Satans, warlocks and tribal chiefs! Were the others rulers of great realms?'

'Yeah, couple of them. Enneco of Pamplona, king of the Basques. Louis the Pious of Aquitaine, king of the Franks, and there was that guy from Narbonne but I think he was only a count. Look, if you don't dress like a Padishah, don't expect to be treated like one.'

'I suppose, if the truth were told,' replies Abu Bakr, 'I *do* think of them as daughters. I think of all my slave girls as my daughters, but especially the Slavs. I should have made that more clear.'

'You told me that Shahrazad was a Bulgarian.'

'I told you that Shahrazad was a Vulgarian.'

'Is Dinazad a Slav?'

'Dinazad?'

'Dinazad! Shahrazad's cadette, the one with the red hair. Is she a Slav?'

'I can't recall a Dinazad. Describe her.'

'Young! Innocent. Slim. Virginal. Demure. Flame-haired. Beautiful voice.'

'There could be no such creature. I feel I may state, with some assurance, that she doesn't and never did, exist.'

'I *know* she exists! I met her! As my head lives, I shall have my Munajjim strike a geomantic sand-table and consider the ascendant. Shahrazad said they were inseparable and now you have separated them. Why? Yaskut min 'Aynayh – you have fallen from my two eyes, Abu Bakr.'

'I think you'll find that, as usual, you have these things all wrong and that Dinazad never existed. Now, do you want to go over these irrigation accounts? We have a problem with our water supply, never mind your Zarb al-Fal and your stargazers. A white substance is forming on the fields. What do you mean to do about it?'

'I'm going to dress in my Arab finery then I'm going to my bedchamber to speak with your daughter Shahrazad. I need to apologise. We had a bad experience in the Rabad today and I fear it was my fault. I took her out for a coffee and the cameleers mobbed us.'

'I hear you took her down to the Rabad wearing transparent silks! Are you Jinn-mad? Yes, of course, I forget. I hear the ghulams are still trying to put down the riot and the mirabs are involved. Eight men have been killed.'

'Marg-i-amboh jashni darad – death in a crowd is as good as a feast. I did ask her to put a tablecloth over her shoulders but she refused.'

'She is not a good woman. She discovers her occiput. Her back hair should not be displayed even to the moon. All women, according to the Hadith, are little of wit and lack religion, but Shahrazad has the morals and the manners of a man, which is to say, she is a slag. She is not entirely to blame for it, as I know she had an unhappy childhood, but a good woman – who is Masturah, well-guarded, veiled, confined within the Harem – guards her unseen parts because Allah has guarded them. Furthermore, a good woman is obedient to man because men have authority over women as Allah has made the one superior to the other – Surah al-Nisa.'

'She doesn't understand. Her reading has done her no good. She is quick to take offence and has no fear of men. Why, I'm *terrified* of her! And knowing she must remain my wife for another two whole months I am apprehensive because she also fascinates me. I never had a wife quite like her. Abu Bakr, what must I do?'

'I know what I'd do if she were my wife and I were a younger man. As you say, she is arrogant and vulgar and needs to be taught a lesson. Now, the Romans had a cure for such arrogance. They slobbered over their own breasts as a kind of spell against Nemesis so I'd have her do that for a start. You could admonish and beat her as recommended in al-Qu'ran but I think, in view of the fact that she may be pregnant to you, better not. No, I think if it were up to me, I'd do another deed of kind on her but this time I'd go through with it, which would give her a nasty shock.'

'But that would mean a repudiation will have to wait another month! We're not supposed to do the deed of kind on pregnant women. Tell me again, Abu Bakr, why Shahrazad wished to be mine.'

'Because she sees you riding by on your horse and says to herself, what a man, so just and upright with such a lovely eyebrow ...'

Titstruck, thinks Abu Bakr, permitting himself a satisfied smile as the Shah, having shaken his kerchief of dismissal, walks briskly through the door then runs down the corridor towards his dressing rooms. It will be worth every dirham, this purchase of the world's most expensive slave girl – a Northern Buzhanian from the Pripet Marshes according to her pedigree, one of a strain bred on the Alfold Steppe by the last Avar khan, acquired by Bulghar khan Krum following partition of the Avar Empire and subsequently seized from an isolated Transylvanian village on the Upper Tisza River by Frankish raiders, to be onsold to the Slave of the Merciful One in Cordoba – if in eight weeks' time, make that twelve, Shahrban is finally cured of his murderous misogyny and so far, so good. Allah be praised!

Shahrban appears before Shahrazad. He has discarded his putrid hufu, a collared Turkic horseman's robe he favours for daily wear, and sports instead a full Arabic robe of honour, al-Khila'ah – a veritable Badlat Kunuziyah, such a treasure-suit as might be found in an enchanted hoard, or Kunuz.

He bends his knee, Salaaming in most worshipful fashion, albeit irony does not come easy to the Padishah. He learned it from watching others. An act of abasement, however, is all the better for clumsy execution – think fellatio – and Shahrazad duly rewards him with her broad, coarse, asymmetric grin.

As well as a tabby silk kaftan with impossibly wide sleeves, the Shah sports drop-pearl earrings, a black, gold-embroidered turband surmounted by a peacock's feather held with a pin of translucent jade, an amethyst corduroy mantle embossed with droplets of Vietnamese tortoiseshell, a crimson astrakhan cummerbund interwoven with threads of Baltic amber wherein are conjoined all manner precious stones including a Brahmani carbuncle, as it were from the hidden hoard of Yafis bin Nuh (on whom be The Peace!), a golden necklace with huge ruby pendant, two leather shoes with gold shoe-buckles and a gold-hilted scimitar in a lapis- and jade-encrusted gold scabbard.

'*That*'s more like it,' says Shahrazad. 'Now you look the real deal. I'm not surprised, that with such low self-esteem, you've had no luck with women. Women like men to strut their stuff. Boy, could Ziryab pull chicks! Let me smell that breath. Phew! I can go for that. What is it, aloes?'

'Khmer aloeswood. Why do I feel we have so much in common, Shahrazad, when you're a woman and I'm a man?'

'Because you're such a big girl's blouse while I'm a bit acca-dacca. At age five I was the strongest kid in the entire Tisza Valley. I could bear the weight of a pine joist over these shoulders of mine. Happy days. I was just one of the boys and no one treated me any different. Hey, your suit inspires me to finish my *Tale of the Lady and her Five Suitors*. Now, where were we?'

'The Lady had made an assignation with the Wazir for the same time and day as the Kazi and the Wali then she'd gone to see the Shah.'

'Gee, you remember. None of the others ever remembered.'

'I wonder if you prefer me to these others? Rest assured I now better understand the situation, Shahrazad. When Abu Bakr said you were his daughter I didn't realise that he thinks of all his slave girls as his daughters so there was a misunderstanding on my part. I accept that a slave girl is unlikely to be a virgin, but there is one question I must ask, if you're to remain my Wasifah.'

'*Concubine!* Hello? We're already married!'

'We must, of course, divorce, in that I am a Levite and cannot marry a whore, divorcee or widow as I deserve better. A wife of mine must be a virgin, but as concubine, you could become Umm al-Walad, Mother of the Child. That would mean you could not be sold and our child will be free and legitimate. Moreover, if the child were heir to my throne, I may feel an impulse to release you. Now, were you ever involved with a blackamoor?'

'Involved with a *blackamoor*? No way!'

The Shah, to his wife's surprise, falls in a swoon, striking out with his hands and feet. He is returned to consciousness by Shahrazad throwing rosewater on him.

'Hey there, Shahwah, don't be such a sook, you'll ruin that beautiful mantle. Come on, the kohl is running down your cheeks because of the rosewater. Sit up!'

'Take off my finery. Why do I feel I must trust you, Shahrazad?'

'I dunno. Something to do with the boobs, no doubt – generally is. Now then, pretty please, can I pluck that eyebrow? It makes you look like a *werewolf*! I can't stand it! Here, let me just quickly glance at it. Eeeek! It makes my *blood* run! It even makes my nipples harden. Must we take off *all* this gear? Can't we leave the turband? Here, let me comfort you. Put your head down there.'

And so they do a second deed of kind and it's good for the Shah though Shahrazad tells a tale the entire time.

'I'm finished,' interrupts the Shah, a stranger to *prolongatio veneris*, 'in case you hadn't noticed. And that's the first time for me in many a year, inside an orifice. No more of the tale. I want to hear more about these others with whom you've been involved. Most women, at this juncture, begin to volunteer the information. If you've only been in Merv six months, does that mean you never saw me on a horse?'

'Wow, you have a *horse*, Eyebrows? Can I ride it? I love horses.'

'You never actually thought to yourself, how just and upright I look on horseback or how attractive and handsome?'

'Oh, someone pointed you out. I thought you were kinda cute till I saw that eyebrow, but I was reading a book, I wasn't looking for action and don't forget, I was married.'

'Married. What do you mean *married*? Married to Ziryab the 'ud master?'

'Noo! Married to this Chinese chick I met in the Harem. Boy, was she cute.'

Alarmed by this latest disclosure, which suggests that Shahrazad may be a Sahikah, the Shah changes back into his putrid hufu and walks through the night to the Khangah. He must seek advice from 'Ali Zindiq. He'd felt quite happy there, for a time, too, and now he feels – gutted.

The ghulams are fighting the mirabs in the Rabad. They've all forgotten what started it.

'Here he is again,' says the Pir, after greeting Shahrban, 'the man who never was.'

'And filled with Love-longing, Pir, as I can think of only one thing.'

'Oh dear. You've fallen in love with this nautch girl. The wise fly settles never on the honey, only on the sugar cubes.'

'I am earth for her treading and dust to her sandals. My vitals are consumed. My love for her is mingled with my flesh and with my blood and has entered into the channels of my bones. What is to become of me? I so enjoyed the deed of kind I just performed upon her. I doubt I ever enjoyed a deed more. She is fat and delicate as a sheep's tail. Mind you, the worst deed ever I did was quite enjoyable. I am a stranger to Nusk but I finished the deed tonight, which is unusual for me, Hamdillah. It was the first time in many a year I completed a deed inside an orifice. See, I generally wait till the execution and do it into my hand. I want to see her again, too, because she mystifies me and then, perhaps, I can be happy again, for another minute or so.'

'It's not just you,' confirms the Pir, 'as it must be competitive. You observe she mystifies others. In sooth, she mystifies *me*! It must be competitive, Shahrban. Let's speak of carnal love which, by its very nature, is competitive. Let's speak of carnal love and Happiness, in particular. Are there lessons here to be learned? Allah save and favour the king! Kurban-at basham – may I be your sacrifice, O Shadow of Allah? I think I should relate (but Allah is All-knowing!) the tale of *The Man who Fell in Love with his Own Feet* or how the Tang foot cloth joined the Lolo neck ring.'

The Man Who Fell in Love with His Own Feet

Or what it means to request 'Chinese' as distinct from 'Spanish' in a house of ill-repute

Passing the night with a prostitute – ten demerits
Composing a licentious book or painting an obscene image – infinite demerit

Kung-kuo-ko

When Duke Long of Dong for reason of state was forced to marry a woman of the Miao, he found her so repellent that he could not bear to look at her. Realising that if he did not consummate the marriage the Miao would rise up, the duke ordered his terrestrial genie, Tong-tzu, Master Tong, to prepare him a love elixir. Tong-tzu, skilled herbalist and natural product chemist, Grand Master of Imperial Entertainments with Silver Seal and Blue Ribbon, an Erudite of the Suchou Academy of Arts and Natural Sciences and Companion of the Honour of the Crimson Fish Pouch First Class, immediately set to work in his laboratory with crucibles, alembic and retort to prepare a potion. Consulting his almanac, using heat and timing, and deploying a sophisticated laboratory technique acquired over seven hundred and sixty-four years of terrestrial life, Tong-tzu distilled yin from a compound of henna, potash, *hauma*, hot blood, mare's urine, issyk kul root, tamarisk manna, citragandha, rehmannia and petraoxymel of carragheen. He then added yang from his jewellery drawer. He now had a Taoist love potion in two components: a phial of clear, bright liquid that changed colour from red to green and green to red, with a small jade lingam fetish to be worn as an amulet. On the fifth day of the fifth month, the day of the Dragon Festival, Tong-tzu sent for Club Foot who'd been sitting outside a teahouse playing mahjong and double sixes.

Provoking another to gamble with money – ten demerits

Club Foot, fearful of Tong-tzu, hastened at once to the alchemist's house which was jiangnan style, a low affair of whitewashed plaster with granite corbels and a black-tiled roof that overlooked the Grand Canal within earshot of Cold Mountain Temple bell.

Serving a genie with devotion – one merit

'I want you to take this love potion to the duke's palace for me,' said the genie. 'As you will see, it has two parts. One is this necklace, the other this liquid that changes colour depending on whether the light that falls on it is reflected or direct. Now listen carefully, Club Foot.

The first thing to remember is that no magic can occur before the phial is broken. The second and more importantly: make sure you do things in proper sequence. Now then, tonight, when everyone is sleeping exhausted by festivities and sorghum liquor, I want you to sneak into the duke's bedroom and place this amulet around his neck like *so*. Then turn to the Miao woman who's lying in bed beside him – I'll organise that – and break this phial over her face. Just snap it between your fingers. As soon as the liquid has touched her face the duke will find her attractive. He may well snort and roll in bed and the jade spear will search for the jade gate, at which point make yourself scarce. There will be no guard on duty. I'll see to that. Now then, whatever you do, don't break this phial before the amulet is over the duke's neck, is that clear? Off you go.'

Working to bring about the success of a good enterprise – ten merits

Club Foot went back to Maple Village to fill in time before night fell. He walked with an awkward, jerky gait that made people laugh at him but only behind his back.

Insulting a disabled person – ten demerits

Carrying the amulet round his neck for safekeeping, Club Foot held the phial in one hand and once in a while would hold it to the light, to watch it turn from red to green or green to red.

Furtively reading a letter addressed to another – three demerits

Using a coin from a string of cash given him in payment by Tong-tzu, Club Foot bought himself a bowl of mustard greens with rice noodles and strange-flavour beans. He ate greedily, leaning against an arch of the cut stone Maple Bridge. He hadn't had a decent meal in weeks.

A nearby bonze who'd been telling fortunes and selling incense on the bridge started to pack away his stall and asked Club Foot for assistance.

Helping another human being in his work – ten merits

'What's it worth?' inquired Club Foot, belching as he finished his meal.

Behaving grossly – one hundred demerits

Tossing the empty bowl in the air, he kicked it as hard as he could off the bridge into the waters of the Grand Canal. No one could front kick harder than he, which gave him respect among the local martial artists.

Behaving brutally – one hundred demerits

'I could tell your fortune or I can give you incense,' said the bonze.

'Tell my fortune,' said Club Foot. 'Now then, how does this table fold?' As Club Foot crawled under the table to inspect the nearest leg, the bonze, thinking he recognised the captain of a passing salt junk, waved. In so doing he struck the table a glancing blow which caused it to capsize, as Club Foot was already folding the leg nearest the bridge wall. Under the weight of incense sticks, Club Foot was knocked backwards and before he'd had time to think, he opened his hand to protect his head.

Damaging a bridge – thirty demerits

There was a tinkle and out fell the contents of the phial, dripping over the soles of Club Foot's feet. The amulet, thank goodness, was still around his neck.

'Look what you made me do, Duck Foot,' said Club Foot. 'Can't you be more careful?'

Grumbling at every mischance – five demerits

'Sorry,' said the bonze. 'Now be quiet as I'm focused on your future.'

'Don't waste your time,' said Club Foot. 'I'm not sure I have one. I'll take the incense.'

Working together as a team, they packed up the stall and put the contents in the handcart.

Amulet depending from his burly neck and incense sticks in either hand, Club Foot followed the milling crowd towards Fang Water Gate. Suchou, capital of the ancient kingdom of Wu, was in a festive mood on this, the Day of the Dragon. Perhaps the people were hoping that rain might fall to fertilise the fields. The dragon, which has the head of a horse and the body of a serpent, sleeps at the bottom of wells and lakes where, upon being woken by thunder, it dashes up into the clouds to make rain. All the houses in the city had a small clay dragon on the roof and there was even a temple, Temple of the Dragon King, next to Military Headquarters. But no one has ever seen a dragon.

Beyond Fang Water Gate, outside the walls, a cut stone bridge led to a small pagoda, where Club Foot would sleep under the eaves in the event of rain. Kneeling beneath the pagoda, he rested on his elbows and tried to find the courage to bend his neck so that he could look under his thighs to see the soles of his feet. This was the easiest way to do so. But he couldn't find the courage.

Sons of the Rumour

Of all external parts of our bodies our feet are the least regarded. Only babies, with their prehensile feet that can grasp the rungs of cots, enjoy putting their toes in their mouth. Most of us hate the sight of them. Adults rarely dispense them so much as a glance as they pull on their boots. If we go barefoot like Club Foot, then our feet become so dirty that we studiously ignore them in the hope that others may do the same. By mid-life we can barely recognise them; in old age we can seldom touch them. Because they are distal from our eyes and hands we scant them, we neglect them. In general, we treat them as we would internal organs; acting as though they didn't exist until they cause discomfort.

Club Foot had no trouble with his feet. They caused him no pain. Indeed they were strong and, like his legs and buttocks, exceptionally muscular, but his toes pointed inward and when he walked, the soles of his feet made no contact with the ground. He walked on two massive calluses on what would have been the back of a Duck Foot's feet. Moreover, his feet dragged behind him as he walked, propelling his torso forward, so he tended to get in Duck Foots' faces, which Duck Foots didn't like. Even so, they often gave him work delivering items for them. They felt he wouldn't be hard to find if tempted to abscond as his hard lot in life had given him a fierce, despondent facial expression – rather like that to be seen in paintings of Bodhidharma, Japanese Daruma, patriarch of Ch'an, or Zen, Indian princeling and Buddhist heresiarch for whom a married butcher can be a Buddha and who, having been thrown out of every Buddhist monastery from India to Canton, invented martial art at the Shaolin convent in the Sung Shan where he founded a Sect – strictly speaking, Vedantine not Buddhist – and this, combined with a powerful front kick and generally strong physique meant Club Foot could cut his way through the traffic easily.

Hoti, that happy, fat, drunken Zen slob, is the preferred public face of Zen Buddhism, but Sons of the Rumour say, with Daruma, that better a saint should weep. We commend *Qabd,* the State of Contraction over *Bast,* the State of Expansion, and why? Because few Zen Buddhists, following Happiness, are able to revert to propriety; this, because they have no longer need for it and because they have burned their books and because they have killed the Buddha.

The Sufic Journey begins and ends in propriety, moving via the Tao.

At night, life became difficult for Club Foot. Intoxicated local youths who never fought one on one liked to gang up and search for victims. A crippled man, sprawled with his peers in Jaspar Waves Square, provided a suitable target.

Wishing evil upon others – ten demerits

Club Foot had scars to prove this and now he lay low after dark. He'd learned that if you don't drink liquor and you don't mix with people and you don't go out at night and you don't make eye contact, you don't get into trouble.

Getting drunk – one demerit
Avoiding a dangerous interview – one merit
Not fixing one's eyes on a pretty person – five merits
Refusing to believe in the virtue of others – two demerits

Club Foot slept alone. Sometimes he'd sleep outside the Temple of the god of Literature near Fang Gate, or in the comfortable rubbish dump by the Imperial Silk manufactory, right by Military Headquarters, but mostly he went outside the walls to the pagoda by the parade ground, to the Shrine of the Emperor's Tablet, to the Yun Yen Taoist Monastery, to the Buddhist Temple at Priest's Ferry Bridge. There he would kneel or lie fitfully till dawn. He could never properly sleep. Of course, if a terrestrial genie ordered you to work by night, you worked by night.

Leaving a good work unfinished – one demerit

Club Foot delayed observing his feet until it was too dark to see them. Perhaps he was afraid to look. It was raining hard now, so he made himself as comfortable as he could and lay listening to the thunder, wondering what next to do.

He had met a few terrestrial genii, mostly round Hokou Hill. They were always old men, virtuous and wealthy, not exactly dead but not exactly alive, ugly and deformed like Master Tong, with long hair and long fingernails. They were impervious to heat and cold and neither ate nor drank, living on air and dew and drinking the Elixir of Immortality. Mostly they rambled about Kunlun Shan, laughing at folk. Ko-Hung, writing in the time of the Ch'in when the Great Wall was completed, records one thousand attested cases. There were also Celestial genii but terrestrials were more common. Tong-tzu, in order to manufacture *shen tan* – the Elixir of Immortality – through the Cycle of the Nine Transformations, needed a laboratory and was thus obliged to rent a townhouse and put himself in a duke's service.

Ssu-ming, Heavenly Governor of Destinies, who keeps account of our human deeds based on reports received from individual consciences on the last day of each month, needs to compute three hundred consecutive meritorious actions, all performed through love of good, in order to elevate any man to the status of terrestrial genie. This, however, is insufficient. The sage must also have control of his breath, must carefully guard his liquefied brain – lost, as a rule, through the jade spear in the deed of kind – but in particular he must have bought and ingested or synthesised for himself an adequate dose of *shen tan*, transcendent cinnabar, the drug of perenniality.

Some fail the exercise through want of courage or merit, others through want of means, but most fail.

Club Foot, who was twenty-two, knew that Tong-tzu was seven hundred and sixty-four. It would be no contest, he decided, if Tong-tzu was angry with his having spilt the tincture.

It might be better if he never found out.

Making false reports – one hundred demerits

Club Foot wondered if his life was coming to an end. To make it worse he was a bare branch – no descendants to offer libations to his souls. In the beginning, his mother, a widow, had tried to correct his feet with strong bindings, but in the end she'd given up the task and abandoned him here in this pagoda.

Helping a widow or an orphan – thirty merits
Receiving an abandoned child – one hundred merits

Club Foot lay listening to the torrents of water now rushing into Suchou's canals – all of them local branches and subsidiaries of the Grand Canal over which Suchou had stood since Sui *Faghfur* Yang Ti completed the last section of the Yangchou–Yangtze canal in Tong-tzu's five hundred and fifty-second year of terrestrial life. Six small canals ran east to west, six south to north through the city, which was three and a half miles from north to south and two and a half miles wide, with walls thirteen miles or so in length and six gates. All the canals were traversed by hundreds of half-moon cut stone bridges every two to three hundred yards, each bridge tall enough to admit the under passage of a single-masted junk.

Tang naval architect Liu Yen had designed five different types of junk for use over the various sectors of the Grand Canal with its many sluices. These vessels, laden with produce, could travel the thousand miles from Yangchou to the two Tang capitals in forty days, while they could navigate the Yangtze Kiang, which flowed forty miles north of Suchou, as far upriver as Suifu in Szechuan, which took more than a hundred days as Suifu was fully sixteen hundred nautical miles from the mouth.

Travelling upriver, these vessels had to be dragged, for so strong was the Kiang that no vessel could make headway upstream in summer using sail, oar or poles. Tracking was done by prisoners of war or criminals degraded to servitude, hauling in teams on bamboo canes, which are stronger than ropes of hemp. Working against the summer rains and the melt of Tibetan ice, pulling through four hundred miles of rapids between Ichang and Chungking, towpath dragging was a job for a Duck Foot. Any man who fell foul of Duke Long and came before a court was always degraded to servitude for life, provided the judge thought him strong and fit. He would be given a pole or an oar or consigned to a Yangtze towpath, and while Club Foot was exempted from military service in view of his deformity, he would not be exempted from the junks; for just as slaves condemned to be guardians of gates were branded in the face and slaves condemned to guard the imperial harems of Chang'an castrated, so slaves who rowed the Yangtze galley-junks had both feet amputated.

Crippling a slave – one hundred demerits

Around midnight the rain eased so Club Foot got up and made his way to the duke's palace, stumping along in his jerky gait, splashing his way through the puddles. As everything has been prearranged, I will go through with this, he thought. If the love potion fails to work I shall claim it is Tong-tzu's fault. At worst, Ssu-ming, Heavenly Governor of Destinies, will deduct another three hundred days from my life for telling lies.

Telling a lie – one demerit

How many days would that leave? Club Foot had lost count.

The duke's palace stood in a group of buildings known as Confucian Temple or Dragon's Head. Dragon Street, which ran due north, formed the dragon's body and the Great Pagoda its tail. The main temple in the complex contained the Tablet of Confucius and a number of gilded boards dispensing wise saws by Mo Ti. Outside the temple was an altar used to kill animals for the Patron of the Soil. There was a library, which included Lu-yen's Kung-kuo-ko, the celebrated treatise on morality – *providing good counsel, three merits* – a hall for the Suchou scholars and a building containing astronomical charts over a stone map of Suchou. The duke's palace stood in the back of a cedar grove behind a large wall. As foretold by Tong-tzu, the palace guards were drunk and the vomitous stench of sorghum liquor was strong, despite the pouring rain.

Inside the palace, Club Foot wandered around till he found the duke's bedroom. There lay the duke, dead drunk, with next to him, a Miao woman. Both had their mouths wide open, presenting an unpleasant spectacle.

By the night lamp shining from a cresset on the wall, Club Foot took his bearings. Old habits die hard; he found himself looking for things to steal, such as might be light in weight and great in worth.

Sweeping away a bad thought as soon as it appears – one merit

Moving silently over the rug which, like the silkscreen and the bedspread, featured a pattern with the golden lotus of the House of Dong, Club Foot tripped on a silk gown that had been tossed onto the rug and fell to his knees. The duke didn't wake; both he and the woman snored on stertorously. Club Foot glanced between his knees and, by the light of the night-light, he could see his own feet for the first time since he'd spilled the potion over his soles. He was still gazing at them half an hour later when the Miao woman, urged to consciousness by a full bladder, stirred, and upon seeing Club Foot in the room screamed so loudly as to wake the dead.

Rising at night, completely naked in bed – one demerit

Before the duke could open his eyes, Club Foot had jumped up and, taking the amulet off his neck, placed it over the duke's head. At this point the duke himself sat, blinked, rubbed his eyes and looked about.

Rising at night, completely naked in bed – one demerit

'What are you doing here, Club Foot?' The duke had been staring at Club Foot's feet for some time by the time he said this. Indeed, it took him so long to say it and he said it so quietly and sweetly, that Club Foot realised he'd done the wrong thing in putting the amulet over the duke's head. I must have it for myself, he thought.

'I'm here to steal that amulet you wear,' Club Foot said, 'and don't you try to stop me.'

The duke instinctively pressed his hands to his throat. 'No, you'll not have it!'

'It's not even yours!' protested Club Foot. 'You know nothing of it! How could you possibly miss something you've never even known?'

'Come, come,' said the duke, 'let's not shout at each other. Perhaps we can come to some agreement. Put your feet up here on the bed and we'll see what we can manage.'

The Miao woman, who despite a mouth full of gold teeth was no fool, started laughing so heartily she made the duke angry.

Properly controlling a concubine of inferior rank – one merit

'What you got to laugh at?' he said. 'You ugly creature, with your big duck feet, how *dare* you laugh at me like that. I'll throw you to the market!'

Throwing people to the market was a cheap and inclusive mode of execution.

'*He*'s the one, the thief in this room you should be throwing to the market,' said she. 'But you can't see it because the rogue has made you in love with his feet and *look* at them! You were never wearing that amulet when we went to bed last night. I saw him put it over your neck as you woke.'

Aghast at the realisation he'd fallen in love with Club Foot's feet, the duke dropped his hands from his throat and Club Foot seized the opportunity. He snatched back the amulet and put it over his own neck.

'Now then,' said Club Foot, speaking confidently, 'I can help you. Do as I say.'

Setting on the right path a friend who has deviated from it – ten merits

The duke, who had never in his life been so addressed by a crippled beggar, was nonplussed. Taking advantage of his stupefaction, Club Foot moved to the silk screen at the foot of the duke's bed and without hesitation started ripping it into ten-foot lengths.

'What do you think you're doing?' said the duke, finally finding his tongue.

'These are to bind the feet of that big-footed demon in the bed beside you. It's scarcely to be wondered at, a man wouldn't want a creature like her. Here! Grab those feet for me.'

Just then, Tong-tzu appeared in the door and laughed when he took in the joke. Of course, it was largely at his own expense but he liked a joke, Tong-tzu. He could always make more potion for the duke and have someone more reliable deliver it.

Seeing the game was up, Club Foot admitted what had happened on Maple Bridge; how he'd accidentally spilt the potion all over his own feet. It wasn't his fault, as he went on to explain, which made Tong-tzu laugh the louder.

'What shall we do with the wretch?' said the duke to Tong-tzu. 'He's made us both look foolish.'

'Throw him to the market,' advised the Miao woman. 'Tie his hands and throw him to the market.'

'Put him on a junk,' advised Tong-tzu. 'He's strong. A shame to waste his strength.'

'Good thinking, Tong-tzu,' said the duke. 'Now let's get that amulet off his neck.'

'Oh no no no no no,' said Tong-tzu. 'Club Foot keeps the amulet.'

'Ah!' said the duke, 'I take your point. He keeps the amulet but not his feet!'

'Man is no straw dog,' said the genie. 'Do you not perceive his confidence? Such confidence Club Foot now enjoys. How respectful I feel of him! And all because he has fallen in love with his own two crippled feet. Something may come of this. All that happens or does not happen in the world being the Will of the Sovereign on high, Club Foot may be destined to join the glorified *shen* of the Dong.'

The duke was offended by this suggestion but Tong-tzu, laughing heartily, went off to make a second potion while Club Foot, arms bound in the lotus-pattern silk, was taken to the prison.

The prison stood by the Prefecture beside the Imperial Granary between the Court of the Provincial Judge and the Temple of Hero Wu-Tzu. The prefect being Duke Long himself, the duke was effectively prince, and in conformance with the thought of Taoist Master Kuan-tzu, a prince, as agent of the Principle in a principality, must decree law that is both opportune and profitable and never give reasons. Give the people reasons and they will dispute obedience. The duke generally changed his laws while lying in bed or fishing.

A prince must dam his people like water, nourish them like domestic animals, exploit them like a field or a wood and treat them, in general, like straw dogs; but above all he must provide them three necessary and sufficient staples: clear if changeable law; the executioner's axe; and a system of financial recompense for spies and informants. There must be no mercy, no pardon, no amnesty; clemency serving to increase crime.

The prison was a series of damp, dark holding cells, a place of remand; to punish a person through incarceration would be both inopportune and unprofitable. A prisoner was held in the prison until he could come before a court; if innocent he was released, if guilty he was punished. The prison walls were damp to the touch and no light shone in there. Owing to his bad reputation and pugnacious disposition, Club Foot was given a cell to himself. The crime had to fit the punishment suggested by Tong-tzu, so the charge was that of lese-majesty, the penalty for which was degradation to servitude with mutilation. Club Foot had been informed of the charge and the penalty, if convicted. There could be no question of clemency; only peremptory inquiry as to innocence or guilt, which wouldn't take long.

On the third day, the duke came to see Club Foot in his cell. The duke held a torch in either hand. Once he'd entered the cell, he dispatched the gaoler somewhere else, so the door remained ajar.

'Here I am,' he said eventually, over the dripping and the silence. 'It's me.'

In the light of the torch, Club Foot was staring at his own feet. He hadn't been able to see them properly in the dark. The duke noticed he'd used the silk from the screens to bind them.

'Take those bindings off,' said the duke. 'If I'm called to give evidence in this case, as I expect I shall be, I should have to say I recognise that silk as coming from the screen at the foot of my bed.'

'I'm glad you've come,' said Club Foot. 'At first I was jealous but then I realised that if no one else had ever loved these feet, I could question my own judgement. I think I know what you're here for but I want it back before you leave.'

'I can't think what you mean,' said the duke. But when Club Foot took off the amulet and held it up, looking into the duke's eyes, the duke found himself reaching out and taking the amulet and putting it over his head.

'We have much in common,' said Club Foot. 'This, I believe, is the first time either one of us has been in love.'

The duke said nothing, just squatted on the filthy cell floor and reached out to touch the feet. 'Why do you bind our feet like that? Why do you bind them in silk?'

'Because my mother did it to me when I was young and how it hurt! I want to see how much my feet adore me, I suppose. I want to see how much pain they are prepared to endure on my behalf. You know I sometimes feel that they love me more than I love them? I even wonder if I'm capable of love, at times. Do you feel that?'

The duke said nothing. At last, he said, 'I can't be completely certain it was you in the room the other night, Club Foot. As you know there is no amnesty here and the charge has been laid against you. You're destined for a galley-junk. Those feet will have to come off. Will they keep on ice, do you suppose? Can we have them stuffed or preserved?'

'Get me a knife. I won't use it to kill a gaoler. And now, my amulet, if you please. Tong-tzu said I was to have it. He is making another for you.'

'Ah no, I fear not. Tong-tzu will be making no more amulets.'

'Why, is he dead?'

'On the contrary. Promoted to Celestial genie. Ascended to the clouds on the back of a dragon at the end of the last month.'

'That would have taken a large dose of transcendent cinnabar.'

'More like twelve hundred consecutive merits. I've made inquiries with my spies and done the computations. There is *no way* Tong-tzu could have acquired nine hundred merits in one month unless … unless …'

'Unless what?'

'I think you know what I mean. "Something may come of this," he said, in regard to your falling in love with your feet. The question is, what? *What* is to come of it? Should we give the amulet to everyone to wear?'

'Do you want to do that?'

'No.'

'Neither do I. This is between the prince and the least man of Suchou. How long before I go to trial?'

'I can fix it. How long do you need?'

'I don't know. As you see, I'm beautifying the feet. I'm shortening them and straightening them, building up the depth of the arch. I want to consummate my love. These feet, before they are lost to me, are going to be the finest feet yet seen. My soles are unlike those of other men, having never once touched the soil.'

'I think perhaps you are innocent, Club Foot. I can't be certain of who was in my room the other night. I wouldn't want to have to testify in a court of law.'

'The Miao woman will testify against me. Just give me back the amulet. I have no quarrel with destiny. How foolish to quarrel with destiny! Men discontented with their fate sometimes accuse the Principle of being unintelligent or powerless. These are inept recriminations. It is the law of the prince of the principality, it is the decree applied. It is my destiny which is being fulfilled. If it displeases me, so much the worse for me. That will change nothing. The Principle does not consult the beings. Heaven, the intermediary of the Principle, is not kind to the beings. The Principle treats the beings as straw dogs. How foolish are those who calculate how they may avoid all sorts of evils! They understand nothing of destiny. One should not cling to any life or refuse any death.'

'Well said, Club Foot! You're a sensible fellow. I should come here more often.'

'Oh, you will come here more often. Bring a knife next time.'

'Why? Here, take back the amulet. No, wait, let me keep it just a moment longer.'

'For abbreviating the feet. I soak them first in urine and blood then I break the toes and fold them over my soles, like so, before binding them with the silk. I'd like to cut the toenails in order to avoid infection. Plus, I want to cut away excess gangrenous flesh from the arch.'

'Is it really necessary to do so?'

'Watch! Judge for yourself!'

The duke watched in silence as Club Foot rose to his sturdy feet and, standing delicately on pointes, pirouetted around the cell with his burly arms arched over his head.

'Exquisite,' said the duke, when the dance was done. 'How beautiful it looked, when the foot, rather than an ugly big stand as per usual, became an extension of the leg. A vast improvement over nature, to be sure. Now they just need to be straightened. Is that what we're aiming for? How long are the feet now?'

'Ten inches at a guess. I can do better than a Duck Foot because my feet are inverted. That's why I'm the chosen – nine hundred merits for Tong-tzu. Something will come of this, as he said. Come back tomorrow and bring me a knife. Now give me back the amulet.'

'Is there anything else you would like?'

'Alum would help contract the tissues and minimise the bleeding.'

'I'll bring alum. I'll contact every herbalist in Suchou and see what can be done. You know, this is a great responsibility, improving the human body, what with Tong-tzu looking down, floating up there in the clouds. Not that the human body couldn't stand some improvement. Walking down the street I often feel I'm among monkeys and then I'm tempted to scratch at my right armpit with both hands.'

'Bring me a ruler as well.'

'Will do. Shall I come early?'

'No! Come later in the day. I can't be taking these bandages off and putting them on all the time. They have to be tighter and tighter.'

So the duke visited every herbalist in Medicine Bazaar to commission, from each personally, a foot-softening emollient. Price was no object to a prince. Normally this was a task he would have entrusted to Tong-tzu but Tong-tzu had risen high. The next day, on his way to the prison, the duke picked up the ointments. They all, of course, contained alum with various animal bloods and herbs, but the smell and appearance of each ointment varied considerably. Where a Greek might have used bear bile, an Arab would use rhinoceros horn. Where an Indian might prefer musk, a Russian would deploy hellebore. The blood of a snub-nosed golden monkey, as favoured by a Lolo, would be replaced by sal ammoniac in a Chinese prescription.

The duke decided to mix them all together.

When he got to the prison with his ointments and knife and a ruler in his hands, he again gave the guard something to do as he visited Club Foot's cell. The two of them put the ruler to the feet and found they were eight inches long.

'Shall I do the dance again?' said Club Foot. 'See how it looks, without the amulet.'

'Oh, all right,' said the duke. So while Club Foot tottered away on pointes – he couldn't actually dance on pointes so he danced on the tips of his calluses on the back of each of his feet – the duke looked on.

'And what did you think?' said Club Foot, having lost his balance and fallen. 'Was it better than before?'

'Marginally, I suppose,' said the duke, incurring one demerit. 'The trouble is always going to be the angle of those feet. They're crooked and I can't see how they could be made straight. They can only be shortened, I suspect.'

'But what about my beautiful soles? You're not being fair to them.'

'I have to imagine them, don't I, as you've covered them in silk. Just give me back the amulet.'

'No! You come back tomorrow for the amulet. You've hurt my feelings now, saying my feet are crooked, even if it's true.'

'Well, in that case, I won't give you the ointment. You can have your knife and ruler but I shan't give you the ointment until you've given me the amulet.'

'When you're gone, I shall take off the bandages and have a good dig at the arches with the knife, then I'll tighten the bandages so that when you come back tomorrow for the amulet, I'm tipping seven inches for the feet and possibly a three-inch cleft in each arch. How does that sound?'

'Pretty good but I can't come by tomorrow, I'm afraid, as I'm busy with affairs of state. I'll try to make it the day after.'

'Six inches. I'm doing stretching exercises for added flexibility in the knee but it may be you who has to consummate the love. Does that please you?'

'No. Something is not quite right here. If anything is to come of this, I can only say it hasn't.'

'But what if I cut off the toes completely and slice the feet to no more than three inches in length, what would you say to that?'

'I couldn't say till I'd seen them. I reckon they'd still be crooked.'

Tears welled in Club Foot's eyes.

Rejoicing over the faults of others – ten demerits

'That was a cruel thing to say.'

'I'm sorry I said it,' said the duke and he was. 'Here, take this bit of ointment. When I come by the day after tomorrow, you give me the amulet and then I want to unbind those feet myself and rub in the ointment with my own hands.'

'Would you like to use the knife on the flesh of the arch? You can if you like.'

'I don't think so. What would be the point? It won't be worthwhile till the ointment has done its job and the flesh has rotted completely. It cost me a lot of money, this ointment. What I will do, is have military engineers design a pair of adjustable calipers to help straighten the feet. The angle of the feet has spoiled the dance.'

'You don't even like the dance now?'

'I like it well enough. I like the *idea*. The notion of a foot appearing as an extension of the leg is absolutely brilliant. Could we achieve the same effect, do you think, with a pair of, say ... very high heels?'

'Of course not!'

'All right then, I must trust your judgement. I leave you to your task. I shall see you the day after tomorrow.'

But he didn't. He never saw Club Foot again, because when the duke came back a week later having been delayed by affairs of state, he found Club Foot had been tried and sentenced and both his feet had been cut off by the executioner and tossed in the canal. As to the whereabouts of the amulet – indeed Club Foot himself – no one knew. Somewhere up the Yangtze Kiang, presumably.

The duke went back to his palace, locked the door to his bedroom, sat on the bottom of his bed and sulked for a week and a day.

Criticising the sages or their writings – one hundred demerits

At the end of the week and the day, a thought having occurred to him, the duke dressed in his silk gown, took a string of cash, and accompanied by an attendant went to the water gate where people drowned newborn baby girls.

Drowning a girl – one hundred demerits
Stigmatising the custom of drowning girls – thirty merits
Saving a female child about to be drowned – fifty merits

By the end of the day the duke and his retainer had two hundred and fifty merits to their credit, in the shape of five newborn females, the parents going off in a good mood, too, with a little cash in hand. The duke took the girls back to his bedroom and gave orders that a wet nurse was to be found, in order they be fed. Their feet, he insisted, must never touch the ground. They were to sit only on the bed.

When the girls were about two years old, the duke began binding their feet. He did it personally. Thanks to Club Foot and Tong-tzu, he had a few ideas here. He used ten-foot-long bandages of gold lotus-pattern silk about two inches wide. He wanted the finished feet to appear an extension of the girls' legs and as he'd kept the foot-rotting ointment he'd meant to give Club Foot, he applied it liberally – indeed, too liberally at first, so he had to procure him a few more girls and he fed the girls only on sticky rice dumplings, which a doctor had told him would soften cartilage. At this young age, the arch was largely cartilage, rather than bone.

Club Foot had the right ideas but he was old and the wrong sex. At twenty-two, his feet were bone, and large and calloused and dirty. In order to achieve the correct result, you had to mould the feet before they'd set.

The duke would never lose sight of how he'd felt for Club Foot's feet.

First, he clipped the girls' toenails and soaked their feet in ointment. Then he massaged their bones and the tissue for several hours until they were soft. Then he broke all their toes except the big one and folded them carefully under the soles, before he applied the silk bandaging. Every couple of days he removed the bandage, washed the feet, carefully pedicured the toenails, then reapplied the bandage, making it tighter and tighter each time. Eventually, after a few months, he succeeded in breaking the arch of the girls' feet, and he ordered they be given a special treat in the shape of gorgeous little shoes that he'd specially made for them out of red silk. Wearing these shoes, the girls were then encouraged to walk about the palace so that the weight of their tiny bodies would help in the foot-abbreviation. The lighter girls were furnished with heavy crowns to wear on their heads.

It was a process of trial and error but luckily, baby girls were easy to come by in Suchou. Sometimes the toes fell off. Laceration of the arch with the knife often led to gangrene and then pus would ooze from the wounds, making them unpleasant to the nose. Four of the first five children had, in fact, to be discarded, but one went quite beautifully and others were soon recruited to the ranks.

The duke called the beautiful girl *San T'sun Chin Lien* – which means Three Inch Golden Lotus. By the age of seven, the compliant little lass was washing and binding her own feet, singing and laughing as she did so in a beautiful high-pitched voice. Tighter and tighter went the bindings. The duke decided to keep her locked from view in a special chamber. He'd never in his life been more excited about a project. This was his destiny. San T'sun Chin Lien had her own exercise yard and a pet cockatoo.

Caging a bird – one demerit

San T'sun Chin Lien was the duke's pride and joy. He appointed a special shoemaker who made her a new set of shoes each time the bindings came off. These shoes became more and more beautiful, more and more exquisitely shaped, more and more magnificent, with delicate little bone heels and magnificent patterns of embroidered silk.

When San T'sun Chin Lien was twelve years old, the duke decreed that no one – not even he himself – was ever again to see her feet unbound and only he was permitted to smell the bandages when they were removed. Oh, the smell of those bandages! Oh, the sight of those beautiful shoes!

Finally came the big moment. After her first menstruation, the duke revealed the girl to the world in a ceremony held in his cedar grove. All Celestials of Suchou gathered by Dragon Head and Three Inch Golden Lotus, whose feet were now more like two and a half inches, showed the beautiful gait of a bound-footed woman to the world for the first time. The men were suitably impressed that while she could move, she couldn't move far or fast, and the women could only imagine the strength of the muscles in her Jade Gate.

Leading back to her home a woman or a girl who has escaped –
three hundred merits
Teaching a wife to behave so as to please her husband –
one hundred merits

'A link with Heaven is here forged today,' said the duke to loud acclaim. 'Here, at last, a civilised female foot. Somewhere in a galley-junk and somewhere in the clouds above are the men who made it possible. I ask you to toast them with me.'

Out came the sorghum liquor and the mare's teat grape wine. And as they drank to the smiling countenance of San T'sun Chin Lien, the supervisor of receptionists was heard to mutter to the secretarial court gentleman, 'Look at those tiny feet, how straight, how beautiful, how respectful! When I imagine the suffering that little creature has endured and I think of removing those beautiful shoes and unbinding those lovely bindings and seeing and smelling and holding the tiny deformed lotus in the palms of my hands, wooo, my desire overflows and my joy becomes uncontrollable. And if those feet were ever to be placed on my shoulders that I could put them in my mouth, or perhaps even eat almonds from between the crushed toes ...'

Putting a stop to a conversation concerning women and girls –
ten merits

'Do not think of seeing those feet unbound,' replied the civilised gentleman. 'You should not look at a naked lotus as if it were a duck's foot! I tell you that if you remove the shoes and seek to loosen the bindings, the Celestial aesthetic will be lost to us and the Mystery of the Bond with Heaven broken.'

Iranian Days (continued)

The Pir then gives the sermon.

'Bismillah – Solve. Go to the Madrasa library, Shahrban, the one that specialises in al-Fiqh, and there you may learn, to your surprise, that under Shari'ah law, Circumcision of the penis is Mustahabb, not Fard; that is, recommended but *not* obligatory. In fact, it is an ancient practice, borrowed by the Jews from the Egyptian priests, universally inflicted upon Islamic boys and not at the age of eight days, the age at which Ishaq was circumcised, the B'rit Milah of Jewry, but necessarily before the age of seven, that being the age of Islamic reason. The commandment in the Torah is to the father, not to the son. Boys, hereabout, are plunged into an icy stream as anaesthetic, the wound being healed with heated sand or salt and turmeric. It is performed on young boys able to endure pain and to respond to pain at reflex level – not to *recall* pain, for pain cannot be recalled. To say or think, "I was in pain," is not to recall pain.

'Why is al-Khitanah not Fard to a Muslim? Isma'il was circumcised at thirteen years, beyond the age of reason, which may be a factor. Perhaps because Ummayad insistence on circumcision of adult converts helped foment the 'Abbasid revolution here in Margiana. Even given that Ibrahim, according to the Torah, was ninety-nine years when he circumcised himself, a sexually active adult man objects to circumcision as painful and unnecessary genital mutilation, repugnance no doubt exploited by Ummayads, especially Caliph Mu'awiyah who vastly preferred poll tax to converts. Paul faced a similar problem in the early days of Christendom, that other Judeaic heresy, and dealt with it such that circumcision to a Nazarene is Makruh but not Haram; that is, discountenanced but not forbidden. In fact, it is common practice among newborn Christians in Khurasan on the grounds of hygiene and morality. Saint Augustine sustained that the rite removes original sin though we observe that clitoridectomy, while diminishing pleasure, promotes lust in a Moslemah.

'In no case, it seems to me, among all the Children of Khalilu'llah, is circumcision Mubah, which is to say, nothing to make a fuss over, neither here nor there, inconsequential. Mutilation of a child is never inconsequential.

'As regards hygiene, removal of the prepuce permits a man wearing a petticoat to urinate without touching his penis. He would thus need to perform Wuzu, the lesser ablution, less frequently but this, I think, cannot be a rationale. Water and sand are everywhere abundant.

'The prepuce exudes a greyish wax that functions as a lubricant to keep the glans as nature intended: soft as the inside of the mouth and smelling like a rotten cheese. Removal reduces the loss, through masturbation, of what a Taoist rightly calls "liquid brain" but where there is a will there is a way and appetency towards fellatio in women is correspondingly abetted.

'As regards sensitivity, the adult prepuce contains fully two hundred and forty feet of nerve fibre, far too many. Joshua excises two tons in weight of prepuce from the Chosen. The penis, like the knee or foot, is a conspicuous piece of poor design, overly sensitive for the world in which it finds itself. They all do it and we have heard from Mawdudus the salutary effects of circumcision on penile function, serving to reduce sensitivity by keratinizing the glans, thus enabling the penis to work harder and longer, and faster and hotter, and increasing, too, the efficacy of the sulcus in removing alien plugs of liquid brain by exposing the sulcus fully on the outward stroke as well as on the inward, but there is more to circumcision than mere mechanics.

'The *pain* it causes is the real purpose of circumcision. Yes, sexual pleasure derives from infliction or contemplation of pain. If you doubt this, buy yourself a mirror or watch two human beings in the paroxysms of congress. A child, peeping on, would think they were in agony and why? Because they are, they just don't feel it. Now, put the child in agony; the child will feel the agony. Cover the wound. Let the child recover from the wound but keep the scar concealed.

'The unveiling, by a lover, of a secret wound inflicted by a tender parent, occasions the ultimate carnal pleasure, presaging, as it does, involuntarily, the bliss of martyrdom, Hamdillah – Coagula. Amen.'

Abu Bakr and the Shah have just performed Salat al-'Asr, the late afternoon prayer, one of their five daily acts of Muslim yoga, or Wazifah. This is the hour at which the guardian angels relieve each other. Four Raka'at follow ablution – Ghusl, in this case, in the Hammam, which involves, in particular, the cleansing of wounds as well as the face, hands, genitals and bronze medallion.

First, facing the Qiblah, the raising of the hands to the level of the ears to open the prayer, the consecratory magnificat 'Allahu akbar', always spoken, then the clasping of the hands, right upon left at the waist above the navel, the mussitated exordium (Surah al-Fatihah –

Bismi Llahi-r-Rahmani-r-Rahim, al-Hamdu li-Llahi Rabbi -l-'Alamin, ar-Rahmani-r-Rahim, Maliki yawmi-d-din, Iyyaka na'budu wa iyyaka nastai'n, Ihdina-s-sirata-l-mustaqim, sirata-lladhina 'an 'amta 'alayhim, Ghayri-l-maghdubi 'alayhim, wa la-d-dallin. Amin) followed by a silent Verse of Sincerity (Surat al-Ikhlas – Qul Huwa-Llahu Ahad; Allahu-s-Samad; lam yalid wa lam yulad wa lam yakun lahu kufuwan ahad), followed by a further spoken 'Allahu akbar'.

Second, the diminution, the bow (Ruku) with the hands on the knees and three silent 'subhana-Llahi-l-'Azim'.

'Allahu akbar' while standing (Wuquf) after, once more aloud, 'sami'a-Llahu liman hamidah. Rabbana wa laka-l-hamd', then the extinction of what has been created (Fana); the prostration (Sujud) with the forehead and the palms on the ground and three silent 'subhana Rabbiya-l-'Ala'.

Then, in the seated position (Julus) on the prayer-carpet (Sujjudah) that which persists (Baqa, the immortal soul) says, 'Allahu akbar'.

'Allahu akbar' again, followed by a second prostration (Fana al-Fana, the extinction of the extinction) then the standing, 'Allahu akbar' which marks completion of the Rak'ah.

After the second and final Rak'ah, the testification, 'at-tahiyyatu li-Llahi wa-s-salawatu wa-t-tayyibatur, as-salamu 'alayka ayyuha-n-nabiyyu wa rahmatu-Llahi wa barakatuh, wa-s-salamu 'alayna wa 'ala' 'ibadi-'Llahi-s-salihin. Ashhadu an la ilaha illa-Llah, wa ashhadu anna Mohammedan 'abduhu wa rasuluh.'

The Shah doesn't understand a word of what he says, whether under the breath or over, but few Iranians, in AD 823, understand Arabic. Most memorise their twelve obligatory verses from al-Qu'ran cockatoo-style. Indeed, most Khurasani Arabs – migrants, originally, from the Iraqi djund garrisons of Basrah and Kufah, pushed along the Achaemenian Great North East Road from the black, if whitening, earth of the Furat through the forests and meadows of the Iranian highlands into Khurasan – speak Dari, a nascent Farsi.

In Tassawuf, the realm of the Sufi – and Sons of the Rumour are ur-Sufis – the Shah remains a 'solitary', a man without a spiritual path and lacking in spiritual tradition. Nonetheless, such a man may receive a spiritual truth. Such a man may even become Happy, if not, as a rule, for long – baptised, in the language of the Roman Church, by the Holy Ghost – though this will confer on him a destiny not entirely enviable, for if the solitary be *utterly* lacking in exoteric tradition – if he be unprepared, as is not uncommonly the case in the calamitous practice of Kundalini Yoga or the scoffing of magic mushrooms – then his sacred revelation is doomed to remain, to his chagrin, untransmissable.

The new-born prophet (and each unbeliever needs a scripture of his own, as Mohammed, on whom be The Peace, warned) finds himself shunned by his peers as a fanatic, an embarrassment worse than any pervert. If the solitary be vaguely familiar with a childhood religious tradition, he will become within it schismatic, or more commonly heretic. In the mystic language of Tassawuf, the solitary – a disciple ripe for understanding but lacking spiritual tradition – must be confronted by a 'Presence', a 'Servant of God' who will assume to him human form.

The Pir must now set loose on the Shah the Hermetic Solvent of the Poisonous Dragon. The Dragon will dissolve the Shah and if all goes well, release the Maiden within him. Then, and only then, can he become Happy and, of course, given his form, he can't remain so.

The Shah, indeed the Pir, must now depend on Providence. There would seem no other course. The Shah is a goose, a view long held by the Wazir and now confirmed by the Pir. Sermons are water off a duck's back and Allah himself cannot help a fool.

☾

'So what do you get up to at this Khangah?' asks Abu Bakr.

'Oh, we talk about things,' says the Shah, 'apart from Duty and Repetition, which involves the playing of drums.' Exhausted from constructing toothpicks, the Shah is sitting, as the sun sets, upon his throne – a marble couch intricately chased as though by Hindu silversmith, set with pearls and emeralds and having for its legs four elephant tusks with a coverlet of green satin purfled with red gold.

'What kind of things?'

'Resurrection. Martyrdom, circumcision, footbinding. That kind of thing.'

'Would you say you were learning anything useful?'

'Not really.'

'Then why keep going back?'

'It's just a way of getting away from Shahrazad and her tales, which bore me to tears. If one more fisherman opens one more trapdoor about which one more spider has pitched one more web-tent to reveal one more ensorcelled hoard in one more treasury with the aid of one more bottle-imp ... I found a pillow in the Khangah, too. I sleep soundly on a sheep they keep there in the courtyard and while I'm not learning much, I do recall that the soul of a martyr is stowed in the crop of a green bird. I hear a lot about Turks and Chinese, Sogdians and Sand People, which could only be useful knowledge to a warden of the marches, but I was hoping to become happy.'

'You have a right to *pursue* happiness certainly, but happy? You?'

'Yes. I was led to understand that that was the purpose of the lodge. I said I would like to be happy and they said that perhaps I could become happy. The Pir said that if I were to listen carefully and take in all that was said I would, eventually, become happy, though I am rather dirty as I find I'm still my old self.'

'Well, that is about to change. This is a special day for you, Shahrban. It is time for your dissolution. It is time for you to confront your black matter, your Khem, in order to convert it into gold. This is a matter of sound judgement so wish me luck. Oxus beefsteak! Now then, did the Pir tell you that Happiness requires both Heat and Timing? Urinogenital.'

'I recall that having been said by someone at some stage, yes.'

'Did he also tell you that the Greatest Medicine is found in the Poisonous Dragon and that our Stone must be Black before it is White and only then can it become Red? Opsoap winebar dopehead downo.'

'He may have done. I don't always listen to all that's said as I don't like being preached at and they will preach me these sermons. The way I see it, all men are equal, but I'm tired of words, Wazir, and I seem to live in a world of talk. Yap, yap, yap. It's all I ever hear.'

'What if a word were to become – upjack arsetit pompchat wishbone – flesh?'

'On my head and eyes, that would be more appealing.'

'I see who you think of when I use the word "flesh". I see it in your petticoat. The spittle is running from your mouth and moistening your moustachios but you've the wrong idea. Cop this, young Shahrban. *Blackamoor!* Ha! Poisonous Dragon become flesh. What's happening in your petticoat now?'

'How dare you use that word in front of me. Haven't I told you never to use that word in front of me? I'll cut off your head!'

'Go on. Cut it off. Cut off every bastard's head, it's all you're bloody well good for. One of these days it may dawn on you it hasn't made you Happy. Now, here's a question you may wish to put to young Shahrazad. Ask her has she ever done a deed of kind with a blackamoor.'

'Well, I'm one jump ahead of you there, sport, as I already asked.'

'I thought you might've. What did she say?'

'She said, and I quote, "Involved with a *blackamoor*! No way!"'

'That would have come as a relief.'

'The greatest relief ever I felt in my whole life, Abu Bakr, because, as you would know, it is the one crime I could never forgive her and she is by far the most interesting wife ever I had. Why, do you realise she has not one single hair over her entire body, apart from her scalp? She hasn't even an eyebrow. All she has is the hair on her head that falls down past her waist and she doesn't even shave her legs.'

'Go on. Fancy that. So you dodged your Poisonous Dragon, now go back and tell her she's a liar because I know for a fact – are you listening, Shahrban? – I know for a fact that she has slept with three blackamoors, all of them slobbering Zanzabari kitchenhands with noses like eggplants and tongues like lampwicks and cheeks like camel kidneys and upper lips like pot covers, all at the same time, and furthermore, it was her idea and she asked them to come back and do it again but they couldn't be bothered, reckoned she was no good in bed – on account of which I demanded and received a ten per cent discount.'

Shahrban, quivering like a fowl with a cut throat, having risen and sat down twice, rises a third time, face like an ox-eye, then, as it were, lashing his tail like a lion, strides off towards the library.

A mite nonplussed, Abu Bakr shouts after this Shadow of Allah, 'Despite being over seven spans from ankle bone to ear and well past her prime at seventeen years, she is still the world's most expensive slave girl! Three million, two hundred thousand dirhams I paid for her, so don't you go taking matters into your own hands up there, do you hear what I'm saying to you? You are not to harm her!'

Shahrban pauses, then turns to address his Wazir. 'Tuff 'alayka! Dirty water on you, Ya Fadawi, lining me up with all these Muhattakat. So they all do it. Well, I'm not surprised, but as to you, Ya Manyuk, you lying, scheming mongrel, you've dudded me for the last time. No Dhu'l-Fiqar for you! Needs must I slay you with the *foulest* of slaughter. Ready yourself, after all manner tortures from Kurbaj of hippopotamus hide – wherewith, if one smote an elephant, he would start off at full speed – to be sawn in half at the waist after dawn prayers with a blunt saw, your two halves to be fired from mangonels into a bonfire so hot that your bones will melt before your flesh; or better yet, I'll harry your house, spoil your goods and sell your women to a blackamoor dish pig then I'll butt you with my head, squeeze you in the ribs, rattle your daggs till your nose bleeds, slit your nostrils, shear off your ears, blacken your residual face in soot, blow you up with a bellows and, having had a gink lead you round Merv bare-arsed and clad only in pink Takiyah, hog-tied and seated backwards on an ass that has seen better days, I'll have you hanged in a pigskin noose, your body burned and your ashes publicly flung in the Rabad cesspool. Have a ghulam organise it. Learn the glad tidings, thy last day is at hand, O Loathsome Pimp! Make ready to answer the summons of Almighty Allah and don thy grave-gear.'

'Hearkening and obedience.'

'Oh, it's you, Eyebrows.' Shahrazad doesn't look up from her book, another Kitab al-Bah among a library of Kutub al-Bah. It's a work of Indian pornography – quite possibly a religious tract. 'I found a ripper here, mate – *Ananga-Ranga Shastra* by Koka Pandit. It's even better than *Kitab al-Izah fi 'Ilm al-Nikah*, the Book of Explanation in the Science of Carnal Copulation. Here's a section describing unguiculation, impressment with the nails – far out! There are seven methods, apparently. By the way, you can last longer by burning a candle of frogs' fat and coconut fibres.'

He grabs her by the hair, drags her to a corner, roughs her up a bit – nothing much.

'Now then,' he says. 'I'll ask you again and this time you'll speak the Truth. Were you ever involved with a blackamoor?' Just as well she won't look in his face. No one has ever seen him quite like this. He's into his red band.

'Let go! You're hurting me.'

'Good. Answer the question.'

'I already answered!'

'Abu Bakr just told me that you have done the deed of kind, not with just one blackamoor, but with three of them all at once.'

'Hello? I was, like, totally trashed?'

'So it's true.'

'It was no big deal! You asked was I ever *involved* with a blackamoor! Involvement, for me, would mean being in love, so I was never involved with anyone, except perhaps my Chinese wife, because she was such a cutie. That was just sex.'

'Then why do it? Why, why, why! Why would anyone do it? Why do yez do it? Why do you let yourselves down and me down at the same time? Why involve yourself with three black kitchenhands with faces like cobblers' aprons?'

'Because of the size of their Mahashim, I suppose. Because I was drunk. Because I wasn't getting any. Who knows why we do it? Do you know why you do it? I felt I was missing out on what the other slave girls get. It's all they ever talk about in the Hammam. Ow! Ziryab could never get it up because he was always so out of it and I suppose I was hoping those guys could make me feel something. Ow! Don't hurt my stomach! I could be pregnant!'

'Not by me, I shouldn't think. Ya Asl, O Vile of Birth, Ya Manyukah, I can't see you as Umm al-Walad and I'm not waiting to find out. Ya Kahbah! Your child, should it exist, is just a clot of blood, not even a morsel of meat as yet, so my conscience is clear. You asked them back to do it again. You asked them back to do it again. *You asked them back to do it again!* And I thought that you were beautiful! I hoped that you were perfect! Too good for me, this woman, I thought, but you're no better than the rest. Why, you're not even good enough for *me*! You're a beast! 'Ifritah! Fajirah! Bloody whores, the lot of you! I'm finished with women. I'll become a kalandar. I'm absolutely filthy. By Allah Almighty, Omnipotent Lord of the well Zemzem and of the Hatim Wall, I shall give away my palace and earn my place in Paradise.'

'Please, Eyebrows. Try to understand me.'

'Don't think to move me with your tears, show me some respect. And stop calling me "Eyebrows"! I'm weeping and laughing alternately, but on the inside.'

'I'm crying for our child. I was never allowed to keep one. Hey, you've got a hard-on.'

'Only because I'm so looking forward to your execution tomorrow. The sight of a woman's gushing blood excites me.'

'I think you should talk to someone about that, I really do. You have a serious problem with women, you realise?'

'I'm talking to you, so you're the one with the serious problem. That's tomorrow morning – early.'

'Understand me and kill me.'

'What's that you say?'

'Understand me and kill me.'

'I can't hear a word you say. You make me lose my senses!'

'UNDERSTAND ME AND KILL ME!'

So the Beast of Merv, seen by his subjects as a Poisonous Dragon who feasts each night on a fresh virgin, destined on the morrow for the scaffold – in his own eyes a deeply suffering, misunderstood, well-meaning man – lets go the blonde locks, leaves the quivering wretch by her box of smutty illustrated tales of fingernails, then walks to the wall of the library and punches, punches, punches it out, till his delicate fists are a broken and bloodied web of skin and bone. He then stumbles, dazed and exhausted, bewilded, confused and defeated, no longer knowing who he is, no longer knowing where he is, no longer knowing what he is and not much caring, down the (Yemeni onyx) stairs of his library, kicking the newell, blinded by kohl and tears – out of the palace, onto the streets of the Rabad, not making for the Khangah, how dare they preach to a Padishah! How dare they preach at all.

When a disciple is ready, the master will appear, as-salamu 'alaykum.

We see the world in a different way in the red band. We must venture there if we mean to defeat the Dragon. Until we defeat the Dragon we cannot release the Maiden.

So feel sorry for the poor atheist. He has never been in the red band. He has not been through the mill. He is a funker.

Perhaps the disciple is ready: 'Ali and his deputy, Abu Bakr, have put pedal to the metal and thus far, the reaction is auspicious – suitably exothermic, with plenty of froth and bubble, while Shahrazad is still alive, unhurt if a bit bruised. To the Dervish of Merv, to a Central Asian Sufi, the Master of the solitary is, as a rule, al-Khidr. This is the Presence also called by the Jews, Elijah, that hairy prophet from the Gilead Desert; and by the Christians, St George; and by the Mandaeans and Sabians, John the Baptist; and by the Akkadians, Utnapishtim; but there are others, al-Khidr being the Green One.

Solve.

It is dawn. Coagula. The Shah has come to consciousness. It is done. He is tired and exhausted and baptised, having been baptised into

Matter. The ark of the city of Merv emerges from darkness in the night sky. As Shahrban crosses the Razuj canal, donkeys begin to bray. Cocks begin to crow.

Then the Azan, the Call to Prayer, from the muezzin on the minaret.

The Shah doesn't like muezzins because the first muezzin was the first blackamoor, Bilal, freed from servitude by the first Caliph, Abu Bakr.

Allahu Akbar!
Allahu Akbar!
Allahu Akbar!
Allahu Akbar
Ashhadu an' la 'ilaha illa-Llah!
Ashhadu an' la 'ilaha illa-Llah
Ashhadu anna Mohammedan rasulu-Llah!
Ashhadu anna Mohammedan rasulu-Llah
Hayya 'ala-s-salah!
Hayya 'ala-s-salah
Hayya 'ala-l-falah!
Hayya 'ala-l-falah
Allahu Akbar!
Allahu Akbar!
La ilaha illa-Llah!

A scaffold is set up in the courtyard, with court officials, cup companions, nabobs, aghas and ghulams, all standing by with arms crossed and feet joined. Many ghulams bear livid scars from their recent fracas with the mirabs. Above, as heads atop the wall, those wretched cameleers, who stand upon each other's shoulders peering down into the yard. They have heard there is to be held, this morning, an entertainment, but are dismayed to see Shahrazad kneeling on al-Nat'a, the leather of blood, with rings about its periphery so that a thong passed through them can turn it into a bag.

Wearing his scarlet Robe of Anger with red cashmere turband, the Shah notes that she is unbound.

Abu Bakr, meantime, buffets his face and plucks out his beard. Facing the Qiblah, he wears his grave-gear and has just completed the two Raka'at death prayer.

'I thought you'd want her dispatched before me,' he side-valves to the Shah. 'I felt you'd want to consummate your act with her before I'm halved. I felt you wouldn't want to see her beating her bosom with an unbaked brick.'

Shahrban nods assent. 'Where's Dhu'l-Fiqar?' he barks. 'Let's get this caravan on the road. By Allah, there is no help but that I must slay you both.'

Abu Bakr produces a knife, the blade of which shines in the sun. It is Dhu'l-Fiqar. Muttering is heard from the cameleers as more heads appear above the wall.

Surely they aren't going to waste that blonde!

'Get those men down from my wall,' says Shahrban but no one moves. He shakes a kerchief of dismissal in the direction of the cameleers, who merely laugh. 'I said, someone get those men from my wall! Abu Bakr!'

'Yes, Lord of the Age.'

'Did you hear what I just said?'

'Yes, Lord of the Age.'

'You refuse to obey me?'

'Yes, Lord of the Age.'

'Very well, Ya Kawwad, O Pimp, we have an audience. We have a public execution and the soil is athirst for your blood. Moreover, I shall have your severed head put between your legs, by your arse, as it were a Jew or Nazarene head. To put that head in your armpit, as it were a True-Believer's head, is too good for you. Where's my sedan chair with its curtains and towel?'

'Couldn't say.'

'Very well. I shall watch from over there behind that tree. Where is the Linkman who will perform these executions? Who will walk thrice round you, brandishing blade about your head and asking, "O King of the Age and Teacher of the Time, sum and substance of revolving Tide, shall I now remove this head from between these shoulders?" as I reply "Yes, by Allah!"? Who will assist Almighty Allah, be He exalted and extolled, in hastening your two souls to the Fire?'

'Wouldn't know. Didn't think to ask.'

There must be fifty cameleers as well as other big, rough men – mirabs, barber-cuppers from the Hammam, ape-dancers, bear-leaders, tent-pitchers – and numbers steadily amount.

Shahrazad gets up off the leather of blood and walks towards the wall, threatening, unless she receive baksheesh from these cameleers, to expose her person. Baksheesh declined, she rips open her shift and, holding apart the torn ends, elbows high, vouchsafes, as threatened in the coffee house, a good perve.

'Ghatti! Ghatti!' the call goes out. The ghulams jog towards the wall, weapons at the ready.

'Ghatti, Ghatti!' May Allah veil them.

'You may have to do the job yourself,' says Abu Bakr. 'Here's your knife. Mind you do it tidy. I can't imagine those lads out there would like to see you make a mess of it. They'd be filthy.'

Shahrazad walks towards the Shah, still holding open her shift. The Shah's knees knock as his member stiffens while his spittle moistens his moustachios; such is the case regarding the Shah. As for Shahrazad, she wiggles her hips like a thirsting gazelle. She has the walk of a wheatfield in a wind and, when she chooses, the slightly swinging gait of a thoroughbred mare. Left shoulder forward, right shoulder back for the delectation of these perving Turkic horsemen, she bends her graceful neck to look from side to side like a young filly. Her eyes are all the Shah will recall as later that day they embrace – never before has she looked him in the eye – too frightened of the eyebrow. Recovering from the sight, she kisses the Shah like a pigeon force-feeding a squab, a technique learned from the Samputa in the Samaniya library.

'Can't you see I *love* you?' she whispers, adding, 'and that's the first time I ever said that and meant it. I ask only that you understand me and kill me. Ana fi jirat-ak! I crave your intercession. Fi 'irzak! Under thy protection.'

'Astaghfiru 'llah,' says the Shah. 'The promise of Night is effaced by Day. Abu Bakr!'

'Yes, Lord of the Age?'

'The quick we can kill but the dead we cannot quicken; thus, it behoveth us to reconsider this matter that Allah may have ruth upon us, inasmuch as Almighty Allah – be He exalted and extolled! – appointeth the issue of long-sufferance to be an abounding good in the world and an issue of patience is praised. You are under our protection and your murder will not escape us. By Allah, there is no help but that we must now forgive you, although you will have your eyeteeth torn, as a lesson, for whatso is decreed unto the creature, perforce he must fulfil and suffer. Have the ghulams clear that wall. This was meant for a private affair. Purchase more ghulams from Binkat at the first slave market of the month. If Shahrazad is to remain here till I have understood her, then I want the palace secure. I will have all cameleers taught their proper place – which is not the Shahristan – on pain they drink a draught of clotted blood. I am going now to my chambers.'

'Hearkening and obedience.'

The two lovers remain on the carpet bed for days, indulging in horizontal refreshments. They taste not of the nourishment of sleep, but pause only to eat puddings made of fatted sand grouse and mountain skink, plentifully seasoned and hotly spiced, drink well-tempered, saffron-tinctured raisin-wine from the Sinai convent and do their needs in the water closet. Immediately after each deed of kind – and Glory be to He Who hath for partner none! – culminating, on the part of Shahrazad, with a peek at the eyebrow – Eeek! – high-bosomed virgin slave girls bring them Al-Milak, an occasion-of-marriage-offer feast: tinctures of cantharides with jackal gall and melted camel hump, drachms of levigated bhang and sherbets of willow-flower water with divers inebriatives – betel, Kusumba (opium in wine) with electuaries of charas, poppy-seed and thorn-apple flowers boiled to a consistency of toffee with sugar, mace, cloves and nutmeg – of which they partake till their ribs feel cold, while the Shah inquires, at first tentatively, about Ziryab. He learns the man is a Barbary Berber, the name meaning 'Blackbird' in Arabic. Not only the world's best 'ud player, but has been down to the crossroads, drinks gallons of wine, keeps a well-stocked Harem, eats mountains of hashish, converses with the Jinn, has opened a chain of women's beauty salons throughout al-Andalus, reformed the Cordoban hairstyle and redesigned the soup spoon.

Even so, the Shah is far more interested in the kitchenhands. How old were they? How black, precisely? How big, exactly, were their members? How long did the deeds last? How many strokes would they have used? Why did she want to do it again if the first time failed to make her nipples harden? Why did she do it at *all*? It is incomprehensible that such a great beauty would want such ugly men but while Shahrazad, like most women, never forgets her roots, one false dawn, exhausted by this inquisition, she bids the Shah depart her. Indeed, she throws a sand grouse at him.

'If you mean to understand me, Shahrban, you're going about it the wrong way. But I'm not giving up on you just yet and I don't want you giving up on me. I only told those kitchenhands I loved them to see what effect it might have. There was no involvement. As I told you, members masculine come in two sizes: too large and too small. I also told you the best root ever I had was with an agha in the Harem. He was no bigger than my little finger but he made the most of what he had. I mean, what's the point in being hung like Ziryab if you can't get it up? I will say this, though, Eyebrows, I won't give my heart to you if you can't get me on the job. No more tyre kickers.'

'I must be in love,' concedes the Shah to the Pir, 'as I take this nautch girl to be the personification of all my good deeds. I can't divorce her till I've understood her as I've made a commitment. I took the oath before Almighty Allah, be He exalted and extolled, but how can a man understand a woman?'

'How can a woman understand herself or, strictly speaking, her selves? Identical twin girls are always less identical than identical twin boys – think it through. A woman is an infinitely complex mosaic of two distinct female principles – one from her father and one from her mother. Thus, we cannot apprehend the female principle by scrutinising a woman. We apprehend the female principle by scrutinising a sinless man, on whom be peace! As the Buddha says in A-han-ching, the feminine sex is, by its very nature, a state of forfeiture and penitence. And as Ibrahim, on whom be The Peace!, says, a woman is hard and crooked as a rib: to which we may add, and who would straighten her, breaks her. Now then, has al-Muqanna, al-Kamarani, Blessings on his name, appeared to you?'

'He has! I saw him in a nightmare! At first I thought it was Baktanus, the chieftain of the True-Believing Jinn, but when I saw that green veil, I said to myself – hello.'

'Wonderful! And did he lift the Qina?'

'He did!'

'Excellent. He has shown you what you, too, must become, which means he approves progress. You are no longer a simple believer if not quite yet a Sufi; you are now a javanmardi, in Arabic, a Futuwwat. Have we heard yet from the ghazis? Rumouroghli! Rumourzada! Ibn Rumour! Allah save and favour the king.'

Shukrat, a burly man with a thick grey beard and a chunk of ambergris wafting through it from a leather necklace, is somewhat hard of hearing. 'After I have done my need in the water closet,' he yawns, 'and performed Wuzu, then covered myself from navel to knee and said the dawn prayer as a missed prayer, I shall tell you of how I converted the Oghuz horde. But first, tell me, why do you murder your wives? I've heard it said you murdered over a thousand women in the past three years. Are you misogynistic? Be quick with your reply as I must visit the chapel of ease.'

'To the contrary. It's because I'm such a big girl's blouse I fall in love with women. Far from hating them, I adore them. I'm the complete romantic. I fall in love with every woman on whom I do a deed of kind and there is no Zenana on earth so large as to house them all. I never want to let a single lover out of my sight. I think of them as I lie in my bed. It's unmanly, I know, but I become obsessed with women: I dote over them, I dream of them, I imagine they love me in return and when I discover they don't, it comes as a shock. You see, they all do it. There is no woman but cuckoldeth her husband excepting Our Lady Fatimah! And even if they never actually did it, they were tempted. I had a wife and ten concubines once, each one of whom betrayed me, since which time my step has become short and my breath shallow. The way I manage the condition, is I try to put a prompt stop to things before they get out of hand. Even so, I just slipped up – I don't quite understand how – with this dancing girl come all the way from Cordoba. It makes me very dirty on myself. Mind you, the one concubine is not that big of a problem but the challenge now is to make sure it doesn't happen again.'

'That *will* be a challenge. Nature always goes too far. May I be your sacrifice, O Kurban-at basham?'

Hashim Wali Abu Muslim

Our settlement was the tashkurgan in which lived the Veiled One, on whom be The Peace, with a well in which he kept a moon on a citadel high above the crag of Saman which is forty miles east of the city of Kesh which is west of the Sogdian Pamir. Atop the crag was a tank we built to contain naphtha to supply a tower which was meant to contain an artificial, gravity-fed gusher which never got built.

Behind our extensive bastion stood a village. Fruit and nuts was all we ate. A stream ran by the mordant store beside our pyrite pit where rain-fed liquor ran off to be boiled down to green vitriol we collected on twigs. We had a stockpile of dye mordants and ink-stuff as a source of cash. Later we built a mint. Prior to the storming of our bastion in AD 783, we made for two years coin engraved 'Hashim Wali Abu Muslim' which became legal tender throughout Sogdiana. Our fortress had a parapet that overlooked a keep with a machicolated battlement that looked down on the walnut grove and inside the keep was a laboratory.

After the Wearers of Black Raiments murdered Abu Muslim, on whom be The Peace, we fought them. They perverted our revolution so we had no choice. Sixteen long hard years we fought. I was a *vispuhr*, a Son of the House, an *Ibn ad-dawlah*, Son of the New Age. I must have been one of the first; I would have been born in '59. We'd People of the House throughout Sogdiana – fifty cities were ours at one point – all dedicated to the abolition of property and the dissolution of marriage.

They called us 'Mazdakites' but we were Manichees.

The Oghuz horde wears white raiments and so too Manichee monks. You can see how confusion might arise.

In summer our walnut grove was a thick dark green, a citadel of leaves. It was our place of play. I shall not forget the fragrance of the leaves as I lay beneath the coverlet. It made a change as well from the sulphurous stench of the mordant shed. There were ferns on the boles of the walnut trunks and branches struck root where they touched soil.

It was a great place for animals. When walnuts fell, a variety of crepuscular vermin would share in the feast. I've seen foxes and honey badgers, wolves and caracal cats, but my favourite animal was the big-eared hedgehog. I had one as a pet. His name was Sohrab and he belonged to the House but I fed him. You'll find them on the Karabil plateau. They're about the size of a kitten with a flat face, big brown winsome eyes and prominent ears. The fur looks prickly but you can stroke it. He liked being stroked, my Sohrab. Don't try to tell me that he had no soul!

It's hard to describe what it's like, living in a house with a sinless man. It is even hard to recall as words can't do it justice.

Peace! You could call it peaceful. On the other hand, you could say it was a blast.

We freed the slaves. Not one slave remained in Sogdiana by 780. Of course, they're back, and what if all that passes on is the lies they spread? I'm speaking of the lies they spread about our Veiled One, how he wasn't of 'Ali's bloodline, as if he would need to be – how he wasn't even an Arab, as if he would need to be – how he was an ugly, one-eyed dwarf who wouldn't ablute or fast or pray with a hundred concubines attended by a single slave. It's true you'd find him as a boy up to his knees in month-old human piss because he was a scourer and scourers work in a fulling vat. Scourers take cloth from the burlers in the grease and give it to the menders in the clean. Burlers are women and so too menders but scourers, like fullers, are always men because only men have the strength in their nostrils and legs to work a fulling vat. Each length of cloth must be rid of dirt and lanolin which takes a full two hours in month-old human piss and pig shit because they add pig shit.

Fair enough, Hashim ibn Hakim was a connoisseur of piss and shit. That's how he learned his chemistry. At one point he had us collecting piss from pregnant mares! He said it would liberate women. He said that if they took two tablets a day of *dong quai* and *gancao* washed down with pregnant mare's piss, they would be liberated from bondage but they didn't like the taste.

Trampling round a fulling vat, Hashim's eyes may water but he can watch every move the dyer makes at the dyer's vat. He can ponder the nature of Allah. He can become the first man since 'Isa, Ruh of Allah, to see Allah's face. Peace be on him!

Then Abu Muslim took him from a vat and promoted him to general. There's anarchy when a prophet dies with problems of succession and Hashim left no Caliph but he left the Rumour and he provided us his covenant and we were his satellites.

Happiness has been, Happiness has gone, Happiness, perchance, may come again and then we'll all be Caliphs.

For months we'd been hearing strange noises from the keep – eruptions, explosions, deflagrations and combustions had us running from our huts to see where lightning had struck. Muslims were gaining the upper hand over us in Sogdiana. Inequality was on the march and private property amassing. This was during the Tang rebellion while Uighurs were looting Luoyang.

Something had to be done. One day Hashim's blind Wazir, Bamdad al-Tabari, comes to the gate, nursing a ball of iron with a cotton wick dipped in goat fat. He points to this ball which was maybe fifty-pound weight, and says, 'Compliments of the Caliph. He would like for you to test it.'

We were to raid a caravan south of Shash in the Red Sandy Waste using this ball with our new machine. The ball appeared to be cast with a raised seam where the wick emerged. We'd thought the wick was a brand. When firing by night it's good practice to attach a lighted brand. We'd no idea what that ball contained. I *still* have no idea what that ball contained.

A cheeky girl, Kamenka, was appointed as our lookout. As soon as she saw the dust rise she was to sound the alarm. We'd intelligence from People of the House lived among the Turghiz. I was ready to light the wick so I had a flame to nurse.

'Here they come!' Kamenka shouts. The men go grinning to their stations.

I lit the wick and I may have done it too soon.

'Kimeks!' says our sergeant peeking through the rocks.

'Baggage mules?'

'Yes sir. Sarts are all on foot.'

'Range? Tell me – *ooh farck, wick's nearly burned through I shall have to – stand back!*'

The engineer leaned over the sling, meaning, I guess, to adjust the wick, but in his haste he brushed the trigger. There was a crack, the trigger released, the counterpoise crashed down, the beam whipped up into the air, the sling released and ball and engineer both were shot over the rocks.

Even before they hit the ground there was a massive explosion.

The iron ball exploded above the caravan. *Noise!* You half-expected to see the Resurrection of the Just.

'This is not nitre,' complained Bamdad when we returned with the loot. 'This is sal ammoniac! And you've a ton of it! Phew, my nostrils are clear now. Put it in the mordant shed. Stack it by the brimstone.'

There'd been a mistake in our intelligence but no matter. Word spread through those escaped Kimeks. We'd plenty of Turkish friends now! The ikshid of Ferghana sent us six she-elephants with jewel-encrusted goads all wearing howdahs with mirrors. The chabish of Shash sent slaves, five Chinese ship-builders captured by Uighurs in Luoyang and with them a caravan of five hundred camels hauling assorted timber – Borneo ironwood, Javanese grewia, bamboo, white Chinese pine – along with a thousand leathern jars that smelled of mustard oil and fuller's earth but were filled with hemp, the nuts of the wood-oil tree, ship-building tools and iron nails, and we were ordered not to liberate these Chinese men.

What Arabs call 'Daylam' is known to the Persians as 'Gilan'. It is a subtropical independent kingdom of mountains, jungles and swamps on the southern coast of the Caspian Sea, occupied by Mazdayasnians. You've had a wife from there, Shahrban. It's next to Tabaristan.

None compares with a Daylamite when it comes to wielding a

battleaxe, so Daylamite mercenaries fetch top price. The 'Abbasids have a blank there on the map. Sassanids could not conquer that shore and no more could the Parthians and it's only just two hundred miles wide and fifty miles deep. It's only just the Elburz Range and two little plains between the range and the sea. The 'Abbasid Caliphate encircles both Daylam and Tabaristan but it seemed that either could be reached by sea, so a plan was being hatched among three parties: the Caliph of Saman, the chabish of Shash and the yabghu of the Oghuz.

The yabghu of the Oghuz had invited us to parley.

Oghuz are known to the Arabs as 'Ghuzz'. Wearers of white raiments, their chief tribe is the Seljuk. They are a Turkic horde moved onto the Low Steppe after the collapse of the Western Blues. They breed the Argamak horses with their heads too big for their necks. They were pagan, but to their north-east they had the Manichean Uighurs building Karabalghasun while to their west, on the Volga delta, the Judeaic Khazars had built the city of Itil. The Oghuz were being made to look uncivilised by Turkic neighbours! Looking south from Bilad-al-Turk they overlooked the city-states of Mawarannahr and divided then between Wearers of Black Raiments and Wearers of White Raiments. We were equally keen to convert them but you'd guess that our faith, with its white raiments, relaxed attitude to alcohol and emphasis on plunder, would hold greater appeal to a Turk than Islam, which has problems with Turks in its stickling over silly little things like the proper way to kill sheep.

I think it's more a question that the Turk abhors ablutions. You would never catch a Turk underwater.

'Take brimstone,' advised Bamdad. 'Show them how we use it between our toes. The yabghu wants a parley with a Man of the House, a Daughter and a Son, so Shukrat! You go with Ostap and Kamenka! You go, too. Ostap, you know what to do. Take the timbers, the jars, the camel caravan and the Chinese slaves.'

The yabghu came to greet us. He wasn't as we'd expected, aside from the white raiments, being young, blond-haired and blue-eyed; he wore a bowler hat.

'Here you are at last,' he says to us in perfect Sogdian. 'The Peace be with you! Salaam. I'd been growing anxious as it's coming on for spring. The ice will soon be melting. I've heard of you, Shukrat, and I've heard of that Sohrab of yours! I never saw a Turkestan hedgehog in my life. We'll go fishing, you and me. You like pork with caviar? What a pleasure this is for me and for the Oghuz, what an honour! Your pavilion is ready. Take your time. As soon as you're ready to parley, we'll have a chat over a fry-up. Join me in some bread and salt. Now, the Muslims have been here some time. I believe they came up from Kat. I said I can't parley till the Mazdakites arrive, which would scarcely be fair. Kamenka, do you like white camels, dear? I don't mean to eat, I mean to cosset.'

'Muslims?' says Ostap. 'What do you mean, "Muslims"?'

'Have I upset you?' says the yabghu. 'Yes, I see I have. Foolish yabghu! I must make amends but how? I know! We'll *execute* them!' He clapped his hands at some Oghuz who were standing by, spitting like sportsmen.

'It's all right,' murmured Ostap, 'really. It will be quite all right.'

'You're sure? You're perfectly *sure* now? You're *sure* it will be quite all right, Ostap?' The yabghu's expression had changed to one of unctuous solicitude.

'It would be no trouble.'

'No no no,' insisted Ostap. 'We don't mind if the Muslims remain. We're not scared of Muslims.'

'Me neither. See, I thought we could have a debate.'

'Debate?'

'Yes, a debate! A debate to discover the Truth! I'm thinking of taking religion.'

'But I can't debate! I'm not a theologian! If only we'd known you wanted a *debate*.'

'Ah, but that's my point, Ostap. That's my point entirely. I don't want the views of a theologian. I want the views of an ordinary, knock-about chap. If a truth can't be expressed to me by an ordinary, knock-about chap, I'm afraid that truth will be of no use to me.'

'That's not the idea,' I heard myself say, 'as the Truth is not for us to use. The Truth is only there for us to be of service to it.'

He stared at me like a goshawk for a time but then relaxed. 'Good point, Shukrat, I take your meaning, I think. Now then, people, off you go and have a decent rest. Why, you must be completely exhausted! Leave your bags. No no no, leave the bags!'

'Dear me,' sighed Ostap as we trudged off to our tent, 'he's everything I feared he'd be and worse.'

'He's a *lovely* man!' protested Kamenka.

'Oh yes, they can be charming when it suits them, but every round thing is not a walnut and every black thing is not a charcoal. Kill us and he knows he won't get his Heaven-Shaking Thunder-Crash Bombos. The last two *da'i* we sent, Kamenka, they buried to their necks in the sand, then played ninepins with the heads.'

In the tent next to ours a boy in black raiments and prayer shawl was rocking. He didn't look up from a book he held in his hand and I knew what book that would be.

A week later, debate began over a meal of barbal and bream. The fish were so fresh they jumped in the skillet. They were to be cooked and served us by the yabghu himself. He made small balls of the flesh of these fish, going in with a crow's-claw and coming up with a camel-hoof, then thrust it into our mouths with the fingers of his right hand. I thought the Muslims would die.

'Who'd like a shot of kumis to wash down that fish?' said the yabghu, hovering with a pitcher.

The black-bearded Muslim man, Nu'man by name, wagged a monitory finger. 'Believers do not drink wine. Salman will tell us why. Salman! *Al-khamr!*'

Salman, the boy I'd seen reading, shut his eyes but continued rocking. He came up with something in Arabic which Nu'man translated.

'Believers! Do not approach your prayers when you are drunk but wait till you can grasp the meaning of your words; nor when you are unclean unless you are travelling the road until you have washed yourselves.

'Believers! Wine and games of chance, idols and divining arrows are abominations devised by Satan. Avoid them that you may prosper. Satan seeks to stir up enmity and hatred among you by means of wine and gambling and to keep you from remembrance of Allah and from your prayers. Salman! *An-nikah!*'

Salman the hafiz rocked to and fro, trawling his memory. According to Zenobia – she told Kamenka – he couldn't understand a word of Arabic but had memorised the entire one hundred and fourteen *surat* cockatoo-style – easy enough given their composition in cameleer doggerel – but he could not always be relied upon and such proved the case here.

Following his muttering, Nu'man could only proffer us the following insight, 'Believers! You have an enemy in your spouses and in your children. Beware of them.'

Ostap began to laugh, spluttering bream into his kumis.

'Salman! *Al-Kafirun!*'

'Unbelievers shall be consigned to perdition. Allah will bring their deeds to nothing. Because they have abhorred His revelations He will frustrate their works. Have they never journeyed through the land and seen what was the end of those who have gone before them? Allah destroyed them utterly. A similar fate awaits the unbelievers because Allah is the protector of the faithful because the unbelievers have no protector.'

'I was laughing at the notion of marriage,' said Ostap, 'rather than the notion of Allah. We, too, believe in Allah, if by Allah is meant the One True God.' He then skolled his kumis, affirming, to the yabghu's relief, its merit.

'And why laugh at marriage, Mazdakite?'

The yabghu motioned to the girls to go out and cosset the white baby camel. They ran out squealing from the yurt, hand-in-hand, thick as thieves.

'Because, by treating women as property, you enslave them and create jealousy among men.'

At this, the yabghu frowned. 'But how can we fight without first boasting of our genealogy? Nu'man, what do you say?'

'I follow Caliph 'Umar,' said Nu'man, 'who forbade Arabs to own land and who said, "Learn your *Nasab*! Learn your genealogies."'

The yabghu then rattled off his own, Turkic-style, to the seventh generation, all one hundred and twenty-seven men with no mention of a woman or a place. We left him to it, laughing, as he got stuck towards the end, the result of the kumis and the inconsequence of his father's father's father's father's father having the same name as his mother's father's father's father's father's father.

Back in our tent, I inquired of Ostap, 'And what do you think? Are we in front?'

He rubbed his eyes. 'The yabghu is not interested in argument, Shukrat. To him we are mere city-filth. He summoned us here to size us up, to evaluate our comparative strengths which he will do on instinct. He wants that Heaven-Shaking Thunder-Crash

Bombos. The barbarian ingratiates himself through religion. The yabghu knows it is the path to civilisation, but he won't want to follow in his neighbours' footsteps to become a Jew or a Manichee. We are Manichean Mazdakites but let's put the emphasis on "Mazdakites". We have the advantage, I suspect, and not just because of our white raiments: we are heretics. Barbarians prefer heresies. Islam is a Christian heresy concocted by barbarian Arabs. It is interesting that Nu'man is a Lakhmid, Shukrat. They were Sassanid margraves: Christians and Manichees forcibly converted to Islam. The same thing happened to the Banu Ghassan, margraves to the East Romans. Arabic Jews like the Banu Qurayzah and Banu Nadir, dead finish. So much for your Muslim "People of the Book". Understand now what it means, boy? It means "taxpayer". It means "non-Arab".'

'You tell him.'

'No, you tell him. You're going fishing with him. This ludicrous notion of genealogy flies in the face of nature. Even so, Fihr, patriarch of the Quraysh, claimed he could trace his lineage back to *Rasul* Ibrahim via *Rasul* Isma'il; while the Gospel of Saint Matthew, the most Jewish gospel, gives us the genealogy of Jesus.'

Next day, the yabghu was in a bad mood having given the kumis a nudge. 'Sit!' he ordered the men and boys, the girls having gone off to play. The girls, I suspect, had served their purpose in having become firm friends, which could only confirm to the yabghu that all women are members of the same tribe.

'Al-Muqanna,' says Ostap, 'the inventor and purveyor of the Heaven-Shaking Thunder-Crash Bombos affirms the time will surely come when men, perforce uncertain as to where they were born, cannot name their mother's mother's mother, and that no man is ever sure of his father or of his mother's father or of his mother's mother's father or of his mother's mother's mother's father because there is many a slip 'twixt cup and lip.'

'Oh, don't worry, mate. We take preventative measures to ensure they don't play up.'

'And how do you do that?'

'We marry them as children. A husband consummates a marriage before they have begun to bleed. Should a husband die, they at once become the wife of their husband's brother and they're never allowed to be alone with a man other than their husband.'

'Disgraceful,' said Nu'man. 'We consider it a mortal sin to falsely charge a modest woman with unchastity; as mortal a sin as robbing an orphan or deserting from Jihad, Salman! *Hijab! Litham! Khimar!*

'Prophet, we have made lawful to you the wives to whom you have granted dowries and the slave girls whom Allah has given you as booty; the daughters of your paternal and maternal uncles and of your paternal and maternal aunts who fled with you; and any believing woman who gives herself to the Prophet and whom the Prophet wishes to take in marriage. This privilege is yours alone, being granted to no other believer.

'We well know the duties we have imposed on the faithful concerning their wives and slave girls, so that none may blame you. Allah is ever forgiving and merciful.

'You may put off any of your wives you please and take to your bed any of them you please. Nor is it unlawful for you to receive any of those whom you have temporarily set aside. That is more proper, so that they may be contented and not vexed and may all be pleased with what you give them.

'Allah knows what is in the hearts of believers. Surely Allah is all-knowing and gracious.

'It shall be unlawful for you to take more wives or to change your present wives for other women though their beauty please you, unless they are slave girls whom you own. Allah takes cognizance of all things.'

'I like this idea of women going round in sacks from head to toe,' conceded the yabghu. 'I find it civilised. Mazdakite?'

'No, because justice and equality must, in the end, prevail,' replied Ostap. 'It may take time, but we cannot regard it as proper to treat women as recommended by the Quraysh. The Prophet and every Arab Caliph are men of the Quraysh. The treatment of women in Mecca was considered disgraceful, even by the standard of Yathrib.'

Nu'man's face went black as pitch. 'Ya ibn al-bazra, O son of an uncircumcised mother, biter of thy mother's uncircumcised clitoris! Have we not heard enough of this man's foul blasphemy, yabghu!'

'Hold thy tongue, thou son of a burned father! Have I permission to proceed, yabghu?'

'Yes, please do so. I enjoy debate.'

'The Prophet Mohammed with all those wives and slave girls was a man of Banu Hashim of the tribe of the Meccan Quraysh, the great middlemen of the Arabs. Myrrh and frankincense caravans from Al-Yemen travel through Mecca. Can I speak now of the Prophet as a man? He never claimed to be anything else.'

'Proceed.'

'When his denunciation of idolatry had threatened Mecca's pilgrim trade, Mohammed's life was spared only when his uncle, head of Banu Hashim, could not consent to his being outlawed through fear of blood-feud. So while most of the seventy-odd True-Believers at the time fled to Abyssinia, the Prophet accepted an invitation from Yathrib, a nearby city-state, to mediate among the feuding clans there. He contrived to unite the Arabs, albeit under the leadership of Yathrib with a few Meccan refugees, but nothing suggests that the Arabs were much impressed by his religion. At best, they tolerated it.

'Sassanids and East Romans having fought themselves to exhaustion in two wars fought over fully forty-five years of the Prophet's life – with Arabs, incidentally, fighting as mercenaries on both sides – the time was ripe for conquest. Within twenty years of the Prophet's death, the Arabs conquered the Sassanids and most of the Romans, but is this "Allah", of whom we hear so much, the God of all the Universe? Or is He perhaps the national god of Arabs, or even the Quraysh?

'Under the Ummayads, who like 'Abbasids were all men of the Quraysh, an Iranian convert to Islam was not accepted as an equal of an Arab. If he served in the army, he needed to fight on foot; he could not fight on horseback. A convert's name as "peasant" could not appear on a salary roll. He had to become a client of an Arab clan, and even though Muslim, was not exempt from land tax unless he migrated to a cantonment. He could even be ordered to be circumcised!'

'Now what's all this about?' said Nu'man. 'You assisted the 'Abbasids to depose the Ummayads. Ummayads have gone to Cordoba.'

'And we now have in place of an arrogant noble, a bureaucratic despot. Your Caliph is still an Arab and still a man of the Quraysh.'

'I suppose you think that in killing Abu Muslim, Caliph al-Mansur did wrong?'

'It could be thought ungrateful, given that Abu Muslim put him in power.'

'Abu Muslim claimed to be divine. Only Allah is divine, my friend. Abu Muslim was a Manichee and so, my friend, are you.'

'That's enough,' said the yabghu. 'I don't feel too flash. Not taking it in. Shukrat, let's go fishing.'

If I'd thought we would wander off to cast silk nets in the mouths of creeks, imagine my surprise on being led behind some reeds to see an eighty-footer with a transom bow and a transom stern sitting on a bank.

It was the work of our Chinese slaves.

'Like her?' said the yabghu. 'As you can see she's a Kiangsu trader. I call her *The Caspian Seal*.'

Two of the three masts were stepped with tabernacle partners at the hull base, while the bowsprit, planted on her larboard bow, raked forward at ten degrees. A small mizzenmast was deck-mounted on the poop, raking slightly aft. Her sails – bamboo laths woven to mats – were rattling in the breeze. You can't lower sail on a Chinese junk. She was twenty-four foot at her widest point which was just aft of midships, with a hull divided by twelve transverse bulkheads into thirteen compartments. These were filled with those thousand leathern jars that smelled strongly of mustard. There was a cuddy under the poop where the yabghu stored his nets. Her bulkhead planks of local poplar were edge-joined and fastened with diagonally driven nails, while her rudder, rudder-post and anchor were all of a strong Borneo ironwood. Her double hull and masts and stiffening planks were of white pine. The *lieu d'aisance* was a wooden cage fastened outside the gunwale and she was heavily caulked in *chu-nam*. She had two lovely big eyes which were painted under long, seductive lashes, both starboard and larboard. A dragon spine was fitted to her arse to serve her as a keel. She was flat-bottomed in the case of running aground – shoal water, the Aral.

'Been to sea?' asked the yabghu, whistling as he played with the sail. 'I was hoping those Chinese men might have stuck around a bit longer but no matter, can't be much to it. Ah, here we come, motive power. Avast yer whingeing, ye lubbers!'

One hundred licorice all-sort slaves then loaded the fresh water and ten sweeps, each about the size of the mainmast of tough Javanese grewia. We pushed and dragged *The Caspian Seal* into the main channel, and scrambled aboard as the yabghu set sail and supervised the setting of the mast chocks. As well as the slaves we had ten Oghuz aboard.

'What fish are we after?' I asked.

The yabghu gave me a conspiratorial wink. 'We're fishing for naphtha, boy. It's to go in the jars then back to your Caliph's lab, sailing through Shash. See, I reckon I'd need some kind of *tiny* Heaven-Shaking Thunder-Crash Bombos that didn't need a sling, something I could carry on a galloping horse, take my meaning, see what I'm driving at, fire from a crossbow? With a quarrel soaked in naphtha, perhaps? So that the quarrel could be made to *burn* and possibly explode? I didn't want to raise the matter with Ostap as I feared it might get back to your Wazir. Anyway, boys are better fighters than men. War is boys' delight!'

It was late March by this time and the yabghu said the river banks would soon become the tops of trees. Without the vines to hold them down, the trees would wash away.

We made our way through the maze of islands into the Oxus delta. We'd no time to waste as we had to get up to the Uzboy channel before the spring spate and it could come any time, depending on the weather in the high Pamir. Pigs were plunging into the water to swim alongside us hoping for swill. An Oghuz archer shot one and dragged it on deck so we had pork for lunch.

Before long we'd fitted sweeps to our rollocks. We had to make haste against that stream which seemed to have donned a coat of mail. Each sweep was the size of the mainmast. There were five each side of the deck with ropes attached to either side on which slaves had to pull. There were ten men to each sweep, five each side, and they stood facing each other with one side pushing as the other pulled. An Oghuz archer beat time on the deck with a drum so the sweeps wouldn't tangle.

'Hevelow!'

'Rumbelow!'

'Hevelow!'

'Rumbelow!'

'Hevelow!'

'Rumbelow!'

This was a Christian galley chant.

It was mid-April by the time we swung onto the Uzboy channel. A northerly was blowing and the river moving into spring spate so all we had to do was steer with that massive ironwood rudder. We pulled in the sweeps and the slaves settled back to play cards. Because of blisters on their hands they held the cards between their toes and played with their feet.

As we travelled the five hundred miles through a soil-less desert of baked clay and mineral springs with mud volcanoes and oil-sand beds and boiling pools of brown acid with shale beds pitted by salt-storms under grey limestone pinnacles riddled with veins of pink and green marble in temperatures that soared from close on freezing at dawn to forty plus at dusk – a country of the fur and of the fan – we had leisure. And the yabghu was keen to revisit certain points that had been raised in debate and so we two sat together by the rudder on the poopdeck as he steered and I watched.

'Do you understand what a horde *is*, boy? It is a group of men who understand the principles of stockbreeding. We must cull and introduce new blood otherwise we become inbred but we do it through women. Look at me with my blond hair and blue eyes! My mother was a Rusky. Tengri picks off weaker men before they can mate and hybrid vigour is assured because men select women for beauty, the more exotic the better. The present Shi'ite Imam is the son of a Nubian slave yet he is still a man of the Quraysh. Women are the one possession a horde will never share as it interferes with genealogy. There, I think, we differ from you Mazdakite Manichees. We prevent our women misbehaving through fear of blood-feud but, more importantly, through lack of opportunity. The notion of men having access to all women strikes me as unnatural. There is always a surplus of women. In nature, a stallion does not have access to all mares. He would like to, no doubt, but the best fighters acquire a harem and defend it as best they can. No man treats another man's son the way he would treat his own unless that boy is exceptional. Men must have some sense of what they fight for and where they're from. They must know their bloodlines. They must train kinsmen never to interfere with other men's wives but by the same token, they must ensure that women don't misbehave. There is no equality between us, you see, because we are not the same.'

'But what if we all belonged to the same horde?'

'We don't.'

'But what if we did?'

'That could not happen before a single empire covers the world. Not before all men and women have the same coloured skin and the same shaped eyes. Meantime, progress depends on warfare. Life is a contest among hordes. My greatest pleasure, aside from drinking kumis and catching fish, is attacking a horde, raping the women, killing all the men and castrating the boys, though I could adopt a boy like you as I find you intelligent.'

'There's not one particle of light in what you say,' I remonstrated. 'What is speaking on your behalf here is the dark matter.'

'Whatever. Clear one thing up. Are Wearers of White Raiments Muslim?'

'Yes and no. We drink wine but we don't eat pork. Well, we shouldn't eat pork. We believe we can transmute Allah, this god of the Quraysh, in the same way Jesus and Isaiah transmuted Yahwe, a Midianite forge-god. We hold that all men, including Arabs, are equal in the eyes of Allah.'

'But if all men are created equal, Shukrat, who's to be yabghu?'

'We'll put it to the vote. Our Caliph is only a Mervi who bettered himself through grace of Allah. He strives to understand both light and matter and would like to interconvert them.'

'You think he would give me a Heaven-Shaking Thunder-Crash Bombos?'

'Fetch him his naphtha, he may do.'

'Well, you've convinced me, Shukrat. You've converted the Oghuz Horde, Slimy Tongue! We wearers of white raiments are now Wearers of White Raiments.'

'We'll never get back up this channel, yabghu.'

'No, but we'll give it a good shot.'

In early May we'd reached the Caspian Sea and the cold nor'easter had become a hot sou'easter. Oh, what a relief to be able to drop anchor and cast out a net, which came in full of Beluga sturgeons, fish the size of men. The rest of our voyage through the Caspian we ate nothing but caviar, washed down in my case with kumis from the master's cabin – clear fermented mare's milk with hints of licorice and sal ammoniac, matured slowly in green bamboo. I couldn't grumble over rations, but how would we get back up that channel? It would mean rowing five hundred miles.

Shirwan was two hundred miles to our north-west. With a favourable following wind we made that journey in two weeks and our spirits were high when the deserted coastline appeared all baked in bitumen. Out came our leathern jars and in went the naphtha. It was a messy business, by gum, and you got black sticky naphtha all over you, standing under a gusher with an open leathern jar and you couldn't get the naphtha off. You'd scrub and pick and soak yourself in water, but all that came off would be your skin. By the time we'd loaded our thousand jars we were black from the spilt naphtha baking on our bodies into tar in the wind and the sun, and the tar stuck to everything. We were tarred and sanded and feathered and salted and we wondered if we might not die, because no one knew much about naphtha, which made you light-headed.

'Is that it, then?' All that remained of the yabghu were his two eyes. 'Is that the jars full? She's riding low in the water, lads. Has anyone noticed the wind's dropped? Let's get our sweeps out. Let's get her back before the wind blows up.'

'Hevelow!'

'Rumbelow!'

'Hevelow!'

'Rumbelow!'

'Hevelow!'

'Rumbelow!'

'Does anyone here but me smell sulphur?' The yabghu was staring at the sail. 'She's moving of her own accord. Get those sweeps in or we'll lose them.'

The Caspian Seal, close to foundering anyway from the weight of the jars, was drifting towards an opening on the shore no more than a hundred yards wide.

'Oh no,' said our Azeri slave, 'we're entering the Bitter River! This is a Place of No Return.'

Faster and faster we sped through the lead-grey waters till we entered the Bitter River, which flows into Kara-Bogoz-Kol, a bay ninety miles wide that acts as a cauldron, boiling off water faster than the Caspian Sea can fill it. Evaporation is so intense in summer that Kara-Bogoz-Kol is twenty foot lower than the Caspian Sea and the Bitter River a waterfall.

Our hands were stuck fast to the sweeps so we couldn't jump out. The transom hurtled down the first cascade then spun in the torrent – and had she been able to shut her beautiful painted eyes, I'm sure she would have. The hull planking rent and we couldn't inspect the damage, so tightly packed were our jars. Then down comes the mainmast and over she goes on her beam, throwing us in the water.

But we didn't drown, you know why? We *couldn't*! There is that much salt in the Black Maw you can't *force* your head underwater. We bobbed about like corks and all the naphtha jars floating as well, just like empty gourds. We had to laugh.

Exhausted, we lay on our backs and went to sleep amid the hull planks of our ruined junk and the wallowing naphtha jars; just fell asleep right there on the water.

It was quite comfortable, actually, until you rolled over.

The Black Maw, Kara-Bogoz, is surrounded by black hills a thousand feet high but utterly bare of vegetation, while all around the water's edge is a brilliant, foot thick layer of white salt against the black rocks. It's not sea salt, it's mirabilite and gives you the shits something fierce. I reached out to a dead herring floating by and ate it. Some of the tar was coming off our skin in the hot, salty water. We all looked like elephants but were glad to find we still *had* skin.

Scambling into a small cove we herded the naphtha jars, scrunching round in the mirabilite on the shore till we had them safe and sound.

'Sogdian boy stay here,' said the yabghu. 'He must guard the naphtha. The rest of us will walk back to the Uzboy channel. She can't be more than fifty miles south and after we cross the Oxus we have access to wells in the Black Sands. We'll raid Sand People till we have the five hundred camels we need to carry our naphtha. The junk has served her purpose. Shukrat, I can't carry the kumis barrel so ration it carefully. We'll be back as soon as we can. You just sit tight here. Amuse yourself by getting all the tar off the jars. If they're to be slung over camels, camels won't want them sticky.'

I watched them clamber over the hill then disappear into the dust. It may have been June or July. As soon as they'd disappeared I removed my raiments and sat back to wait.

If I beat the gulls to the dead fish being sucked into the Bitter River they still had juice. I ate lobsters and caviar and rationed my kumis so I had a swig each day. I girded my loins in the fur of a dead seal I found washed up in the salt which I got to before the hyenas. Hyenas did the rounds daily.

There was only dust and salt and sand and the vapour bubbling off the water but I settled in. What a contrast to what I'd known! Every night when dusk fell, I waded out through spindrift of sulphurous scum, preferring to sleep on the water where I felt more safe from hyenas. Then I would dream of the walnut grove and stroking my little Sohrab.

Each time winter came the salt in the bay would crystallise, which made sleeping awkward. I was always glad when spring returned and the salt went back into solution. I got to know the moods of the Bitter River pretty well. Eventually, I could predict the weather just from listening to it. I had my camp east of the cascades in a cove protected from southerlies. I had to be camped close by the river to get to the herrings before the gulls.

Sometimes it rained – never much, but that was a busy time for me as I had to collect fresh water from the depressions in the rocks. Even so, when the water fell distilled from the sky it was brackish. Today, I'm the only man I know who can drink water from a desert well.

One day they reappeared, coming down the hyena track. By cleaning a naphtha jar each day I'd kept a calendar and each one of those thousand jars was clean by the time they returned.

'Where's the yabghu?' I asked.

They shook their heads.

Most had died on the terrible trek from Kara-Bogoz to the Uzboy. Having crossed the Uzboy, they walked up the Atrak River to its headwaters in the Dry Mountains. The camels, dromedaries, they'd seized from caravans on the Merv–Baghdad road – twice, as they'd had the misfortune to encounter Caliph al-Mahdi on his way from Rayy, which led to the skirmish in which they lost both the yabghu and all their camels. The yabghu, dying, enjoined his freedmen never to forget that naphtha, but for the sake of the Oghuz horde, to reaquire the five hundred camels and to rescue that naphtha and take it on to Saman.

We loaded the naphtha onto the camels and returned through the Karakum Desert, with camels eating camel-thorn and drinking water from the wells – skirting Margiana so as to dodge Arabs – making our way back to Sogdiana then upriver from Kesh and on to Saman, a journey of some six hundred miles.

I never again saw Ostap and Kamenka. I dare say Kamenka is making life difficult for some long-suffering Oghuz man.

I was a hairy-arsed fellow when I returned early in '83. I'd been away five years. Old blind Bamdad felt my face as the Men of the House unloaded the naphtha. They dumped the jars temporarily into the pyrite pit.

'Good God,' said Bamdad, 'he's been living with the Jinn, this cove! He's half man, half salt. Do we know him? Is he someone we should know?'

Then came the storming of our bastion.

For years, the army of Caliph al-Mahdi, the Wearers of Black Raiments, had been mounting assaults on our Sogdian cities and grinding us down, yet our army was denied use of the Bombos. We were ordered to retreat and hold fire. The Arabs gave us quarter till fifty thousand satellites were bailed up in Saman.

With so many extra hands on deck, that naphtha tank went up fast. If a Mazdak Tower was ready to light when the Arab army arrived, said Bamdad – and it was only just downriver in Nasaf – then the Oghuz, our new converts, might appear to reinforce us: in any event, the Veiled One had something up his sleeve. He was setting those Arabs a trap.

The naphtha jars were taken from the pit and hauled up the cliff-face hand over hand. Into the tank went the naphtha. Down below us was the mordant store, piled high with nitre, alum, brimstone, sal ammoniac and the pyrite pit, which fed past the well with the moon, into the lab.

Each dawn, the People of the House would beg the Caliph to show them his face and on the morning of the day the Arabs finally arrived, he acquiesced. Bamdad had men moving through the crowd, handing out pieces of smoked glass.

The Arabs had a new trebuchet. To test the range they loaded a boulder and slung it at our castle but it fell in the walnut grove.

Their next projectile was smaller but the trajectory was higher. This missile sailed over the bastion and looked set to clear the crag, but clipped a corner of the naphtha tank and out spilled all the naphtha. I'm trying to think of how much there would have been – a thousand leathern jars, close to thirty thousand gallons rolling down that crag, all over the mordants into the pyrite pit.

The Arabs began pounding on the gate. I sped off to where I'd last seen Sohrab so I didn't actually hear the blast although I'm told it was heard in Kashgar. Some say I'm the sole survivor. It wouldn't surprise me. It was night when I woke covered in blood and spread-eagled, my ears ringing with bits of bodies all over me. Clearing a breathing hole through all that flesh took me hours. I was staring up at the night sky when I saw the second moon appear, moving left to right. I watched it disappear until my neck was stiff.

Ninety minutes later, there it was again, moving left to right across the night sky, and again it disappeared. This went on all night. Come dawn, I gritted my teeth and forced myself to stand.

Saman was gone. One small piece of bastion was all that remained. The castle had disappeared. The crag was obliterated.

For two whole months that second moon could be seen in the night sky. It passed over every ninety minutes. Everyone over a certain age in Sogdiana recalls it. The Oghuz, the Turghiz, the Kimek and the Karluk could speak of it, as it was visible from the steppe. Nowdays, if people wonder what it was, they say it was a comet. It was nothing of the kind! It was a covenant. It was al-Muqanna's covenant with mankind. As to that Arab army? Gone. We'd won a great victory over them.

Iranian Days (continued)

The Shah leans back to await the inevitable sermon that follows a tale and if he'd a timepiece to consult he would do so, to ensure the sermon didn't go over time for how he hates to be preached at. The thought of Shahrazad's perky boobs induces, as always, a melancholy in him, but he can't wait to get back to his chambers to set them abounce. Only the deed of kind has power to take his mind off his miseries though he quite enjoys Duty and Repetition, on the odd occasion when the drummers go off.

The burly Shukrat, however, nods quietly to the Pir and the Pir nods to the Tartar who, unbeknown to Shahrban has sneaked up quietly behind him. The Shah's arms are grabbed and pinned to his coccyx and before he knows quite what's happening, Shukrat has grabbed and rent the Shah's hufu and is reaching between his legs.

'Hey! What do you think you're doing?'

Shukrat gives an unpleasant smirk. He licks his lips and starts to rub his groin with his ugly fat fingers. 'I'm looking forward to this,' he says, 'as you're just my type. I prefer men to eunuchs and women as I can use the scrotum for a bridle and I suspect that you fancy me, too, for you've been coming on to me all through my talk.'

'I have not!'

Shukrat clutches the Shah's groin and squeezes. 'I know three hundred and two words for this thing,' he says, 'and four hundred and sixteen for its use in coition. How are you liking that, then – is it as good for you as it is for me? Are you up for a little pygisma a posteriori, a bit of buttockry? I reckon that if I'm enjoying it then you must be enjoying it, too. See the effect you've had on me? Why, you've made me lose control, you wicked Alegomenos. I can't be held accountable for anything I may do now. You've tempted and enticed me. O you wicked Agathonian, you led me on with that eyebrow.'

'I did nothing of the kind,' retorts the Shah. 'I detest you! I abhor poofters.'

'As to that, I can only say you didn't put up much of a fight. He didn't put up much of a fight, did he, lads? Going round, flashing that eyebrow as if to say, help yourself.'

'The fight went out of me only because you exert some power I don't understand, but that doesn't mean I enjoy what you're doing. You know I can't be enjoying it. My member is smaller now than when you began. Doesn't that tell you anything?'

'Not really. Wait a bit – woo, here we go – crocodile brain kicking in – I'm on the job – want to watch? I'll rub it into the eyebrow. I'm going to need a bath.'

'Ya Ja'dan! Wa Ghausah! Ya Musibati! Wallahi! Ho, to my aid! O my calamity! Musulmanan to the rescue!'

'That's enough of the Epipedesis,' says the Pir, smiling. He nods to the Tartar, the Shah's arms are released and Shukrat, after a high five with the Pir, retires to the Hammam.

'I suppose,' says the Shah to the Pir, 'you're aware that a sexual assault is a capital offence?'

'It's only your word against his. You didn't put up much of a fight. You could have stopped him easily if you'd screamed and struggled harder. Did you not see the way his expression changed when you got him on the job? Did you like the way he ground his teeth? Did you see his pupils dilate?'

'I never, in my whole life, saw anything so horrid!'

'Well, now you know how a certain young person must have felt at a certain time of life. Pardon's the word.'

And with that, the Shah, hand on heart, is shoved out in the alley and the Khangah door slammed shut.

The poult breeder sees him trembling as he walks by the cage and takes pity on the man. 'Ya Hajj,' she says. 'O Pilgrim, don't you be quizzing me again. Don't you be making me speak of my income! Merv is full of publicans and harlots. I'm selling no poults to the palace which was my principal customer and kept me in business these past three years and now, to make matters worse, I've chipped a tooth. See? This was in the cucurbits. You'd bite that, would you not. I purchase my cucurbits from Tiberias as I've a relative works at Magdala, salting sardines from the Sea of Galilee. You'd take this for a cucurbit – same shape, same size, made of solid copper – feel the thing! Feel the weight in that! It would sell for ten golden dinars, I warrant, at the brass market, and I was meaning to take it there but then I sees you walking by and says to myself, and you thought *you* were miserable! Here, you take it, you poor miserable little creature.'

'I can't.'

'Yes you can! Do yourself a favour. Ya Tai'is, O you poor miserable wretch, go buy yourself a decent suit of clothing. Make large your sleeves! Get yourself a turband! Smarten yourself up!

Take this and put it in your mouth, for safety's sake. I hate to see a Mervi man wearing a Jallabiyah.'

'You're too kind. It's been a long while since anyone showed me a kindness.'

'Well, publicans was never a popular breed and working for the Beast o' Merv, what would you expect? He's had more women than Sulayman, that man. You can't tell me it's right.'

'Yes, well this is a thing which Allah hath decreed unto him ere He created him. So he is not to blame, for Destiny so wills it that men must needs lust after women and 'tis the bounden duty of the women to defend themselves against the men so the sin lies with the women. Now, I feel this small copper cucurbit is more than I deserve.'

'Maybe so, but if we all got what we deserved, mate, we wouldn't be gettin' much. Go on, take it.'

'You're too kind. May Allah requite you abundantly.'

'Careful of that lead bit at the end. Don't break the seal. It looks to have the maker's mark in graven talismanic characters like the tracks of ants, which may increase its value. What do you think it could be?'

'No idea. Work of art?'

'I broke my tooth on it. That much I do know. You comin' back this way?'

'I should say not! I was just sexually assaulted in the Khangah!'

'Wouldn't surprise me. They brought the wolf to the Madrasa that he might learn to read, but when, quoth they to him – say A, B, C, D, quoth he to them, Lamb, Sheep, Goat, Kid. If you do return, fetch me some salix for this tooth.'

'Ya 'l-Ajuz, Ya Hajjah; O Mother of Sulayman, can you tell me what a tyre kicker is?'

'A tyre kicker is a time-wasting pauper who when he sees a cart for sale walks around it kicking the steel tyres as though he had the necessary.'

'And when doing the business how could I tell if a lady is on the job?'

'Ya Akh al-Jahalah! O brother of ignorance, when on the job our underfelt becomes all moist and sticky. Our nipples harden, engorge with blood, and our cheeks may become flushed. If we haven't shut our eyes, you may see our pupils dilate. We may grind our teeth.'

Abu Bakr is quick to see the kumkum up the sleeve. 'What's that you have there?' he asks.

'Oh, just a little piece of scrap was given me by an old woman. Allah Karim, who raised up the heavens without columns and spread out the earths like carpets in mercy to His creatures. I'm keeping it to remind me of the fundamental decency of folk.'

'You've a deputation of mirabs waiting to see you, Shahrban. They slept in the Divan. Wouldn't talk to me – insisted on speaking to the top man. You recall your Divan? Down the corridor and to your left. And put on a decent pair of bag-trowsers!'

'Send a slave with salix to that woman who sells the poults. It was her give me this, in a gesture of compassion.'

'Hearkening and obedience.'

An audience chamber should impress an audience. The throne of the Byzantine emperor rises mechanically into the air. Ummayad caliph 'Abd ar-Rahman the Third will use a mercury-filled bowl, so designed that a courtier's lightest touch will set it aswing whereupon myriad light beams trained through ceiling apertures of translucent marble reflect from the pulsating surface to flash round the audience chamber like lightning bolts. The oft-empty throne of Harun ar-Rashid in Baghdad astonished many, but the audience chamber of Shahrban al-Mutliq of Merv, now seldom used, amazes none. It is in need of a good dusting. Gasping and choking as he fights his way through endless successive pairs of velvet drapes the Shah espies, asprawled upon a carpet, a nonagenarian. Twice a day, the Shah is meant to hold Darbar here. And once a week he is meant to act as Mufti, holding the Book of Judgements, Kitab al-Kaza, but he does none of this.

The man before him at present is the chief mirab of Margiana. He is wrapped in his Patoo, his winter blanket – cold, the audience chamber.

'Aren't you the lad used to sit on his horse in the snow all night?'

'That was some time back. How may I be of help?'

'Good question. I cannot seem to impress on your Wazir the gravity of our plight.'

'Try me on,' says the Shah, squatting on the carpet, 'but make it brief as I'm busy.'

'I'll give it you in a word, Sahib – salt!'

'Not sure I follow.'

The chief mirab motions to a colleague intendant who hands him a water-filled flask. 'Taste this,' says the chief mirab, thrusting the flask at the Shah.

'Oh no! I trust no man!'

'Come on, Shahrban, it's only water from your dam. Taste it and tell us what you think.'

'Not really such a big drinker of water. Perhaps not the best person to adjudge.'

'Taste it!'

'Oh, all right. Give it here.'

'Well?'

'Bit salty.'

'Bit salty! We have here one of the largest oases in Khurasan. Now, most oases rely on Qanats and wells to channel springs but we have our Murghab River which provides us sweet water and washes down fertile silt for our every need. Do you know, perchance, the Chinese word *zhi*?'

'I don't speak Chinese.'

'It means "to rule" but it also means "to regulate the waters". I'm asking for your full attention, Shahrban. You have surrounded yourself with fools – Turks who know nothing of irrigation. Who in his right mind would set a nomad to supervise a mirab?'

'I would have had my reasons. Now, you mention salt as a problem. Where does the salt come from? If, as you imply, someone is poisoning our waters, rest assured they will be dealt with. Good day.'

'Not so fast! The salt has to do with your mania for cotton. It has to do with the amount of water the textile industry consumes. I told your Wazir, I said to him straight, I said, if you don't act to return this river to the system practised under the Chosroes, you'll live to see what's happened along the Dajlah happening here. Are you aware, Shahrban, of a situation that arose just last month when a huge, important caravan of dignitaries was stopped on the outskirts of your city by ghulams and every merchant in that caravan, along with every pilgrim and every cameleer, forced at knifepoint into a field of cotton and not allowed to resume their journey until they'd picked every boll? And then, when they got to their lodgings, they were given to drink a glass of brine and told they couldn't have a bath because there was no water in the well and you want to build a bigger barrage and line all the canals!'

'You don't think that might solve the problem? I would have been following advice.'

'*Whose* advice? There's only so much water to be had. We get hardly any rain. All our water comes from the river. Now, if you line the canals to prevent seepage, the wells will fail. Build more fields and you're putting the best water on the worst soils. But it may be too late. A civilisation chokes on salt. We've ruined this oasis given us by Allah and all for growing bloody useless cotton. We're heading back to desert, Shahrban. Down below the dam they can't grow wheat anymore, only barley and alfalfa. You don't see the salt that covers the fields because the farmers wash it off. They waterlog the fields to the point where the drainage ditches can no longer cope. If you got out of your palace more, you might understand my point. They drown their cotton, every summer, to a depth of over six foot and three foot of that is to wash off the salt that formed after the last harvest, but the more salt they wash into that river, the more water they need. We're on a waterwheel and what about drought? All our fields will become pure salt, fit only to grow desert tamarisk.'

'I'll get some slaves straight onto it.'

'I presume you jest. You might as well ask your slaves to stop the waterwheels from creaking. No man can stop a Sakiyah from creaking and no man can remove salt. We've ten thousand slaves removing silt. It's true more silt is coming down since they cleared the headwater foothills but I'm told that only pistachio burns hot enough to fire steel, I wouldn't know. I do know that all the slaves in the world cannot rid soil of salt. What's that you have in your sleeve?'

'Ah what, this little copper thing? Just a piece of scrap.'

'Show us it here. Why, this has been underwater a thousand years! Where's it from?'

'Couldn't say.'

'Too heavy to be solid copper – must be something inside. What's this writing on the lead seal? Gramarye, I'd say. Looks to me like Square Hebrew.'

'Give it back, it has sentimental value. I'll think about what you've said, though, my word I will. You've given me food for thought. Ala mahlak.'

'The time for thought is over, my friend. It is time for *action*! We demand you rid this oasis of cotton!'

'A tall order. May Allah offer you another oasis. I shall see what can be done but in the meantime, to put your mind at ease, I saw, in a vision, the end of Merv and it was not caused by salt.'

'*Zhi* – remember that word.'

Before he knows quite what he is doing, the Shah is walking back towards the Khangah. Good God Almighty, the force of habit, isn't it a shocking thing entirely? He baulks at the thought of destroying the economy and doesn't want to kick his wife's tyres. While standing outside the Khangah, he sees the induction of a new Son of the Rumour. The Pir is allowing the inductee to quench his thirst from the Wondrous Cup, Umm al-Ka's, a chalice of Shiraz that never needs topping up. Placing his hand on the man's breast, the Pir says to him in Dari, 'You are now the Treasure Chest of our Tariqat and lode of our Rumour, code of all we advocate and forbid. Henceforth you are the rectifier of believers on our Way and, by God's will, al-Bab and home of our science of Ta'wil, the inside of our Rumour and the rumour of our Rumour. You are blessed in your beginning and in your end, blessed without and within, blessed in life and in death.'

'Ah,' says the Pir, on noticing the Shah, 'here he is, the man who never was. Come in, my friend, and Sa'adah – wordly prosperity and future Happiness. Ya tayyib al-Khal, O nephew of a good uncle, what's that you have in your hand? Looks like a kumkum. Now we were speaking, I forget the context, of Cordoba, capital of al-Andalus. Between there and Feringhistan on a wild plateau, is the old Roman fortress town of Leon. I'd like you to meet the Roman Catholic Bishop of Leon. He is become a Son of the Rumour. He has just pledged the troth of the Prentice to the Shaykh, al-'Ahd wa al-Misak, though it is a shocking thing entirely that he rejects the True Faith and gives partners to the All-Wise and magnifies the Cross and bows down before a pigeon. Allah save and favour the king!'

Vermudo the Deacon, *mutilado de guerra*, face deeply scarred, all-but-cleft athwart by a galloping horseman's sabre, wine still dribbling from the crevice in his chin, tries hard, but unsuccessfully, to smile. 'We have something in common,' he mumbles to the Shah through what remain of his teeth. 'I, too, was Lord of an Age.'

The Tunic of Santa Eulalia

'Father, when I'm grown I shall find the tunic of Santa Eulalia!'

I was breathless having run all the way from the *Bierzo* and my father was gloomy because my brother Aurelius, king for six years, had just been killed in putting down revolt among the slaves on our estate. He had left no sons and the Palatine nobles had elected Silo, husband of Queen Adosinda, to succeed, because I was thought too young.

Among Visigoths the king is warlord.

My father would sit in that church all day to keep out of the rain and listen to the river. But Silo was building a church in Pravia, rough looking thing, too, *mas feo que Dios* – uglier than God – to Santa Ines. That was to house a phial of God's Mother's Milk and a pinion snatched from the right wing of the Holy Ghost at Pentecost.

'Who is this Santa Eulalia?' My father, though a bishop, didn't know much about religion.

'She is patron saint of the Visigoths, Father. Abbot Diego says that there are no Visigoths in the Cantabrias but I assured him that we are Visigothic here.'

'What would he know about Visigoths? *Basta*! He's only a Celt. Did I waste twenty-five gold solidi sending you to Compludo? Have you learned to read, Vermudo?'

'I'm making progress. The abbot says I'm brilliant. I don't want to be king of the Asturias, Father. I prefer to be a monk.'

'Well, you're not to be one. Any *jornalero* could be a monk.'

Father had been both blinded and ordained, which suggests that his brother Alfonso must have seen him as quite a threat. He'd missed out on becoming king himself when King Favila was killed by the bear, because Uncle Alfonso the Catholic had married Favila's sister. Now, had Father married Queen Ermosinda, he would have become king because Adosinda was Ermosinda's daughter.

I could see there was no point discussing Santa Eulalia with my father, so I returned to Compludo next day.

'Abba Diego! Abba Diego! See what I have found!' My impulse when I found a new butterfly was to tell the abbot.

'Where have you been, Vermudo? You left here Whitsontide. It doesn't take a month to get from Cangas to Compludo. What's that you have there? Prior complains that every book in this library is pressing a butterfly. Where'd you score him?'

'Arroyo del Naranco near San Glorio.'

'Don't go chasing butterflies there. You'll be eaten alive by bears.'

'They don't bother me. See the bright ocelli and the hour-glass-shaped red patch on the upper forewing?'

'Is that a skipper?'

'Ringlet. I saw a lot of fritillaries on the heath as well but we have them.'

'You'll be wasted as king. How many butterflies have we now between Cangas and Compludo?'

'More than a hundred and twenty, Abba, and I'm still finding new ones.'

'Even so, your father pays me to teach you to read. And we have just time for a short lesson. Let us turn to Lucan, our great Hispanic epic poet, born in Cordoba and died in Cordoba aged only twenty-seven for plotting against Nero. Sentenced to death but, turning informant, allowed to name his poison, so hired a surgeon to open his veins in the bath. Ooh, that's right, he's in the scriptorium being copied. Damn! Hand me that Gospel.'

'How would you choose to die, Abba, if you were given a choice?'

'I won't be given a choice. I'm heading for white martyrdom here with a fortified, steadfast mind. I won't be leaving Compludo. It's not possible and never was to lead a Christian life outside a monastery.'

'I mean to find the tunic of Santa Eulalia, Abba, when I'm grown. My ambition is to be a greater bishop that Masona.'

'Certainly better than being King of the Backblocks. I would seek that tunic in the Merida cemetery basilica, not that we know what goes on there, since Lizard-eaters moved in. It may have been transferred to Cauliana. Now read this quickly for me, please, as I hear the bell for sext. Did you know Lizard-eaters forbid the ringing of bells in Cordoba as it interferes with their bellowing from the minaret?'

'Can I read instead from *The Lives of the Fathers of Emerita Augusta?*'

'*Anamchara! Anamchara!* I've done a wrong thing.'

'What have you done now, Tearful One?'

'Wet the bed.'

☾

We had to have a soul-friend and mine lived in a cave. There were hermits living in caves across the Bierzo. They were a concern to the abbot, because he couldn't keep a close eye on them and didn't know what they were up to. Once in a while, Prior Adelgaster and Abbot Diego would take holy water and ropes and go out to forcibly ordain some, but they were good at hiding. Hermit Mocholmoc agreed to be my soul-friend, because he liked butterflies too, but it was a perilous commitment, as he used to insist, because if he imposed on me a penance commensurate with the gravity of my sin, I would likely dodge it; whereas if he imposed no penance, the debt of my sin would fall upon him.

I wasn't to be his soul-friend: his soul-friend was an angel. Mind you, I wasn't yet nine years of age: too young to be a soul-friend.

His *cueva* was ten miles from Compludo in a limestone *tajo* near a beech forest. There were lots of butterflies about, mostly fritillaries, and plenty of birds. A colony of storks had nested over the cave and there were rock thrushes and stonechats and rock buntings in the gorge, and griffon vultures and booted eagles on upcurrents looking for linnets, and yellowhammers and citril finches that had strayed out of the woods, and blackbirds scrabbling about in the undergrowth where only martagon lilies grow because the canopy of a beech forest is so dense. Beyond the cave was a stream and a small *marisma* which filled in late summer with spikes of yellow gentian, wolfsbane, alpine roses and brook thistles – all attractive to fritillaries – while outside the entrance was Irish sessile oak and – can you believe this? – a mat of Irish spurge and Kerry butterwort. It was the sight of these had persuaded Mocholmoc to live in the cave because he was Irish. He came from a place in the west called *Corca Dhuibhne*, and he'd been a monk in a monastery because as he said it was a 'thin' place

– perhaps the thinnest known with only the thinnest of membranes dividing apart the Two Worlds, but Vikings had captured him and taken him along with most of his fellow monks to Cordoba, a thickish place, where he'd been sold in the slave market to Lizard-eater 'Abd ar-Rahman, to become one of five thousand 'mute' slave-soldiers. He was given a sword and a horse and sent with Berbers and Slavs and Blackamoors and other Irish ex-monks through the marches on annual raids into Aquitaine and the Asturias, because a Lizard-eater may not tax another Lizard-eater. And once on the way back from the Asturias, descending this very stream with a collection of men's heads banging about in a bag tied to his horse's neck for display on spikes in Cordoba outside the Rusafah Palace, he'd seen this cave and thought to himself – I am living a lie here. So he'd sneaked off and hidden among the beech trees and now he lived alone in the cave. The heads he'd given to the brown bears.

He was the thinnest man I ever saw. I could see his every bone. Regarding gluttony and lust as the sins that had brought Adam undone, he lived naked – nothing before, nothing behind, with sleeves of the same – *imnochta*, according to his Rule of Columba – *imnochta do gresdo sachem ar Christ ocus ar na soscela* – detached from the world, following the teachings of Christ and the Gospel – eating only when hungry – *gachas*, acorn porridge for the most part, watercress, food becoming the wise, though he had a firkin of butter he'd nibble on the eve of the two Easters and the two Christmases; sleeping only when sleepy and spending most of his time in the stream up to his neck in the water which allowed him to maintain *crosfigell* – the cross-vigil – with water supporting his arms as Hur and Aaron supported the arms of Moses during the battle with the Amalekites. He recited each day the three fifties, and after each psalm, alternatively, the *Magnificat* or the *Cantemus*, because, as he said, artwork produced for a king by a son of life should be gilded. I heard him chanting the Charm of Mary in his high, clear tenor as I came through the forest.

Under his Rule, he was meant to live *I fail primh catrach* – close to the seat of a bishop – which would have meant Compludo in his case, but we never saw him. Irish hermits didn't like our Iberian Rules and we lived under the Rule of Fructuosus, San Fructuoso, a Visigothic metropolitan of Braga who had founded Compludo. Our Rule was loquacious. Mocholmoc, following Saint Ailbe, believed that two thirds of piety is silence, but we never stopped talking in Compludo. We had to reveal every one of our thoughts, visions and dreams to the prior, and I had reading lessons, and every one of the eight canonical hours we observed in prayer.

'Tell me why you wet your bed,' he said. 'But first – was it urine?'

'Not really.'

'Oh dear. Let me cross myself. Did you tell the prior what you dreamed?'

'I did but he didn't believe me. It was a dream of a woman's tunic.'

'I don't believe you, either. One week on nettles and nutshells, for lusting in your heart. Here, take these nutshells. You can pick the nettles on the way back.'

'I don't believe I was lusting in my heart for a woman's tunic!'

'Your bedsheet says otherwise.'

I didn't return to Compludo that night. I went straight back to Cangas where Father put me to work, tending cattle on our estate. The head stockman was Gad, one of our many Jewish slaves. All Jews in the time of King Sisebut the Poet had been baptised but even Jews who were practising Christians were still circumcising their sons, and circumcision is forbidden to a Visigoth on pain of scalping.

When Silo died in 783, Fruela the Cruel's infant son, Alfonso the Chaste, was proclaimed king, but Mauregatus seized the throne, and no sooner had he gone off to no-man's-land to engage with Lizard-eaters, than all Asturians sickened with a mortal undulant fever. He got back from his skirmish to find us sick as dogs. That afternoon, I got a call he wanted to see me. I found him, dripping wet, sitting under the palace thatch.

'Vermudo,' he says, '*hombre de confianza*. What has happened? What in God's name has happened here since I was at my skirmish?'

'The Lord is punishing us, Mauregatus, with an undulant fever. Did you not know God may appoint a king in order to chastise a people?'

'But Bishop Fruela ...'

'Dead.'

'And Bishop Franimian?'

'Dead.'

'Who is calling on Santa Ines and Santa Maria for help?'

'No one. They are powerless, anyway. I'm off, tomorrow, to Merida. Could I speak with the Mozarab?'

He'd brought back in chains a Mozarab who answered to the name of 'Ibn al-Kuttiya'. We call them Mozarabs – *Musta'ribun*. I'd never before seen a man wear jewels. 'Son of the Goth' and myself took a short stroll along the sea cliff where Pyrenean lilies that grow in the grykes are a haven for the dappled whites.

'I am a monk in a monastery,' I told him, 'and what I cannot understand is how a Visigoth, raised in the language of Ildefonsus, would choose lizard-speak.'

'No, because you live here in the Iron Age,' he replied. '*Look* at the place! Look at your *palacio*! *Cortijo de labor!* Nothing but a wattle and daub hut with a mud floor and thatched roof. I am a poet and if I can write in Arabic a thousand lines, each ending in the same rhyme, why would I bother with Latin and Greek?'

'But why come here to fight us?'

'Adventure, *señor*. I want to write a *Kasidah* and it must have a battlefield scene. An ode should commence with an erotic prelude and, as a rule, the poet is travelling alone through a deserted landscape when he happens upon an abandoned encampment where dwelt a woman he once loved. An ode must include celebration of horses and it must end in a battle.'

'What did you think of Merida?'

'Tiresome, filthy place full of Berbers and *mawalladun*. Storks' nests on the aquaduct. The wali would rebel were it not that the Yemenis are always at the Jordanians' throats.'

'Did you notice a cemetery outside the walls?'

The next day I said goodbye to my wife Amalasuntha and my little son Ramiro and set off to Merida to find the tunic of Santa Eulalia. The time had come for manhood.

I went south-west along the *Duero* to the monastery of Dumio, which was founded by Martin, who'd been a hermit in Egypt. It is an *ermita* and since we depopulated Braga, the abbot there is bishop of Braga as well, just as Abbot Diego was bishop of Astorga. Galicians round Dumio were notoriously pagan so Martin wrote them a book entitled *De Correctione Rusticorum* in order to try to stop them worshipping their Mother Goddess, Atacaina. I told the abbot I was writing a book on the impact of Islam on monastic life, so he advised me to visit the urban monastery of Agali. I didn't like to tell him the purpose of my quest, because he was Galician and Galicians don't like Asturians. And Asturians don't like Galicians. Even so, and mark my words – nothing will come of this cult of Santiago de Compostola! As if St James went to Spain. We have the Real Thing in Oviedo: I saw to that. We have, in our church at Oveido, the relics of Santa Eulalia, and she is patron saint of Galicia *and* the Asturias.

I found the cemetery all right but I was ill with fever and delirious the entire time I spent in the basilica. I wouldn't know what went on. I returned to consciousness, with blood upon my saddle-pads in clots like bullocks' livers, to find I was on a horse that wasn't mine, it was midday and I was about to return that pickaxe I'd borrowed from Dumio.

'What have you been up to?' said the slave who took the pickaxe. 'You've ruined this pickaxe. Look at it! No good for anything now. I hope that's not your blood on your sleeve. What's that you have in the sack?' He took the sack off my horse and opened the mouth to peer in. 'Hmm, as I suspected – bones. Human female longbones, skull and pelvis of a tall, lanky creature, maybe twelve years.'

'Let me see,' I said, jumping off the horse and rummaging through the sack, but it was as he implied: no tunic.

I began to see her in my dreams. She was a tall, pale girl with grey eyes and black hair, methought, and carried her head on a long neck tilted to the right. Once in a while she would startle me by violently tossing her head to remove from her eyes a lock of hair that persistently annoyed her. Her white face was freckled and her breasts unformed buds. She was no conventional beauty and yet she possessed divine poise. When I woke, my eyes would fill with tears and my head pulsate. I knew Santa Eulalia loved me as much as she'd loved Masona.

'Praise be to God,' I would whisper, as my heart filled with devotion. 'Praise be to God for the love of my darling, the Holy Virgin Martyr Eulalia!'

When I got back to the Asturias, I found Mauregatus dying. He asked to see me on his deathbed.

'Before I am gone,' he said, 'from this splitting headache and the fever that I suffer, I mean to ordain you, Vermudo, as bishop of all Pravia. I won't take no for an answer. It is a marvellous thing entirely that you have retrieved these relics.'

But as he spoke, a posse of Palatine nobles came galloping up.

'Don't do it!' they said. '*Por favor!* Vermudo the Deacon for king! We hear how he killed fifteen Banu Kasi with a pickaxe and then he stole the wali's horse and made off with the relics. Take no notice of Mauregatus, Vermudo. He's likely as not to recover.'

But he didn't. He died that very night and next day I was crowned king of the Asturias.

It was 788 and I was nineteen years old.

King Vermudo the Deacon! I held the relics throughout my coronation. I wouldn't let go that sack. I had to take the sceptre in my left hand.

Over the next two years, the Asturias recovered, thanks to the intercession of our Holy Virgin Martyr. The cattle and people regained their health. The hay in the hay meadows flourished. There were more hands to harvest the barley harvest than ever before as it was a time of peace.

I banned skirmishing. I told my Palatine nobles that when next we fight those Lizard-eaters we shall fight them in a proper battle on a proper field, as we did once at Covadonga, when we kicked their butt.

I kept my palace in Pravia though I prayed at the church in Cangas. I functioned as deacon in either place as I would not appoint a bishop. It is to the deacon to assist the priest, according to San Isidoro, in all that is done in the sacraments, to lay the table and to drape it and to declaim both Gospel and Epistle. I can do that. I can both read and write and I had an amice and alb and girdle and stole and maniple and chasuble all inherited from my father and I would hold a candle in my left hand with the sack in my right.

In 791, as we left for battle, each man in the Asturias on horseback, I was touched when my nobles presented me a silver pickaxe, with handle inlaid with agate.

☾

I gave the war cry: *Todo por la patria, Señoritos! Todo o nada! Todo por la Virgen de la Salud muy milagrosa!*

The emir of al-Andalus at the time was Hisham, father of Hakim. I've heard it said he was a pious, ascetic man who completed construction of the mosque, but to Santa Eulalia and me, he was nothing but a filthy, lizard-eating heretic. I sent an envoy ahead asking Hisham to meet me in battle at Leon but what I didn't know was that he'd already left Toleto, leading his slave army towards my eastern frontier of Castille. This was bad but what was worse, a second army of jihadis under command of Yusuf ibn Bokht – a general battle-hardened through years of warfare between Hisham and his brothers – had just left Merida moving over the *Meseta* towards my southern border and Yusuf ibn Bokht was to give me the mother of all hidings.

We went through Covadonga. I never saw more damselflies over the glacial lakes! Bogbean blues, azures, large reds, dragonflies, four-spotted chasers, keeled skimmers, emperors and ruddy darters. Butterflies though, nary a one. That's odd, I thought, I should have expected a few copper fritillaries. But not one; a bad omen. And the night before the battle I'd a nightmare in which Eulalia ignored me.

Our armies confronted each other on the outskirts of Leon. Thousands of men all shouting, emptying their bowels and using the product to poison their arrows. I held up my sack of relic bones and brandished them before leading the charge, but everything went badly wrong as Asturians weren't used to fighting in strict battle formation. We got in each other's way and I was wounded in the face, to the point where all I could do was cry, 'Quarter! Quarter!' like everyone else.

The Arabs didn't bother chasing us, preferring to collect heads from our dead. Alfonso the Chaste was among us unhurt so I abdicated in his favour, there and then. In my final decree as king I made myself bishop of Leon, then I went back down alone to my see, afraid to confront the families of all the Asturians who wouldn't be returning. I still had that sack, though. My word, yes, I wasn't about to part with my sack of relic bones.

Egyptian vultures were eating the remnants of our dead, picking the bodies clean. They had so gorged themselves that for days I could knock them down with a stick.

Over the next ten years I did nothing much. I had one Leonese parishioner who lived in a typical Berber earthenware beehive hut and we had no common tongue. He was Basque and kept merino sheep. Three times every Sunday, I would preach sermons to him. When bored, I'd busy myself rearranging the battlefield bones, strewn about everywhere now by bears, to form intact formations. I cleaned the brains, like a Mauretanian Jew, from the few remaining heads and salted them. I then gave the skeletons a Christian burial. Aside from this, I rarely left Leon except to attend Church Councils, at one of which Bishop Diego, my old mentor, asked did I still see Mocholmoc. 'Your soul-friend would hear you out,' he said, 'if he were still in the cave. And if I were dreaming as you say you do, every night of grinning heads on sticks, I would confer with my soul-friend. I would get it off my chest whatever it was led to my ruin.'

'Well, I don't know I am ruined,' I said. 'I have seen better days, it's true, but these are the bones of a Holy Virgin Martyr I carry in this sack.'

'Is it right and proper, Vermudo, to carry them round as you do?'

Sometime that winter Lent I went to see Mocholmoc. It was cold and wet; the Irish speak of 'cold, stormy hell'. An Egyptian vulture was chasing a long-eared owl outside the cave. I saw a black woodpecker. I made a note to check the gorge come summer for woodland browns as I was short a woodland brown in my new collection. Then I started calling for Mocholmoc as I couldn't hear him chanting.

'*Hola!*' I shouted. 'Anyone home?'

He emerged from the stream that ran by his cave. He'd been lying on the bottom in the gravel. 'You again!' he says. 'What have you got there in that sack?'

'Only the bones of a Blessed Virgin Martyr, the relics of a saint like yourself. I mean to keep them by me.'

'And does it help? Do you dream or do you wake in bliss?'

'Oh, I dream. I dream each night of men's heads on sticks, which is why I'm here. I want to know why things have gone so badly for me when I've done nothing wrong.'

'You may have done nothing wrong,' he said, 'but have you done anything *right?* Doing nothing wrong is a virtue associated with old age. Did you find that tunic of Santa Eulalia, Tearful One? That was your ambition.'

'These,' I said, 'are the bones of that very martyr in this very sack.'

'Did you hear what I said? I said did you find the *tunic?*'

'*Lo siento,* it wasn't in the basilica.'

'Then you will need to find it. Your relics are incomplete. You will have no rest till you do.'

'I wouldn't know where to look for it.'

'Oh, you won't find it by looking.'

'What is to be my penance?'

'I want you tomorrow to heed the words of St Columbanus, Tearful One: hold your tongue when suffering a wrong!' And with that he went back down underwater. I waited half an hour but he didn't resurface.

Sure enough, the following day, a posse of Palatine nobles came over the hill from Oviedo to arrest me, so they said, for complicity in a plot against Alfonso the Chaste. They destroyed my butterfly collection, took my sack of relics to be buried in the chapel of San Juliano and conveyed me in chains to Compludo, there to spend the rest of my days in a sentence of perpetual exile. I was to be denied Celestial Medicine except on my deathbed. I was to sleep each night on nettles and nutshells except for three days each month which I would spend in a grave with a freshly dead body. During this three-day black fast I would not eat, drink or sleep, but earnestly make cross-vigil on the corpse at each of the seventy-two canonical hours. During Holy Week – *Semana Santa* – each year, I would be taken from my cell, stripped naked before the *retablo*, and given seventy lashes, with full genuflection and cross-vigil to be performed between each lash – this, while still legitimate bishop of one of the three oldest sees in all Spain.

Mocholmoc warned me to hold my tongue so I said nothing as the false charges were read and the unjust punishment pronounced.

And this was twenty-one years ago. For twenty whole years I said not one word but as you see I was in the end released, for here I am in Merv.

The white martyrdom for which he longed was eluding old Abbot Diego and one year come Pentecost he had me taken from my cell. He was in the library peering through my old butterfly collection which looked pretty shabby and neglected.

'Twenty years,' he said, 'and in all this time you have said not one word. I can't imagine what is going on in your head. I thought it cruel of Alfonso to deny you Celestial Medicine. I can't see how a man could survive one week without the Eucharist. In any event, I've made a decision. I said to Adelgaster, I said, if Vermudo survives this Holy Week, I mean to release him into the woods to procure him his nettles for his bedding and I don't care what Alfonso thinks. And if we never see him again, well, that's just too bad. *Hasta luego*, Vermudo! Take this little palm leaf.' He handed me a cross of palm from the recent Palm Sunday. They grow palm trees in Cordoba.

I took my palliasse to contain the nettles and left the convent grounds. It was mid-spring, late May, *Semana Santa* having come early.

Before I'd walked a mile I realised I wasn't the same man as before. I was more fragile yet at the same time more appreciative. Twenty years on bread and water had ruined my physical condition, twenty years without speaking or reading a book had destroyed my brain while twenty years without Celestial Medicine had withered my soul. I hadn't seen a butterfly in twenty years, either.

It was a warm, cloudless day, I recall, with nary a breath of wind. I walked up through the golden ash, wych-elm and small-leafed lime to discover a glistening hay meadow all adrift in butterflies. I seated myself on the moist grass in the middle of the field – it would have been midday – surrounded by kidney vetch, mountain cornflower, bloody cranesbill, musk mallow, white asphodel, spiked rampion, bastard balm, Solomon's Seal, woodcock and sawfly orchids, purple loosestrife, ragged robin, marsh ragwort, pink lousewort, great sheets of devil's-bit and all about me, butterflies – swallowtails, green hairstreaks, grizzled skippers, black-veined whites, silver-studded blues, purple-edged coppers, clouded yellows, large wall browns, common brassy ringlets, heath fritillaries, marsh fritillaries, purple-edged and sooty copper fritallaries, long-tailed fritillaries, mazarine blues – and through the dancing of this rainbow were the green beech trees in the middle distance with their translucent leaves, the meadow being utterly surrounded with a beech forest one hundred feet high.

I heard myself suddenly sobbing, as the door opened on another world.

I had found the tunic of Santa Eulalia.

When that night I returned, laughing and singing, to my convent, Diego was concerned. 'Vermudo,' he said, 'I very much fear that you have been institutionalised.'

I laughed and jabbed him in the paunch. 'Not the case! It's just there's nowhere I prefer to my cell, dark and damp though it be. There is no company I prefer to my own, stale bread is my favourite food and water my favourite beverage. There is no bed I prefer to nettles and netshells unless, of course, it be a grave containing a freshly dead body; and I do look forward to my next seventy lashes as I feel they do me the world of good.'

'Yes,' he said, 'this is the worst case of institutionalisation ever seen. But it is pleasing, at the same time, to see you smile and to hear you speak. What brought about the change, then? Fresh air?'

You know, I felt not the slightest compunction to tell him what I'd found? I was too *Happy*. I was too Happy to want to tell anyone anything, but Abba decided I should confer with Mocholmoc, now I was speaking again.

So next day, still dancing and singing, I went to see my soul-friend, the anvil of the stream.

'I'm sending you on pilgrimage,' he said before I'd spoken a word.

Na tri choisceim – ta's ag cach
is fearr shiulas neach go brath
ceim d'fhoisru an othair thais
ceim d'oilithre, ceim d'eaglais

All men know it: the three best footsteps a man shall ever walk are the step to visit the sick, the step of the pilgrim and the step to the church.

'You need to find the tunic that goes with the bones, Vermudo.'

'That won't be hard,' I said, 'as any old tunic would do. You see, the bones I had in that sack were not the bones of Santa Eulalia. They were just the bones of some poor little Roman girl. The bones of Santa Eulalia are the mountains and the crags. Her tunic is made of the petals of the flowers and the green leaves of the beech, embroidered with the wings of butterflies and studded with the stars of the night sky.'

'You've crossed to the other side,' he said. 'You've gone behind the Curtain. Try to stay there. But do find the people a nice little tunic to go with the bones, even so. They would appreciate that. It will complete their reliquary. Find that city in all the world where are manufactured the world's best textiles and order a nice cotton tunic. That can be your pilgrimage. But don't forget, Vermudo, you must return to Compludo before you die, in order to receive on your deathbed, Celestial Medicine. Off you go! Take your time! *Adios* Bishop Vermudo.'

Iranian Days (continued)

'As for my sermon, Shahrban, I give you simply the Rumour as expressed in the Symbolum fidei of my Metropolitan, Elipandus of Toleto; and let the words of his mouth and the meditation of his heart be acceptable in thy sight, O Lord, my strength and my redeemer.

'Si conformes sunt omnes sancti huic filio Dei secundum gratiam profecto et cum adoptivo adoptivi et cum advocato advocati et cum Christo Christi.

'If we live lives as pleasing to God as the life that was led by our Brother Jesus, then that same Grace that was shown to Christ Jesus will be shown to us, so that we, too, will be adopted by the Father and the status of the Son of God bestowed upon us – *et ille Christus et nos Christi.* Amen.'

And after Duty and Repetition, 'Does anyone here know where I could find someone who reads Square Hebrew? I want to translate this lead seal on my little copper cucurbit. And if a Mozarab can learn to speak Arabic then so can I. Thanks to your talk, Vermudo, I mean to make a bigger effort on my Arabic.'

'Mawdudus is away today,' says the Pir, 'but try any synagogue. Mind you, the ignoramus would be unwelcome. Have you studied Torah, Mishnah, Gemara, halakha or aggada?'

The Shah would normally walk up the alley past the poult concession, but today he heads off towards the Razuj canal, a feculent fosse a-flow which serves the Rabad as sewer. He knows of two synagogues in al-Harah, the Ghetto. There is one in the patragars' quarter, the alley of the china-menders where Jews sit cross-legged, bracing broken bowls between their legs while mending them with a bow drill, wire and glue of lime and eggwhite; and a larger by the dyers' guild-hall where votes are cast by hands stained red with madder root, purple with Tyrrhenian mollusk shells, yellow with larkspur livers, crimson with mulberry woodlouse scales, white with Irish cerussite, red with Kermococcus vermilio, mauve with Crozophora tinctora, green with Cornish malachite, blue with woad and indigo with indigo. But before he actually approaches a Mervi Jew or even a 'chalas' – despised 'half-done's', those Jews who converted to Islam – he intends to memorise the writing on the seal, even make a copy for himself, because Jews everywhere have a reputation for deceit and double-dealing and if, as the mirab suggested, this copper cucurbit *has* been underwater, it may have been part of the Temple treasure taken off to Toleto, in other words – the very thing a Shah might wish to bequeath to a son and heir. If possible, the Shah will himself translate the seal, with the aid of a Hebrew–Dari dictionary.

He sits on the bank of the Razuj canal, glances about him and, satisfied no one is looking on, takes the cucurbit from his sleeve and holds it to the light. As always, he is confounded by the sheer weight in this little gourd-shaped bottle, which seems almost too heavy to be made of solid lead.

I shall pull the seal off completely, he thinks to himself, and be done with it, but as he rips the seal with his teeth, he sees a red smoke emerge, which quickly expands. Spiralling heavenward, it trails over the rubbish-filled canal until, having reached the full height of the sky, it condenses into a sun-tanned 'Ifrit, a Jinni built like Brad Thorne, whose red turband touches the cloudless sky even as his upturned, winkle-picker boots span the canal. His head is the size of the concrete dome of the Pantheon in Rome, his arms as long and tough as the hardwood beam of a trebuchet, his hands like winnowing forks, his legs as vast as the mainmast of a salt junk plying the Yangtze Kiang, his mouth the size of the cave in the Thawr mountain where hid the Most Praised One – on whom be The Peace! – his teeth the size of the steles that bedeck the banks of the Orkhon River and his nostrils ovals like ewers that sit by every Hammam bath. Furthermore, his eyes are as bright as the chandeliers that light the Samaniya library.

As the Shah beholds this 'Ifrit, clad entirely in a dull red cope, his side muscles quiver, his teeth chatter, his spittle dries, his member shrinks and he feels a need to void his bowels and bladder, which he does, bepiddling and besoiling his bag-trowsers.

The 'Ifrit, crossing his arms behind his back and thrusting a finger up his fundament, peers down upon the marzban before him and says, in strained contrition, 'There is no god but *the* God and Sulayman is the prophet of God,' adding, 'O Sulayman, thou Apostle of Allah, slay me not! Never again shall I gainsay thee in word nor sin against thee in deed, for well thou knowest I am Jattunas, a ducking and diving Jinni, one of the Judeaic Jann who helped thee build thy Temple, but I sinned against thee, Sulayman, for when going out to ease thyself in thy water closet, thou entrusted the four-jewelled seal-ring on which is written the Most High Name of God, Shem ha-maphrash – 'Ism al-A'azam, the Ineffable Name of Allah – to thy concubine Aminah, I alerted Sakhr al-Jinni to impersonate you and to steal that ring, containing the crystals presented you by the Spirits, the Birds, the Winds and the Earth, which he did, reducing you, for forty days, to abject beggary. But when after forty days you recovered that which had meantime been thrown in the main, there to be consumed by a mouth-breeding fish, you sent your Wazir, Asaf bin Bakhiya, to seize me; and that Wazir brought me to you against my will, in bonds, Sulayman, whereupon you bad me embrace the True Faith, the Faith of Mohammed, who made salvation general, which I refused. Then taking this cucurbit, this tiny copper kumkum in which your concubine Aminah was wont to store her rosewater, you shut me in it and stopped it up with lead seal on which is written Shem ha-maphrash, the Hundredth Name of Allah, and then you gave orders to your Jann to cast me in the midmost of the Sea of Galilee, where I abode these one thousand seven hundred and forty-seven years, during which time I conceived the notion: "Should Sulayman someday choose to release me, then I will open the bowels of the earth to grant him his one wish, whatso'er that wish may be. So peace upon you, Sulayman ibn Da'ud, and upon thy father, and thy will be my command."'

'Canst thou, 'Ifrit, rid the oasis of Margiana of salt?'

'Too easy. Not. A. Problem. Just ...'

'Wait! Wait. 'Ifrit, by the power invested in me by the Most High Name, I *command* thou bestow on me a virile member longer and thicker than that of any blackamoor!'

'And would it want to be black?'

'Ay, w'Allahi. I imagine so.'

'Cut or uncut?'

'Cut.'

'Ya Maulaya, O my Lord Sulayman ibn Da'ud, I hope you have thought the matter through. You won't be able to wear shorts now. Urinogenital: Oxus beefsteak. Opsoap winebar dopehead downo if upchat arsetit pompchat wishbone Ka-spronka. Done.' And so saying, the Jinni reconfigures himself in a puff of smoke which heads off to a nearby Chapel of Ease, Al-Mustarah, the haunting place of Jinn-Father Abu al-Tawaif Iblis.

The Shah's first need is to wash himself as clean as a sewer will permit. He then takes the empty cucurbit to a nearby scrap metal dealer. Shortly thereafter, clutching a dinar, he decides to visit a public Hammam. His heart is pounding for never before has he entered a public bath. There is no clout hanging over the door to indicate women are bathing so the Shah enters the Maslakh, or change room, where the keeper sits by the pay-chest.

The keeper gives the Shah the standard formula of entry. 'Ya ibn al-aur, ala-judi-k! Whatever you think's a fair thing, O son of a hard-on. But pay on the way out.'

Hands are clapped and a boy runs up who wears a pair of horsehair bag gloves. Smiling, the Shah strips off his bag-trowsers, hangs them on the earthen rack, then dons a pair of bath-clogs as the baths, being in a poor sector of the Rabad, have a mud floor. The attendant, chastely averting his eyes, then escorts the Shah to the steam room where he scratches the soles of the Shah's feet with pumice and rubs his back with the gloves, periodically holding, for the Shah's delectation, a dirt-roll stripped from the Shah's skin. When he adjudges the process complete, he withdraws. The Shah stands, and flexing his shoulders, strolls off, through mostly Turkish cameleers, towards the baths. Then, taking a Minshafah from the rope, he wipes his face thoroughly, and enters, without hesitation, the coldest bath. He emerges to total, flabbergasted silence, broken, eventually, by,

'Allaho A'alam! The runt's mother mates with a black ass!'

The Shah takes this in good part, throwing his head back and laughing heartily, so as to almost swallow the dinar. He hadn't been game to look down but he can feel something aflop. His trowsers having been laundered gratis and after a quick shampoo, he pays and strides off in high spirits towards the Shahristan.

He can *still* feel something aflop.

And two days later, a delighted Abu Bakr confronts the Pir. A high five becomes a resounding high ten.

'Done!' says the Wazir. 'It worked a treat. By the virtue of the Fire and the Light and the Shade and the Heat, it went as you predicted. He made that wish you predicted he would make and now, as expected, he cannot get it up – too big. He's out of action. Women of the world may sleep abed in peace.'

'Alhamdolillah! He'll be back. I'm expecting him.'

And sure enough, he is. 'Could I have a word in private?' he says to the Pir outside the Khangah.

'Any time,' replies the Pir. 'My breast is the grave of secrets.'

'I made a poor decision. I met up with this Jinni from the subtle world who granted me a wish and I didn't think things through for I have now ruined my entire life through depriving myself of my one pleasure. I am absolutely filthy.'

'Bismillah. Was he one of the Jann who helped Sulayman, on whom be The Peace, build the Temple?'

'He was. He was a diving Jinni possessed of free will and capable of grasping Reality. I found him confined to a kumkum for having refused salvation.'

'Many a Jinni took part in building the Temple. And where was the cucurbit found?'

'On the seabed of the Sea of Galilee.'

'Have you considered trawling the bed of the sea for a second cucurbit?'

'That would take up all my time and who would defend Merv?'

'Abu Bakr.'

'But what if I spend the rest of my life looking for something that isn't there?'

'That can only happen if you become addicted to the search. I suspect it depends on your wish. What was it?'

'By the triple oath of divorce, I am too ashamed to say.'

By next morning, Shahrban has made a decision. He will take all the coin from his mint, raise taxes on cotton to replace the deficit, and set off with nine ghulams for the Sea of Chinnereth, as the Sea of Galilee was known to Sulayman ibn Da'ud, on the twain be peace.

The party travels through the Caspian Gates and on through Ecbatana to Baghdad where Shahrban has a game of chess with *the Believer* on a square field of well-dressed leather and is soundly thrashed. Next it's up the Furat River, across to Tadmur and from that ancient oasis via the Vulture's Pass to Dimashq. A quick prayer in the cathedral-Mosque, then on across the Golan Heights to Galilee. The entire journey, on horseback, takes less than a month; this is the beauty of the Caliphate: in facilitating transit it expedites trade. It is now possible to sell shrimp from As-Sindh in Antioch, frankincense from Ma'rib in Urganj, lapis lazuli from Badakshan in Qayrawan and asbestos men's jackets from Kapisa in Tabriz.

The nine slaves and the Shah rent a house in Kfar Nahum. This is the region 'Isa ibn Maryam, on whom be The Peace, cast out Jinn so there are Jinn about. The Shah dispatches the ghulams to interrogate local fishermen to ascertain if cucurbits are still being caught in the nets. The sea itself is only small, thirteen miles by seven, but so deep the Shah is obliged to shelve all thought of draining it.

No fisherman ever heard of a metal bottle in a net.

'They're lying,' says Pishaq. 'There's a monastery called Tabgha, Master, with a Church of Loaves and Fishes.'

And the archimandrite of this monastery confirms that a cucurbit, sealed with the *shem*, the Most High Name, was in the monastery till a novice recently disappeared.

The Lava Desert of the ancient Geshurites in Manasseh beyond Jordan, east of the Sea of Chinnereth, contains within it the ruins of Golan, a Jewish city of refuge. And it is to the Lava Desert that Shahrban now repairs alone. A Jinni with free will can be a Lord of Knowledge and living in the Lava Desert are Judeaic Jinn, Nazarene Jinn and True-Believing Jinn. It is a 'thin' place, Manasseh beyond Jordan – thin, in the sense of pertaining to the porosity of the membrane between the Two Worlds – the Talmudic 'Curtain' – a place where the dirham tends to drop as to the nature of Happiness; indeed, in conjunction with Gilead to its south, it is as thin a place as any – thin as *Corca Dhuibhne*, Seed of the Goddess, in modern-day Kerry; thin as Kapilavastu and Kundagrama in the Himalayan foothills; thin as Balkh and Tus and Chisht on the Khurasani steppe, for this is the Biblical Wilderness, home to Elijah and John the Baptist, a dangerous place to work on your tan while enduring a forty-day detox.

When, after forty days, the Shah has not returned to camp, his ghulams search for him at Philippopolis and find him wearing a loincloth he made for himself from the skin of a dead camel.

They open his spittle with bread and camphor-apricots as he

reports, 'There are any number of Jinn out here in this Lava Desert, lads – winged troopers bearing standards and colours, willy-willies and sand-devils with round holes for mouths so that their speech is whistling – but none may approach their campfires and they tell me a Jinni only grants a wish to pay a debt. Now, the only man to whom these Jinn were indebted was Sulayman – on whom be The Peace – Sulayman, who had seven hundred wives and three hundred concubines, which makes me second most married Muslim man.'

'We have a new wife and all for you, Master, a Jewish Magdalene lass.'

'May I be triply divorced and be she lovely as a moon, she can be of no use. Take her back. Now take a look at this. Can you believe it won't work? It won't harden. When we get to Kfar Nahum I will ask you to take a purse of cash, go up with it to Dimashq and commission a jeweller there to build me one thousand pearl-encrusted kamakim, each about the size of this member and while there was a time when the size might vary – depending on who was measuring it and what they wore – those days are over. Bring them to me by the Waters of Meron as I have confected a scheme based on a tale of Shahrazad's.'

When two weeks later the kamakim arrive, the Shah decides to target a village within sight of Mount Hermon where lived, in days of yore, Banu Elohim, sons of God, giants who lived in chastity until they saw the daughters of men. The village has fields all round where Shahrban means to create a diversion. He has bidden his ghulams organise a demonstration match of buzkachi, a rough sport from the Turanian steppe never before seen in Galilee, and no sooner has Pishaq – a former professional player, a chopendoz – decapitated three calves, gutted them, filled their bodies with sand, sewn up the bellies, then called for tanks of water in which to soak the bodies to increase the sport, than the village all but empties, as folk spill into the chickpeas to cheer on the contestants, leaving behind, as the Shah intended, a skeleton crew of scullions.

Dressed in hufu, the Shah then starts trundling his handcart through the streets, declaiming, 'Gold cucurbits for copper! New scent bottles for old! Pearl-encrusted kumkum for any old copper thing at all with a lead seal.'

Hallal, the circle of justice, has been drawn on the chickpea field in lime. In the middle lies the headless calf, entitled to be the body of a headless man – about eighty pound weight. The ghulams, responding to a pre-agreed shout from a delighted Nazarene, rear their horses then lunge forward, jostling fiercely as they grab at their sodden prey. To do this, they must hang from their saddles by their boot-heels, gripping their whip-stocks in their teeth. All wear the turband – except Pishaq who wears the wolf-fur cap of the chopendoz – high-heeled boots, sheepskin jackets and trowsers held with rope belts.

A post has been erected a mile off by an irrigation ditch and the Turks hurtle through the chickpeas, chasing the man with the calf tucked under his leg. They flog and thrash him, striving to dismount him while grabbing as they do so at the calf. A score is made by encircling the post and hurling what's left of the calf on hallal.

The game will last as long as it takes all three calves to be torn to bits. By this stage, Shahrban has disposed of his bottles and many a kumkum found its way onto his cart but none, regrettably, with lead seal. Despondent, he is trundling the cart to dispose of its contents in a ditch when he happens on a freestanding house of iron-plated swart stone with, between two marble benches, a door of teak and would you believe, the knocker on this door is a cucurbit with lead seal?

He rips the knocker from its mount, then opens the door. Fearing to be set upon by dogs so sensitive in smell they could tell if a man were chaste, he finds, instead, a lovely pavilion with murmuring fountains of alabaster lionheads spouting water as diaphanous as diamonds amid a garden of sweet-scented roses with about it birds warbling the praises of Allah and reciting the names of the mother of Moses at the end of which stands a raised dais on which is a golden Takht and on this Takht an elder sitting with before him exceeding store of books and dispread at his feet a waist-shawl of white sandal edged with ambergris and eagle-wood at which he is making fumigations, conjurations, adjurations and recitations of words not understood of any.

Shahrban decamps into the perfumed wind under the clearest of clear skies, with the kumkum he supposes purloined from the Nazarene monastery. He wants to open it in the very place he opened the first, so a month later he is back in Merv on the banks of the Razuj canal, where off comes the seal and out comes a Jinni.

It is a Marid, not quite so large as an 'Ifrit. 'Adsum!' says the Marid. 'Labbayk. Te Deum. Here I am. Gloria Patri et Filio et Spiritu Sancto sicut erat in principio et nunc et semper et in saecula saeculorum, O Solomon Davidson, thy slave the Nazarene Jinni Sidus, is between thy hands. I am come to do thy bidding, before the world ends, by the Truth of the Messiah and the Faith that is no Liar. In nomine Dei miseratoris misericordis – ask me thy heart's desire, Solomon, before the world ends, for well thou knowest I owe thee one now.'

'I wish only to unwish a wish that already unwisely I wished.'

'You were haply granted a wish, Solomon, through intercession of some other Jinni?'

'I was. It was the Jewish ducking and diving Jinni Jattunas.'

'And you returned that Jinni to his bottle?'

'Ah – no.'

'Do I hear you aright, Solomon? On you be The Peace, but you say the Jinni is out of the bottle?'

'The Jinni is out of the bottle, thou speakest sooth.'

'But Solomon, once a Jinni is out of the bottle ...'

Well, it seems the Jinni being out of the bottle, the wish cannot be undone.

'Of *course* you couldn't get it up! Look at the *size* of the thing! What were you thinking? By the virtue of the Virgin, you can't expect your heart to perform *miracles*. You can't expect your blood to stiffen corpora cavernosa in a thing that size – not before the world ends: not with a normal heart. You didn't think things through. To get an erection in a member like that, you would need a bigger pump. You will need a heart larger than that of any Nazarene saint.'

'Well, just do as you must. Do what it takes. I have unfinished business, before the world ends, for which I need a functional member masculine.'

'I hope you have thought the matter through, Solomon. Peace! Done. You now have the biggest heart in all the world.'

'*Urk!*' Shahrazad is first to see the new member in all its pulsating glory. 'I hope you don't expect me to accommodate *that*! You want me to lose the child?'

'Is it the biggest you ever saw?'

'Yes, and by far the ugliest. I suppose that pleases you.'

'Bigger than Ziryab's?'

'Certainly longer.'

'Thicker than Ennico's?'

'His wasn't that thick. I never *look* at them! I hate the very *sight* of them! *Urk!* I'm always expected to *handle* them, of course, whatever that's about.'

'Handle this.'

'Oh, Eyebrows, have you no sense?'

'What's the matter, Shahrazad? Frightened you might get on the job?'

'Wipe that smirk off your face. I'd like to know where you got that thing.'

'Yes, and so would the whole wide world but I'm not telling. If you won't accommodate it, I shall have to find someone who will. I want to test it out. It's not for decoration. Well, it's not *just* for decoration.'

'Do as you like. Just don't bother me. This is my best chance yet to catch up on my reading.'

'You must promise to give it a try, though, as soon as my son and heir is born.'

'Eyebrows.'

'Yes, O Dear my lady Shahrazad?'

'Are you thinking of taking a second wife?'

'Bismillah, you're jealous! The nerve of it! Can you imagine a thing like this would not want to be at work?'

One week later, a distraught Wazir again visits the Pir. It's after dawn prayer and the Sons of the Rumour have gone off to their work.

'Salaam. Ya Bismillah, fetch me a cup of tea, 'Ali Zindiq, and make it strong. You have no idea, mate, the *carnage*! The state of the sheets! It's not entirely blood. He's going through all the harlots in Merv now, three at a time. Is this going to plan?'

'Be my three wives triply divorced, I warned you when he left for Galilee he could procure him a second Jinni as he has the persistence of a sitting hen. With you be The Peace and the mercy of Allah and His benediction. Not every wise man is saved by his wisdom nor every fool lost by his folly. We can only hope it was a Nazarene Jinni and not a Jew or True-Believer. How many harlots remain in Merv?'

'Too few for mine. I can't have cameleers complaining they can't relax in Merv. We'll lose our status as cotton entrepot.'

'Is he still using Dhu'l-Fiqar?'

'Calls his new member Dhu'l-Fiqar. No woman has yet survived a deed of kind with the thing and these are working girls. Oh, you should see the smile on his dial. He's a bad man, Hamdillah.'

'Dinazad must give him Da'wah, the call that will tell him that he is the son of a King who must throw off his raiments. But first, we need a trigger.'

'We do. We need a terminator, a large strong creature with robust constitution, built like a buffalo bull but emotionally vulnerable. I know such a one.'

'Not some local almah?'

'Oh no – Hottentot – Hottentot from Ifikiyah, that Hottentot Princess. I met her at a function in Baghdad. Of course, they were covered up down there, but ... Phwoar.'

'Isn't she with that travelling circus?'

'Only because her embassy fell behind in the rent. She's actually a very sweet girl. Well bred, too, royal blood – her father lives on Pombe beer as thick as millet gruel, she says, and sleeps on a bed of slabs that slope to drain off the liquor he makes in the night. It may have been the Caliph's idea that she should earn a little on the side because she fell in love with him. Got this thing for powerful men – haven't they all. He told me, with a laugh, that he was no match for that Hottentot. She'd spit him out like a watermelon pip, he said, when she got on the job.'

'That's the lass we want. Where is she?'

'Circus was on its way to Balkh so they're probably somewhere near Bamiyan. Don't worry, I'll sort it. I'll have Dinazad ready as well, for Da'wah.'

'Promise that Hottentot the royal hand of our Shah in marriage. She must stay with him and eat of his salt. We'll have a slap-up wedding with al-Walimah. Tell her he fell in love with her on sight when he saw her in the tent show. They're genuine then, are they?'

'Oh my word, yes, no question of it.'

'Alhamdollilah! Praise be to He who fashioned such booty from dirty water.'

'Shahrban, I think it's time you took a break, mate. Three times a night every night would overtax any man.'

'I don't feel tired. I can't wait for the next, bring her in! I never felt such energy. This is the way that things were meant to be, I see it now. You know what I like best? I love to see the expressions on their faces when they see Dhu'l-Fiqar and then, when the ghulams have pinned them by their shoulders to the sheet on the carpet bed ...'

'Oh, spare me the sordid detail!'

'Sordid? What do you mean? I am answering a call of Nature, Abu Bakr. A call of Nature, that as a True-Believer, I am obliged to observe. There is no monkery in Al-Islam. By Allah, were my life the price of their favours, 'twere no great matter. Does not Surah al-Baqarah say, "Women are a garment to you, and you a garment to them"? And does not the Hadith attest, "I fast and I break the fast. I pray, I sleep, I go in unto my women, beware! Whosoever deviates from my Sunnah is not among my followers"? These are my legally married wives, Abu Bakr. This is a call of Nature to which I am attending. I can't be held accountable for any untoward consequence.'

'And you don't feel sorry for these women?'

'Ha! I haven't yet found one I feel I can trust.'

'What about Shahrazad? What's to become of my daughter when she's delivered of her child?'

'I don't know. We shall have to wait and see. That will be up to Almighty Allah, be He exalted and extolled. You know that blackhead wife of mine, that stinking armpit did the runner on us – any chance of getting her back?'

'I shouldn't think so. But I have organised a wedding for tomorrow night and you are to be the groom. I found you a second wife, Shahrban.'

'Excellent! Where's she from and what's her name and what's so special about her? Is she a dark-eyed virgin aged about fourteen, chaste and fair, as lovely as corals and rubies, whom neither man nor Jinni has soiled and who never in all her days has lusted after male kind?'

'Expect those in Paradise, but no, she's pretty special. She's a dark-eyed girl, another daughter of mine – in fact, she's a blackamoor. Her name is Marjanah but you could call her Umm al-Ka's.'

'Mother of all Cups?'

'Umm al-Ka's meets Dhu'l-Fiqar – that should be quite a contest. She's besotted with you, Shahrban.'

'You said that about Shahrazad who has no eye that can look upon me.'

'Shahrazad, as we know, is a brazen hussy. Umm al-Ka's is a coy girl, over the moon at this chance to become the second wife of so prominent a man. Let's just hope it works out. I think you'll find that, in her own way, she's as interesting as Shahrazad.'

'No other woman could be as interesting to me as Shahrazad.'

'Wait till you see Umm al-Ka's.'

'You weren't here when the circus was in town,' whispers Abu Bakr to the stunned groom. 'What do you think? Lovely white teeth, hey – winning smile. Her father has given us a Jihaz of cooking pots, matting and bedding carpets. These, of course, will remain the bride's property in the event of divorce. Let the singing girls now trill their joy with Zagharit and Walwalah and beat the tabrets, while the wedding guests prepare to enjoy a banquet of delicious meats and sweetmeats. An orchestra will soon be here. Are you feeling well, Shahrban? You've gone a trifle pale.'

'I don't know this woman's family name.'

'Oh, men don't know much about women. A name is the least of our concerns. They falsify them. Now, don't drink too much of that Shiraz – you'll need to be on your game.'

Marjanah is very much her father's daughter when it comes to knocking back the beer and is soon excusing herself from the bridal throne every ten minutes.

'I have a bad feeling about this,' says the Shah.

'Shahrban, that's only because every man in this room so envies you! Why must you have all the luck, up here in the Sadr, the place of honour? It's time you two lovebirds left for the bridal chamber. Mind how you go! She's a bit unsteady on her feet.'

'She hasn't said one word to me all night.'

'Ah yes, but she keeps glancing towards your thighs. I can tell she's keen to give you a night you won't quickly forget. Satuq! Pishaq! Escort the Shah and his good ladywife to the bridal chamber. Better have the ladies-in-waiting join you, at least till you're up those stairs.'

'Hmm,' says Umm al-Ka's, 'dey done tol' me you 'ad a pecker 'n a haff. 'Zwhy Ah'm here. T'ing is, Ah cain't easy lay on diz big butter mine. Mind if Ah gits on top?'

And five hours later, 'Hey, come on boy, you tard? You tard or somepin? You tard awready? You ain't finish yet! Ah'm on give you one more frill 'afore dat sun come up.'

'Oh no you ain't. Satuq! Pishaq! This, I swear, is *my* blood on the sheet. It's true, I'm tired, Marjanah.'

'Seems like you done wrote a cheque dat yo ass cain't cash.'

Champ rarely quits when he's in front; champ never knows when he's beat; that's what made him a champ.

☾

Donkeys bray; false dawn at last and another night mercifully over.

Da'wah.

The Azan of the muezzin: according to the Hadith, 'A'ishah reported that when Harith ibn Hisham asked the Messenger of Allah, peace and blessings on him, 'O Messenger of Allah! How does revelation come to you?' The Messenger of Allah, peace and blessings on him, replied, 'Sometimes it comes to me like the ringing of a bell …'

Da'wah.

The cantilation of the Mervi call to Subh is a powerful, resonant call from a powerful, resonant baritone voice, using, in AD 823, the 'reading' of the 'reader' al-Qisa'i of Kufah – one of seven authoritative Qira'ah of al-Qu'ran that correspond, in the Sufic mind, to the seven levels of Heaven, the seven Ahruf of scriptural meaning, from the most bleedingly obvious to the most inner and obscure by which, according to the Hadith, al-Qu'ran was 'sent down'.

Da'wah.

The predawn call to Prayer from the muezzin resounding over Dar-al-Islam – in Egypt, a blind muezzin is preferred who cannot take advantage of the minaret's height to overlook neighbouring households – generally, in the noughties, either the reading of Abu Bakr Asim of Kufah in the transmission of Hafs or the reading of Nafi of Medina in the transmission of Warsh – has rung, like the ringing of an angelus bell, in the heart of many a visiting census-Christian enslaved by intoxicants but ever so physically fit and secularly street-smart, to divert him, briefly, from partner to recall, briefly, his parlous spiritual plight; but Shahrban has heard it too often, so it cannot serve the Shah as Da'wah.

Da'wah.

Now Dinazad from the Dingle (*Corca Dhuibhne*) – captured by Vikings, sold in the mercado of Cordoba – knows three druidic songs: a reel, a lament and a lullaby. Following 'disappearance' at the instigation of Abu Bakr, she has practised, long and hard, on the lament. Erse, coarse, harsh and sung in her sweet, unwavering voice – the words are of no more significance here than the Arabic words of al-Qu'ran.

Whoso wrote the lament had listened, long and hard, to seabirds. Whoso wrote the lament had fallen from Grace in the eyes of Christ.

Now Dinazad is heard to sing in the room next the Shah.

And the floodgates open.

Da'wah.

Bismillah, thinks the Shah, as my head lives, what have I *become?* Good God, I'm nothing but a sleazy pervert! Astaghfaru'llah! I pray Allah's pardon! In choosing before Shame Hell-fire, I am now fallen into both! Almighty Allah, be Thou exalted and extolled, O Ya Sattar, Veiler who veils the secrets of Thy creatures, Veil me! Hide me from retribution! O Allah, veil me with twofold veils, one from my Shame in this world, the other from the Flame in the world to come on the day of the Great Understanding when neither sons nor wealth will avail aught.'

He weeps and sobs and bites his hands till his tears have worn trenches in his cheeks and his gall bladder is like unto burst and the floor is awash and the carpet asoak. He weeps as the Companion 'Umar wept (recalling how he buried alive his baby daughter who, while the grave was being dug, patted away the dust from the Caliph's hair and beard). He cries till he can cry no more then sleeps and when he wakes, he cries again. This goes on forty days and forty nights and if the shades of his many victims could see him in such distress, why, they would be unmoved, which makes it the worse: for it is to women that we turn in our distress. To whom else, for comfort in our troubles, may we turn? In despair, the Shah, in his mind, searches through all the women he has known, seeking the one who might understand him, the one he might enfavour with his trust, but none measures up.

One day, he looks from where he sits on the floor to see Dinazad, chaste as a sheltered ostrich egg utterly untouched by man or Jinni.

'I'm going downstairs, Shahrban, to fetch me water. My throat is dry. Do you want anything?'

'Bring me a ptisane or medicinal water,' he says in a weak voice. And then, after she has gone, quietly, so she can't hear, 'I don't want to possess you, Dinazad. I have a feeling it may destroy your repose. I want the *repose* you enjoy. I want it for myself. I want to be *like* you. I trust you and would not suppose that you could make droppings or drippings.'

A breakthrough, yet thinking over it later from her perspective – another breakthrough – he sees what a selfish thing it is to have thought and cries even harder.

And after a further forty days, Abu Bakr appears in the door.

'Don't waste time on a sleazy pervert, Abu Bakr.'

'Don't be so hard on yourself, son. There could be no greater perversion than romantic love, of which you were never guilty. And if a sleazy pervert, what could be expected of a man whose father was a sleazy pervert and whose mother was a slag? Never blame yourself, son, always blame your parents; after all, it's their fault you are the mess you are. Now, I have two pieces of excellent news. First up, Umm al-Ka's just missed a mense so let's keep our fingers crossed; second, you have been selected from a prestigious field of applicants to speak on behalf of all Khurusan at a conference shortly to be held in Cordoba entitled "Silk Road: Implications for Future Ummayad Policy Directions".'

'What, is there a road somewhere made out of silk?'

'No, no. We are to think of the Silk Road as all those routes plying through Sogdiana, Ferghana and Bactria en route from Luoyang to Sur. When first I heard of this conference, I thought to myself,

Inshallah! I know the very man to give the Mervi perspective. So I took the liberty of putting forward your name and I am completely over the moon that you have been selected. It will ease you out of your miseries. It is wonderful news that you have seen the error of your ways but you just can't sit here, bawling your bloody eyes out the rest of your life.'

'I suppose no one feels sorry for me?'

'All the saviours are *very* sorry for you but the sooner you pack your valise and head off for a change of scene, the better. Why, it will do you the world of good! Our Stone must be black before it is white and only then can it become red. And think of this: you haven't had to bring a buffalo over a desert. There's a man down at the Khangah now who's just done that very thing. Off you go! Check him out. It will do you the world of good to get some fresh air.'

A crowd of boys stands outside the Khangah. The Shah can see the cause of the excitement is indeed a buffalo, a beast seldom seen in Merv. Urchins clamber over the big grey creature, lifting her legs to inspect her hooves, pulling at her tail, squeezing her bag; despite which, and despite her massive horns and head, she quietly chews the cud. A placid, domesticated creature, she is fastened to a lintel by a string through her nose. The Shah infers there are Zutt about, for the buffalo is a creature of the Zutt and only to be found in those hot swampy regions of the Caliphate where live the Zutt, but if this buffalo walked into Merv as seems likely, then either she came via barge to Ormuz thence Huzistan from Kashkar in the swamps of southern Al-Iraq, or from As-Sindh following river courses through Zabulistan, a land where dwells the feared White Hun, who has preserved independence, so that the province of As-Sindh is not connected to the rest of the Caliphate by land but only by sea.

The Shah eases by the buffalo's nose as the Pir opens the door.

'Shahrban! Salaam and Allah Yahdi-k, The Peace upon you and may Allah direct you in the right path. How's it going there, mate? Kurban-at basham – may I be your sacrifice, O Shadow of Allah? You look a touch the worse for wear.'

'Almighty Allah has dealt with me harshly, 'Ali Zindiq. I'm taking to the bottle. I must listen hourly to the giggle of the daughter of the vine as she gurgles from the gugglet so I was wondering, if I were to call by every day round now, would you be so good as to let me to fill my gugglet from Umm al-Ka's? That would save me a deal of cash as I mean to drink all day every day.'

'You're not quite ready for Umm al-Ka's. You're close, but not quite ready. Here's a man I'd like you to meet. I asked him to call by from Al-Iraq. He brought his buffalo over Dash-i-Lut, the Great Sand Desert, in celebration of which feat I *will* give you a tad of this Shiraz as you listen to his tale. There you go, Shahrban, to celebrate your progress, here's your first tipple from the Wondrous Cup. You're doing quite well on the path to salvation, for to use the language of Kitab al-Jafr, our Stone must be black before it is white and only then can it become red; *or*, in terms of Tasawwuf, as we're all in woollens here, the Soul that inclines towards Deeds of Kind must become the Soul that *repines* of Deeds of Kind before it can find Peace and Happiness. This Gypo has a tale and a half. Allah save and favour the king! Kubera! Tell the Shah your tale anent …'

Cartouche Chiseldorf

After the conquest of our Zutt homeland – an ancient fertile plain irrigated by the two great streams Sindhu and Mihran – the cruel and capricious Ummayad general Yusuf ibn al-Hajjaj removed my family with hundreds of other Zutt along with our buffaloes to Al-Iraq. Many Zutt remain among the marsh Arabs of Kaskar. My father Prasannacandra is descended from these deportees while my mother is the daughter of R. J. Wilson, a runaway blackamoor.

Zutt deserters from Sassanid armies had previously been settled in Antioch. Caliph Walid would later deport thousands more from Kaskar and from Antioch these Zutt were consigned by Caliph Yazid to Mopsus. Mopsus is on the Jayhan, and the Wadi of the Jayhan, which opens into the Gulf of Iskanderun, is congenial to buffalo, being a warm, mosquito-infested swamp. It was here in Cilicia Pedias on the Mediterranean coast that we 'Gypsies' – as we are called by Arabs who think we come from Egypt – developed our world famous mozzarella cheese. But we are not just makers of fine cheese; we are world renowned for cheesy music! We are the boys for your party. Uncle Lapa for years played tambour in the world-renowned Gypsy Kings.

This is going back some time but people still speak of the Gypsy Kings. They were primarily a wedding band catering as well to bar mitzvahs and such was their fame that boundaries drawn by men on maps meant nothing to them. They crossed in and out of the Caliphate through the Cilician Gates at will. No border guard ever wanted more than an autograph for his daughter. The Gypsy Kings were as popular over the Taurus in *Dar-al-Harb* as they were this side of the Taurus in *Dar-al-Islam*. They often travelled to play as far as Iconium and Homs. They once did a wedding in Constantinople! Uncle Lapa said they were treated there like kings – real ones. But Uncle Lapa was more than just a master of the tambour; he had a flair for languages. He could assimilate any tongue to such prodigious extent that he was known to the Barmakid wazir in the court of Caliph al-Mahdi as the one man in the Caliphate sufficiently fluent in Arabic, Sanskrit, Sindhi and the Prakrit of Ardamagadhi, as to be appointed court translator when the Qadi of Multan in the province of *As-Sindh* – a man of such justice he could decide causes between beasts and birds – conducted his inquisition into the beliefs of *Shvetambara*, a sect the name of which means in Sanskrit *al-Mubayyida*, or Wearers of White Raiments. I don't suppose I need conjure here of all places the reaction to this in Baghdad – not that the poor bloody Jains concerned had ever heard of *al-Muqanna*. They were just Jain ascetics who wear white robes and live in monasteries, as distinct from *Digambara*, fanatical monks who live alone, stark naked in the forests.

So Uncle Lapa was obliged to leave the Gypsy Kings and present himself to the court of the Qadi sitting at Valabhi in a place called Surashtra, across the Rann of Kutch to the east of the Caliphate, where an inquiry was to be held as to whether *Shvetambara* were *Ahl ad-Dhimma* – people entitled to protection under Islam and so a measure of autonomy on payment of *jizyah* and *kharaj* – or rebels like the Oghuz horde, loyal to the Khurasani Abu Muslim the Manichee, in which case they would need to be crucified.

The hearing was scheduled to take place during the Abiding Festival, a retreat held by *Shvetambara* during the Monsoon. According to Uncle Lapa it rained buckets on and off the entire time. Valabhi was a pleasant place, he said – swampy, humid, mosquito-ridden – not too far from the Gulf of Khambat on the Arabian Sea and just beyond the borders of the Caliphate in a place called Gurjarat. Gurjaras are nomads like the White Huns, who swept down the Valley of the Sindhu, made themselves at home in the Thar Desert and continued on through Rajputana into the Deccan. At the time of the inquest they were thought to be busy subduing the region of Benares.

The court heard that the monks of *Shvetambara* spend most of their time on the hoof, divided into *gana*, each led by an *acarya*; but during Monsoon when the ground pullulates in vegetative growth they dare not travel because, according to their faith, plants have souls. They call the soul the *jiva*. Indeed, their first monastic vow is *ahimsa*, a pledge to refrain from harming lifeforms. Uncle Lapa said they spend most of their days muttering *Airyapathiki*, their formula for atonement. You can't easily make a move without harming some lifeform or other.

People in the courthouse had to shout to be heard over the rain. Each session began with a chant in *Ardamagadhi* of the Jain *Namaskara Mantra*. The court then filled with White Clad monks along with local lay Jains – Zutt, Muhannas, Sammas, Lakhas, Lohanas, Nigamaras, Kahahs, Lorras, Bhattis, Thakurs, Burfat, Sahtas, Jokhia – tribal peoples from the Punjab, Rajputana and Gurjarat, plus a few Arab blow-ins, and every day this naked *Jinakalpin* with a piece of bone through his nose who didn't possess a fly-whisk, according to Uncle

Lapa, let alone a robe, and who would stand stark naked in the middle of the aisle in the posture of bodily abandon, *kayotsarga*, making a puddle on the floor as the water and ash ran down his legs. They roll around in the ash and mud to stave off insect bites. According to Uncle Lapa he smelled as if he hadn't wiped his bum in a thousand years.

At first they tried to ignore him. But he was a big man.

Namaskara Mantra is to the Jain the foremost auspicious thing of all auspicious things:

Homage to the *Arhats*!

Homage to the *Siddhas*!

Homage to the *Acaryas*!

Homage to the *Upadhyayas*!

Homage to the *Sadhus*!

Then following *Salat az-Zuhur*, the midday Muslim prayer, began the day's session.

Day One.

Representing *Shvetambara* was the learned *acarya* Haribadhra. He was a tall, bald-headed Zutt in white raiments who, according to Uncle Lapa, endlessly wielded a whisk-broom as he spoke. All *Shvetambara* carry a whisk with which to dispel mosquitoes – this more for the mosquitoes' benefit than for their own – and the whisk is their one material possession, aside from white raiments and a begging bowl.

Here was a problem with which to begin and an inquisition must begin somewhere.

'I'm told you are generally on the hoof,' said the Qadi, 'with no fixed abode. How then can you have monasteries and libraries? How could you be People of the Book, *Ahl al-Kitab*?'

To which Haribadhra replied, in the words of Uncle Lapa, 'That is a good question. *Shvetambara* do not possess books, it is true. We are utterly dependent on the generosity of our layfolk. *Dana*, the virtue of religious generosity, is the foremost virtue in a lay Jain and if we need to look at a sacred book we ask a layman to open it. We have many sacred books. We are not permitted to touch them ourselves through having dirty fingers. We cannot wash our hands through fear of harming animalcules.'

'Steer clear of the mosque! I am concerned as to whether or not you are People of the Book, *Ahl al-Kitab*. Now, you say you possess a book. Were you given a Revelation by a Prophet?'

'That is a good question. "Each nation has its Apostle" – *Surah Yunis* 10:47, and again, "We have sent forth other Apostles before your time, Mohammed; of some We have already told you, of some We have not yet told you" – *Surah Al-Mu'min* 40:78.'

'Hmm, I see you're well-prepared for the inquiry, Haribadhra. You speak as a *Hafiz*. I know of several *Huffaz* who do not understand Arabic and yet have memorised *al-Qu'ran* from the seven oft repeated verses right through to *al-Nas*: the Grace lies in the Resonance of the Utterance not in the Meaning of the Words. "We have made *al-Qu'ran* easy to remember but will any take heed of us?" *Surah al-Qamar*."'

'Our *Sutras*, like your *Surat*, Sahib, were first transmitted orally. They are known as the *Purvas* of the twenty-third Fordmaker *Parsvanatha*.'

'And have they been subsequently written as *al-Qu'ran* is written?'

'Just as *al-Qu'ran* on stones and palm leaves was arranged in one hundred and fourteen *surat*, so our *Purvas* are arranged in a canon of forty-five texts divided into five groups.'

'Rubbish. Bullshit.'

It was the Sky Clad Jain. In contrast to *Shvetambara*, whose initiates rip out their hair in five handfuls, this particular *Digambara* monk possesses, provocatively, the scorpion sidelocks of a prince. But no one has ever seen him before, no one can tell the court where he's from and in this he resembles the first *Jina*, the Fordmaker *Rishabhanatha*.

Indeed, he has the nipple-whorls of the *Jina* but no *srivatsa* – that characteristic, echinodermatous cicatrice over the bone between the pectoral mounds. In contrast to the White Clad monks who sit about in chattering groups, the Sky Clad monk stands alone. He has no whisk, no robe, no begging bowl and answers to a name which Uncle Lapa translated to me as Cartouche Chiseldorf.

The Sky Clad monk possesses *tapas* by virtue of his practice of *parisahas*, the twenty-two discomforts: hunger, thirst, heat, cold, mosquito bites, the nuisance of an unrestrained penis, of not being free to be aroused by women, of avoiding disgust at White Clad slackers, of blisters caused by constant trudging, of sore knees caused by meditative sitting, of drowsing uncomfortably on bare earth exposed to attack from jackals; the putting up with endless insults, the threats from patriarchs, the beatings from soldiers; of having while so proud a person to beg for slops and to drink from household drains; of having to exude complete contentment despite suffering frequent fevers and diarrhoeas; of having to put up with cuts from sharp grasses, of never being free to take a bath or wipe one's bum; of seldom receiving from ignorant Brahmins the respect that is one's due; of having to behave modestly while conscious of possession of supernatural powers; of having to avoid despair in the face of loneliness, self-doubt and suicidal depression – and then he makes an hypnotic gesture whereupon the rain ceased.

The courtroom fell silent. Above the song of a *cakravaka* bird spoke Cartouche Chiseldorf in a soft voice, the voice of one who speaks but seldom and then mostly to himself.

'This *Murtipujaka*, this image-worshipping, dogma-worshipping Wearer of White Raiments before you, deludes himself and yourself. The words of *Mahavira* as the twenty-fourth *Jina*, the last Fordmaker on this continent of *Baraka* in Rose-apple Tree Island are now lost and forgotten. Just as well! Over the centuries since his departure they would anyway have been corrupted through repetition. Just as well! He who would gain *moksa* cannot do so through reading books. He must somehow contrive to visit a continent where a Fordmaker presently lives. That is not too hard. Why, there are fifteen Fordmakers on Grislea Tomentosa Tree Island in the continent of *Hairanyaka*. I was there recently.'

'Remove this gentleman from court,' said the Qadi. 'I fear he is unwell.'

So Cartouche Chiseldorf was ushered from the courthouse into the monsoon rain which had recommenced but he came back next day wet as a beetle, according to Uncle Lapa.

Day Two.

'So you worship an idol,' said the Qadi to Haribadhra to open the second day's session. 'I see it in the temple over the road, a fifty-foot-high statue in sitting meditation with white enamel eyes. I see women pouring milk on it, dabbing it with sandalwood and saffron paste, anointing its legs with inguda fruit oil, waving incense and butter-lamps at it, draping it with garlands of kadamba blossom and laying before it mangoes and guavas with rice-swastikas on chaplets of *ketaka*. Are you aware that those who build idols will be asked on the Day of Judgement to bring them to life? When The Most Praised One, Blessings on his Name and upon his Family and Companion-Train, cleansed the *Ka'abah* of idols and icons, only one was to be spared: the icon of *'Isa* – on whom be The Peace! – in the arms of Our Lady *Maryam*; this, because these two, unlike others, did not cry out when they were born. This idol of yours, good monk – did it cry out when it was born?'

Haribadhra has observed there is a Buddhist abbot in the courtroom: he must have guessed something was afoot but what he didn't know, the Qadi was planning to catch him in a clever pincer-move. Even so he ignored, said Uncle Lapa, the Qadi's actual question.

'That in my view is an ordinary question. We believe that in *darsan* the worshipper is in the presence of a Fordmaker even as the Christian believes the body of *'Isa ibn Maryam* is in the bread and wine. Such delusions do no harm. The building of temples – *jina-bhavana* – and the *puja* of the *murti* of the *Jina* are for laymen. As monks we have no contact with the *murti* because of our dirty fingers. *Jina-bhavana,* the building of temples in which to house a *murti* of the *Jina,* is one of our seven *punya-ksetras.* It is to be encouraged.'

'Let me guess a few of the others,' said the Qadi. 'Feeding *Shvetambara?* Clothing *Shvetambara?* Providing *Shvetambara* with books and whisks? Giving *Shvetambara* accommodation?'

'You imply, Sahib, we give nothing back. That is not true! We allow men and women to practise *dana* and so free them from the tyranny of Brahminism.'

'Rubbish! Bullshit!'

Oh no: it's Chiseldorf again and today he reeks of *bhang.*

'On the continent of *Nandishvara,*' explains Chiseldorf, 'in the Island of Rejoicing of the Middle World – that island visited only by gods where they congregate to celebrate festivals – there are no fewer than fifty-two *Jina-bhavana* that have existed through all eternity, the *murtis* in which are regularly visited by *Siva, Vishnu* and *Krsna.* Just as well! There are indeed *Jina*-images, many of them images of future *Jinas* including that of the twenty-fifth *Jina Padmanabha,* in heavens and mountaintops throughout this universe which, as I attest through personal experience, is in the shape of a cosmic man standing with arms akimbo of variable width but fourteen *rajjus* high, a *rajju* being the distance traversed by a god flying for six lunar months at a speed of just under ten million miles per second. Given that the universe – which as I further attest is uncreated and eternal like the *jiva* – just as well! – assumes the form of a cosmic man, is it not perhaps pardonable to let these fools worship their *murti* of the *Jina* provided always the *murti* has *prana*? A *murti* must have *prana*. Has the Qadi seen the *murti* of the sixteenth *Jina* in the temple over the road? That *murti* has *prana*.'

'Have this gentleman removed please and see he does not return. He is beginning to annoy me.'

So Cartouche Chiseldorf was again ushered out to the temple over the road on this occasion but next day he was standing at the back of the court like a flamingo, said Uncle Lapa, on one leg.

In the meantime, the Qadi has motioned for the Buddhist abbot to take the stand.

'In the name of God, the Compassionate, the Merciful – can the Striver Buddhist give us an independent idol perspective?'

'He can. It is true as your Prophet says they should not exist.'

'And why not? Why should they not exist?'

'Because the *Jina* like the *Buddha* is a liberated being, freed from the Cycle of Death and Rebirth. The *Jina* through harsh austerities, like the *Buddha* through meditation, has become a *siddha*, a liberated soul, never to be reborn. To depict or sculpt a *siddha* as a being is a gross misrepresentation. The Fordmaker – *Arhat*, 'Conqueror', *Jina*, *Mahavira*, *Vardhamarna*, call him what you will – is only a human being like ourselves who lived and preached in the lower *Ganga* Valley one thousand years ago. He was an exact contemporary of the *Buddha*. Indeed the *Buddha* would appear to have been at one time a disciple of the *Jina*. *Mahavira* means "Great Hero", *Vardhamarna* "Increasing Wealth" – ideally the Jain layman will be as wealthy as the Jain monk is poor. The Jain layman is destined to be reborn at best in Jewel hellground: the Jain monk is heading at worst for the lowest paradise heaven. There he will be reborn as a goddess. The *Jina*, like the *Buddha*, was a married man of royal blood who fathered a son but, like the *Buddha*, he found this world as pleasant as a porter does his shoulder-yoke and, like the *Buddha*, achieved *kevala-jnana*; following which he wandered about stark naked for thirty years teaching. He was an *arhat*. There were many *arhats* then: who knows how many achieved omniscience? They were better days. But one thing is certain: we do not know what they looked like. No living man has ever seen an *arhat*. So we should not focus our minds on what we think they looked like because we don't know.'

'I have seen idols of the Buddha in Balkh – plenty of them up there. Big fat fleshy Greeks with curly lips; frightened the life out of me.'

'You won't see idols like that in Valabhi, Sahib. Footprints and wheels only.'

'And what does our White Clad Jain have to say to all this? Any comment?'

'I see the problem. The problem exists in all but one *murti*, the *murti Jinantasvamin*. *Jinantasvamin* was carved in the lifetime of *Mahavira* as a raincloud for the peacocks of the mind.'

'So you don't deny the problem?'

'I said I can *see* the problem! No one denies the problem. It all comes down to the needs of the layfolk and the skill of the sculptor.'

'Rubbish. Bullshit. A *murti* must contain *prana*. That is all.'

And so concluded the second day of the contest; Islam to win, Buddha the danger with Conquering Hero well back on the rails.

In the evening if weather permitted Uncle Lapa the Translator took a stroll round town. The Qadi and his wife, who hadn't long been married, retired each night to the bungalow early.

Day Three.

'Is it possible Haribadhra, that *Khatim ar-Rusul* the Seal of the Prophets, *Sayyid al-Kawnayn* Liege Lord of the Two Worlds – *Mohammed* our Most Praised One – is a *Jina*? I'm trying to be helpful.'

'No, not possible.'

'Well, it seems some people you just can't help. Why not?'

Now Haribadhra, according to Uncle Lapa, had obviously been dreading this moment. Since the fall of the *Rashtrakuta* Dynasty five years before, Valabhi lacked protection. It is the duty of a Hindu monarch to protect ascetics in his realm but Valabhi, now unprotected, was exposed to attack from Islam. Haribadhra muttered the Fivefold Salutation before he spoke.

'As I understand it, your Most Praised One was born two hundred years ago?'

'Two hundred and fifty to be precise – in the Year of the Elephant.'

'Too soon. You see, Sahib, *Shvetambara* live between the Rivers *Ganga* and *Sidhu* to the south of the *Vaitadhya* Mountains in the civilised region of this continent of *Bharata* which is one of seven continents on Rose-apple Tree Island in the Middle World at the centre of which rises Mount Meru. Human beings are confined to the inner two and a half islands of this Middle World, each of which contains seven continents, but only in the civilised portions of the continents of *Bharata* and *Airavata* – together with such portions of the continent of *Mahavideha* as lie beyond the *Kuru* enclaves – does Law of *Karma* apply. These are the the Places of Action and a *Jina* – a Fordmaker, an *arhat* – must be born in a Place of Action.'

'Then is not Arabia a Place of Action? I am continuing to try to be helpful.'

'The appearance of a *Jina*, Sahib, is not just a matter of being in the right *place*; it is a matter of being at the right *time*. Within the civilised portions of *Bharata* and *Airavata* – but not, significantly, within the Places of Action of *Mahavideha* where the Fordmaker *Simandhara* is always to be found – a time cycle operates, each turn of the wheel of which takes several billion years. As the wheel ascends, human life progresses through six eras: extremely Unhappy; Unhappy;

more Unhappy than Happy; more Happy than Unhappy; Happy; and extremely Happy: then as the wheel redescends conditions deteriorate: extremely Happy; Happy; more Happy than Unhappy; more Unhappy than Happy; Unhappy; and extremely Unhappy. Extremely Happy people live for many thousands of years, are born as pairs of male and female twins each six miles high with their every need – *ragas, toddy, pan* and the like – satisfied by Wishing Trees. Extremely Unhappy folk by contrast die as a rule in their mid-teens. They are reduced to one foot six and spend their entire lives picking through tips where they mate with everything they see.'

'So we move from paradise to hell?'

'Oh no. This is the Middle World of which I speak, Sahib, the world of humanity. Gods, it is true, live on *certain* islands in the Middle World but mostly in heavens of the Upper World and even in the highest hellground, which is known as Jewel hellground – this being the hellground to which are consigned unchaste human beings – as well as the interstitial spaces between Jewel hellground, the stars and the lowest paradise heaven. Heavens are divided into paradise heavens and heavens beyond the paradise heavens: there are twelve paradise heavens, fourteen heavens beyond the paradise heavens and five unsurpassed heavens that lay above the heavens beyond the paradise heavens.

'Goddesses, incidentally, live only in the first two of these paradise heavens; they can, for purposes of trysting with the gods, visit as high as the eighth. Peripatetic, interstitial, stellar and gods of the first two paradise heavens perform, in the manner of human beings, deeds of kind on goddesses. Gods in the third and fourth paradise heavens are content with fondling goddesses; gods of the fifth and sixth paradise heavens are content with kissing goddesses; those in the seventh and eighth paradise heavens are content to look upon goddesses; while gods of the upper paradise heavens where goddesses never venture content themselves with reminiscing over goddesses they have known. Gods in the heavens beyond the paradise heavens have no thought of goddesses while souls in the slightly curving space – that crescent moon above the Upper World – belong not to gods and goddesses but to liberated beings that dwell there in a state of omniscience and bliss.

'Below Jewel hellground is Pebble hellground and then, in descending order, Sand, Mud, Smoke, Dark and Extremely Dark hellgrounds. Individual hells are situated within these hellgrounds. There are three million hells within Jewel hellground, two and a half million within Pebble hellground, one and a half million within Sand hellground, a million within Mud hellground, nine hundred thousand, nine hundred and ninety-five within Dark hellground but only five within Extremely Dark hellground. Demons like gods are spontaneously born without the need for parents.

'Gods are too Happy and demons too Unhappy to achieve liberation. Rebirth as a human being is a necessary but insufficient condition. *Moksa* – liberation from rebirth – can only in practice be achieved during eras when human beings are able to conceive of its desireability; in practice, this means when they are either more Unhappy than Happy or more Happy than Unhappy. It is only during these two eras that Fordmakers are born.

'Now, seventy-five years and eight and a half months after the birth of the twenty-fourth *Jina Mahavira*, the continent of *Bharata* passed from a more Unhappy than Happy era into the present Unhappy one. Eighty thousand years must now elapse before the wheel again ascends into a more Unhappy than Happy era and not before then will conditions again comport with the birth of an *Arhat*. The last *Jain* to achieve the status of *Siddha* was the monk *Jambu* who had hands and feet like lotus flowers, the neck of a spiral conch, thighs like two elephant tethering posts and a waist that a woman could encircle with one hand.'

'Rubbish! Bullshit!'

'Oh, not him *again*,' protests the Qadi, face like an ox-eye. 'Enough is enough! Get this filthy creature out of my court and *keep* him out! What, in the name of Allah, the Pitiful, the Merciful, must a Qadi do to be obeyed in Valabhi? Guard!'

'Sahib, the man has *tapas*. He is a Jain *Vidyadhara*, an adept of *Durga* and *Vetala*. He makes himself invisible. No one saw him come in the door! He lives on wild rice-water. He never sleeps but merely rests in a state of *yoganidra*.'

'What nonsense! Clear the temple over the road of *pujari*, escort this gentleman to the temple, usher him in and shut the door, then lock it and throw away the key. I need to think over what I've just heard. My head is spinning. Court adjourned.'

Shaking his head, the Qadi goes off to debrief his wife over a meal of pickled pomfrets while Cartouche Chiseldorf is herded into the *jina-bhavan* opposite where sits in meditation with his big enamel eyes the great Valabhi *murti* of the sixteenth *Jina*.

Next morning when the temple door was opened on a cavalcade of rats, Cartouche Chiseldorf has disappeared but also missing is the fifty-foot-high idol of *Jina Santinatha* of which now all that remains is the greasy-grey, fruit-strewn plinth on which it sat.

Dissension immediately followed over who had committed this outrage. *Shvetambara* who venerate the sixteenth Jina as *Averter of Calamities* laid the blame squarely on the Qadi. The Qadi in turn blamed the lay Jains, though how they could have moved that *murti* without attracting his attention, given he was doing a deed of kind on his wife at or about that time in the bungalow adjacent to the courthouse opposite the *jina-bhavan*, is moot.

'Whoever made off with that *murti*,' said the Qadi, 'has made a blunder if he thereby supposes that I will be diverted from my inquiry.'

But in fact, according to Uncle Lapa, without the goodwill of the local lay Jains it became impossible to proceed. Within a week of the loss of the *murti* the courthouse was effectively deserted. Even *acarya* Haribadhra now declined to appear. Furthermore, the Qadi had to face the unpalatable fact that he lacked back-up; the nearest *hajib* was off at the *Hajj* and no *djund* in Surashtra; the Qadi could order in troops but they wouldn't leave *as-Sindh* during the Monsoon.

And the rain, according to Uncle Lapa, just kept pelting down. The Qadi began spending all his time with his wife, the tree to the creeper of his hopes. This, on or about the bungalow bed. They hadn't been married long.

'*Jina Santinatha* could hardly be an historical figure in my view.' The Qadi must now address either Uncle Lapa or his Zutt guard, these being the only people aside from the Qadi who now come to court; before going home the Qadi makes a point of turning up for half an hour each day. 'Yes, according to my calculations he would have had to have been born at least four billion years ago. Furthermore, he is not a god but a man. Therefore, *Shvetambara* in Valabhi worship divine men. The Wearers of White Raiments who worship divine men are Manichees and Manichees are the one sect to which we cannot grant *dhimmitude*. We can never accept the Manichees as "People of the Book". We detest them! Disgraceful rogues, they have it all wrong and yet have wheedled their way into every Book there is. We know that they have successfully wheedled their way into the *Gospel*, the *Tao-te-Ching*, the *Avesta*, and more recently the *Sutra in Forty-Two Articles*. Everything I see here in Valabhi leads me to conclude that they have long ago wheedled their way into the *Purvas*. Oh yes, I sense here the presence of an unseen foreign – what the hell is going on out there? What *is* that commotion?'

'The rain has stopped, Sahib. The Monsoon is over. *Shvetambara* are leaving Valabhi, walking slowly, eyes to the ground.'

'Bludgers! Drifters! We shall crucify every last one of them. My inquiry concludes tomorrow. I have come to my decision.'

Later that night a massive crowd of people descended on Valabhi. The Qadi, who'd been doing the business on his wife, rushed to his verandah to see thousands of Pratihara Gurjaras from Rajputana, most of them women, flocking down the street: townswomen of the merchant classes, braided hair and anklet-bells atinkle; coarse, dark, untouchable *sudras*, toddlers clinging to their hips; wives of the warrior caste on fine Arab horses fed on *ghee* and *kodrava*; and last but not least, Brahman ladies with necklaces of pearl, rocking in camel carts.

'Fetch me my elephant,' the Qadi said to his guard. 'I intend to get to the bottom of this. Have my translator ask these women where exactly they are going.'

As the elephant was having must glands painted in fresh vermillion, Uncle Lapa presented himself to the Qadi to give his account.

'A local woman had a pregnancy-longing, Sahib, for some dry and bitter myrobalan fruits. When her husband went off to search the forest, he found a *lingam* of Lord Siva. These ladies, recent Hindu converts, are on their way to anoint the *lingam* and beseech it for offspring.'

'As if this place hasn't offspring enough,' said the Qadi, mounting his elephant. 'How far out of town is this *lingam?*'

'Not far, Sahib.'

Goading his elephant, rut-juice pouring from its temples, the Qadi entered the forest. He saw before him a row of *swastikas* within a row of coloured chalks, and following them by the light of the moon discovered, to his consternation, a *murti* not unlike that of the sixteenth *Jina* that had disappeared from the *Jina-bhavan*. The gold leaf over the brass was gleaming in the moonlight. The big enamel eyes were shining brightly. But whereas in the *Jina-bhavan* the *murti* had been sitting in cross-legged meditation, here it was sprawled against a myrobalan tree, its arms hanging limp by its side, expression on its face like a stunned mullet and between its wide-open legs, a big black *lingam*, shaft propped on a stump.

'This is the work of Cartouche Chiseldorf,' observed the Qadi. As he spoke, a group of *Shvetambara* entered the chalked alleyway. They walked as always elephant-slow, eyes downcast to avoid lifeforms. As soon as they saw the women approaching the *murti* with the buffalo milk, they shouted and ran forward in rage, caring not where they trod. A tussle broke out with White Clad monks attacking the Hindu pilgrims with whisks and the pilgrims responding by kicking, screeching, spitting and scratching like monkeys. The Qadi, fearful for his elephant's welfare, ordered his guard to call a cease fire. The presence of the guard and the elephant between them restored the glade to order and shortly thereafter Haribadhra whispered something in Uncle Lapa's ear. 'He wants you to resolve the dispute, Sahib, in the courthouse. Will you do it?'

'Inshallah, I must await the *djund* from Multan. Oh, very well, why not?'

Day One, inquiry Two.
'And we say it is *not* a *lingam*! A *lingam* must be hard and firm! The member of the *murti* seems hard and firm but only because the *murti* is made of metal. Why the very *notion* of a *Jina* possessing a *lingam* is contrary to common sense. The *lingam* is anyway black. The *murti* concerned is covered in gold! If the Qadi would examine the *murti* of *Jina Parsvanatha* who stands in *kayotsarga* he would see the tiny member. The member of a *Jina* to a *murtipujaka* is always so tiny as scarcely to

be seen. This thing that extends so fat and thick to the *Jina*'s knee is the work of black magic.'

The Qadi's wife now entered the courthouse to sit, discreetly, in a rear pew – the first time she'd been seen in public, said Uncle Lapa, and while she wore a black *niqab*, she had nice eyes.

The Qadi was so nervous to see his wife in the courtroom he lost composure. 'Gypo, ask the Pratihara lady what she has to say, I mean, on the face of things, I don't like the notion of – well, you know what I mean.'

The pilgrim chosen to present the case for the *lingam*, as one of the few pilgrims who spoke Sindhi, was a high caste woman with a high-pitched voice and a brief but cogent message. 'She says, Sahib, that if you in any way attempt to interfere with their devotions to Lord Siva they will immediately inform their kinsmen so that ten thousand thousand Prahitara horse-archers will descend upon you to drive you from Gurjarat with a bloody nose and give your army the Mother of all Hidings.'

'Hmm. I see. Gypsy, inform Haribadhra I find the lady's argument compelling. I am forced to conclude that the member of the *murti* in the forest is indeed the *lingam* of Lord Siva. The Door of *Ijtihad* is now closed! Hamdillah, thanks be to Allah. Court will rise.'

An army of jihadis en route from Multan was heading down *Shatt as-Sindh* towards *Khalig Khambat*. They were destined to sail on to Canton through the South China Sea as reinforcement to a garrison sent thirty years before to Emperor Suzong by Caliph al-Mansur.

Night fell: exhausted by deeds of kind and now feverish, the Qadi slept. He woke, round midnight, to a full moon shining on him and the sweat pouring off him.

His wife had gone! He knew where to look for her.

Pausing neither to mount elephant nor rouse guard he ran into the forest. Sure enough, there she was, with the pilgrims, anointing and caressing that *lingam*.

When at last the army arrived in Valabhi, they razed the city to the ground on the Qadi's order. They destroyed all temples, Buddhist and Jain alike, leaving not one standing. They left not one *murti* intact. They devastated the holiest site of *Shvetambara* in the Middle World but White Clad monks had meantime drifted off to Rajputana and were not pursued.

As to the *murti* with the *lingam* of Siva? The enamel eyes had been stolen during a storm by Chinese boatbuilders, and what remained the Qadi smashed before his wife's very eyes with his own hands. He had the metal melted to a chamberpot which he took back home with him to Multan. But the *lingam* he was forced to detach from the *Jina* so as not to upset the *Siva-babas* and it is still there, stuck in the ground, garlanded and receiving daily offerings. Naked women dance before it from time to time.

Iranian Days (continued)

After he has told his tale, Kubera looks quite thoughtful. 'I met up with Uncle Lapa in Dimashq recently,' he says. 'We were sharing a jar of old Greek wine, a fat lamb, fresh fruit, flowers and confections near Bab Faradis. It was there he told me the tale I just recounted. After a second jar of wine, he thought for a time then said, "I often wonder if I did the right thing back there, Kubera. You see, I haven't been entirely candid. Cartouche Chiseldorf spoke a language I'd never heard, but I didn't want to lose my job after having been forced to travel all that way, and as Cartouche Chiseldorf always included a few words of Prakrit, I made it my business to fill in the gaps. This requires a deal of skill. What I conveyed to the Qadi in Arabic, as having come from the mouth of Cartouche Chiseldorf in Sanskrit, was actually my own construction, an improvisation based upon what I was hearing from Shvetambara, who spoke in a Sindhi vernacular and the Prakrit of Ardhamaghadi.

'Am I, in part, responsible, for the destruction of Valabhi?

We shall never know. But for whatever reason – and I put it down to bad conscience – I committed to memory the words that Cartouche Chiseldorf had spoken, which I kept in my head through recitation. I have no doubt it was a Scythian tongue as it sounded a bit like Latin. It was reminiscent of Dari, too, though with more subtle fricatives. In any event, whatever it was, I could make neither head nor tail of it. Then years later, while busking outside a caravanserai in Halab, a pair of round-eyes passed me by, speaking another tongue I'd never heard but which rang a bell. I chased after them and laughing off their pathetic offer of small change, inquired where they were from. They said they came from an oasis called Khotan in a place called Altishahr. They were speaking Khotanese. I repeated to them the words that Cartouche Chiseldorf had said in the court at Valabhi. They listened with interest and said it had to be a Khattite tongue, Luvian, a long-dead language not spoken for at least a thousand years though related distantly, as I'd suspected, to both Khotanese and Tokharian, as spoken in Kucha and Yar-Khoto. Tokharians – your forebears – are the ancestors of the Yuezhi, the Saka people who migrated from the region of Altishahr during the Han Dynasty to take over from the Greeks as the Kushan Empire, north of as-Sindh, in Tokharistan.

'I asked them if they'd be so kind as to translate Cartouche Chiseldorf's words for me. And this is what they told me that Cartouche Chiseldorf had said:

Murtipujaka are deluded. Shvetambara do not exist. Arhat does not exist. Mahavira does not exist. Baraka does not exist. Jambu does not exist. You are on your own. Moksa is burning off the karma. Hairanyaka does not exist.

Nandishvara does not exist. Jina-bhavan does not exist. Jiva, the soul, is blissful and omniscient, uncreated and eternal – just as well! It is merely obscured by karma that may be burned off with the twenty-two discomforts. There is no such thing as rajju. Murti does not exist. Prana does not exist.

'But as to that "Rubbish" and "Bullshit", it seems I wasn't far from the mark.

'It is all unreal, Rubbish, while at the same time it cannot be all in the mind, Bullshit. Amen.'

'Enjoy your fresh air?' says Abu Bakr, when the Shah reappears in the ark. 'And now you're off to Cordoba.'

'I never give presentations and I don't know the way to Cordoba.'

'Deacon Vermudo, who's feeling unwell, is on his way back to Compludo so he'll accompany you and you can take your two nabobs, Mubarak and Hilali. As your party will speak both Latin and Arabic, you have a choice of land or sea routes.'

'I'll take my two ghulams, thanks. Is there some reason you want me out of the way?'

'Is it any wonder you can't sleep when you don't trust anyone? Take whomever you like. Now, I've asked Dinazad to sing you a lullaby to help you get some sleep. She'll be here shortly, in fact, here she comes.'

'You know, if all the women in this world were like Dinazad, Abu Bakr, this world would be a better place.'

'If all the women in this world were like Dinazad, Shahrban, this world would cease to exist. So yea, thou speakest sooth.'

The journey to Spain is a nightmare. Vermudo is too ill to speak and actually dies on deck, off the coast of Ibiza, pleading for Celestial Medicine. In due course, the Shah's presentation in Cordoba, though well received, leaves him perplexed. Introduced to the rostrum by an Ummayad who seems to have confused Merv with Mashad, Shahrban delivers a carefully memorised speech on the textile trade with particular focus on qutn as native to Margiana, allowing ten minutes for questions, but there are none.

By forgoing notes, he can study his audience and soon detects a faint but growing smirk – distinguished from the smile, as involving only one half of the mouth and sexy in a woman, too, betraying a divided cortex (Shahrazad, needless to add, has it in spades) – and wonders whether they are laughing at his undivided eyebrow. Or do they think that what he says is ludicrous? No, they just find beguiling his unfamiliar Khurasani accent. This, the Shah proves by switching mid-sentence from mention of qutn as a thirsty crop to a consideration of the silkworm, a topic on which he can extemporise having kept them as pets as a boy: how eggs must be preserved cool, hatchlings warm and moulters hungry; how the worms themselves, on leaves, must neither be too close together nor too far apart; how, after moulting, they must be sparsely fed but when fully grown copiously so on fresh-picked mulberry leaves which may be neither dusty nor withered; and of how they are so very sensitive towards any untoward noise that they must be forewarned, in a quiet whisper, of any stranger to a village.

The smirks do not broaden at the jeu d'esprit. Indeed, they appear to have fixed at a rate independent of what is being said. Dropping silk, the Shah moves on to a confession of his distrust for women but no one demurs, even though he mentions the consequence, in a confessional aside.

He concludes it wouldn't matter what he said and he is right. He could say anything. His audience responds, not to what he says, but to the way in which he says it. His quaint, broad Khurasani accent amuses these Cordoban sophisticates. And given the effort he's put into his Arabic of late, this comes as a blow, so that after the silence that follows his presentation he bursts into tears. The audience, touched by this unexpected gesture, if a trifle discombobulated, rises to its feet in loud applause, on the assumption that all Khurasan would do as much.

Later, directed to a dinner being held in a noisy bodega in the barrio, the Shah – longing for dates and cream – is fed fish soup, palmitos, asparagus and spicy sausages at a long, wax-burned table warmed by braziers of olive pressings. The tables are awash in wine so the Shah quickly becomes garrulous and charming, but on return from a visit to the loo finds himself excluded from conversation, the women now shrinking from his every solicitude, the men ignoring him completely. Because he is, au fond, an 'Abbasid vassal and the black 'Abbasid flag is here accursed; nor may mention be made of Caliph al-Ma'mun during Friday prayers.

Staggering down a lane on his way home, the Shah sees, displayed on a wall, a poster of Ziryab. It advertises a chain of hairdressing salons and features a lean, black cassia-pod of a man wearing a fur-trimmed cloak; all teeth, hairbangs and earrings. Feeling obliged to rip the thing down, the Shah gives the top left-hand corner a sharp tug, noticing as he does so that someone else has beaten him to it. But to scratch this poster off the wall you would need one of Ziryab's patent eagle quill picks.

The Shah and his ghulams have rented a two-storey townhouse that is built, Roman-style, around a patio. The murmur of water sprouting from bocas onto naranjos would be the sound of Cordoba if only Cordobans themselves could be persuaded to shut up for five seconds. From a tile-floored upper storey the Shah can survey the grey-green maquis – ilex and cork oak, cistus, lavender, lupin, myrtle and arbutus. The river below, with its sandy shallows is, like the buildings on the nearside bank, light brown. The Shah can see a group of muleteers – yunteros – watering teams of black mules. As they do so, they chat up women who are washing clothes on a sandbank. It is odd to see people watering mules and washing clothes in the middle of the night but Cordobans, as the Shah is learning, prefer siesta to sleep. The conference goes into recess every day after noonday prayer with the next session scheduled for 3 am the following morning. Having made his contribution, the Shah intends to boycott remaining sessions but as he's been obliged to lease the townhouse for a minimum three months, he is left with a question of what to do. Possessed of no inner resources, he could always get stuck into his toothpicks, but why not, instead, seize an opportunity to do something a bit different? The idea is Pishaq's, Shahrban only ever having had the one idea. Why not become a labrador, say, and hoe olives in the bancales? This would allow the Shah to learn what it meant to do a hard day's work. Or if that lacks appeal, why not study? Why not, say, learn to sing? Ziryab has a conservatory in which students are taught to sing; Ziryab, who hands across his 'ud to be untuned by an audience prior to recital – a student of Isaac of Mosul, the first to systematise Arab harmony, the Mystery at the heart of Islam, it being impossible to listen to an expert cantilation of al-Qu'ran without horripilation.

The Shah is no sooner snoring on the carpet than he wakes to a noise would freeze the very blood. He can hear, somewhere close by him, a woman being tortured.

No! A thousand times no! A thousand and one times no!

The groaning and moaning steadily increase but the Shah is on his feet and stumbling as a terrible, agonised screaming begins.

In the bedroom he irrupts to see what he takes to be a horseshoe arch over another horseshoe arch but closer inspection, in the dim light, reveals it to be Satuq, doing the business on a local drunken blackhead.

'What's your problem?' spits this blackhead, face red as a rose. 'Can't we enjoy privacy? Would you please respect our privacy?'

Mumbling apology, Shahrban retreats and goes back down the hall to stare at the ceiling till dawn.

And when he wakes at midday, he finds Satuq and Pishaq have decamped, taking with them all the cash.

Toto abandonado. And how he trusted those ghulams.

When, after a few days, Shahrban goes out on the streets to beg bread, the first vehicle to appear is an ox-cart, owned by a man in search of labradors.

'Hey Eyebrows,' says this man. 'Yes, you! Salaam. You lookin' for work?'

Heart pounding, the Shah clambers onto the cart which is then driven over a bridge making for jarales, a heath covered in gum cistus, whither converge many carts, for a morning wolf-drive. Along with Visigothic hermits, the area contains marauding wolves in the habit of descending nightly on the campina and killing sheep. Guard dogs, obliging the lesser ablution every time they are touched, are thin on the ground, so it is thought only a matter of time before the wolves attack a pueblo.

The beaters – Shah excepted, all able-bodied, unemployed local farmhands – dine that night on chickpeas, rice, bread, olive oil and wine and, at first light, after a slug of aguardiente, head off shouting and bashing at the cistus.

'Hevelow!' shouts the Shah, joining in. 'Hevelow! Rumbelow! Hevelow! Rumbelow!' But he can't keep up. He is not as fit as the others and is soon left behind. By nightfall he is bushed – lost, defeated, abandoned – it doesn't get much worse but worse is to come. He finds a rough track that seems to go nowhere – up and down through the forest –and pursues it till exhausted, whereupon he falls flat on his face to weep.

Come midnight, he hears the sound of creatures approaching. They are not wolves but boars, black as the ink in which are written the sacred words of Allah, rummaging round the forest floor looking for acorn mast. When they scent the Shah, they begin running towards him. Affrighted, he scampers up a small cork oak, ripping open his leg.

He is now back in the red band. He knows no human being can help him. He needs God's help but in order to reach God he needs a saviour, a semi-divine intermediary between himself and God and semi-divine status tends, in an Iranian mind, to be hereditary.

As if we didn't have problems enough. But we came here for a conference on the Silk Road. So let us now search back along the Silk Road, retracing our steps through the Ummayad Emirate to the 'Abbasid Caliphate, disembarking at the Mediterranean port of Sur perhaps, across the deserts of Syria and Parthia at camel-speed though Khurasan, on down through Kashgar and Khotan to Dunhuang, an oasis-pass at the eastern end of the Tarim Basin, conflux of all roads from India, China, Gandhara and Sogdiana, where ferment of Indian, Syrian, Iranian, Hellenic and Judeaic soteriologies has given birth to surely the sweetest saviour that ever this world has seen: Kuan-shi-yin, catechist of Amitabha Buddha, Mithraic God of the Pure Land. As Chin Dynasty p'u-sa, Kuan-shi-yin has both moustachios and beard; by the time of the Ming, the 'white-robed Guanyin', a porcelain murti, will be female, though significantly lacking the characteristic lotus feet of a Ming lady.

Now harken to the words of Dharmaraksha of Dunhuang:

'Whatever strife a man is in, should he invoke Kuan-shi-yin, Kuan-shi-yin will immediately harken to that man and free him from his strife. Whoso invokes Kuan-shi-yin is safe from fire and water. Whoso invokes Kuan-shi-yin is proof against robbers and demons. If a condemned prisoner invoke him, the blade that is meant to decapitate that prisoner will break upon the prisoner's neck. The convict who invokes Kuan-shi-yin will be delivered from his shackles. If, in a caravan of travellers, there is one devotee who invokes Kuan-shi-yin, the entire caravan will scape all dangers, because of that devotee. With Kuan-shi-yin, there is no need to supplicate with elaborate ritual: it suffices to cry, in distress, from the bottom of one's heart, "O Kuan-shi-yin!" Whoso invokes Kuan-shi-yin is proof against lewdness, spasms of hatred, unintelligence and callous and jealous behaviour. Every woman who has recourse to Kuan-shi-yin to attain a child – whether gifted boy or charming girl – will see her wish fulfilled. All men should have recourse to so powerful and benevolent a p'u-sa as Kuan-shi-yin! His desire is solely to work towards the salvation of all sentient beings. To this end, he will certainly assume any form he deems necessary, appearing now as Buddha, now as p'u-sa, now as Brahma, now as Indra, now as Vaisramana, now as Vajrapani, now as king, now as brahman, now as monk, now as a man of the people, now as a nun, now as a woman of the people, now as a child – in short, whatever form he feels will be best heeded by the individual he means to save. Invoke him!

'Have every confidence in him! If you have been thrown into a pit of fire, invoke him and the brazier of coals will immediately change into a cool pool. If, having fallen from your ship into a tempestuous sea, you are surrounded by sharks and seamonsters, invoke him, and the waves will refuse you and the sharks and seamonsters reject you. If, in falling from the height of a mountain, you invoke him as you fall, your fall will be suspended and you will remain in mid-air as the sun is suspended in the sky. Invoke him, and the wicked ones preparing to destroy you will fail in snatching a single hair of your head. In his name, a brigand who would seize you will become humane and compassionate, no executioner will have the will to strangle you, all bonds and shackles will be unable to confine you and no poison will sully you. Every charm cast upon you will be returned against its author, all tigers and serpents will avoid you; floods, tempests, sandstorms and avalanches will do you no harm.

'For those who invoke Kuan-shi-yin, in whichever world of the six they may dwell, the way of punishment will be closed and they will be reborn, not in the hells, nor in the beast-world nor in the world of hungry ghosts, but in the Pure Land of Amitabha Buddha, there to be delivered from illness and old age.

'O penetrating, pure and compassionate regard of He who Listens to the Sufferings of this World, Kuan-shi-yin! O Light without admixture of Matter! O Sun of Wisdom piercing all Shadow! O You whose Compassion illuminates all beings like Lightning, whose charity covers all beings like Soft Dew! O Kuan-shi-yin, who extinguishes Hatred and Discord, Dispute and Litigation! O You who gives Peace to man, even in battle, may we think of you, Kuan-shi-yin, unceasingly! May we never doubt you, so Pure and so Saintly, Kuan-shi-yin, be you our Support and our Strength! Comfort and Protect us, in danger and in pain, in suffering and in eventual death! Help us to fulfil our duties! O You who considers all beings with your Pity, O Ocean of Compassion, we invoke You!'

The Shah has never heard of Kuan-shi-yin, but he is a man of the Silk Road and his cry is heartfelt and his remorse real. He thinks, spontaneously, of all the khutbahs he heard back in the Khangah as he cries from the depth of his massive heart – the largest heart, remember, in all this world of the six – using a voice that becomes the world's loudest voice and is heard in Mauretania, 'Yazata Atar! Ya Muqanna! Yesu Jidu! Santinatha! I know my crimes are as black as the bristled swine below me on the forest floor but I *so* regret them! Let me not find mercy here before I have tasted Happiness! How long this toil and torment wherewith I am liver-smitten? Let me not die here, unless it be written from All Eternity by the Will of the Creator of Souls. I swear, by the irrevocable oath of triple divorce, I shall *never* do a deed of kind again! And if thou slay me, I shall be a martyr on Allah's path.'

Immediately – *immediately!* – the swine scatter as a man comes galloping up on a white horse. He is a warrior, returning with a sackful of severed heads from a skirmish in the Asturias. The horse breaks to a canter, then, frothing and sweating, to a trot, as it underpasses the Shah, who leaping from his perch follows his saviour with a sword all the way back to town.

He has to jog, though, and it is ten miles to the Puento Romano, through chug-chug of nightingales and eventually, down through goat bells and dwarf iris onto a cobbled mule track. He never ran so far or fast in his entire life.

Cordoba seems deserted. The horseman, bypassing the Damascus Palace, stops at the fence of the Rusafah Palace, set amid al-Rusafah, the garden in which al-Hakim crucified, one by one, three hundred rebels – al-Hakim, poet-emir who put down revolt among his concubines by writing them beautiful poetry; al-Hakim, who crucified the father of a rebel leader with the severed head of his son hanging off his neck.

Dismounting, the horseman takes the severed heads from his sack and impales them, one by one, on the upright bars of a metal railing, lifting each as high as he can, then thrusting it down spitefully in a splatter of fluid neck first.

The Shah, complacently watching, is enjoying his first-ever runner's high; the strange languor produced by the body's own opiates. He would be unaware that his member is badly bruised. The Arab horseman then mounts his horse and departs while the Shah wanders down to inspect the severed heads.

OO! Cramping up in the right calf like a man being crucified or impaled, woo! Ho! Toes up! Haaaa – that's better; phew.

All the heads have a Saminid eyebrow and the closed eyeballs move in unenlightened sleep as the faces wince and grimace. They have something they need or want badly to say but the Shah can't lip read and the heads can't speak.

Picaninny dawn: the muezzin, voice trained by Ziryab, cries the Azan, the Call to Prayer, using the reading of Qurra 'Abu 'Amr al-'Ala' of Dimashq and the severed heads turn towards the phallic minaret of La Mezquita which is built on the site of a Christian cathedral which was built on the site of a temple to Janus, two-faced Roman god who looks both forward and back, the god of doorways and transitions.

Friday today, thinks the Shah, and I really should find my way to the mosque as I have much to be grateful for.

The Sahn of La Mezquita is planted with orange trees, naranjos, a native of South-East Asia. Patio de los naranjos, the dark leaves of the naranjos, the flitting butterflies among them, the great marble lavatory cistern supplied with al-Abarik, the ewers for Wuzu, all so peaceful and natural. Catching a glimpse of the cunt-like Mihrab beyond the Zulla, the sanctuary, which is seventy metres square and divided into eleven naves and twelve bays by one hundred and ten columns pilfered from the Temple to Janus and San Vicente's Cathedral, of marble and jasper and porphyry, buttressed, above the abaci, by Visigothic hexafoil arches in two tiers, like a harem of rose brick and white stone arses mounting arses of white stone and rose brick, the hypnotic potency of the illusion is such that the Shah swoons, falling forward on his face impelled by gravity and, striking hard his forehead, is rendered insensible.

Forbidden Transitions from Crystalline Kingdoms

Can you hear me?

Excuse me, sir, can you hear me?

The captain has turned the seatbelt sign on.

Oh.

Al Morrisey – short, powerfully built Jew with the hard face of an Irishman, now in his early sixties, balding though concealing it by shaving his head in the manner of a Carthusian monk, still running the City to Surf in under one hundred minutes, just – is cramped aboard an Airbus A340-600, flight VS 201 that left Sydney 1435 in some long-distant time zone and is now thirty-eight thousand feet over Siberia skirting Kazakhstan en route from Honkers to Heathrow. The cabin lights are turned off on this *Voyage au Bout de la Nuit*. Al pushes up the porthole shutter, but nothing to be seen out there, Al.

Total estimated flight time in durance vile 23 hours 50 minutes.

Economy, but good enough for billionaire Chuck Feeney, who part funds the News Hour with Jim Lehrer, only decent thing on TV, seat over a wing, e-ticket booked the day before on impulse.

Return flight available 9/10/07 no worries.

Prostate not too bad – able to induce a relieving micturition at the disabled toilet in the Honkers lounge and of such is sexagenarian happiness. There have been occasions after a longhaul – and this may be your last, Al – when you pissed and later ejaculated blood and Pastel complained of the taste. Benign geriatric prostatic hypertrophy. You do not leave your window seat for the duration. Even the thought of someone waiting outside to use a toilet inhibits and the public urinal was ever out of the question, which curse has afflicted your entire life and debars all thought of journey on the trans-Siberian railway or the Chinese Silk Road tourist track that now links Urumchi in Sinkiang with Almaty, capital of Kazakhstan, through the Dzungarian Gap. And you've been reading voraciously, over the past decade, of Central Asia with its religious pammixia.

In your forties you could oft get a flow going on a plane by reciting some half-forgotten formula such as 'methyl, ethyl, propyl, butyl, amyl, hexyl' or 'Nemu tahasa bhagavhato arahato sammu samuhubdhasa' with the concentration required to recall a fading sequence serving to relax the sphincter, but nowdays the dispiriting dribble that so often cuts off mid-flow will dampen your crotch if not mopped carefully with tissue or kerchief at session's end. Memories of heading home with urethritis, struggling to keep the mind off all thought of Pastel's gorgeous legs in those last, long hours between breakfast and touchdown during which female passengers arrogate the toilets to moisturise their faces. You have, at times, come off a plane bleeding from every orifice like the victim of a haemorrhagic fever, but nowdays you hydrate to straw-coloured urine the day before a flight and drink nothing aboard except that welcome glass of wine with each dinner.

So here you are on a longhaul, man with no income of which to boast, racking up the credit on the weak Australian dollar. Tell us why you do it, Al; come on, tell us why you subject yourself, at your own expense, to economy longhaul. Well, suicide is not an option: you're committed to care of your mother, who's now in her early nineties and you can understand why Primo Levi threw himself down the stairwell.

That freebie to London via LA! New Zealand Airlines. Told you wouldn't need a visa.

No one ever visits this great land without visa! Don't you want to see Disneyland?

Travelling in transit on to London, only passing through.

Passin' though *LA*! You *kiddin'* me?

No transit lounge: they had to put you out on the street where you could have disappeared and resurfaced in an amnesty. You could have become American, like one of Pastel's old flames. He told you, unprovoked, that he'd been her lover but she couldn't recall him. He actually used the word 'lover' to you, the cunt. His drummer, emboldened by her reputation, raped her. That, she did recall, and saw fit to complain to you he'd torn her jeans and wouldn't kiss her.

You could be working LA today instead of cruising the seas with the Paddy Shaw Showband.

Imagine trying to transit the US today without visa!

Strange dream just then concerning ... *Persia*?

Why *Persia*?

Why dream?

Why sleep.

In *Wajd*, enlightenment, there are no dreams. No more nightmares, no more psychic conflict to resolve. Ah Lost and by the Wind-Grieved Ghost, come back again!

Pastel was reading that book when you left, *Co-dependent No More*.

I cross all bridges with joy and ease. The 'old' unfolds into wonderful new experiences. My life gets better all the time! I am SAFE! It's only CHANGE!

Speaking of which, it's hard to sleep, sitting up for twenty-four hours across innumerable time zones when the man next to you hogs the mutual armrest. May he be afflicted with the deep-vein thrombosis. You'll be sweet, Al, though your time will surely come, because you ran for nearly one hundred minutes on Sydney's recent holy day, the second Sunday in August. *Very* nearly, *far* too nearly; ninety-nine fifty-eight to be precise, much mirth over this on the Tuesday (Gehurr gehurr, cue Disney Goofy laugh) but no one with whom to share it because you now do the run, more precisely the jog, alone. There was a time when three blond children, even Pastel would join in, but now they are too busy. Twice, in recent years, with a son and grandson, but now you run alone with sixty thousand people.

Oz does the body well – credit where credit is due.
The only two Australians universally admired even ...
Bzzz ... Robbie McEwen and Stewie O'Grady?
Correct.

The City to Surf has become a useful marker of your physical decline. You run a minute or so slower each year, which doesn't sound like much, but over thirty years amounts to half an hour. You would like to train harder but injuries – relentless minor injuries of knee, calf and thigh – see you, inevitably, running less as you tend towards the minimum training necessary. You have knees damaged from motorcycle accidents and cattle kicks on the *shtetl,* and you need your legs for bass drum and hi-hat, so you run the minimum possible. You walk with a limp but run without and swim from the Point to Alley Break daily; kayak off Deeban Spit; no Chris

McCormack, you are nonetheless Shire dinky-di, holding off the ill-effects of your alcoholism with nutrition and exercise. Each morning you check your pulse and feel if you could palpate your liver with your fingers, which if you can't – under your right ribcage – you may have a drink with lunch.

And sometimes you may say your prayers, but conscious no one is on the line.

If prostate would permit, you could squeeze an extra two minutes by getting to the front of your start instead of slipping down onto Park Street at the very back of *les poursuivants*, but you could never have been a professional athlete as you can't provide a urine sample; you could never urinate on demand. You can't use a men's urinal, even if no one is about – they might come – preferring solitary walks in places you could whip out the old boy unobserved. Pastel says this indicates having been sexually abused as a child, but isn't circumcision sexual abuse? People attack the Aborigines for sexually abusing their children but they're only children themselves and handling the penis of a twelve year old to cut it with a flint or a razor *is* abuse. It depends on definition, but then again, you have the snapshot. You took a snapshot and a vivid one. You were in the bath. Was the bath on a kitchen table? The bath, a small plastic affair, had deep scratches at the distal end. You even recall the gist of what you said, in mild protest.

'What does it matter? It's only used to make wee wees!'

The snapshot is of Grandma – your mother's foster mother as you recently learned on sighting the paperwork – head turned to one side stifling a laugh. Unexpected. You do recall your gorgeous mother – had she even *seen* that paperwork? – plying your glans with oil; some problem with the annular scar where the shaft met the glans, not to be confused with What the Priest Did. Why do we not fight them off? Whatever the motivation, you took a snapshot. You can still see Grandma shaking with mirth as, flicking through your album, you can see the priest's pupils dilate. Better leave the bloody thing alone. Let the skin adhere to the shaft.

The future casts a shadow on the past.

Was this snapshot taken before or after that snapshot of chasing naked blondes? Pastel says a premature sexualisation betrays sexual abuse and she should know because what a face she came home with that day she finally realised she'd been raped, after the conference with the prison dykes. She'd thought it was all perfectly normal and who's to say it's not? Some men are doing life for what others walk away from and boast of. It was all she'd known, poor girl – no one misses a slice from a cut loaf. They were hairless blondes you chased, Al, you being so dark and hairy. Striving for hybrid vigour in the offspring, hey. Your father ran off with a blonde and you would run off with a blonde and there they all were, romping round as in an Escher woodcut. Clones. It was an underground venue with red walls, unsavoury type of place, very likely a nightclub. Blondes prancing in a circle – all as comely as the pocket-Venus Pastel or the tall, statuesque Pretzel – but would you even have *seen* a naked blonde at this age? You wonder what you would have done with one, had you managed to catch her. Do we need to be taught? Women seem to move their heads up and down instinctively *et de virtute locute clunem agitant "ego te ceventem, Sexte, verebor?"* Juvenal. What Marcus Aurelius calls 'the attrition of membranes' is an instinct, or appetency, but you took a snapshot of that dream, only dream ever produced one. So it must have significance.

This was back in first class with Rene Rivkin at Rose Bay Infants. What a sweet boy. What a charming child! And yet, like Pastel, apparently despised his own appearance. When you read of his suicide in his mother's Darling Point apartment after prolonged, public disgrace, with his wife Gayle having given him the broom after thirty-plus years of marriage and five kids, you wished, on learning how he cried all day at the thought of Silverwater, that you could have put an arm around his shoulder, even as he once put one round yours the day you fell over on the asphalt under the Moreton Bay figs and took the bark off your knee. You do recall his intelligent smile even as a boy of seven; this, long before the Joe's Café disbursement of gold Rolexes. You can't recall another classmate from then but you recall Rene and there he is, looking down and to his right, lost in thought, as though thinking of all the money he intends to make – and don't they all do it? – insider-trading. He's just in front of the blackboard. Always precise, the snapshot, in its relative positioning, detail and angle. Rene had an unusual name and what a sweet, intelligent face under that optimistic mop of curly hair. What a pair of sweet little, bright little, cute little Jewish boys, the pair of you.

So, is it over with Pastel? It is not looking good. You think you've caught her at the very moment of blowing out the pilot light.

... took a snapshot ... very moment ... that *cheesy* look ...

Seem to have gotten yourself the sack after thirty-plus years with three kids to add to your preceding four and they would all do it if they could. It is not just Gayle and Pastel. Men be warned! If they can do it, they will do it. The kind of man they needed to become financially independent has become a trial to them. It's a question of having the necessary. Anita Keating did it – tired, no doubt, of hearing the words 'John Howard' over the breakfast table. One stockbroker, one politician, one jazz percussionist – all best in class but rendered obnoxious and tedious through ostracism. Pastel says the trouble with you, you remind her of poor old Gunnar, another righteous man done down. How she hated her father! And through your whingeing it's as though he's come back from Cooma to disapprove of everything she does. The way you see it, all old Gunnar ever did was complain about Aussies tealeaving tools and he didn't like Bob Menzies and thought men should be in charge of women. A married man cannot shrug his shoulders at injustice. That's what women don't understand. They would like you to be Christian but only when it suits. Not in bed. They cherry-pick the ethics. What married man dare ask the Lord to Cleanse the Thoughts of his Heart! Anita, a former Dutch air-hostess, has access to the parliamentary pension and if they have the necessary, they will do it. Men be warned! It's only because of your mother, Al, you have the necessary here. Ten-plus years of caring for her and this is your pay off: divorce.

Your mother loves you dearly. She's been generous towards you. You love her dearly in return. At times, you were angry with your father having abandoned you with a dumb showgirl, but what a *heart*. What *anima*, what *spiritus*. What *psyche*, what *pneuma*. What *Nafs*, what *'Aql*. Decrepitude has attenuated your mother's legendary *anima* while dementia has destroyed her minimal *animus* yet her *spiritus* remains strong. She often says, 'I love you, darling,' over and again, and not just to you: to anyone. It led to misunderstanding in the hostel. Demented men were found in her close company. Along with 'I'm sorry', it is the one phrase she can still utter fluently and she says it with such intensity that no one could be in any doubt but that she means it. Of course, it helps her survive but she has acquired, through loss and suffering, what Isaac of Ninevah called 'the merciful heart'. You often see it manifest in dying folk. The trouble is, keeping someone alive as long as medically possible is tantamount to slow, protracted torture. And as long as you countenance that, you will be complicit. And if you refuse to countenance it, you will be charged with murder.

She was such a warm, beautiful woman, so popular, so very full of love and verve and yet you, her only son, are an anthropofugal solitudinarian. What happened, Al? During her pregnancy, your father left her for a blonde, arguing you weren't his son at all – it was wartime so allowance must be made – and you were raised by grandparents until you were six. In those days you seldom saw your mother, except in the papers, or heard her, except on the radio, because you were too young to visit a theatre. She partied hard but when, from time to time, she'd reappear to shower you with gifts and kisses, how your heart would ache again when she'd gone again. Not that your grandparents didn't treat you well and love you dearly; it's just that your mother was so effusive. Quite an actress and still an actress. Popular with the AINs who say she has 'personality'. Won an acting scholarship to the Royal something-or-other in London at eighteen but her foster parents wouldn't let her take it up. In her mid-thirties she reappeared with a man she'd married for security – so she said – though there must have been more to it than that, because they stuck it out. You had to go live with them. Well, you didn't mind living with her, but you weren't too sure about him and the feeling was mutual. You were in the habit of getting into her bed after he'd gone to work, for cuddles. Snap! He returns one day unexpected to find you in bed with his wife. The face in the doorway is not a happy face.

So she made bad marriages and cheated on both her husbands. No detail of her love life now remains unknown to you because she confessed all, as one does to a new lover, early in dementia. Dementors be warned! So warm and instinctively seductive, so beloved by her grandchildren, who cannot now, regrettably, find the time to visit her, she probably loved you more than anyone else. Poor creature, stripped now of all human dignity. She has, as Nora observed of Joyce, a very dirty mind. Quick off the mark at the hostel with off-colour suggestions, where her loving nature made her popular with staff and saw old men fighting over her, what few there were. Now she's in the nursing home they're mostly bedridden. The fact is, great female beauties cause collateral damage in their young. Pastel is no different. That decade living with your mother as a boy has left you badly scarred, though it's taken you fifty years to realise this is why you're such a bastard. She was always fighting with that husband, who positively loathed you, because you so resembled her first husband, who positively abandoned you, claiming you weren't his son at all, and even as a parting gesture of goodwill, giving her the money to pay for an abortion. The things we learn from our Dementors! You're pretty sure she didn't know who your father was, at first, and when she realised that you were the son of her estranged husband, decided not to tell him. He being the Bert Newton of his day, everyone felt they knew him, so you were often quizzed about this man you'd never met. She insisted you keep his surname where Bill Clinton's mother had more sense. If she hadn't treated you as a lover maybe your stepfather might not have treated you as a rival. Thinking back on it, he was jealous and given reason, but you can't really bear to think back on those years of the soft cop and the con cop. You can't even look at the snapshots.

So, are you a team-player, Al Morissey? Have you good interpersonal skills?

If it means losing that precious house, they won't do it – no way! Oh, you'll go quietly, Al, but, hey, let's see you do it with a *smile*. Come on! Pastel has plastered the house with all the photos she can find of you beaming. Many date from your late twenties and feature the big, stoner smirk. No wonder you don't feel at home anymore in your own home. It's been a while since you smiled like that.

The whisky ain't workin' any more, Travis.

You suddenly recall walking through a dark, wooden transit lounge where it's 3 am. A couple of zombies are staggering about, apart from which, the place is utterly deserted. The shops and all the booths are closed and you've lost your way, trying to find some out-of-the-way cubicle.

You're halfway through a door when – snap! You take a snapshot.

High glass walls, so dark and yet so vivid. You don't recall what city it is; you can't recall what *country* it was! Dim lighting. Dark wood everywhere, big doors – big high glass doors – another snapshot, but taken some place that was not quite dream and yet not entirely real.

Like Cronulla, the Jewel of the Shire.

'Nulla must be the only place on earth where a local paper can run a feature entitled 'Olympian of the Week'.

'In line for junior sportsman this month we have Brad Browne of St Aloysius ('United in Christ, Making a Difference') recently crowned NSW under-eight cross country champion, nice one Brad; Royce Jones of Cronulla South Primary ('Play the Game') who placed first in the under-twelve surf ski at the recent Gold Coast Australasian titles, well done Royce; and Chase Stanley of Endeavour Sports High ('Valuing Individual Potential and Achieving Personal Best') for scoring two tries for New Zealand in their recent defeat by the Great British Lions in the third of three Rugby League Tests at Wigan; congratulations, Chase.

'Senior sportsman this month is tight, too, what with Ian Thorpe breaking his own world record in the eight hundred metres freestyle at the world titles (keep up the good work, Ian); Ricky Ponting, Glenn McGrath, Stuart Clark, Michael Clarke and Phil Jacques doing the Shire proud in the recent cricket Test match against India in Bangalore (top knock, Pup); Greg Welch taking out the Hawaiian Ironman (much improved change-overs, Greg); former world surfing champion Mark Occhilupo for a stunning win in the Bells Beach Rip Curl Pro (back to the Point now, Occy?) and Michael Diamond for adding to his numerous Olympic gold medals yet another world trapshoot title (now let's get some of those Indian mynahs out of those palm trees).'

☾

The Irish orchardists who worked Arcadia next to Kit's at Penrose – John O'Brien senior and John O'Brien junior – toiled from dawn till dusk for all but six weeks each year, but in those weeks returned home, without fail, to Oireland. Not uncommon practice, actually, in the old southern highlands, but no one could have done it before the longhaul. They would have been stranded in Dimdim.

With your first wife/longtime friend and your two eldest daughters, you went to the States once on the world's last passenger liner; oh, you go way back. In your early twenties, *Ellinis*, Chandris liner, via Tahiti and Panama on to New York with the tea chests; so you've seen Hispaniola from the sea and you really should have taken a snapshot but didn't have your camera. Off to Penn for the prestigious Ivy League postdoc, intending to hang out with Philly Joe, dealer to the stars which didn't happen because he was teaching, of all places, in Hampstead then later went to Paris to work with Archie Shepp.

O'Briens' plot in Arcadia is now the last Penrose orchard. Those carefully nurtured trees are being ripped out to make way for alpacas. No money in small orchards now, only endless work and despair. Once we had dreams of a pastoral future. What happened to those dreams, Al? Kids don't want to know and the women are now bailing out, off into the cash economy as fast as they can hightail it.

Apropos of the longhaul, Milesians say of the Fairy raths of *Tuatha De Danaan* that when it is day here it is night there and when it is night here it is day there and when it is winter here it is summer there and when it is winter there it is summer here.

You won't be getting on the Tube in London – bad memories of Cromwell! You will go straight to Ireland because by this stage, ethnically Jewish, you are, in fact, Christian Gnostic. You've jumped the fence. Among the charlatan alchemists of Rudolfine Prague were some genuine mystics, among them Michael Maier – converted Jew of Hesse, court physician to Rudolph the Second – and Maier makes clear, in his alchemical emblem books, that the Stone of the Philosophers is *only* for the converted Jew. The two great Spanish Christian mystics, St John of the Cross and San Juliano, were both ethnic Jews of *converso* stock, ipso facto 'Jews' – Jews to Nazi Germany, even Bondi Road or Acland Street. Is there such a thing as a 'secular' Jew? Not at this late stage when some have blue eyes and some have black, some have red hair and some have blond. If all goes well, this ordeal, undertaken at what looks like the end of a second marriage, will urge you into the red band and make something of you at last. Drummer who could *enlighten* folk with his bodhran? That would be good.

The Talmud presents Jesus as bastard son of Miriam, a ladies' hairdresser, begotten on her by Joseph during her menstrual period and thus a born magician. There is much from the Talmud in the Koran; six centuries of post-Christian Judeaic thought has fed into the Recital, even as it takes much of its Christianity from the Apocryphal Gospels.

You know what a tacho is, Rene? We know you don't drive your own vehicle, but next time you're ashing your cigar, check out the dash on your Ferrari and there behind the steering wheel, is a round dial with a red band and that's your tacho. It measures engine revs. You would want your chauffeur to be getting into the red band from time to – what's that? You say you need a *new* chauffeur? Oh no, I'm sorry, I'm busy at present – but you wouldn't want him staying there, because if he did, the engine would seize. A comparable Irish experience here will push our animus from carer's depression into a *mania* where – if all goes well and we get to move to the other side of the Curtain – we will speak to spirits and they will speak to us and for this, we must needs venture to that 'thin' place where ten years back was put the kybosh on our promising musical career and where we became enlightened, but only for a space of weeks.

Could that enlightenment have lasted *longer*? Could *Shekinah* be with us today, Rene?

Shh! They don't understand, Al, remember? Talk of sodomy won't offend but don't, for Chrissake, mention Jesus; they'll think you worship at Hillsong.

Where nothing could be further from the Truth.

It's hard to get a handle on such things in saintless Dimdim. Pastel says the inmates at Kenmore asylum rave on about God all day, but she doesn't go on to mention the priests in the Goulburn cathedrals. Someone from work has given her to read *The God Delusion* by Richard Dawkins, and *The End of Faith* by Sam Harris and *God is not Great* by Christopher Hitchens and she's reading them, Pastel, who never read the Bible in her life. Mind you, she'd know what's in it. Then again, she understands quantum physics, as do her friends. One of them, having read the Dawkins, is now on 'spiritual detox'.

Little doubt that love you felt for all mankind would have seen you in Kenmore; thank God you had the saving grace to see it. Your daughters insist you came back from Ireland with raging schizophrenia superimposed on your normal bipolar, so you keep quiet, if only because, as Emerson says, men descend to speak. Nothing of note has happened in the decade since – disregarding losing everything – but nor have you read in those years of voracious ecumenical reading anything to suggest you were in any way deluded. Faith, to an Australian, *is* insanity: indeed, the word for extreme asceticism (self/harm, anorexia, insomnia) is '*geilt*' in Irish, which means lunacy. It was the real deal, Al. You'd like to believe otherwise now it's gone, but the facts don't bear this out.

What a series of snapshots you took! What an album of signs and wonders.

There is pleasure in madness that only madmen know.

You cried on the phone to Pastel but you well recall how she feels because you've done it yourself – composed but impatient. It is hard for the one doing the breaking up to observe their victim's disbelief. It is always a strain, as Isaac of Ninevah says, to *sin* against *love*. He equates hell with compunction. She wanted to speak to you before you got on the plane but not to retract – just to wish you well. She's had you up to here. You can't blame her. But now you have no one to talk at and you do struggle to converse with this woman you had no idea existed, a woman who suddenly emerged from a woman you thought you knew well and trusted but bent, it seems, on ridding herself of you, once for all. You are not quite sure why she rang. You are not quite sure of anything, except that modern marriage, in the absence of utter poverty, has a thirty to 35-year span, max.

Because it is no longer needed! No longer needed and goes on for too long. This generation of Boomer women who grew up under the power of disgruntled patriarchy or, in the case of wogs like Pastel, worse – disgruntled exilarchy – married young and envy their daughters. Now they see before them a window of opportunity and seize the sill with both hands. Think not to dissuade them!

You have tried to explain to Pastel how women *cannot* demand sanctity and sex from the same individual man, but they are bent on so doing because they've only to open their legs or have them forced apart. You've noticed, for instance, from reading *Cleo*, that there is, to a modern woman, one moral tenet only: a guy must *never* cheat. Women demand fidelity as the signifier of commitment, but partnerships are only there to be broken and in a world where there are no chaste women, men obsess about the size of their penes. So that every time you log on your fuckin' email, it's 'Bam! A rollickin killer kok in yr pants' from Hugh Naildit; 'Freak the girls out with your gigantic schlong' from Didier Skoracik; 'Subject her to a punishing ride' from Karen Rockmode; 'Show the world that giant you've been hiding' from Wun Hung Lo; and 'Smooth talking may get you in her bed but a massive member will keep you there' from I. Seymour Furburger.

These Boomer women are about to give surviving Boomer menfolk the flick and the men can't see it coming. *You* didn't see it coming, Al, and you, of all men, should have seen it coming. You keep thinking, oh, it's just a matter of time before things return to normal and I am back settled in my customary seething indignation, but you notice the longer this goes on, the more composed she becomes; which you are no doubt meant to note and approve. She will be seeking support from family and friends who will be giving it in spades. You, by contrast, would not seek to share a humiliation. And all because you complain all the time, apparently, about your failed career and your mother and your lost farm and what's happened to the environment, and you drink too much and won't socialise and she's exhausted by two demanding jobs which she won't give up, not to mention her garden and friends and children and grandchildren and no one can help you or wants to, because you have alienated the world, so that now – sucked in – you are surplus to requirements.

There are no grounds for divorce now, anyway: no one is ever at fault. 'Your honour, he gave me every reason to believe he might *raise his voice*! As, in the past, he has been wont to do.'

Divorce granted, costs awarded.

You visited a funeral parlour before you booked your flight. You made sure Pastel had the number because should Mum die while you're away, her body would need to be embalmed pending cremation. You are not taking a mobile. You will be incommunicado for seventeen days. Pastel could execute the will, but no provision for co-attorney.

Suicide, though popular in Cronulla, with Steve Rogers, Rugby League legend most recent of a long line, through the familiar combination of alcohol and anti-depressants – Burton remarks the chronic melancholy of those who live under the brightest skies – is not for you an option. It would set a bad example to your eldest daughter, for instance, who is just as mad as you are and often threatening self-harm. Others might lose respect for you. But you can't be fazed to work anymore on your drumming technique. Where would be the point? People claim you trample over the top of small combinations, that you're too loud and busy. Younger drummers are not interested in what you have achieved because all they know about you is that they never heard of you, which is all they need to know. They would never think to ask *why*. They would never question what they have been taught. That would imply a degree of independence of mind.

How do I get to be a *successful* drummer? not:

How do I get to do things on a drum kit that have not been done.

It's fucked. Toynbee and Spengler saw it coming. The Great Lie – if I've heard of him he's good and if I haven't then he can't be – portends the end of democracy as we know and love it. Spengler thought this inevitable while Toynbee begged to demur; the point is, how do we *deal* with it? A Christian response is to take it on the chin while the inclination of a married man is to whinge or to run into the street bearing arms.

You knew it was fucked when you saw Billy Cobham described by some arsehole in the *Herald* as 'bombastic'. Billy Cobham *bombastic*!

That's *just* the kind of thing that you keep reporting to Pastel. And twenty years ago she would have listened enthralled. Pastel, aka Ingeborg Hakonsen; woman who witnessed your enlightenment and dismissed it as just another male ploy to shirk responsibility.

And she may be right.

There *is* something in us does not want to be involved with other people. That kind of thing comes at a cost. Ten years ago you were needed by your family. Today your wife cries and says she can't *stand* you anymore and while she still loves you, sort of – the way you love a powerless person eyeless in Gaza – she doesn't want to live with you because you are too *intense*. By which she means mentally ill for, like Frank Zappa, you have an aura that's pure angora, apparently, and too much to bear after a hard day's work when she has courses she wants to take in the evening.

She doesn't mind having sex with her ex, but you find it increasingly difficult to whisper in her pink ear, 'You know, I think we could have a great *past* together?'

But you don't *need* to work, Ingeborg. We could sell the house and unit and you could be demi-semi-co-dependent and …

What? Be in your *power* again? No way! I'm going to work till I'm *seventy*. And I need to put my money into my super for my retirement. It's sad but true that you're a great drummer, Al, and a pity no one wants to play with you now, but we're *exhausted* and you're so strong and all you can think to do is to make yourself stronger, so no one can help you. I've tried for thirty years. Until you learn to *deal* with the fact that the world has moved on and that you are not the only man who has put his entire life into his work and now can't cope with being redundant – because Libby's husband, the Qantas pilot who lost his job, is just the same; and do you know, women, in that situation, would get together? – then you will be continue to be what you have become. You won't like what I'm about to say now, but have you thought of seeking professional help?

She has the *fear* that you may *appear* at any hour at all of the night or *day* to deliver a *spray*.

So there's only one way forward, solitude – O Solitudo O Beatitudo! – because as you may recall, Pastel, I stumbled into Peace and Happiness once and was content until I saw the sadness in your eyes.

I wasn't sad! It's just I had to come all that way down with the key.

Oh no. I saw your expression of hurt when I said I didn't need to talk to you anymore (and took a snapshot).

I was *glad* you didn't need to talk to me anymore! Go back to Ireland, go on! I'm so *glad* you're actually *doing* something about yourself!

Not shape up or ship out, but:

Shape up *and* ship out.

Do you suppose that God can be kicked away and whistled up again when it suits?

I wouldn't know. As you say, I'm just a heathen Scandinavian. I *do* know I can't *stand* you anymore. You have to keep going back to my past and *charging* off it! I *can't stand* it! I can't *stand* you, Al! You are *so bitter*! I can't *stand* it! *I can't stand it! I can't stand it!* I can't stand it. I can't stand it. I can't stand it. I can't stand it. I …

Oh, that's enough. Me, me, me, I often wondered how this would end, Mimi. I knew it would have to – because just look at my poor mother, a wealthy woman reduced to being fed mush and left with two cheap smocks. Nothin' is forever, kinda like the weather, but I wouldn't have spent all that money on the house if I'd known this was going to happen. I'd have saved more.

I'll pay you back, *not*:

You come home because I still love you and we can work this out, *but*:

I'll pay you back. Hey, maybe you can find someone more suitable. One of your old girlfriends? A younger woman? As you say, I could never really understand drummers.

Are you *kidding*? You think I want to go through *this* again? Besides, I don't have the money now to have my *tatt* removed.

I'll pay.

It's alright until others become involved and then it gets nasty.

We must only hope she just doesn't jump that fence.

I feel the same way, Al. I've been with men my entire life. I'm *over* it. Try to understand that it's nothing personal. I now choose to spend my time with *positive* people, *sane* people, people willing to honour being alive by having *fun*! I got involved with guys when I was just thirteen, as you keep reminding me. Fifty years of slavery! It's time for me to do what *I* want to do now, before it's too late. Try to understand – or not. Thanks to you, I won't die wondering what sex is all about.

Well, I guess I love you enough that I want you to have what you want for yourself, Pastel.

Can we still be friends?

Oh, you mean I could keep cleaning the gutters? But there'd be none to listen toomy when I'm feelin' gloomy. Sorry. If only you could understand what losing the farm and seeing my mother in supermax has done to me. She was my only family, and without those cows, I'm lost. You picked a fine time to leave me. When we met, it was *you* had the past and I was the one with the future or so I was assured by Buddy Rich no less – *perii*! But I'm warning you, Pastel, you hook up with someone else! You try to install someone else in my house!

I've been faithful to you, Al.

Oh, don't start that again.

You have no energy for younger women. And you *do* see things from her perspective. Would *you* want to live with yourself, Al, if you had a choice? You're not such a fun guy these days and you used to be able to make folk laugh (Gehurr gehurr, cue Disney Goofy laugh). Your mother always said it was your saving grace. You've been drinking a bottle of wine a night and sometimes two, because it's so cheap. Oh, it's so criminally *cheap*! Clearly, the first thing to do is to stop drinking so much cheap wine.

Zawanul died. Always on some trip or other, according to Cannonball.

Your wife is old, your honeymoon is over, the liver is telling you to stop drinking – you've hit the wall, buddy.

So, destination Temple Borf, Ibiza on Guinness in the rain.

It did the job last time.

Sitting on a longhaul, one's moods oscillate, unprovoked, from joy to despair and *eroticism*. Once, flying home from London, you woke with a start thinking of Pastel and the realisation you would shortly be having sex with that extraordinary body produced in you an *ecstasy* in which every nerve quivered and shuddered as though under the influence of some first dose of some baneful drug while everything in the darkened cabin became suffused with light because that's what she does to men. Despite the belly and bingo wings – lately become what the Dutch call *dikke stukje*, as distinct from *lekker stukje* – the legendary legs remain: chunky, shapely, dancer's legs and her friends, her daughters and now her daughters' friends all persist in telling her how 'gorgeous' she is; whereas no man in his sixties has anyone to tell him how 'optimistic' he feels, how well his long-term memory works.

It's a deadly emotion, passion – destructive, exhausting, high maintenance. We shall be glad when it's over and *love?* Love should be reserved for God. Children with parents obsessed with each other grow up as orphans, as Stevenson observed.

Godless men start clinging to their wives when they reach a certain age. Regrettably, the womenfolk don't start clinging back.

More recently, occupying the aisle seat on a domestic flight from Brisbane, a young woman's naked arm on the mutual armrest fell in contact with your own and neither saw fit to withdraw so the contact became eroticised. You developed, mercifully in part concealed by your seatbelt, a throbbing, oozing erection, which your neighbour must have noticed because at length she arose from her seat and, insisting you remain just where you were, eased her bum across your lap before heading off to the toilet. You understood by this that she was offering you a blow-job but only if you were man enough to accept her challenge, which you weren't. Others would have noticed, you weren't drunk, it wasn't dark. In fact, it was mid-morning and no one else had even left their seats as it was only a one-hour flight.

What is it with these young women today, they will give a blow-job to a total stranger? That said, they don't know how to kiss. Imagine having to marry one. You do feel sorry for your sons there, but not so much for your grandsons, as this cannot go on. Pastel was bad, maybe worse, as a pioneer of sixties sex, but this was because the working class didn't believe in foreplay then and now no one does. And sex between solitary animals, as we observe them in the wild, is a brutal, painful affair instinct with mistrust.

They expect to begin with a blow-job. Women introduced the blow-job to the heterosexual world. Let this be put on record. Men are accountable for anal sex but women introduced the blow-job. This was back in 1971 because they'd read about it. Men, at first, were taken aback. It took years before we asked for it, decades before we demanded it. *Nemo repente fuit turpissimus* – no one became filthy overnight. Juvenal.

In the eighth century Rule of Tallaght, a monk who in waking hours – note those 'waking hours' – was guilty of self-abuse by 'looking at a woman who pleased him or from salacious thoughts or through indecent words' was given, by his confessor, his *anamchara*, a week's penance.

In contrast, according to the Rule of the Fianna, a White Boy could not refuse a naughty so Diamuid hooked up with the rootrat Grainne, betrothed by her father, High King Cormac Mac Art, to Fionn MacCumhaill.

That happiness which began for you in Ireland (putting paid to the French concept of '*apenis*') lasted a few weeks – but what weeks! Back in Dimdim, conscious of the need to come down, you wondered if you could. It seemed, at the time, impossible, but Dimdim is a great place to come down and in the end, you made it back. And the last state of that man is worse than the first (which, being translated, means 'capable of loneliness') but you felt you had to go back to your family because your youngest daughter was still in school and Pastel couldn't have coped back then because she didn't have a full-time job and was not yet her own woman.

A man's foes shall be they of his own household. Matthew XX, 36.

If, as individuals we choose someday to regroup, it won't be as families: it will be as brothers and sisters in Christ, Buddha, Mahavira or Mani.

From the Rule of Comghall of Bangor, 'If you have withdrawn from the world, remember that you now walk a path of suffering. If you have a son or a family and have decided to leave them, you are to regard yourself as dead; you must not seek out your relatives or even think about them.'

Hard call, Comghall.

Every person you saw walking by on the Esplanade, you saw with the eye of a confessor. With the eye of a Padro Pio, you saw through all their pain and ignorance, it *burned* you! It *hurt* you! You wanted to *rush up and help*! You wanted only to help, but could you have helped anyone? By means of a bodhran? No good laying a religious rave. You had no money, nowhere to go, nowhere to live. You could barely speak, let alone work. The farm had gone, your mother was in respite and you'd destroyed your own prospects.

Coltrane wanted to be a saint. When asked, towards the end of his life, what he wanted to do next, he said, 'I want to be a saint.'

I wanta be there in that number when the saints go marchin' in.

You might have ended up with a cult like Bubba Free John. This would have been out in the bush somewhere – Jonestown South and the Children of God. Given your voracious sexual appetite, maybe as well that didn't happen. You would have gone out, like St Kevin in Glendalough, to live as a hermit, but weak-minded folk would have gathered round you because you would have had *charisma*, in Weber's sense of the word. You would have had *conviction*. Whether or not you can now win back your Clarity, we're about to learn. If, as alchemists insist, it's a matter of heat and timing, conditions are auspicious.

Of course, it won't be up to *you*: we can only prepare.

Have you, perhaps, ill-treated Pastel, to get out of the marriage? She claimed on the phone you don't like her and never treated her as a wife. Well, you never *pretended* to like her! She's a New Age goose, all crystals and pecuniary affirmations, an evangelical Hindu, a devotee of Lakshmi. And you always thought of her more as a concubine, which she anyway prefers. You respect her and desire her. You have, over the years, tried to get out of both marriages, both ways – down into the hell of promiscuity, up into the heaven of virtue – but you're still with Pastel who has longtime had you by the short and curlies. Your passion for Pastel persists, but directed towards that Pastel that was actually some years before your time, the really notorious one *that you never actually met and concerning whom your imagination is free to run riot and does*. Meantime, whatever it is between you, it has legs; you're horrified to realise you're still having sex with a sexagenarian. Imagine reading that in the papers at twenty. 'Man in his sixties admits to having sex with a sexagenarian!' Urk! Yuk! The Quest for Australia's Sexiest Sexagenarian. Yet for her, it was all about sex from the outset. She made that painfully clear. So you think you can root, Australia. She was attracted to you, initially, because you weren't 'coming on', later insisting you would 'need to do the business' – and oh, the frisson of horror thereby induced in you, the great romantic. But the sexual challenge thrown out by this frigid, foul-mouthed beauty proved irresistible.

And she quickly fell in love with you, let's run that again, and she soon succumbed to the self-sabotage of addiction and co-dependency and because of her great beauty you married her and now, multi-orgasmic, she can't recall that she was ever ill and wants only to be dead again.

The Holy One, blessed be He, had the same problem with the Children of Israel.

Pastel is not the kind of girl who needs a cuddle after sex; *you're* the kind of man who needs a cuddle after making love, which is why you're always in such trouble with women – you can't let go. You're a failed womaniser. Like a fish in a fish trap, you can always get in but you can never get out. You're not a *real man*. You don't even like dirty jokes.

Too much oxytocin?

Insufficient serotonin.

You can't relate to other human beings but you were quite good husbanding cattle because cattlemen are, generally speaking, tough-minded introverts.

If there was one thing you never wanted to be, Al, it was to be divorced.

Go back to your poor, sultry mother for insight. Now demented, incontinent, incapable of feeding herself, thinking you're her father, at times one of her lovers, in her twenties a great showgirl beauty, what was called back then a 'soubrette' – warm, exuberant, not so smart as to pose any threat to man, with a nice touch of the tarbrush, and well-endowed (12D). One night you woke and listened to her crying and screaming as she was being raped in her bed. Great Days!

Furthermore, they continue – how she screams today when she's being bathed. Buttwipes know what *that* means. A sexually active granddaughter now with a sexually active mother – who would have thought it possible? We live, in the West, far too long.

Pastel, far smarter, blonde sixties pin-up, go-go dancer supreme, *grande horizontale* mistress of various Sydney racing identities, ex-denizen of a demimonde that terrified you then and terrifies you still, yet the greatest medicine, according to Rhases, is in the Poisonous Dragon, so stick with it, Al; this experiment must continue, as the monk's experiment continues, unto death.

When first you saw her she was in a cage, undulating over the dancefloor at the Cubana; Pretzel and Charmaine in the other cages, and you were playing drums in the house band. In those days women had no objection to go-go dancers dancing over the dance floor in cages.

Wait a bit, wait a bit – did you just say you're a *black* man, Al?

No no, it's just that Mum is mixed blood. No birth certificate, no adoption papers and frankly, no big deal – Stolen Generation high yeller. Linda Burney? Marcia Langton? Pat O'Shane? Dawn Casey? Frances Rings? Leah Purcell? Lois O'Donohue? Pat Turner, Rhoda Roberts, Karla Grant? That opera singer from Oatley? Bev Manton? I could go on.

They're black. Moreover, not all of them are stolen.

They're not black. Take another look. They're mixed bloods.

They're *black*! What planet you from? They may be yellow but they're *living black*. You're a fascist. We can have nothing further to do with you. Barack Obama is black. The Reverend Jeremiah Wright is black. Colin Powell is black. Karla Grant is black. Anthony Mundine is black. Tamana Tahu is black. Wesley Enoch is black. Johnathan Thurston is black. Patrick Johnson is black. Stephen Page is black. Troy Cassar-Daley is black. You see when a black mates with a white in this society, the product of that union is black. And when *that* black mates with a white, then the product of *that* union is another black, and when *that* black mates with yet another white, then the product of that union is yet another black. Get the picture?

Then how many whites must a black man fuck before he could cease to be black?

As many *shiksas* as a Jew needs to fuck, Al, before he could cease to be a Jew. So you're a Jew as well as indigenous? Pull the other one. You're actually a blackajew.

I am not a blackajew. I am *Australian*. I'm dinky-di and wish I could say I was proud of it, but I come from the world of showbiz where Jews and mixed bloods meet and mate. Roy Rene was Jewish and my father wrote his material.

You should be proud to be a blackajew.

I am not a blackajew! You're only Jewish if your *mother* is Jewish! It was my *father* was Jewish. My mother was raised Catholic, as was I.

Why would you come to this arsehole of the earth, Al, unless you intended to make a fresh start?

Why indeed. As for Mum, she's from a generation did not regard it as an honour to be black. Indeed, it was seen as a *disgrace*.

Times change and the wise men change with the times.

Oh yeah. Hey, you know what comforts me here?

What comforts you there, Al?

That weird, zany ambivalent *wit* so pathognomic of Chassidism permeates the first known work to mention the Holy Grail.

You mean by Chretien de Troyes?

Chretien de Troyes.

Now, why would a blackajew inflict on himself a second dose of the Showgirl Blues? Because you're not supposed to *marry* showgirls: you fuck them backstage.

Freudian *shtik*: to make things right, to get things straight, to *understand*!

And now the beautiful, spirited daughters, the beautiful, spirited granddaughters – countless in their number, endless in divorces – the fighting off of other men can never cease.

Model comes in just the one colour ... black ... but we can offer you the full range. You prefer a light black or a darker black? Export model uses pitch black. What you see there, that's Paddy black ... very popular black, no, that ain't white! That is actually ultra-light black. You take your time.

And who wouldn't want to walk away but to be *asked* to walk!

And Jesus answering said unto them, The children of this world marry, and are given in marriage: But they which shall be accounted worthy to obtain that world, and the resurrection from the dead, neither marry, nor are given in marriage: Neither can they die any more: for they are equal unto the angels; and are the children of God, being the children of the resurrection. Luke XX, 34–37.

Oh no! You left your bodhran beater in the disabled toilet in the Honkers lounge. It must have fallen from your pack as you replaced your transparent plastic toothpaste bag.

No matter, you can always buy a new bodhran beater when you buy yourself a new bodhran in Dublin.

Time to explore the modern world, Al. Feeling digital?

Does the hen have eggs? We shall have to check that clacker with our *digitus impudicus*, the one we raise in our road rage, meaning, 'sit on that and spin'.

Brought up all your kids without a TV in the house, here – please accept this bar to your Dragon's Tooth, Antissa Twenty-One – even so, they managed to see plenty of it at their friends' homes, but the thought was there, the fix was in and Pastel did it tough.

Now you don't watch TV. Serious! You don't go to the movies. You don't go to the theatre. You never went to the opera. You don't go to the ballet. You don't go to the pub, for fear of getting in fights. You have no friends in common with Pastel, indeed, you have few friends – mostly the waiter who brings you your bill along with your Irish coffee, by which stage you're usually feeling pretty genial. Beasts and books are more your thing. When at sea with the Paddy Shaw Showband, you stay in your cabin and read Latin psalms. Good money with the showband – good money on those cruise ships.

Only time Al Morrisey ever saw a movie or a TV show was on a longhaul and it's ten years since he took his longhaul to Ireland and that was his last longhaul. Ten years ago, we couldn't choose our entertainment on a plane. It was foisted upon us.

What was it Juvenal called Ireland? Juverna – not Hibernia, Juverna '*arma quidem ultra litora Iuvernae promovimus et modo captas Orcadas ac minima contentos nocte Brittanos*'. That's from the second satire, the one against the baleful effects of poofterism.

Back of the seat in front of you now, your own private entertainment system, the V-Pod, with five hundred hours of video games and movies for your distraction. Sixty hours of movies! What price now, Dan Brown?

Okay, let's see what they're watching here, let's get ourself into that red band. This is where it begins. It begins on the plane.

Harry Potter! How can they swallow this notion that a *woman* would know what a young boy thinks or feels? As to this quasi 'Philosopher's Stone' that introduced Harry Potter to his enthusiasts, J. K. Rowling does not understand alchemy. Could this be a problem? There is a limit to what may be gleaned from the well-thumbed *Brewer's Dictionary of Phrase and Fable* but Pastel, who has adult friends who read this tripe, says it doesn't matter, that J. K. Rowling tells them all they want or need to know.

Harry Potter and the Philosopher's Stone, Monty Python and the Holy Grail, The Life of Brian – is this how it ends? The most sacred of Western men's business misconstrued by a woman having been mocked shitless by a claque of British queers? J. K. Rowling is a false prophet, Pastel. She is perfectly normal, thank you very much. She has no siddhic power; she can't even levitate or manifest food in the manner of a Sai Baba. All she does is turn literary lead into fool's gold, the currency of late Capitalism.

Okay, what have we in riposte that Pastel might understand? Okay, Harry Potter *cannot* find the Philosopher's Stone, which *is* the Holy Grail, the New Pearl of Great Price, the complete and perfect inhibitor of selective serotonin re-uptake, because a little child has no desire to be a little child again. In the absence of sexual maturity there can be *no possibility* of sublimation, no intimations of immortality, no Mystical Marriage, no manifestations of Godhead, no surcease of internal narrative; it's as simple as that.

Ah, that's not so simple, Al.

Okay. It's *crap*! Can't you people see that or don't you people care?

And that just makes you look like a Muggle.

Okay, so it may be crap and maybe even evil crap, but isn't it great that children are *reading* it? Are you an enemy of reading?

Hermetic: 'impenetrable', as in 'hermetic' seal. J. K. Rowling impenetrable?

Hmm. So you can choose categories. Okay, choose 'crime'. Scroll down.

Zodiac: set in a time when everyone smoked, this film tells the tale of a psychopathic true-life San Francisco serial killer who was never caught. Fast forward.

Young couple parked in a car, headlights, shot to death. Fast forward.

The star is the guy played that ... oh no what's this? Shit. That's sick. That's *fully* sick.

A pretty young blonde, hands tied behind her back, is being stabbed to death and we get to see her blood splash up and hear her scream.

Drop a Temtab, get a few hours' sleep, Al: big day tomorrow and you have to stay awake as you've no accommodation booked. You have to function.

Oh no, you're awake again already.

Prostate not too bad. Hit a button, any button, some TV now, perhaps? *CSI* – we've heard of that on the Jewish/Scottish book show: endorsement enough. The little boy opposite is watching it; he's not sleeping. That's the third time he's run this program through. He's no more than seven. His parents are crashed out in the seats behind him.

CSI Miami: a pretty young girl's heart is being pierced by a nail from a nailgun which we get to observe as a kind of explanatory video footnote. Rewind, there's the heart pumping, see, the nail rips in and the blood spurts out.

CSI Las Vegas: a drunken man is being decapitated by a slow train.

Turn to TV pilot *Dexter*: a psychopathic forensic expert turned serial killer by night cruelly vivisects Miami lowlife who have evaded justice. It's a comedy. 'Slick and intelligent. Michael C. Hall received a Golden Globe nomination.'

Oh, that's enough of the visual.

Some music now, perhaps.

Timberland, 'Kill yourself'.

Amy Winehouse, 'Rehab'.

Rihanna, 'Push up on me'.

Chemical Brothers, 'No path to follow' *(to FX of coke being snorted)*.

☾

It's happening. The Gnostic puts in a fix and the solution seeds. You are beginning to *notice* things. Your gaze is holding them longer and slower. Always the first step, the revulsion, the disbelief in what they crave: sex and death and drugs, pretty much. Can't they see what they've become? Don't they notice what's going on, don't they *care?* Their lust for sex and death which betrays their ignorance grows ever more insatiable but they can't see it.

Actually, this can only go on for so long because there are just so many ways in which to die and fuck and get out of it. While Juvenal was frothing at the mouth over the power of the poofter in Rome (*magna inter molles concordia*), John the Divine was writing his Book of Revelation on the isle of Patmos (*etiam venio cito amen*). There comes a turning point and it can't be that far off.

Jesus should be back now any day.

You were fifty-two when you first went to Ireland. You went with Greg Hare, who played bass beside you at the Cubana when you were both nineteen, with Pastel, who would have been only seventeen then, in the cage, already married but didn't wear a ring. You'd worked with Greg on and off since you were both fourteen. He would appear, from time to time, to introduce you to some new musical trend. He introduced you to The Band, The Who, Steve Reich, King Tubby; he introduced you to Grandmaster Flash and Weather Report. You played together at the El Rocco in the days of the old Three Out, but only Tuesday nights.

He drove down the many miles of dirt in the Holden, still driving the same car he bought when he was twenty. You'd moved to Goongerah. He was still in Orange. Coming in from the milking you found him shooting the breeze with Pastel, chiacking with the daughters.

Hey, listen to this, he says. He's smaller than you and ostensibly asexual, which makes him someone with whom you can relax. He puts on a CD. It's shy FX 'Original Nuttah' from 1994 – one of those seminal jungle tracks, as familiar to aficionados of neurofunk as to votaries of jump-up.

What's that supposed to be?

That, my friend, is *drum 'n bass,* you 'n me! Me 'n you! We haffi brock a smile 'n don bother screw dis one dedicated to all massive 'n crew we haffi getta lively inna dance venue.

The daughters are lovin' this.

Tape loops and drum machine. I'm surprised.

Is he still woodshedding, Pastel? Does the man still p-p-p-practise in the w-w-w-woodshed?

Three hours a day, Greg. It's called 'networking' – as on a fishing trawler.

Hey, *strong* man! Come with me. I got ideas, Al.

Let's walk down by the cattle.

No! Let's not walk down by the cattle. So how many cattle you got these days, Al?

Forty head.

And does that return you a g-g-good income?

Ten, f-f-fifteen grand a year. I won't submit to a judging ring.

Nah, that wouldn't be you. That's not a good income. Mum gone? I didn't notice Mum.

I like cattle. Yeah, she went to an old people's home as I couldn't go on. No respite. Three years she was here with us. Twenty-four hours a day in the end and no one who hasn't done it could possibly understand what it involves. I had a cow in that condition I'd be prosecuted. It was like having an untrainable dog. To make matters worse, she thought I was my father in the end and started paying out on me. I heard more about her love life than ever I wanted to learn. You know what one of the nurses told Pastel? 'Your mother-in-law has the morals of an alley cat.' This, at the age of *eighty fuckin'-plus*! Does it never end? My father claimed I was the son of some Kangaroo she'd been screwing. It was Pastel pulled the pin. I was prepared to see things through but Pastel pulled the pin. It's her or me, she said.

I always liked your mum. To tell the truth, I *fancied* her – I like big tits, sorry, but it's all about tits for me – so there you go. I think it's a disgrace the medical profession would allow people to live on when they've lost that part of the brain that controls shame. We all have these sexual urges. Strange to see Pastel in a place like this, though. Why'd you hook up with Pastel, Al? If it's not a rude question.

You mean, as distinct from Pretzel or Charmaine?

If it's not a rude question.

Because she is a rude girl. Satisfied? She's also easy on the eyes. She has been a good trophy wife. I like beautiful blondes and I prefer the Nordic type. I know you liked Heather.

Yeah, I went to school with Heather.

Yeah, I went to school with Heather, too, and I still talk to Heather. Heather is my best friend. It's just I wore her down. I wear people out. Don't worry. She understands. Our kids are going great. So what you got in mind, Greg?

Something is formatting. Is this where you practise?

Yeah, but for what I wouldn't know.

Is this the w-w-woodshed? Where's the wood?

It's a killing room. It has good acoustics.

You kill things in here.

Look, now and then I have to knock a killer, okay? You wouldn't understand. I don't butcher them myself, so I don't have a saw. I take the quarters into town on the tray under a tarp.

I see you still got your Ludwig kit.

Oh yeah. Well, I mostly work on the practice pad. For what I wouldn't know. The whole scene is fucked. While Mum was here

I couldn't lift a stick. I couldn't turn my *back* on her, man! She'd yell and scream all night. Pastel couldn't sleep. I couldn't take my *eyes* off her! I literally couldn't take my friggin' eyes off her and I think those years off the air did it for me, at my age. Carers of the frail mentally ill have the lowest Australian Unity Wellbeing Index of any marginalised group – fully forty per cent falling in the range of extremely severely depressed. I just can't seem to shake it. I'm not the fun guy I was. The whisky ain't workin' anymore. It's not as though it's over, either. She'll see me out.

Play us your one-stroke roll with your left hand, Al. Could you still do that, even though extremely severely depressed? Let's see how long you can hold it. Let's see if you could hold it for, say, two whole seconds. I'll time you.

So you pick up a stick, Al, and you relax your wrist and strike the practice pad and keep the stick quivering, as only you can do, as far we know, for maybe twenty hits a second for almost two seconds.

Hmm. Now do it harder, Al. Okay. Check. Okay, now do it on the snare drum. I'd like to hear it on the snare drum now, please. Hard as you can, Al.

Stop giving orders! We're not having sex.

Faarck! You know there's no one else can do that? You fuckin' *amaze* me, Al, you sound just like a d-d-d-drum machine!

Thanks. That's the payoff. See, if I was out there suckin' cock I wouldn't be able to do that.

And what are you practising for again?

I dunno. You don't suck cock, you don't get work. Mishima says the lion runs up and down because that's what it means to be a lion.

I tell you what, you're a pretty good drummer, man, but we're both fifty years of age and jazz is dead. Once in a while a technical prodigy will come along like yourself or Jaco, but by and large, it's dead finish. I admire you for sticking at it and doing what you're doing here. Session work of the kind I do no longer has meaning, either, because in the past, when that red light went on, I had to nail it. Now all I do is kick for touch. It's all ProTools and sound compression. But you and me, *we* can do it live.

Do what live?

Drum 'n bass! It came out of breakbeat and acid house. You always were the best samba drummer outside Paulo. In fact, you're the *only* drummer I know both *strong* enough and *fast* enough to *play* drum 'n bass live! The young ravers like it one-seventy, one-eighty beats a minute, Al. They like it *fast as*. Bass comes in half that, hiphop speed. I got the bass if you got the drum. I'm puttin' down sub-bass these days, man, so deep you don't so much *hear* it as *feel* it. It's more like a pressure than a sound wave – nothin' over twenty Hertz. That's where it's gone, that's how they like it. 'Course, they can't *dance* at one-eighty beats, only when they're peaking; most of the time they just kinda stand there and sway about. Well, I can dig that. I got the amps to drive the twenty-one inch sub-bins. It's a very loud, bass-heavy thing, this drum 'n bass. You need a factory or a warehouse, ideally. In your car, unless you wind down the windows, you could rupture an eardrum. It mostly has stuff come over the top but we don't really need that – vocals and all – bass is the one thing they need. See, they're all trying to crawl back up.

Who's 'we'? What you just played me at the house sounded like a TR-808.

Yeah, well, that's all they got. It's all they got, Al. What they mostly use for bass is one loop from Kevin Saunderson's line on Alex Reece's 'Just Another Chance' from '88. They call it 'Reece Bass'. They distort it, compress it, compact it, flange it then overdrive.

Which is just what I'm trying to get away from.

Yeah, and you got away from it. You know 'Amen Brother' by The Winstons? That's a house-tempo breakbeat they use a lot. I'll send you a copy.

Don't bother.

You know Carl Craig's 'Bug in the Bassbin'?

Look, we're too old for this!

Bullshit! Think of Stewie Spears. You like Aphex Twin, Al? They call that *drill* 'n bass. Let's call ourselves 'Farmfunque'. Hey. Live techstep.

I'm not interested.

Al, you took that spunky blonde out of the cage, why? You fucked over your entire family for Pastel, *why?*

Pastel and I have a family! We are strictly legit. Don't talk to me about Pastel. You wouldn't understand. She fell in love with me, man, so I had no choice. A chick like that falls in love with you, you got no choice. You wouldn't understand. I can still see her saying, 'You won't break my heart, will you, Al?' This was out at Cotter. Anyway, by age twenty-six, she had stopped drinking. *Jeune coquette, vieille devotee,* she was on this New Age kick. She's still on it. She was, as you know, a great dancer, but she could sing a bit. Those were the days Don Banks wanted to put her on the Music Board. He was always hanging round the Lotus. At twenty, she went back to Canberra with her husband. Everyone, from Gorton on down, was trying to get into her pants but at age twenty-six she was a *reformed character*! It's just that no one noticed. I had no idea of her past, man, absolutely no idea. Had I known what she'd been up to, I wouldn't have gone *near* her. Everyone seems to have known about it but no one told me. She's leaked a bit of it to me, over the years. I can't *deal* with it! A Muse is a Wound that will not Heal. See, I felt sorry for this beautiful creature that everyone else was shunning when I, of *all* people, should have shunned her. Either that, or avenged her. It's just I know I'd do it hard in jail. Beware of Pity, as Stefan Zweig said. I was the wrong guy.

I hear she's done some dreadful things.

Oh yeah, well, haven't we all. That said, I don't like it how she mutters the mantra when I annoy her. I liked it better when we threw stuff ... Okay, all right, fuck it, why not.

You won't regret this, Al. Well, you may do, but here's an opening into a new world. See, they use different drugs to us. Novelty – we'll show what can be done. I got a drum 'n bass contact in the UK which is the home of drum 'n bass.

I would have thought it came from Detroit.

Yeah, it did, but it was looking for a home. I know this amazing drummer in Aussie, I said. Nothin' beats a live show, Al. Play us that single-stroke roll again.

You're *incredible*! You do not lose any volume. How *do* you *do* that? You think you could play real hard and fast without a break, for, say, half an hour?

Al Gore and his *Inconvenient Truth*. Let's watch that, to finish the flight on a thoughtful note, *not* because of the implications for male-driven overpopulation and female-driven materialism with the light thus cast on the monastic nature of the frugal Dark Age Irish Celtic Church which, as Toynbee remarks in his volume on Challenge-and-Response in *A Study of History*, was less reminiscent of Christian than of Buddhist or Manichean institutions; *not* because of the 'science' because you can't do science without a control, no, because here's a man who suffered an injustice and has held together his marriage.

How did he contrive that?

Heathrow 0525, touchdown in the fog. You walk the moving walkways, now removing your shoes, now queuing in sidewinders, now exhibiting your toothpaste, now being frisked, now through Customs, now through Immigration, now thankfully down that long corridor to the homely Irish departure lounge where all around you are Londoners who only just got out of bed. You managed a quick urination, too, which has put you on top of the world. God damn it, you feel as a man *should* feel!

You pick up a paper from the seat beside you as you wait to board. It's a supplement with a feature on Sherman George, fire chief in Missouri, who in recognition of the one hundred and fiftieth anniversary of the St Louis Fire Department was made honorary grand marshal for the one hundred and thirtieth Veiled Prophet Parade, the nation's most spectacular Independence Day Parade, featuring giant helium balloons of Uncle Sam, Michael the Eagle, Liberty Bell ...

British Midlands flight BD 121 to Dublin now boarding through gate ...

Veiled Prophet? Isn't he from *Lallah Rookh* by Thomas Moore? Mokanna, the Veiled Prophet of Khorassan? How did *he* get to St Louis? His sect merged with the 'Ismailis to become the Assassins of Islam, thanks to whom we now remove our shoes in every airport.

One hour and twenty minutes later, Dublin, 0820. Welcome home, Al Morrisey. It has nothing to do with ancestry; nothing to do with that friendly Irish craic and Guinness gargle; you're home. Just think of yourself as Irish. Think of yourself as Irish and living where every Irishman wants to live – Cronulla Beach.

Step aboard a double-decker and alight in O'Connell Street Upper.

Hey, that massive needle opposite the prick with the stick – that wasn't there.

Dublin is a homely place: locals prefer Sydney. Harvey Norman is here now, using the Oz accent to good effect in ads – we de man: Go Harvey. As part of the same building complex that houses the

Book of Kells, you pass, on the corner of Pearse and Sandwich Street Upper, Trinity College Visitors Car Park. The alcoves at the back of the parking lot are filled with builders' waste and buddleia, the brickwork is grimy, there's a crudely demolished arch and you can see all the panes of glass in the station roof still missing after ten years.

Low-rise Dublin is a Georgian shambles behind black metal rails held with cable ties. You would come to the Pearse DART to clear your head with a Wicklow walk when you were camped at Belfield, to confirm how much you love Nature. So you love this Pearse Station in this grotty shit of a city. Fifty metres behind the enclosed glass walkway of T. C. North East Corner Development Indoor Sports Complex and Science Gallery is the grimy black ornate Victorian iron rail overpass on four brick piers where the lime green and yellow DART carriages rumble into *Staisun na b Piarsach*. And what a façade on that station: shield bosses and broken windows and three flagpoles but never any flags, presided over by Apostle Andrew on the Catholic church next door which bears the motto 'Deo Optimo Maximo Sub Invoc B Andreae Apostoli'. All of which combines to give a feeling, straight off the longhaul, that nothing here is *real* – not the eyes, not the setting, not the city – a feeling that strikes with the force of *déjà vu*, especially when moving, under the watchful eye of *Janus*, from clinical depression to mania; jet-lagged, sleep-deprived in such meaningful surroundings where you underwent the most important epiphany which left you, for a time, Peaceful and Happy.

Why are you always depressed, Al? Is it insufficient serotonin? Is it because you drink too much? Is it because you are damned? Is it because you have known Peace and yet continue to sin? Or is it perhaps bad karma, something done in some previous existence.

That poster opposite Trinity on Pearse advertising *The Bourne Ultimatum* with the slogan 'Remember everything. Forget nothing', is unChristian yet plastered to the side of The Light House, which bears the slogan 'John 8.12. Jesus spake to them, saying, I am the light of the world' with the painting of a lighthouse and at the back of the Light House, the Grace Bible Fellowship building that meets on Sunday in the Grace Chapel.

'It is more dreadful for the Gnostic to be expanded than contracted for few can remain within the limits of proper conduct in expansion' Ibn 'Ata' Allah . You'll stay at the Holiday Inn tonight because you need a bath and some crisp cotton sheets. You booked your room at the airport. Good thinking to lash out on soft pillows and a double bed for the first night, not that you will sleep, Al; this is Dublin. Is it coming back; has it ever gone? Not for one moment. What we should do now to fill in daylight hours is go visit the panther.

It's happening; you know because you're close to those tears that trickle down your cheeks on Sunday when you take Communion. As it says in the Rule of Ailbe, monks should follow the abbot to the cross with melodious chants and abundance of tears flowing down emaciated cheeks; and again, in the Rule of Mochuda Raithin, it is the duty of the abbot to encourage the seniors, weighed down with sorrows and sicknesses, that they may invoke, frequently, the Abbot of the Archangels, with floods of tears.

The path to Salvation through Extreme Severe Depression.

Once in Abu Bakr's time, folk from the Yemen came to Medina.
When they heard a reader in the mosque chanting the Koran,
tears fell from their eyes.
We were like that once, said the Caliph, but our hearts have
since grown harder.

What did you do on your first day in Ireland, ten years back, while you waited for Greg to fly in from Ibiza? You did what you're doing now:

you caught the DART out to visit the Joyce museum in Sandycove. You picked your way from Bloom's Hotel in Anglesea Street through a legion of T-shirted, paunchy, hard-faced, prematurely white-haired Irishmen down College Green to Trinity, past the Bank of Ireland, on past Doyle's Pub with the plaque that reads, 'There is a good time coming, be it ever so far away', and on down Pearse past Gardai Headquarters, under the Guinness ad ('If only everything flowed so freely') onto the DART at Westland Row.

Grand Canal Dock – now that's modern – but Dublin Bay, looking north towards Howth Head, is as ever.

It was off Howth that the Sons of Tuireann finally regained consciousness, all badly wounded having made their three shouts from the Hill of Midcain.

There was hope then. Now there is no hope but there is knowledge.

The Irish had only monasteries. It was the Norse built the towns and sited a mere five miles from the first Viking settlement in AD 840 at Black Pool (*Dubh Linn*) was Tallaght Monastery – piecemeal requisitioned as a convenient Viking takeaway.

Olive-striped green seats with yellow handles, the smell of the bay at low tide, the ear-splitting 'door-closing' beeper; it was on this very DART, returning from Enniskillen, that you took a snapshot of the young man you'd thought might have been the panther because till he turned his head to one side you'd thought he was a woman. It was a Saturday evening and later, when the panther duly appeared, she'd hair like that young man – long, black, luxuriant, curly – Parisian by name Zora.

God, how you love this city, the site of your resurrection! Mind you, it doesn't love you because it hasn't loved anyone since 1994 when 68-year-old Father Liam Cosgrove died in a gay sauna after last rites had been administered him by two other Roman Catholic priests who happened to be in the building; this, one year before Father Daniel Curran was jailed for seven years in Belfast on thirteen counts of sexually assaulting boys; and Father Michael Cleary, spokesman for the Catholic Church on contraception and divorce, was exposed as having twice impregnated his housekeeper in Harold's Cross; and the Catholic Archbishop of Dublin, Dr Desmond O'Connell, was forced to concede he had indeed authorised a loan to paedophile priest Father Ivan Payne. All this, a mere three years after Bishop Dr Eamonn Casey of Galway allegedly diverted one hundred and twenty-five thousand punt from the collection box to an American divorcee, Annie Murphy, the mother of his son, Peter.

You alight in Dun Laoghaire, where the stub-nosed Sterna Line ferry docks, and stroll along the pier where Samuel Beckett discovered, one wet winter's night, his nihilistic vocation. Because what else remained? The little maestro, like Charlie Parker, had exhausted the form. Yet still it goes on. We want our meal to continue. Our meal must never end! Bang bang bang with the empty tankards on the trenchers! But all that remains is pepper and salt and sugar and mineral water – Roddy Doyle, Maeve Binchy and the pellucid Colm Tóibín.

Walk the seashore, Al, to the Martello Tower at Sandycove.

And there he is. Leave him to you! That snarling, glossy panther in the fireplace amid the chairs, the bed, the hammock, the thick granite walls that slope up to the narrow windows in this Fort Denison look-alike, the coal in the scuttle, the fuel stove, the table with the Chinese blue and white, the kero lamp – nothing has changed here, what's to change? There's the trunk, the grey wall heater, roped off against intrusion. In 1904, Oliver St John Gogarty rented this Martello Tower and James Joyce of UCD with Dermot Chevenix Trench, deeply disturbed son of the archbishop of Dublin, came out to visit and sleep in this dark, circular tower where Trench had a nightmare of a panther in the fireplace, and drawing his revolver, fired at it. Gogarty, shouting, 'Leave him to me!' seized the revolver and shot down the saucepans over the little maestro's head. Joyce, shaken, walked back to town that night. He could tell when he wasn't wanted. Ten years on, in the first chapter of the greatest modern novel in the English tongue, Trench has become 'the ponderous Saxon Haines' and Gogarty 'stately, plump Buck Mulligan'.

There he is, the varmint. Leave him to you! You paid him no great mind when you saw him here ten years back yet that same night at Bloom's Hotel you had the mother of all nightmares. It featured this very panther. He was tearing at your throat, stabbing you in the back and firing a nailgun at your heart. You tried to scream but couldn't, and then you were sitting up in bed as if a film of you being shot in the head were being run backward.

Trench shot himself in the head over a woman in 1909. Those were the days in which men killed themselves for love.

Pastel! Don't let it end this way, please. Even so, we know it must, as all things do: we should regard all times as past, all gold and jade as smashed, all carpets and brocades as worn through.

We need a snapshot of this porcelain panther. Snap!

Done.

Back at the Holiday Inn, watching Or Tee Eee and reading the *Irish Times*, you discover that Dublin has just endured its wettest summer since records began in 1954, the Baldonnel pluviometer recording rainfall 232 per cent above average for June, July and August. It appears you arrived on the very morning of August 24, St Bartlemy's Day. There is much talk of this because the Curse of St Swithin's, which dates from July 15, AD 971, says:

St Swithin's Day if thou dost rain

For forty days it will remain

And it has. Forty days of relentless Irish weather which ceased the morning you arrived.

St Bartlemy's dusty mantle dries

All the tears that Swithin cries

And what a mixed blessing, for such as like to sleep a' night for the Irish are now pouring onto the streets in party mode.

Hey, you didn't think you were going to *sleep*, Al? Friday night in Dublin! Just before midnight, you're woken by a brawl on the corner opposite as children, still on holiday, run to the disturbance from every quarter. Now guards arrive, sirens ablare. The voice, in these parts, is used as a weapon, contempt for other beings being expressed in its very volume, although the mobile, over the past ten years, has obliterated privacy worldwide.

Hopsom jopsom hopsom jopsom FOOKIN'! Jopsom FOOKIN' IDJUT! Jopsom jopsom JAYSUS CHRIST! Jopsom FOOK OFF!

Even little Dublin girls at play squeal and yelp at the top of their lungs and harken to the men roar themselves hoarse as they barrack for TV soccer in the pub. To an outsider, this is all very disturbing, but the Irish seem unaware of their own aggression. What is most striking is the loathing expressed in the usual Irish expletive, the most commonly heard word among young people of either sex being the adjective 'fookin" uttered with characteristic plosive venom so that what you hear, as you lie in your bed, hour after hour, is:

Jopsom hopsom GO ON, FOOK OFF! jopsom FOOKIN' jopsom hopsom GO ON FOOK OFF, FOOK YA! Popsom FOOK OFF FOOK YA! Popsom jopsom jopsom popsom and they can't see a conjunction.

☾

Now half-twelve and wide awake so t'ink might as well go visit Temple Borf. Should stort now to make our way t'ere, a mere ten-minute walk and safe, given t'e entire population of Dublin is now out on the street, celebrating the first fine night of summer on the first fine night of autumn.

August is *Lunasa* here, more properly *Lughnasa*, the great harvest festival named after the Celtic sun god *Lugh an Laimh Fada*, Lugh of the Long Arm. *Lughudunum* in Gaul was the Roman name for Lyon, site of a vicious rhetorical contest instituted by Caligula in which the defeated contestant was brutally humiliated.

For a Celt, being cast out was brutal humiliation. It was called by the early Celtic Church 'white martyrdom'. Without family or tribal support, life quickly lost meaning. Ostracism led to loss of income, reputation, status and eventually wife, family and sanity. Needless to say, it was eagerly seized upon by the Celtic monk, even as he shaved his head in imitation of his shaven-headed slave.

'I have no interest in anything not monastic and secluded! I care not whether or which, provided it be secluded and monastic.

'What a trial it is to go to vigils as the wind burns my ears. Were it not for fear of the Lord I would ignore the bell, my little sweetheart.

'Adam, Samson and Solomon were all deceived by women. Anyone who listens to a woman will be in grave danger.'

Rule of the Grey Monks.

Or, in the dictum of Caliph 'Umar II, *Shawir hunna wa khalif hunna*: consult women and do the contrary.

There is a good time coming be it ever so far away. Shane MacGowan of 'Pogue Mahone', whose idea of breakfast is a bottle of Baileys, see, does this mid-morning interview, horsh time 'n all to be awake. 'Fire away,' he says to his fancy, swigging his Baileys straight from the bottle. 'If I should Fall from Grace' is a fine song by Shane MacGowan.

If only everything flowed so freely, Shane.

There is a good time coming be it ever so far away.

Pastel has changed more than you have, Al, over the past thirty-five years and for the better so be pleased. It is proper that she can no longer relate to that woman barred from so many a club, thirteen-year-old mug lair frozen in the body, and what a body, of a woman – gauche, brash, butch, unbelievably beautiful burlesque queen – and Noughties Burlesque, me darlin's exploits a taboo that no longer exists. No perve who ever saw Pastel dance has forgotten how when, bored, she would cross her eyes and stick out her tongue, bridging up to the broad-shouldered bars of her cage like an All Black in a haka. None of the other girls had her sense of humour, but she's moved on, do you see? She's her own woman now as her feminist friends attest.

She is the greatest artist ever came out of that capital city; Rosalie Gascoigne having been Kiwi. And likely the greatest burlesque dancer Australia ever produced, but you don't figure in her fans' fond recollections of Pastel – any more than you figured in her fans' fond recollections of your mum. Each of them built a reputation with no help from yourself. In men's minds you had nothing to do with either one of them. You're a postscript.

There's a brief glimpse of you coming onstage as the sticky fingers reach for the remote. Because by the time you entered their lives they were on the verge of retirement.

Pastel actually won your heart by dancing for you in private, soon after your 'first bite of the cherry' (her words).

The way the yearning flickered across her face was like an electric storm.

She yearned for respectability.

Feminists: they have worked to destroy the marriage. It is interesting the different reactions incarcerated men have to their women jumping the fence, which is well-nigh universal practice on the inside among women. Whereas to a Muslim it's cause for suicide, the kafir hopes he may be in for a threesome. 'I wouldn't care less!' he'll tell you. Odds on he's watched a fair bit of porn in which vixens, for entrée, lick each other out. Dream on!

Most beautiful women are not sexy and most sexy women are not beautiful. It may well be that to be both, a woman needs to have been sexually assaulted as a child.

Pastel was 'Elephant' at Ainslie Primary where she towered over the boys and had breasts by the age of ten. Today, this would be put as a prompt stop to 'bullying'. At thirteen, on Gunnar's instigation, she was dragged through the courts – which arrested her mentally and physically – over a crime committed on her by the likely lad who, moving on from schoolgirls, fucked the local countryside to become the Sheik of Scrubby Creek, a noted vigneron – a crime that would these days bring him a slap on the wrist if it went to court.

He got off with a bond.

In the *Arabian Nights* they would have both been put to death.

Pastel's pudendum, as chief exhibit for the prosecution, was examined by the court and, on completion of the trial, consigned for display to the playgrounds, toilets and locker rooms of Canberra High. By age fifteen, she'd thought rape was the norm. Aged twenty-three, punk in microskirt and with the deep cleavage, she was a young mum asking for it. No jury would have convicted. She liked to dance to the gut-bucket jazz of brothel-born Louis Armstrong. She'd jump on a table, drench herself with a jug of beer, then do her thing. In her company you once met the drummer who raped her aged twenty-five – ugly Dago dimwit, half her size – and offered to cut his throat or, at least, teach him how to play, till she confessed she'd asked him back to try something she read about in one of those porno magazines her desperate husband was feeding her, ar, what do you do. You never heard of *any* woman doing a thing like that, what *do* you *do?* He was no kisser but he was a teller, the Dago dimwit – they like to brag and how it used to turn your gut when you had to listen to it at the band table, between sets, as an Emerson-reading virgin of sixteen. From all this, you learn that this is what can happen when a spirited girl – with or without complicity – is raped.

'Urinogenital', the word that says it all. When 'genital' is first encountered in the context of 'urino' a burlesque act takes shape.

You don't really like sex, Al. What a pity you're addicted and what a pity these New Age women, in their demands for 'acceptance', cannot accept that when you give a man your heart, you confer on him your shame. Pastel should have unloaded all that shit onto some celibate confessor. The instinctive male sexual response, if possessed of appropriate capacity, is to go in harder, to go in deeper and as often as possible with killer sperm.

It is absence makes the sperm grow meaner.

You will never get over Pastel. She is one of a kind, like to that devyl in form of faryryste maydyn tempted sir Percyvale but chonged unto a smoke and a blak clowde when he made, leyde by her naked, the sygne of the crucifixe in the forehed of hys. *And then sir Percivale made grete sorrow and drew hys swerde unto hym, and seyde, 'Sitthyn my fleyssh woll be my mayster I shall punyssh hit. How nyghe I was loste, and to have lost that I sholde never have gotyn agayne, that was my virginitie, for that may never be recovered after hit ys onys loste.'* You can't expect another woman to follow after Pastel. Okay, so she lied to you about certain aspects of her past but she says she's been faithful to you in a tone that brooks no argument. There are degrees of fidelity. She now enjoys her work in a maximum security men's prison. You've long had to deal with what you well know to be endless Platonic power-plays. It was actually your suggestion that she should apply for the job. She likes a male audience, flaunts respectability, enjoys rejecting advances, and it comforts the incarcerate with women on the outside to meet a woman he can't seduce. Regrettably, the job has reawakened a lust for giving counsel. She's the jail 'deal with it'. Should ever you complain, she drags you to a mirror to meet the man responsible for your problem. She seems to press your 'mother' buttons, even as you seem to press her 'father' buttons for her. Who was that prophet married the temple prostitute, was it Hosea? The consort of Simon Magus, Jesus' Samaritan rival, was Helen, a temple prostitute from Ephesus, Temple of the Great Mother. Such women pack a punch. Pastel's past has become your Poisonous Dragon and you have fucked yourself stupid.

Fleurs du Mal. She says she never did it for money and never with more than one guy at a time because she was clean. Had there been go-ey or smack about in the sixties, she'd have been into it.

She *constantly* told the band table she was locked in a sexless marriage. It was only the truth from a tomboy but she came across as a nympho.

The law can't deal with rape. God knows what she tells them in the jail. What prevents rape is lack of opportunity and fear of retribution from a woman's kinsmen. Today, they take it in their stride. You've read of one Australian girl; violently raped in Thailand, who couldn't be bothered taking a flight back to Thailand to give evidence in court. And they wonder why they get blown up.

There's an Arabic word *fitna* means a combination of sexual tension and political discord. It is *fitna* afflicts young Mustafa from Punchabowl when, acting on text-message misinformation and revved up by Sheikh Hilali, he shivs a convict Aussie dog after the Cronulla riot, December 2005, when Shire drunks, congregating outside Northies Pub by the Bali Memorial in memory of 'Our Girls', seven St George and Sutherland Shire girls blown up at the Sari nightclub in Kuta October 2002, were waving bastardised Union Jacks from toned arms emerging from T-shirts proclaiming 'WE GREW HERE, YOU FLEW HERE'.

'LEBS OUT' (grossly unfair to the Maronite)

'SAVE 'NULLA'

'WOG FREE ZONE'

Even a bestiality slur upon 'the lascivious prophet', as he was known to Victorian evangelicals, and why in God's name would you print a gormless comment like that on a shirt when it's on record that the Most Praised One – Blessings on his Name and upon his Family and Companion-Train – deflowered 'A'ishah, daughter of Abu Bakr, aged ten when he was fifty-three?

A line in the sand had been crossed when a bunch of Leb hoons, visiting 'Nulla to kick sand in faces and perve on the likes of Kathy Lette, decked a North Cronulla lifesaver.

Decked a volunteer *life*saver, I mean ... do they want *war?*

They want jihad but they'd like a slice of Aussie slut.

As it says on the Memorial, 'Seven young girls set off for fun, to relax and soak in some Bali sun, but the news broke out and rang in our ears, our girls had been killed and we cried many tears, we wish we had known that that "goodbye" would be our last, how could we have known that your future would be our past? How do we right this terrible wrong? For all of you we must stay strong, we will try to move our lives forward as our goal, you will always remain deep in our hearts and soul.' Written by the families of those lost and there are photos of the seven young girls on the revetment of the water fountain in the shape of the seed of *Banksia robur*, Shire native: Jodie O'Shea 29, Michelle Dunlop 30, Renae Anderson 31, Simone Hanley 28, Francoise Dahan 30, Charmaine Whitton 29, Jodi Wallace 29.

Seven old maids set off for ... Nah, doesn't sound right; yet in the *Arabian Nights*, the brides and grooms are fourteen years of age.

You still recall the window in Nando's bending back and forth under the weight of a thousand arms. You recall the constable winking at you (signing with the eyelid, *al-Khalaj*) as he ran down the mall outside the Commonwealth Bank followed by a braying drunk, peroxide-headed grommet squad, with you and your daughter having threaded your way through to Michael's to buy some green king prawns. Always good king prawns at Michael's. They positively glisten.

Your daughter was visiting from far north Queensland and luckily for you both, she wasn't wearing a headscarf.

Interesting, the alliances that formed in the days after the riot: Chocolate Drops and Coconuts would see themselves as Anglos, with Abo's firmly siding with the Muslim. Indeed, the urban yeller fellers spilled out of Redfern on the train hoping for a bit of action but had to settle for abuse from passing cars.

And you got put on the Leb, who'd never before been racially targeted. Indeed, you had to leave town for a time till things settled down.

'Is he one of them?' you heard it said to another Surf Club member. They weren't young men but they were younger than you. You were coming back from Gloria Jean's on the Tuesday, this under the Rissole rink at the edge of the park behind the beach. Folk were edgy, with retaliation having been effected out of all proportion to the initial drunken Anglo assault (on a Jew and a Greek). The blue-eyed boys were looking for men of 'Middle Eastern appearance' and you'd made the mistake of meeting their hard-eye.

'So, you a Muslim, pal? You still livin' in the Dark Ages?'

'Nah, he's that guy from over the road runs the Mother Forget shop, Woz. He's okay. How's it goin' there, Eyebrows? No worries, buddy.'

'I hate all Mustafas.'

'Ah, Woz, he's an old man, pal, and he's wearing a *crucifix*.'

'Okay. I'm out o' line but I bet he don't worship in the Elephant House with Bruce Baird. How would *you* feel if you had your fuckin' missus dissed and now your car trashed and your herbed fish stolen off your barbecue at Shelly's once and a friend of your sister *murdered* in the Bali bombings? How would *you* feel?'

You were tempted to reply 'I have a bronze medallion from North Bondi, Fuckknuckle, and won a junior beach flags' but didn't want to bust your cover.

Won the junior beach flags. That was a great day. Good elbow block. Learned to swim under Alf Vockler at the Watson's Bay baths.

Now, think of all those chicks you could have raped, Al, if you weren't such a gentleman; all those chicks you stripped or part stripped in your twenties on an understanding it would go no further. Was *that* sex? Can we notch that up? If not, it isn't *fair*!

Mantra in the all-male correctional institute: it isn't *fair*!

Mantra in the all-female correctional institute: gimme gimme *gimme*.

On the one hand, we repent our sins; on the other, we could never get enough of them.

What exactly *is* sex? Where does it begin? Let's ask this young lady, *excuse me*!

Oh no, she just did a heel on the cobbles – well-oiled, hard-faced, bottle blonde in her mid-forties, the kind that pours out of the lifts Friday night at Jury's Christ Church wearing microskirts and mouseketeer ears to wiggle down Parliament past the bouncer on the Maccas (!) for a night of debauch in Temple Borf, having flown in possibly from Manchester earlier that evening. This one has her stilettos by the straps but lobster-face there in his paunchy T-shirt with number one grizzled crewcut leaves no doubt that this is an all-Irish affair.

Fook Sake, woman! Jaysus Christ, Fook Sake.

Quid enim ulla negaverit udis inguinibus sive est haec Oppia sive Catulla? Deterior totos habet illic femina mores. Get an old slag on the job and she'll give you anything you want because all an old slag ever wants is to get sticky round the micky. Juvenal.

Let's see if it still exists. There is the side wall of TBMC opposite – Good God Almighty, it's Barnacles Budget Rooms.

You walk into Curved Street to find a man urinating against the front door.

Does that mean the place is closed? Not necessarily in Temple Borf where a pool of urine trickles down the steps of every darkened door, but the borf – those neat little circular Temple offerings – are always a few feet from a wall. There's something to be said for rain.

Now *that* borf, that could be Abrakebabra. And that, that's Pizza Milano. That's Purty Kitchen for sure while *that,* smell the saffron? Charlie's Oriental Express.

Go back to bed, drop a Temtab. What made you think you could fit in here?

First light, late August, just before six, is the best time of day in Dublin. For a full fifteen minutes the gulls get a look-in as surviving revellers are now too drunk to 'fook' and the streetsweepers have yet to arc up. From between occasional tyres on roads can be heard the cry of Liffey herring gull: *Da wah wah wah wah wah wah wah wah ...*

Dublin City streetsweepers in yellow vests featuring the three castles of Dublin Town sweep detritus off footpaths onto the cobblestones for collection by machine. The pigeons are into the borf and the takeaway wrappings. Butts, beercans, broken glass, the stench of urine in every door and outside TBMC a boisterous resonance of bottles being rolled cobbleward by testy broomsman.

Not one burly bouncer in black with earpiece on any door; like vampires, they cannot stand the light of day. Not one Dixie cup by blanketed body on any footpath; it is yourself and the sweepers, Al, though at seven-thirty machines arrive, brushes bouncing off the bollards.

You will book a Barnacles Budget Room for tonight as they are conveniently central, right opposite the Wall of Fame in fact but someone may first need to hose away that pool of piss in the door as you're an early riser and didn't bring gumboots.

Greg looked the part here, knocking back the black stuff at the faux '30's bar in the Turk's Head with his cheesy cobweb elbow tatt. Bit of a Touretter, constantly shouting, 'Call the G-G-G-Gardai!' or 'I demand to speak with the T-T-T-Teashock!'

The Wall of Fame is two years old. You will be looking straight at it from Barnacles Budget Room tonight if for some reason you can't sleep. You will have only to go to your window and there they'll be, all staring back, twelve musical celebrities on the side wall of Temple Bar Music Centre with Paul (nobody knows why Elvis took it all) Brady in the top right corner. There's Sinéad, Christy, Shane, Van – no Gilbert of course – U2, rightly bigger than the rest with a youthful Bono not yet sporting his trademark straw-coloured specs. Ask that painter who just started painting the awning in Cecilia Street, what's the score with TBMC?

Ah, thank goodness, it's only shut for refurbishment.

Now, where was that tromb player busking? Wasn't he up here somewhere on Sycamore Street? He had a black eye and an ear stud and his tromb had seen better days, too, but for some reason he stood in the Olympia Theatre stage door. Over and over he played the same tune as if he were playing it just for you, Al, as if he were sent to speak to you alone – *ma'lak Yahwe*, Angel of the Lord.

Be there in that number when the saints go marchin' in …

And you'd suddenly realised that this trad jazz standard which you'd long associated with *evil* was a hymn.

Seventeen Sycamore Street and the crystalline clusters beginning to form. Solution is approaching saturation.

Opposite where that tromb player busked a crowd formed on the cobbles last night, outside this four-storey brick Georgian building with a video camera trained on the yellow stripe that leads to the door and on that massive door in silver letters in the biggest script to be seen in all Dublin:

SIN

That's the name of it. You stare till you feel the need for insular minuscule, the smallest script to be seen in all Dublin – in which is written the Book of Armagh AD 807, but the East Pavilion of Trinity Library Colonnades won't be open yet so you decide to breakfast at the Maccas in O'Connell which will take you past Forbidden Planet, the comic book emporium with its windowful of monsters on a par with the vinyl sleeves in All-City Records (Ugly Duckling, A-Trak AKA THE I SPINNA, Monkey Boy Breaks) or, amethyst purple and malachite green, the nymph-naked skullduggery on display in the Dublin Head Shop up the street from Barnacles.

That's where the panther was squatting in front of that iron fence with the black spikes impaling the red Coke can, outside Trinity main entrance in front of Goldsmith on his plinth with his pen and book. She was awaiting a number ten bus via *An Lar* to Belfield. She wore high-heeled wedgies and microskirt and squatted like a Muslim man about to take a leak. When first you saw her, having walked up from Pearse DART after the false alarm, your blood froze.

She got you right between the eyes.

She had you in her sights and she was up for it, too; she was giving you a glad-eye for no other reason than to test your Christian mettle – *ma'lak Yahwe*. Your thoughts *immediately* turned to the nature of *Dreams* and *Forewarnings* and what these say, but when you got on the bus you sat next to her to learn more. She was in Dublin to learn to speak English and this was her last night. Desperate? Rootrats often target older men.

You would not have survived her. You would have followed her to Paris where she'd have mauled you over as Pastel did, only worse. You were meant to be a one-nighter.

Which makes you feel – cheap.

She was lodging with a private family in Donnybrook. You made no attempt to hook up but you recall thinking as she got off the bus, *why am I letting her go?*

Because, if we are going to fuck, the anima wants a fertile womb. As quoth Imam 'Ali (whose face Allah honour), 'an old woman is deadly poison.'

Now we go in to see the Book of Armagh. Get your NSW Senior's Card ready, Al.

A favourite snapshot of Pastel is of dancing with this beautiful blonde, of touching her body for the first time, albeit chastely, on the floor of the Chopsticks Nightclub in Civic having gone there down Northbourne Avenue with the band in which you were both working, Pastel as vocalist – she could no doubt tell you the date – during which time she had a vaginal orgasm only didn't know what it was. As she would put it when co-dependent, 'I wasn't alone anymore.' And as you were leaving the venue, she ran up the stairs to kiss you.

And now it's over.

You can still see her, in that red dress, running up the stairs, blonde locks flying. After she'd had the orgasm, you did a strange thing; you both extended your arms in what you now realise was *crosfigell*, the cross vigil prayer position beloved of the Celtic monk in which Kevin prayed at Glendalough for so long that a bird is said to have nested in his outstretched palm.

There'd been no impropriety. Heather had not long given birth. You held each other in recognition as it had become a scene from one of those Jain narratives, one of those soul biographies that relate the tales of pairs of souls reunited over successive embodiments. You like the Jain concept of the universe as uncreated and eternal. It comports far better than Genesis with your physical intuition.

A snapshot you took of Heather at fourteen shows you both sitting in a park near the Conobolas. She's a bit above you and to your left and it's dark and she's saying, 'I'm not perfect!' and your head spins, you think you're going to faint, you little incipient Cathar.

Go on, the voice was saying in your head that night at Belfield after the panther got off the bus. You lay awake all night until the suitcase wheels began. Don't stop!

Go on, said the voice, go on; don't stop now, my darling. We're nearly there. You did the right thing, you'll be rewarded. You turned your back on Satan the Stoned. We're nearly there. Push! Push!

And then you thought of that Irish girl you met in Hobart once who had the sweetest, blithest laugh of any woman in the world, a laugh that would not have survived a carnal encounter and you pushed past her as well and *whoomph*! She was your gatekeeper. Because you went right through and beyond this carnal world, right through the Veil of Separation bypassing all the human women, they're only creatures, and solution crystallised and you could have held the beaker upside down in your hand.

Then you did a strange thing. You were no longer *thinking* but you felt impelled to get out of your bed where it must have been round dawn and you went to the communal kitchen where you took a fork from a drawer and struck the kitchen tap with it over and again, to listen *intently* with your ear close to the tap because it was *important* for you to know just how the sound of that ringing ceased – this long before you'd read of the affection Irish monks had for the bell in the *cloch teach*. Bell casting, developed in the eighth century, was a jealously guarded monastic secret, and the monks would make a shrine for their bell just as they did for their sacred book. Did the resonance stop suddenly or did it merely *fade*? You determined that while it must have faded it *seemed* to stop suddenly and content with this quantum insight and for some reason relieved you went back to your bed exhausted and slept soundly for an hour or so and when you woke – *She* was there – Mary, Shakti, Shekinah, Isis, Cybele, call Her what you will – and the journey of your life was over.

Why can't journeys end when they are over?

You had made the Mystical Marriage at the age of fifty-two but hadn't yet stabilised.

'Rarely come the Divine intuitions except of a sudden, lest the slaves should claim them as the result of their preparations' Ibn 'Ata' Allah. That sudden consciousness of the switching off of all masculine (read sinful) impulse with concomitant loss of all desire to grouse, fight, fuck, eat, sleep; the dramatic, overwhelming sense of looming, benevolent *female* presence – the disappearance of time, hence of narrative – the phenotypical transfiguration, the doctrinal emphasis on the importance of stabilisation: could it be that the spiritual discipline of entering the red band in a thin place – the path of Christian virtue – may lead under favourable circumstance to non-pseudo-autosomal shutdown of certain Y chromosomal genes presently misconstrued as 'junk' – for there could be no 'junk' in a chromosome, only ignorance in an observer – accompanied by corresponding activation of certain 'junk' regions of the X with selective inhibition of serotonin re-uptake? Could *this* be the Mystical Marriage? We all contain within us a nascent Virgin: only in the male can She give birth to a eunuch.

☾

Nuns were forced to live outside the Celtic monastic enclosure. They got something from Christianity but what, no man could say (especially when he saw them venerating Joseph).

Ah, don't start crying in here, Al, for Chrissake, pull yourself together! Who's to say *She* won't return in your hour of death? That will be up to you. You have a template. And you know it works because you had an aftershock that time you got lost in the Wilderness a year or so after Belfield and you'd been screwing Pastel and smoking bushbuds and drinking dry the Yarra Valley.

Study this interlacing 'carpet' page on the Book of Kells here and pull yourself together – come on. You know you can do it, you've done it before. Admire the knots, the whirligigs, the crypto-Islamic ornamentation not unlike the effect of la Mezquita in Cordoba. Written on the vellum of one hundred and eighty-five calves, the hair removed by soaking the skin in shit and then scraping it with a knife and you've done that as they won't tan a single hide anymore. You've also thrust your gloved and lubed left fist up many a cow's arsehole searching for that squash-racket handle of the cervix into which to insert the metal needle warming between your teeth as you've been a cattleman and you can artificially inseminate and preg test.

Christ, you miss your cattle. You miss your cattle more than any human being you ever met. It was a shame you had to cut off their heads. You've buried, in your time, a fair few heifer heads from those home-kills.

So *this* is what we should do with our male calves. We should make *gospels* of them so that nothing goes to waste. It doesn't say that here but these pages are male. Better than pulping old growth forest.

And that Christ child there is a red-headed man: Book of Kells, 800 AD, Virgin and Child by the scribe known only as 'the Illustrator' showing four red-haired archangels, six red-haired saints, four red-haired something-or-others and one red-haired Mary nursing one red-haired adult Christ-child.

And we can recall how he feels, which is not the same as being in Her Arms again.

Soviet philosopher Ivanov writing in 1920 – and, bossa nova excepted, nothing much has happened since of cultural note – in the common room of the Convalescent Home for Scientific and Literary Workers in Moscow to his good friend the atheist Gershenson installed in the opposite corner of the room, writes:

> 'A man who has faith in God will not consent at any price to see in his faith merely one of the constituents of Culture. On the other hand a man who has become a slave of Culture will inevitably diagnose Faith as a cultural phenomenon whatever may be the exact definition of Faith that he goes on to work out. He may define it as an inherited outlook and an historically determined psychic habitus, or define it in terms of Metaphysics and Poetry; or define it, again, as a socially formative force and an ethical standard: it all comes to the same thing ... the real point is this: our faith in an Absolute – in which we are already in touch with something that is *not* Culture – is the issue on which our destiny hangs. If we have this faith it gives us an inward freedom which is veritably Life itself; if we do not, our unbelief condemns us to an inward enslavement by a Culture that has long since become godless ... Faith alone – and by "faith" I mean a complete renunciation of the Fall of Man, for which Culture is another name.'

So God created man in his own image, in the image of God created
he him; male and female created he them. And God blessed

them, and God said unto them, be fruitful and multiply.
And the Lord God said, it is not good that the man should be alone;
I will make him an help meet for him.
Feminas ad imaginem Dei factas non esse.

Buy a few postcards of the Book of Kells for the granddaughters, write something witty on the back, now go book yourself a Barnacles Budget Room for Saturday night.

The anomalous northward extension of the Azores High brings fine weather to all Eire. Farmers, smiling, arc up the long arms of the headers to harvest what will prove a record cereal crop. Meantime, back in Dimdim, the wheat crop fails over two weeks from harvest in drought – the latest it's ever been known to fail, after all that rain in May with no follow-up. And in Temple Borf, thumping house music continues till 'late' (4 am) from F.U.N. Fitzsimmons (4 floors, 4 bars, 4 DJ's all 4U) and SIN.

It is ten years since you first visited the Temple Bar Music Centre with Greg, there to meet the man from London, home of drum 'n bass. This was to be your out-of-town tryout. You'd rented a kit from Drum Depot near the hags with the bags by Ha'penny Bridge and needed to mike it up and do soundchecks. There were people in the foyer didn't look like clubbers.

'They'll be for Eochaidh,' confided Cellach the agent.

'Who?'

'Eochaidh! He'd be on before you in the other room.'

'And what kind of music does Ekegg play?'

'Traditional. That's his flier, next yours. Do you read Irish, Greg?'

'No.'

'Then don't bother reading it. Eochaidh don't speak English. Well, he does but his father won't encourage him.'

'I like the sound of that,' says Greg, 'and I like the sound of Ekegg.'

'On hearing you was a farmer, Al, Eochaidh's father asked me to give you this. It is a traditional goatskin winnow. You put the grain in here and shake it to separate the chaff 'n all. It comes with this little knuckle-headed beater which you bang on the skin to frighten birds, so. Now.'

'He's joking, Al. That's a bodhran, traditional Irish drum.'

'Tell Ekegg's father I mean to catch the act.'

'No! You must *not* catch the act, Al, as it could throw you out!'

'Any chance of – sniff sniff?'

There's no path to follow.

'I shall see what I can do, Greg. Every chance I should imagine.'

You're in a bad mood now because no one tells Al Morrisey what not to do. Seething, you walk to the wall to peruse the fliers. Two shows tonight and an afternoon matinee sponsored by the Arts Council, which flier is not for the casual reader.

Ceol ilghneitheach, iltreitheach a sheinneann an Ua Duinchdheannanach, ceol a chiumsionn an uile mhothuchan go slachtmhar dilis. Nil aon amhras na gur seiftiuil an cumadoir e chomh maith.

Oscloidh an t-albam 'Duinchdhan' seo domhan ur os do chomhair nach dtraochfaidh do chluas go deo agus ar iocshlainte don chroi agus don anam e.

Eochaidh Ua Duinchdhan Feodoga isle

Conor Ua Duinchdhan Giotair bioghuilli

Caoilte Ua Duinchdhan Giotair Leictreach agus bioghuilli

Fionnuala Ua Duinchdhan Mearchlair

Dubhlitir Walsh Bodhran, triantan

Niall O Clery Dordghiotar

Buiochas ar leith ag dul do bhaill an teaghlaigh, do mo chairde agus do na ceoltoiri.

And then Eochaidh walks through the door the man was last night urinating on.

They're children. Band of little Irish buskers.

You turn to Greg who's as white as you are but can think of nothing to say to him.

Brilliant! The pair of you go on to play what the papers all call the best live drum 'n bass act ever heard in Dublin ('Al Morrisey a veritable drum machine, Elvin Jones of drum 'n bass'), but next morning you have fled to UC Belfield wit' the bodhran, leaving Greg and Cellach no forwarding address and it's over. You have blown it as per usual but you've blown your last chance, mate, because that was it.

So. Now. Is it possible you never really *wanted* to succeed, Al, at some deep psychological level, at all at all? Is it not also possible that you actually *loathe* this world, Al, and every hydrogen-bonded creature that creepeth upon the earth? Because if all went well you were booked to play London the following week and all went well but you spent the weeks you were meant to be in London wandering Belfield as far as Donnybrook and Stillorgan then cycling Kerry and Clare on a pushbike, off with the fairies.

It was over before it began when, contrary to Cellach's advice, you *did* stick your head in backstage to listen to the children play and it proved a fateful five minutes. Cellach was right. Cellach was on the money. Four of the children had red hair, presumably the three brothers and their sister, and the band used two guitars – one acoustic, but played in a way you'd never heard rhythm guitar played – with bass guitar, bodhran and low whistles, and the girl on a kind of rhythm stride piano, all very effective.

The low whistle has, on the melancholic, the effect of oboe. It smacks of *huzn*.

And *huzn* is your Sufic *maqam*.

They were playing a polka that had an ancient quality. You recall every bar. You often hum it to yourself to lift your spirits on a bushwalk. You would have been humming it the day you got lost in the Blue Mountains and saw the ring of trout. You found the CD in Killarney as no one in Dublin ever heard of Eochaidh and you made everyone listen to it and everyone says, it has to be traditional, that polka, but it's not. It was composed a mere twelve years ago by a little boy in Dunquin.

It is the real deal. It is not factitious; it is not, say, Philip Glass as compared to McCoy Tyner.

Irish music can uplift the *chi*; Negro music, of the kind they spin in SIN, pushes it down into the *muladhara chakra*. The odd thing is, the beat is the same in both.

Those children were playing with fire and someone should have put a prompt stop to them because they were working the region capable of transporting a primed soul into the Philosophical Stone-become-red, known to the Irish as *Tir na nOg*, Land of the Ever-Young. It is the realm of the suicide bomber. It was *mystical* music; it was music of great druidic power. The Irish have music can make a man cry, make a man dance and make a man drink, whereas drum 'n bass can make a man fuck, make a man fight and make a man dance.

It got you between the ears. If you want to play the blame game, Al, it destroyed your worldly prospects because it set in motion that chain of events which made you take a powder and saw you do a runner and yet, and yet – others don't seem to get off on it. Oh, they listen politely enough when you force it on them because you're a strong man and can grow obsessive when drinking late at night. You played that CD endlessly till it wore out and you never burned it.

No worries. They will have it in Killarney, mate. You will have it again by the end of the week.

And wasn't Pastel annoyed, as well, when she heard what you had done! It was then you realised that all they really care about is money and status.

Rule of Tallaght: 'A layman came to Mocholmoc Ua Litain seeking spiritual direction. "What is your present condition? Are you living the life of a married man?" "No," came the reply, "It is three years since I had anything to do with the wife I had." "Did you promise this to anyone?" asked Mocholmoc. "No," he again replied. The holy man then remarked, "That is too long a period to have cut yourself off from the devil without turning to God."'

Up early Sunday to the cry of herring gull and the sound of breaking bottles after three hours' broken sleep. Stagger off to the Grafton Street Maccas to read a virgin *Independent on Sunday* and drink coffee.

Now Tojo is dead. Max Roach – Tojo because of his circular Coke-bottle lenses – father of modern bebop drumming, to the drum kit what Joyce was to the novel. He lived into his eighties having begun his working life, it says here, at nineteen in the band of Coleman Hawkins.

Coleman Hawkins.

More coffee, please. Thank you.

The most famous Colman, who took up his cross bigtime, was third abbott-bishop of Lindisfarne. He oversaw the collapse of the Celtic Church and with it, the long-drawn-out demise of the Far Western Christian Civilisation, now in its final throes at SIN nightclub. At the Synod of Whitby in AD 664, St Colman of Lindisfarne argued the case for Celtic Christendom as St Wilfred argued for Rome. Unsuccessful and having a temper on him like Jerome, Colman stormed from the synod, taking all the Irish and thirty Saxon monks from Lindisfarne, and returned, headland hopping in a currach to Connacht via Iona, where he founded a monastery on some remote offshore isle, the name of which …

The name of which …

The name of which *was*?

The name of which fookin' escapes us.

Can't remember a *thing*! Losing the memory. More coffee, please.

Fancy Tojo dying. Everyone is dying.

And everyone not dying is losing their memory. How *awful*, the company of folk in their mid-sixties! Women clinging to the fading glamour, paunchy, alcoholic men so dismal telling you again everything they told you the time before. It would be nice to hear, now and again, from the grandchildren, but they are too busy.

Pastel says it's not that they don't love you, Al. Aren't you glad they have a life? But you have to text them, in that you have nothing, as they see it, to offer so you're out of the loop.

With neo-Romanesque front and dark, Georgian interior, the Church of St Ann's on Dawson is a mere four hundred yards from SIN but a whole lot quieter. If the Irish Catholic Church in 2007 is in St Brigid's Nursing Home with Polish buttwipe attendant, the Anglo-Catholic Church of Ireland is dead as a dodo, with two Dublin cathedrals, Christ Church and St Pat's, effectively museums and St Ann's – parish church of Bram Stoker, author of *Dracula* – so little in demand you find yourself, at 8 am, the sole communicant, a first in your experience. Nonetheless, your personalised service is beautifully conducted before a splendid reredos Lamb proclaiming 'Holy Holy Holy' and the acoustic compares favourably with the central chamber of the Red Pyramid. The priest has a resonant Northern Irish accent and treats you to the old liturgy, which it is meet and right so to do. Tears moisten your cheeks as you kneel alone to receive at the rail. What stunning silence after the thumping of Saturday night in Temple Borf!

And he took the cup, and when he had given thanks, he gave it to them: and they all drank of it. And he said unto them, This is my blood of the new testament, which is shed for many.

'Bram' Stoker. Now Bram is not short for 'Abraham', it is short for 'Abram'. What is that saying, Al?

Settle for nothing. You are getting tired. There is a display for the World Wildlife Fund on St Stephen's Green at present, where the sun is shining, the peonies are in flower and the crowds have gathered to feed the ducks. 'Spirit of the Wild' by Steve Bloom: prints of endangered wild animals, primates prominent. To your surprise, you detect *huzn* in the face of the silverback gorilla. It is clear as crystal.

You are regaining capacity to read faces.

You must somehow stay on your feet if you mean to see again the Lurgan longboat, the Tara Broach, the Cross of Cong and those many glittering golden hoards of Bronze Age gorgets and ear-spools because the Museum is closed Monday and tomorrow you're out of here.

Kill right now for a good Clare Valley cab sav.

Folk in Cronulla should understand that you do *not* erect a Bali memorial opposite a Hog's Breath Café!

As you walk down Grafton in the sunlight you pass the by-now familiar buskers; the little Korean girl with violin, the man dancing a tango with his female dummy and that dreadful piece of PaddyWhackery, the stage Irishman in cloth cap who is camped beside the tart with the cart pretending to play bodhran. He has a ghetto blaster he affects to accompany, playing along to The Furies and Davey Arthur, but he makes his money principally by having his photo took. He can't play – can't play for shit. Once, when he was up between a pair of young Spanish tourists, you were tempted to snatch his bodhran to show the world what a *drummer* can do but let's leave that for Doolin, Al, and those pick-up sessions in O'Connor's pub where musicians gather from across the *Gaeltacht* and maybe Eochaidh will surface, who seems to have disappeared off the face of the web.

That will be an interesting evening. Nothing an Irishman better enjoys than having an Aussie show him how to play!

You choose The Atlantic on Suffolk and discover the menu features 'chef's Persian specials'. When the blond man comes to take your order, you ask, Is this a *Persian* restaurant, mate? Are you guys Iranian?

Polish.

Hmm. It is Sunday, 26 August 2007. You order eggplant tagine with a glass of Shiraz.

Opposite the façade of the Bank of Ireland in College Green over the road from Trinity College, 'Tommy Moore's roguish finger' has earned itself a brass *Ulysses* plaque embedded in the pavement, as always, riddled with gum. You get to see the gum defacing every pavement for if ten years back you stared at the crowns of the trees to keep out of trouble, today you keep your eyes downcast to avoid the evil eye. You're aware you have an expression that folk can easily misconstrue. It smacks of *huza*.

Sometimes they think you're spoiling for a fight. Sometimes they think you're looking for a fuck. All you want is for that Lost and Wind-Grieved Ghost to come back again, that grace, that Sufic *hal* that raised you, briefly, to eternal life.

They don't understand a mystic in Cronulla and that is their problem entirely. Tommy Moore, high above the pavement, has a flip-flop stuffed under his cape that must have involved some cackling drunk scaling his ten-foot-high plinth. Tommy Moore wrote *Lallah Rookh*, the name of the pub in City Road where the Wentworth building now stands and which was the favourite watering hole for the scientists of Sydney University. There was a Veiled prophet in *Lallah Rookh. Sidere mens eadem mutato. Lallah Rookh* was set in Persia. There is *no way* this Polish menu can be alluding to *Lallah Rookh.*

Something is about to happen involving Persia.

Meaning *crystallises* when in the red band in a thin place. If there were no building opposite you'd be looking straight at the number ten bus stop.

Why? Why is this region of Shane MacGowan's dirty old town so thin? Why is the World of the Seen so close to the World of the Unseen here? *Animus!*

Loading.

We don't know. You once tried to explain to Pastel what you did on your postdoc at the highly Talmudic University of Pennsylvania, where everyone was a rude, argumentative Jew, many of them Nobel Laureates. You took a few magnets off the fridge door in a failed effort to demonstrate how a bipole can take up two positions in a magnetic field to create the phenomenon known as NMR, nuclear magnetic resonance, if the bipole be a nucleus, as it flips between aversion/aversion and attraction/attraction.

You were working, in the Biophysics Unit, on the world's first two-twenty megahertz NMR.

Romantic love is the folly of seeking to fix a flip midway and we need another glass of this excellent French wine, *Garçon*!

You start thinking again of how She does it and as you do, She does it. As you muse over your red on the nature of *meaning,* meaning irrupts. You become aware of the muzak, and how long since you heard *that*? How long since you heard 'Tower of Strength'? Fifty years? You've a snapshot associated with that song. You can't think of the name of the guy who had the hit but that's him: it's no cover.

Eochaidh's brother had a similarly affecting vocal mannerism. On one track he sucks his breath to make a whistle that so freaked you when first you heard it, you wept; it was so blithe and soothing. You never heard anyone else do either of these two things and now one of them is doing it on the muzak at the Atlantic Restaurant in Suffolk Street, 1 pm Sunday, 26 August 2007.

That black dude singing 'Tower of Strength' came down the stairs at El Rocco one night when you were seventeen, sitting in beard and duffle coat listening to Mike Nock play 'Billy Boy'. You were so impressed you took a snapshot. He was the first American negro you'd ever seen in the flesh, a big, black handsome dude with a hit single and all the white chicks flocking to him. The Three Out and management were equally delighted to see him in the door where he stood a long time, basking in adulation he would not have enjoyed in Philly. Come to think of it, he puts you in mind of the Blazes Boylan Heather once fucked, to pay you back good and proper. He was a good-looking guy, too, and quite a guitarist.

Marriage never recovered. You can dish it out but you can't take it.

Can I have the bill, please?

Museum opens at 2 pm. You are walking with eyes downcast, thinking of the nature of the Veil between the Two Worlds, those of the seen and the unseen, your eyes fixed and there are people's legs about, coming and going to either side, when suddenly – *very* suddenly – you're looking in the eyes of a dead man.

He fell outside a shop called Oasis and his skull as it hits the concrete – his arms don't extend to protect his head – makes a sound you will never forget. His head turns so his procumbent eyes hold gaze with your own. He is looking at a blue screen. You don't need to move the focus of your eyes one centimetre.

There's no mistaking a dead man drop. He falls at the speed of gravity. You've seen it in cattle many a time.

Bystanders are aghast. No one speaks or moves. They await a cue and as you're closest, you provide it.

Well, someone has to and you *have* recently refreshed your Senior First Aid Certificate at Kirrawee Golf Club. You must now recall how many breaths they want these days, between the chest compressions.

The first thing to do is put him in recovery position. That much you do recall. Your brain is working apace – what comes next? As you place your hand under the head to roll him, you feel the sticky blood.

Nassau Street now comes to life, everyone full of suggestions. 'What should I do?' asks one sensible girl. You ask her to call an ambulance.

'He's goin *blue*!' barks a Yankee matron and she's right; he is going blue. '*That's not good!*'

'He's havin' a *seizure*!' says someone else but he's not having a seizure. You bend his right knee under his left leg and roll him onto his right side. A man checks for pulse.

'No pulse,' this in a pallid whisper.

You'll have to go through DRABC. How does it go again? Shit.

No vital signs, blue in the face, not breathing – no pulse but a pulse is easy to miss.

Can you hear me?

Excuse me, sir, can you hear me?

The captain has turned the seatbelt sign on.

'He *cain't hear* you! He's goin' *blue*! He's havin' a seizure!'

'He's not having a seizure. He's all right. He just KO'd himself.'

'He's not all right if he's goin' blue!'

'Oh, shut your face, would you, please? He'll be *all right*.'

And you see the consciousness return to his eyes. He's green-eyed, slight, late twenties, thinning red hair, well-spoken, not drunk, not drugged – Irish. Realising, horrified, where he is, he scrambles to his feet. He's young and fit and lucky. Had he gone down at that speed backwards he'd have likely fractured his skull. Never give an occipital Glasgow kiss – martial art precept. People report that a fracturing skull – as in the Melbourne fracas that led to the death of cricketer David Hookes – tinkles like a breaking wine glass.

The shopowner now emerges to report ambulance on the way. The victim, of course, wants none of it. People offer him clean tissues to help staunch the blood. A broad Australian accent will put him at his ease.

'You came down pretty hard on your head, mate. It's lucky you're Irish. Hey, did you feel okay before you fell?'

'Just a little – odd.'

He'll be okay till the zambucks arrive. You seize your chance to slip away.

Now you're in shock. It's not about him and not about you but he wouldn't know that. *You're* in shock. Before you can reach St Ann's Church, you're in tears. You keep walking as you can't think straight. But this is not a time to think.

Thin place there, outside Trinity. Best move off, just carry on, visit the museum as intended.

You won't be staying at Barnacles tonight. Back to the Holiday Inn.

And now, for a short but memorable time, you have access to *Two Worlds*.

There is blood drying on the palm of your left hand. From time to time in the Museum you glance down at it.

Did it happen in the *real* world? Check. You didn't imagine it.

Was it *unusual?* Yes, it was unusual. You couldn't have created it.

It was a sign, a Sufic *karamah*.

In the treasury you begin drumming the fingers of your right hand in powerful, complex patterns, first on the glass case that holds the book shrine with the bossed Celtic cross with the cusped arms; then against the glass case that holds the belt shrine with the bronze buckle with the silver and niello inlay. An attendant rushes up to stop you before you set off an alarm.

Then said Jesus unto him, except ye see signs and wonders, ye will not believe.

People only listened to Jesus because of His signs and wonders. Prophet Mohammed – on whom be The Peace – couldn't offer signs and wonders so he just said, 'I'm a great poet.'

And he wasn't wrong, having been the greatest poet the world has yet seen.

Australia's best-known poet is Rudyard Kipling. We will remember him.

There is an exhibition of bog bodies from across Europe – black-brown, leathery human bog bodies, strangled or throat cut then tossed in a bog as human sacrifice. Three of them, the Sueve and two Celts, still have hair and the hair is red as though stained with henna. It's odd to see this wavy, orangutan-coloured hair adhering to orangutan-coloured vellum. Would the bog stain keratin red? You can't see how.

There's a young, modern Irish girl with orangutan-coloured hair perusing one of the bog bodies. Snap. The man who fell on Nassau Street had orangutan-coloured hair. Snap. Up on St Stephen's Green right now are prints of genuine orangutans. They have humanoid fingers and fingernails.

You glance down at the dried blood on your hand. You wish you never had to wash it off. Because if it washes off, the experience will fade.

Something important is striving for your attention which has to do with red hair.

What happened today was not the doing of a Divine Mother.

What happened today was the doing of a Divine Father – The Holy One, blessed be He, or Allah, be He exalted and extolled. It was meant to demonstrate *Power.* It was meant to provoke *awe. It was like a lightning bolt!*

'As long as fear is weak, so will penitence be, and where there is little penitence there will be little devotion. The person who does not fear God will not love him.' Alphabet of Devotion.

And that is the entire problem. Modern Western Secular Man, Cronulla Man, *does not fear God.*

Mustafa from Punchabowl fears Allah. Allah says to him, in Bali – do Me a favour. Rid Me of these infidels. See how they fornicate and drink alcohol in the place where they worship the monkey?

Book yourself in, tonight and tomorrow night, at the Holiday Inn, Al. Have a short holiday. You need your bodhran bad now. You need a bodhran bad because you need to reproduce that sound. What else can you do? You're a drummer.

We must work while it is day and we must not quarrel with Destiny. How foolish to quarrel with Destiny! How foolish to complain we're only a drummer.

Monday morning finds you sitting quietly in a coffee shop overlooking Grafton Square as you wait for the World Wildlife Fund shop to open. You're looking down upon 'rangas' crossing at the traffic lights below. What a cheap but satisfying form of Dublin entertainment! With the sun out, the redheads of Dublin glow like copper wire. Nowhere else in the world does auburn hair look as good as it does here. It's the light, the watery, east coast Dublin light.

There's a stout, middle-aged lady with red hair.

There's a young office-working girl with red hair – long red hair.

There's a student with red dreadlocks.

There's a boy with red hair, in a school uniform, skipping along.

There's a baby in a stroller with red hair being pushed by a mother with red hair.

There is never long to wait. And this hair is neither strawberry blonde nor titian but *flaming auburn*; it is orangutan-coloured hair – the hair of Grainne.

Noting you buying all the orangutan cards, the girl in the shop cites a UN report called *The Last Stand of the Orangutan* which advised that one thousand orangutans burned to death during forest fires in Borneo in 2005. The continued logging of old-growth peat forest – largely for Ikea sawlogs and high-grade photocopy paper pulp – in both Borneo and Sumatra is forcing these apes, thought to number in the wild fewer than sixty thousand, to forage oil palms planted to cater for burgeoning biodiesel demand in a warming world striving to reduce dependency on fossil fuels, and increasing Tim Tam and KFC demand in consequence of utter failure. Local hunters are paid to kill them as pests. Characterised by the slowest reproductive rate of any terrestrial species, this 'wild man', this 'lecherous she-ape' is in fact an exemplar of primate virtue, with males adopting an eremitic lifestyle as vegetarian anchorites and females assuming the role of mother-goddesses, in oestrus only once every nine years, with youngsters clinging to their mother's belly or back, until by age eight they're the weight of a full-grown human being and yet still they cling; still they cling. Safe in their mother's arms, unaware of their father's existence, though it's not all sweetness and light: possessed of canine teeth like tigers, these lads could give you a nasty nip.

Pot-bellied like gorillas but unconcerned by their appearance.

You take out your Lonely Planet guidebook to find Colman's island.

Page 479. *Inishbofin Island, some 9 km out in the Atlantic from Cleggan, is a haven of tranquillity … Inishbofin's historical figure of note was St Colman, who at one stage was a bishop in England. He fell out with the English Church in 664 over its adoption of a new calendar and exiled himself to Inishbofin, where he set up a monastery.*

There's a ferry from Cleggan. *Getting there and away,* see Clifden. Turning back to Clifden you notice on the facing page, *Roundstone Musical Instruments, open 9 am–9 pm daily, July–Sept. It makes and sells the bodhran, the goatskin drum beloved of traditional Irish musicians.*

Within the hour, the bookings are made. Train from Dublin Heuston 11.10 am tomorrow, hire car Galway airport, pick up a bodhran in Roundstone, catch the late ferry from Cleggan to Bofin in time for dinner at Murray's Doonmore Hotel where the weather is inclement – advised to bring raincoat.

That hire car will sit idle for three days in a ferry parking lot but you *must* make this last pilgrimage, Al – while you still have a chance and the pilgrim frame of mind. If Skellig Michael was about sex, then Inishbofin is about death. Either hallow – St Colman now, St Finan then – interceded for you.

You had actually wondered whether to visit Skellig, yet it was off Little Skellig, looking in the eyes of a gannet, that you became a son of life. And if that can happen off Little Skellig, then something may happen on Bofin.

Gannet Dreaming – you have Gannet Dreaming. The whole of Ireland is a white Dreaming. Your mother is likely three-quarters Irish. Mixed-bloods came from the vicinity of missions, whence Irishmen were doing things their mothers never taught them.

'On one occasion Dubhlitir came before Maelruin urging him to allow his monks to have a drink of beer on the three great solemnities of the year. Maelruin replied: "As long as they are under my rule and keep my ordinances they will not drink in this place anything that brings about forgetfulness of God." Dubhlitir answered: "My monks drink beer, and they will enter heaven along with yours." "I am not certain of that," replied Maelruin.'

And indeed, you don't feel *transfigured* the way you were ten years back. Maybe because you're still on the turps. *She*'s not here, which is a disappointment. You go to 12.45 pm Holy Communion at St Ann's to find a woman celebrant. You then return to your coffee shop to continue perving on redheads.

You must now bring animus to bear on redheads, these offerings made to Lugh of the Long Arm and thrown in bogs. People will say it is the bog died the hair red, no – the hair was always red. Celtic gods like red hair. It is not only the world's orangutan population under threat. The gene for red hair is recessive, and down to 1–2 per cent worldwide. You carry the red-hair gene because your three children with Pastel are blonds, the youngest strawberry blonde and your own hair, when young, was titian. Now to preserve red hair redheads should marry only other redheads but redheads themselves would not find other redheads as attractive as a non-redhead does. In democracies, sexual imperative to mate with folk our fathers would disapprove rules, while in patriarchies, arranged marriages, built around alliances, reinforce genotypes.

Poles and Nigerians will presently destroy the world's best stash of redheads even as Muslims destroy the orangutans of Kalimantan – in despite of the fact that Malays regard the orangutan as possessed of superhuman wisdom. But the red-haired gene will not disappear and human redheads will continue to emerge as though spontaneously from non-redhead stock. A superstitious future humanity may well regard their emergence with awe – all the more if it can be shown that this gene originally arose from cross-breeding with Neanderthals.

Hey Al, are we game to visit the bookshop on the ground floor?

Browsing, you pick up a book on stained glass in the chapels and churches of the Kingdom of Kerry. You open at 'Epiphany', the visit of the Magi at Little Christmas from the Gospel according to St Matthew, the first of twelve scenes commissioned by the Josephite Convent in Dingle from the great stained-glass artist Harry Clarke. The first figure you see is a black Persian prince, one of the three Wise Men, those Magians who set out from Qom, south of Tehran, home of Ayatollah Khomeini, and whose bones now rest in Cologne Cathedral.

Flicking through, you come across Brendan the Navigator, Kerry's patron saint, from St John the Baptist Church in Tralee. This window depicts St Brendan without tonsure. He is raising a dead man. Oh. You didn't know Brendan raised a dead man. You search the index though you're now hearing the angelus bell as on Or Tee Ee One at 6 pm. Here we are: from St Mary's, the Pugin pile in Killarney. 'St Brendan raises a man from the dead through the power of God' in English, under Christ doing the same thing for the widow's son, in English. Brendan is here given a Roman tonsure – wouldn't that have Colman spitting chips!

You return the book to the shelf. You return yourself to the Holiday Inn. You did say, on immigration, you were here for holiday.

Be chary of jumping to conclusions, Al. You've heard the phrase 'delusions of grandeur'? You must know that every golf club in the world now possesses a defibrillator for raising men from the dead; still, be equally wary of dismissing a wonder, a Sufic *mu'ujizah*, a miracle, as it may just be your mission to restore the Celtic Church, the Church appropriate to our times. Touched again with a fleeting Augustinian sanctity outside Allhallows.

Buy a copy of *The Times* to read in bed. Important to keep on an even keel.

Oh dear, the news is all bad – Celine Conway, 29-year-old blonde from the condemned Sean Tracey House on Dublin's northside, on a two-month holiday at the Costa del Sol to escape the damp in her wet, condemned flat while awaiting a new council house, was iron-barred by her partner, Sean Hickey of Buttercup Drive, Darndale, in front of their three young children, to such extent she had to be identified from the ring on her finger.

It's time to move on, Al.

Explanation one: a young man, unused to sunlight, suffers sudden syncope, swoons, hits his head hard on the concrete and knocks himself witless. He happens to come to as a passing first aider prompts him and gets to his feet.

Explanation two: a young man is caused to drop dead through the power of God, in order to bring fear to the heart of a wicked but gifted drummer looking on, who is then given power to return the young man to life, as a sign the Celtic Church *is* indeed the True Church of Christ.

A bumper cereal crop is coming in that would have been ruined had that rain continued.

Christ is dead. Christ is risen. Christ will come again.

This *hal* does not involve the *Shakti*. Allah has no Shakti: to attribute to Allah a partner is the Muslim crime of *Shirk* – pluralism.

Bodhran in hand you are sipping a stout outside the Cleggan pub waiting for the *Island Discovery* to take you over to Bofin, the second sacred Irish isle to be trashed by Vikings – this in the year 795, the year in which they also raided Iona and Murray in Sligo, enslaving the monks and grabbing chalice, paten and book shrine from the *dairthech*. In 824 they returned to attack Skellig Michael, enslaving Abbot Etgal.

Six pm, Tuesday, 28 August; stratocumulus cloudmass covering the Bens but when the sun comes out to illuminate the azure bow on a nearby trawler; *what* extraordinary clarity in the Atlantic light. You can hear the bleating of sheep on that hill a mile across the bay.

A little old-fashioned pre-school girl, very pale with blue eyes and a mop of black hair, plump, wearing a dirty light blue dress and a pair of scuffed shoes, is skipping up and down the street outside the pub, talking to herself.

'Hello,' she says to you.

How nice to encounter a little girl who has no fear of speaking to strange men. She would never do that in the Shire. The kindness of strangers becomes, to a solitary pilgrim, the token of God's Love.

'Are you crying?'

'No.'

'Why you crying?'

'I'm not.'

Folk waiting to board the late ferry all hold shopping bags. They're Bofin Islanders off the bus having been shopping in Clifden. Most farm income in these parts comes in the mail.

'Is that a drum you have there?'

'It is.'

'Can you play it?'

'I can.'

'Play it.'

'I'd rather not.'

By the time the ferry docks in Bofin, *Insula vitulae albae,* Isle of the White Heifer, it is 8.15 pm. Spectacular late light emerges from under a cloudmass to illuminate on the harbour headland the ruins of Cromwell's barracks, built over Bosco's Castle, Bosco being a Spanish pirate in league with Grace O'Malley who used to lay a chain across this harbour.

As on Aran, lights from the mainland mitigate a sense of isolation.

You walk to your hotel. There is light drizzle. Everyone is friendly. You were the only stranger on the ferry. It is rather late in a wet season.

The place has a legend: in the time of *Tuatha De Danaan*, the Tribes of the Goddess Dana, it was covered in thick fog. One day, two fishermen made shore and lighting a fire, dispersed the fog – by the loch behind Doonmore Hotel in fact, Loch Bo Finne.

An old woman appeared through the fog, clutching a drafting cane and driving a snow white heifer. Upon seeing the fishermen, she struck the calf with the cane, turning it to stone. The fishermen then wrested the cane from her, struck her with it and she turned to stone but the stones are no longer to be seen.

That problematic but undeniable lust for 'strange' women is satisfied fully in you by Ingeborg Hakonsen of Viking stock. Indeed, she provokes in most Australian men stupendous lust – which must have something to do with potential hybrid vigour but also contains undertones of purchase, perhaps even of capture and possibly vengeance for atrocities committed by her vile ancestors.

Give her one for me, says Colman.

You find you are still capable of *sexual feeling*. That's odd – indeed worrisome.

The dining room, very crowded, has red tablecloths, artificial red roses on the tables, red napkins in the wine glasses and the menu looks promising, too; seafood chowder, beef, salmon, French and Australian wines.

Everyone in this dining room has red hair.

The twitcher from Belfast with his booming voice ('fancy dinnerrrs') who sounds and looks like the Rev Ian Paisley has red hair. His long-suffering wife has thick red hair, braided.

Their three colleagues at the same table are balding red.

What looks like a social science academic working his way through a bottle of Rosemount red has red hair – *and* a red face. You'll see him tomorrow roaming the knoll outside the pub, looking for mobile reception.

Those two stout matronly sisters, with nothing left to say, have red hair. They could be twins.

That thin man with his young wife, who says 'Jesus and Joseph!' at her children's table manners, have red hair, as do son and daughter.

The three burly labourers, billeted from the roadworks gang, have red hair. The one with the beergut has the room next yours; he'll be snoring all night. He'll be forced to lie on his back. You'll hear his every breath and fart. They're drinking porter they brought in from the bar.

The teenage waitress has a red plait.

There are sixteen orangutan-coloured redheads in this one room.

You're the only one here without.

This, you cannot deal with. Head spinning and breathing hard, you grab your bottle of plonk and retire to your room. The boards along the hallway creak and you're thinking, as you're blinking back the tears, is *this* it, then? Is this where I die?

It was off Little Skellig you became a son of life and received a guerdon you subsequently lost or, strictly speaking, forfeited.

Now, pull back the curtains and open the window and stare at that moonlit island in the sea. You pick up the bodhran to find the sound the dead man's head made as it hit the cement. As you hit the drum, you stare at that beautiful anvil-shaped island out there under the moon.

In your forties and a student of karate – how we deceive ourselves – your young instructor would walk round the class as it went through basics and rest his hands, briefly, on shoulders. 'Too stiff, Al,' he'd say to you. 'Relax. You won't get speed till you relax.'

'I am relaxed.'

'No, you're not. I can feel the tightness in your shoulders. Try to relax.'

'I can't relax when I keep getting beaten up all the time.'

'You keep getting beaten up all the time because you're so tense, Al.'

'I don't feel I am tense.'

'We don't know it's there till it's gone. Have you heard of Daruma? He invented karate but also Zen. It's a cycle we must somehow break. No one can do it for us. Think of karate as practical Zen. We put ourselves through all this pain and boredom just to get *hip*. Now, I've told you the secret. It's not about fighting. You can do it through meditation. Once *hip* – and it happens when you least expect it – the tension lifts. And then you realise how tense you were. Do you know what causes that tension, Al? *Death*. We're afraid of death but we don't know it because we never think of death. Now come on, bring your non-punching fist right back to your belt. That's better.'

You took a snapshot of a gannet flying low off Little Skellig. There'll be surely one in this bird book.

Page 31. *Magnificent ocean-going birds which wander far and wide from their breeding colonies. Gannets are often seen from headlands and from the ferry. Almost all the West Coast gannets originate from a colony breeding on Little Skellig.*

Were it not for the odd Australasian gannet plunging into the waters of Bate Bay, a place where men still row boats, you'd be unable to live in Cronulla: you would go mad. You'd spend all your day staring out to sea like those greater blackback gulls that sit on the ridge above Loch Bo Finne, playing a CD you've been listening to of late – *Red Lanta* featuring Art Lande – another seemingly lost jazz talent on piano with Jan Garbarek on flute, recorded in Oslo in November 1973, the very month you started work with Ingeborg Hakonsen at the Lotus Chinese Restaurant in Canberra; the year Heather bore you the elder of your two sons, the one with the dark hair; the year of your final scientific publication in the *Journal of Chemical Physics*.

Why a gannet? Well, why not. It seems that the great feature of Skellig Michael as a monastery was the adjacent gannetry and not just as a food source: watching a gannetry during breeding season is like wandering down a nave in la Mezquita in Cordoba; the mind is immediately thrown into a state congenial to meditation. Something, too, in the *beauty* of that gannet set off a détente in the siege engine of your mind and you were hoist into a state of *bliss*. It happened suddenly and, as predicted, you felt the tension in your shoulders lift. You became immortal when you *saw* you'd been here before.

Eternity: you've lost sight of it for like Shane MacGowan you have fallen from Grace, Al, and Eternity is again just a word.

'Whenever we transgress the three renunciations of our Baptism, that is, the world, the flesh and the devil – those renunciations that transform a son of death into a son of life – heaven is closed to us unless we first dip into three pools: the pool of blood of flagellation, the pool of sweat of hard labour and the pool of tears of regret.' Alphabet of Devotion by St Colman macu Beognae of Lismore.

Here's a sketch of nearby islands. That island out there in front of us under the full moon is High Island. It could be – five miles?

High Island. Storm Petrel nest in its unique 7th century monastic ruins. Peregrine is also among this sacred isle's population. High Island is only accessible in the calmest weather and by a short, steep climb.

The fescue grass on High Island in the absence of sheep will be ankle-deep and clotted in barnacle goose guano.

Celtic monasteries, in the seventh century, were clustered round the tomb of the founding saint and based on a ring fort. The space between the rings, if there were more than one, was for cows and kale. The inner enclosure contained the cells of the monks, the guest house, the refectory, the oratory or *teampal,* usually an 'oak house' or *dairthech* if there was oak about and from the eighth century on, a high cross. If there was wood on Bofin – and you'd need willow to make a drafting cane – those structures would have been wattle-and-daub except for the oratory, always of stone or oak, and the high cross. The *cloch teach* or bell tower – that emblematic phallus, the Christian Mystery in stone – came later.

Where there was no mud or wood, as on Skellig Michael and High Island, stone *clochans* were built for cells. Many survive as Vikings couldn't be bothered pulling them down whereas they would happily torch anything flammable.

Life may never be as meaningful again as here and now – as on this night, as in this place. We need both heat and timing. As Yamamoto says in *Hagakure,* 'How things end is important.'

Kill yourself, go kill yourself.

Pastel can look after Mum. It is time to penetrate the Ultimate Mystery, Al, but first, a visit to Colman's Abbey to show respect to another great loser.

When you returned from Skellig you were in Eternal Life. That's why you weep when the celebrant says, 'The Body of Christ, the Bread of Heaven, keep you in Eternal Life' and 'the Blood of Christ, the Cup of Salvation, keep you in Eternal Life.'

You can't believe you committed a sin in going back to Pastel and the kids, that is the problem. That is the *big* problem. You couldn't *function* as an angel. You didn't want to *do* anything. You've read how Daruma spent his later life staring at a wall; well, you'd have been happy to do that – staring at a wall a breeze – probably the wall of Kenmore Asylum. St Barsanuphius of Gaza, who avoided the sight of other human beings, spent fifty years in unceasing repetition of the name of God. You'd have been happy to do that – unceasing repetition of the name of God a breeze. You lose appetite for things of this world when you wake each day in *ecstasy* and you could literally feel something *warming* your brain, as you daily woke from dreamless sleep. You were in a state of *Wajd,* Sufic divine inebriation. You were never so happy since your first intimation, your first real mystical feeling, for you'd become again a babe in a mother's arms – a *Real* Mother this time, but no good for any work.

Your first mystical feeling came to you after your first orgasm which didn't involve sex. It was between you and *Her*. You woke in your grandparents' bed at Katoomba – you can still see the waterstains on the ceiling from the snapshot – after a nocturnal emission. You would have been six. You didn't know what had happened but you lay a long time thinking, what a wonderful world we have here.

It was downhill all the way once people became involved. The first is always the best. The first stone wall ever built, Imhotep's wall in Saqqara, Egypt, is the best stone wall. Better than these walls on Inishbofin.

The lesson seems to be that there are *two* kinds of enlightenment, one involving God, one involving Mary and if Islam is correct – maybe Christ went too far.

Got it! That's the sound we want! That's the sound the world awaits. Knuckle backfist, left hand choking the skin. Let's do it again.

Try that in Doolin, O'Connor's pub, with just the one beat on the first beat of the bar.

Half-twelve and here they come. Been strolling in the moonlight, playing children's games on the bench now, right below your window. Young islanders, men and women both, all pissed as newts.

Hopsom jopsom hopsom jopsom FOOKIN! Jopsom FOOKIN IDJUT! Jopsom jopsom JAYSUS CHRIST! Jopsom FOOK OFF! jopsom hopsom GO ON, FOOK OFF! jopsom FOOKIN jopsom hopsom GO ON FOOK OFF, FOOK YA! Popsom FOOK OFF FOOK YA! Popsom jopsom jopsom popsom now think of the monks on High Island chanting their midnight office in front of their high cross under the full moon.

If it is hard renouncing this world while loving the neighbour who creates it – and to love your neighbour as yourself you must first *rid* yourself of yourself, which is what women can't understand – it is harder having a celibate priest scold a copulating layman unless that layman be given a second *chance*: because one fuck and you're out. Sons of Abraham, by tradition, don't get a second chance. *It just can't be right!* Druids believed in rebirth. And you *know* you've been here before, Al, sometime between the sixth and twelfth centuries AD, you were here or hereabout. You *know* that. You just know it.

The sun is arise.

Bofin fisherman superstitions: 'You would not be wanting to see the seapies on the hills or the shadows of the hills on the water. You would want no talk of cattle or fowls or rats. You would not want to meet with a red-haired woman on the way to the harbour. If you did, you would go straight home to bed.'

Seven am. Why, you must have nodded off. You are still fully clothed.

You can no longer tell if you're asleep.

A couple of pied wagtails, of the twelve pair nesting on Bofin, roam the beer garden and the gravel carpark where that bastard with his bodgy starter was coming and going all the long night.

Suicide on the rise in Ireland. Ten per cent of those who attempted last year were under the age of twelve: one was six.

Pub now dead quiet. Still very hazy and mild. High Island covered in cloud. You start your pilgrimage to Colman's Abbey, the last throw of your die. It's three clicks to the ruins of an Augustinian abbey which stands on the ruins of Colman's abbey which stands on the ruins of Flannan's abbey. You set off down the Low Road which will take you back past the harbour. There are red hens wandering the lane, sheep on the grassy bank. Everything is wet. There has been a clearing shower. To your left you pass a typical low Irish wall, mainly freestone reinforced with wire fencing affixed to windsplits of treated pine. The verges are brightened with crisp wrappers and flattened milk cartons. You hear linnets and magpies, wagtails and a rooster. Herring gulls laugh: *Da wah wah wah wah wah*

Sheep bleat: *Heh heh heh heh heh heh*

In the West, roosters crow '*Cock-a-doodle do!*' In the East, '*Uzkuru'llah ya ghafilun!*' (Remember, or take the name of Allah, O careless one.)

You stop to peer through a six-bar gate bent in the middle where someone has run over it with a tractor. Through it is a field in which a curlew probes a long, sickle bill amid some fat Charolais cattle. To your right is a helipad. On the shingle, rock pipits pick through the seaweed.

Fences here are to keep stock out. Plenty of grass in the lanes. The lower strand of every fence above a drain is thick with wool. There are cow pats on the road.

Don't be thinking to yourself, 'I could live here', Al. That's got whiskers. Think, rather, 'I could *die* here'. That way you can remain here.

It might have been a garden once within that ringlock fencing affixed to those concrete pillars but now contains only upturned forty-fours, one large blue and white recycling bin, several piles of gravel, three concrete pipes, some duckboards, some steel reinforcing mesh and a rusty van. The house that belongs to the yard is a slate-roofed bungalow with nettles and thistles for garden serviced by a power pole at forty-five degrees guyed by a rope attached to a spike.

All of which says the missus has taken off, to the mainland, no doubt.

The rain starts and stops. Now, here's a place with missus still in residence. It has a garden with carrots, spuds with haulms just beginning to die off, onions, turnips and peas and some plastic children's toys on the lawn.

Quite a few houses now. To the right you're looking at the Connemara coast across the signal tower on Gun Rock. You pass an upturned currach weighed down with ropes attached to Besser blocks. Colman arrived in one of those but they're not a one-man operation; minimum crew four rather like a Bate Bay surfboat. You can't take that to High Island.

There's a big, fat, Irish bumblebee working some yellow vetch. You can't help but smile at the single-minded dedication. When you kept bees in Penrose and Goongerah, they would not work in weather like this. Your mood is lifted by that bee. You're thinking, I could maybe take the bodhran to O'Connor's pub which is not that far south and see what effect it has if I go

Death
Death
Death
Death

You once heard a street Leb being interviewed on SBS after the Cronulla riot, shown leading prayer during Ramazan in a boxing gym. So, quite devout, yet kept saying, 'Goddamn' as in 'I'm a Goddamn Aussie!' so does not see God as Allah, because he would never say 'Allah-damn'. That man can never know Mary. He could never *conceive* of Mary. The Christian Mystery is not for him but he fears Allah.

If Allah is not the Holy One, blessed be He, then Who is Allah?

How deeply a Christian, perusing his scanty congregation of

geriatrics, resents the sight of all those tough young men spilling from Lakemba Mosque!

But there's a problem for the lifesaver, too: Osama bin Ladin, supposedly the great saint of Islam, is fucking four women!

We should be so lucky.

Mustafa from Punchabowl envies and fears modern Western debauchery. We fear and envy his Eternity and contempt for Death.

We have the technology but have lost control of our women.

The Muslim has his wisdom, part of which says Christ went too far.

And we can't defeat someone who has no fear of Death. Deep down, we're fucked and know it – but deep down. The War on Terror brings to mind what Augustine said to his fellow citizens, following the sack of Rome by Alaric, the Arian Visigoth, in AD 410:

You desire to enjoy your luxuries unrestrained and to lead an abandoned and profligate lifestyle without the interruption of any disaster or disease. Your desire for peace, prosperity and continued economic growth is not prompted by any pious purpose of using these blessings farsightedly, in sobriety and temperance; no, your purpose rather is to run riot in endless fine dining and debauchery and thus to generate from your prosperity a moral pestilence that will prove a thousandfold more disastrous to you than the fiercest of enemies.

As for Cronulla Woman, she has no fear of man, no fear of God – no fear of Allah. She loathes Mohammed, on whom be The Peace, as much as she would loathe Jesus, had not Paul conflated Jesus with Mithras.

Five big plastic recycling bins beside a number of rusting vehicles, some abandoned, by a pier under a sign saying, 'No long-term parking'. How Irish is that? You laugh and laugh but your mood swings back as you near St Colman's Church. Surely the Tykes haven't had the gall to canonise *Colman?* You can't bring yourself to enter the place, which would anyway mean traversing a sodden strip of ply over a cattle grid. It's the ugliest kind of Irish church – grey stucco with two hideous metallic silver painted angels on the gateposts. To your left, a grotto, with a sky-blue cumulus-white (that is, Irish-coloured) Virgin being adored by some woman. We're all potentially women: we all have that untapped X chromosome inside us but hers is in a Barr body. The yard of grey pebbles is surrounded by fuchsia and to the east is a shipwreck memorial for seventy-one drowned locals, mostly Laceys, Tierneys and Lavelles.

The sun emerges as you head up the hill. It'll be good to escape the sound of the dredge and the rear of Day's Hotel by the pier, a squalid, noisome, corroded, rubbish-strewn midden complete with porcelain toilet.

You want to *get* there! You start to accelerate.

By Ann-Marie's craft shop an extraordinary chorus of song erupts, thrilling your heart. Skylarks! Males marking out territory, singing atop the power poles. Bofin is skylark central, fully fifty breeding pair.

You start jogging then *running* down the lane, bursting in anticipation. You think of the Children of Lir, the sea god of *Tuatha De Danaan* – Aodh, Fionnula, Fiachra and Conn – who were turned into swans by their jealous stepmother Aoife and under a nine-hundred-year curse 'till a cold bell peals, to bring belief in the word of the Lord throughout this land' and as they heard, on Inishglora in AD 432, the tolling of the bell that would bring an end to their immortality, they gave to the skylark the secret of birdsong, charging him to take it to every bird in the world.

And there it is: your pilgrimage is over. Beyond Granny's Lake with its yellow waterlilies and reeds, you glimpse, to the *clunk clunk* of a stonechat, a ruined Augustinian abbey behind what is now the Bofin graveyard with a backdrop of sea and the Rinvyle Peninsula and Ballynakill Bay on the Connemara coast. Nothing here. Just the usual small, roofless stone oratory filled with wet nettles, one or two lichen-encrusted cruciform gravestones and that's what's left of Colman's early retirement package. There was constant brawling, it seems, between the Irish and Saxon monks, prompting Colman to shift the Saxons to the mainland where their monastery, 'Mayo of the Saxons', became renowned for scholarship.

Flat and despondent, you trudge back past the dredge for lunch in the bar of the Doonmore. That's two meals now you've paid for and missed. A raven flies by that hasn't properly absorbed the skylark's lesson. Near the pier you encounter a man about your own age sitting on a seat with a couple of plastic shopping bags by his feet. He's taking a breather. You're sweating in T-shirt, shorts and running shoes: he's wearing gumboots, tweed jacket, cloth cap, woollen shirt with necktie and waistcoat. He'll be living on an acre or two of poor land up Cloonamore way in a house that would fetch two million euros from a Dutch merchant banker who will then use it for a holiday home and keep it empty ten months of the year.

You're knackered. After lunch with a pint of the black stuff, you shower and while shaving your head, catch a glimpse of your own handsome face in the bathroom mirror. Good god, are those *your* eyebrows? You need to take to them with a pair of scissors, Al. You look like Bart Cummings.

High Island out there, in the shape of an anvil: you need to think of some way to get over but you won't be able to think at all if you don't get some sleep and soon.

Pull the curtain. Couple of Temtabs.

You wake in a sweat, imbued with déjà vu. All this has happened before and it's *not even real*!

You take a short walk. There's nothing else to do here except drink. Turning right instead of left takes you to Doonmore; through a gate along a green road to the ruins of an Iron Age fort called, as they always are, *Dun Mor* – Big Fort. There will be nothing more to it than a slight protuberance in the soil, a defensive earth ring.

On the way there you hear a wren. They hunted wren here on St Stephen's Day as in Kerry they climb Carrantouhil. The book says that chough nest among fulmar on the seacliffs and as you've never seen this West Irish crow with red feet and vermilion beak, you're keeping a close eye out but what you see instead through light drizzle will be the last snapshot in your album: the awful metaphor of Inishshark, a mile across Shark Sound.

Houses, a dozen or so, not yet completely unroofed. You can make out the church and what must be a school or possibly a hall. You can see the entire north coast of Shark Island, the cosmos of Shark. Through a squall of rain now, you can see the Iron Age field boundaries. Back in the fifties, in the days when in Dublin opposing captains in the All Ireland football final would genuflect and cross themselves then kiss the ring of the prelate before he bounced the ball to start the game, the Dail was skint and there was neither money nor will to build a pier for Inishshark. By 1960 there were insufficient able-bodied islanders left to man a currach.

Today, with helicopter pad and EU membership, access a breeze, but you realise, not for the first time, as you sink down into your heels, mesmerised by this sudden representation of *your entire life and thought* – that the state immediately following clinical death yet preceding decay – as the tattered garment yet clings to the flesh and the unseeing eyes behold a blue screen – has resonance for you, so that you prefer Inishshark given over to the barnacle geese rather than afflicted with a brand new Keating concrete pier.

What time is it? Casting a cold eye, you see your watch has stopped.

As you climb Dun Mor you meet, descending, your stocky, red-haired neighbour from the roadworks gang. What's he doing up here?

'Hello!' he says. 'Fine weather!'

Yes, you agree. You like intermittent drizzle, it cools the blood.

You ask has he taken a day off.

'I have,' he says, 'hurt my arm! Hurt my elbow here. And where are you from?'

'Sydney.'

'Sydney! I have a son on Coogee Beach. I'm from Mayo. There's a lad down there cutting peats. Have you seen him? Well, I'll be off. God speed!' He holds your gaze just a little too long, like a pervert, with his green eyes.

Ma'lak Yahwe. A red-haired Angel of the Lord has just given you, an outcast, a blessing. Sobbing like a toddler through tears and convulsive jerks you can see the blue van into which a man is loading peats. A pair of choughs flies by, making their onomatopoeic call. Five miles to the north is mountainous Inishturk, population ninety and possessed of six little splashes of white; one comes and goes down low, a wave breaking on the west seacliff; the other five would take the collapse of the German economy to shift; dwellings of indigent sheepfarmers on the south-eastern hill.

The green road brings you to a cross overlooking a group of stags. You are now close to sea level. The plaque says, 'To the memory of Edward Mull and Richard Mathes, former students of Kansas University at Lawrence, who lost their young lives by drowning here at the stags of Inishbofin on Feb 3 1976. May they rest in peace.'

Your mind turns to your eldest daughter, in serious mental anguish since leaving home to run off with the raggle-taggle gypsies-O, but won't go near a church. Part of the reason you came away was to work out how you can *help* her but she refuses guidance and why wouldn't she, when it comes from you. It's hard to know what to *do* with her and you do blame yourself. If only she could understand that what we call mental illness is less chemical imbalance than alchemical judgement. If only she would understand that Christ died to *redeem* her. Not just save her – *redeem* her. You gave her that Guanyin figurine you found in your mother's lowboy but Guanyin is only a saviour. Guanyin is not a redeemer. And Christ died to redeem us. And if Christ is the fulfilment of the Law then Mohammed, on whom be The Peace, is an arch-revisionist Patriarchist-roader. There's a gannet.

Hey! Let's wait to see if he dives.

He's diving. Plummeting down, he's a gannet. Smack!

But he doesn't resurface and what's this? A mass of dense low seacloud is heading straight towards us – a huge *fog*bank heading straight for Bofin.

Better turn back. Wouldn't want to be caught out here wading round a peatbog in a fog. The quickest and safest return route is via North Beach Bay and Loch Bo Finne where the two mute swans and their seven grey cygnets swim and cavort. But you haven't gone one hundred metres when the fog moves in, a fog so dense and thick that you can no longer see your *hands* let alone your feet.

You'd best stay where you are till it lifts. But it doesn't. The wind has gone. What seems like half an hour elapses and the *silence* is like that in St Ann's Church. You hear nothing – no sound from the sea. Even the birds are silent though mute swans, as the name implies, don't have much to say. The island has gone silent.

You start to creep like one of those creatures that creepeth upon the earth. The green road will take you to Water Dog Cove – Otter

Cove – just west of North Beach and beyond the gate it's metal road but you'll have to get there. What if you're stuck out here all night? Surely, the fog will lift. Instead, it seems to intensify. The wind has dropped and there's no movement in the air.

Slowly, on all fours, you make your way down the boreen. Should ever you stray to left or right, you find yourself sucked into bog.

What was that? You hit your head on the gatepost. That's good, because once through the gate you're on metal road. You get to your feet and walk forward like a man. The fog by the lake is a little less dense. Straining your eyes you can even see reeds. If you keep walking you will eventually come to your hotel.

There's a swan on the grass, no, wait a bit.

Maaah!

It's that snow-white Charolais heifer calf from the paddock up the road. She must have gotten through a fence. And now, out in the fog, she's shitting herself, as will be her mother. But you can't hear her mother. Spooked, the calf scampers off, galloping down the lane. She's from that paddock where the greater blackback gulls sit staring out to sea.

You stumble, literally, into a red Passat that's parked in the middle of the lane. You observe it has no flat tyres. Peering through the passenger side window, you can see a figure slumped at the wheel. It's that red-haired waitress from the Doonmore. She's having a bit of a kip. Well, drinking all last night as she was, she's probably tired. Better sleeping it off at the wheel than trying to drive in this.

Could a fog stay down as long as this? Shouldn't it be lifting?

Straining your ears, and indeed your eyes, you can hear nothing and see nothing. There are no Honda ninety's to be heard and the dredge has stopped work. No birds call. Bofin is normally buzzing with little songbirds.

Wait a bit: there *is* a sound to the north. What sound is that? It's coming from the direction of the open sea but it's not waves. The sea is dead calm now, millpond calm. You can get that on the Atlantic.

You walk back past the Passat to where you saw the errant calf. But the calf is gone; she must have found her mother on the hill.

The fog thins slightly. You can make out a male stonechat, with black head and russet breast, sitting on a fencepost. When he sees you, he throws back his head and bursts into song, breaking the spell of silence.

What *is* that sound? It is a kind of regular bell-like tinkling over an intermittent water slosh. It could be Airto Moreiro going off with some weird Brazilian percussion instrument.

You make your way down to *Uiamh Mhadaigh Uisce,* Water Dog Cove, where peering out to sea like a greater blackback gull, you can see something looming up out of the fog and making for the shingle.

It looks like the *Havingsten.* Good God, it's the *Havingsten,* the *Sea Stallion,* thirty-metre replica Viking longboat on display at the Liffey Annexe having been sailed out from Norway. Are they taking her down the coast? She's fitted with sixty rollocks and the sound you heard was the sound of the oars plying from behind the sixty shield-umbos on the gunwales. The painted prow is fitted atop with a lion-shaped brass weathervane off which rattle the eighteen chains you mistook for tambourine. She's shell-clinker built, with thirteen layers of pine atop and oak below, caulked with wool soaked in tar and held together with seven thousand iron rivets and square roves, planks painted blue and red and yellow with woad and cinnabar and orpiment and in the dead calm her yard is stayed on three massive yard chocks next to a thirty-metre mainmast rising off a keelson rigged with six sheet stays of horsehair and walrus skin, one fore and five aft. Displacing twenty-five ton but riding low in the water on a one-metre draught, she can carry a ballast of sixty tons of loot and accommodate forty slaves.

There's ringing in your ears. You watch the oars withdrawn and the aft-mounted side rudder swung hard astern. The stocked iron anchor is dropped in four foot of water and now men with blond moustachios in 'haat Havaberk' leather/bone helmets, stretching down over their eyes to form swimmer's goggles, in cross-strapped leather leggings, all wearing short-sleeved woollen tunics, some holding iron chains with neckloops, others two-metre long yewwood longbows and one, a pattern-wielded Ulfbehrt sword from the Rhineland, wade ashore in sullen silence and no, this is not a re-enactment, Al, for all those faces are Gunnar's face.

That's not good. You must be hallucinating. You sink to your knees, close your eyes. Pray. The *ringing* of the tinnitus drowns out the tinkle from the weathervane and when you open your eyes the men are gone and the longboat has disappeared so you would seem to be demented.

Be careful what you think.

That calf is coming back down the road. You can hear her footsteps.

Shut your eyes and keep them shut. Reach up the back of your hand and feel the wet muzzle of the white heifer.

It is vital that she trust you. Stress will vitiate the meat. Walk her round to under where the hook hangs off the block and shoot her with the Remington rimshot. Now cut the throat while the heart still pumps. The tongue lolling from between the teeth, so beguilingly greenish, will brine up a treat. She's likely never been drenched so may have the fluke. Lose the hooves. Ease the thread of the gambrel between the Achilles tendon and the bone and lower the chain till the gambrel fit on the hook now hoist up the carcass till the head is off the ground and cut off the head. Bob's your uncle.

Open your eyes. You're looking at a blue screen. Every which way you turn your head there's nothing to be seen but a blue screen. Jaysus!

Hopsom jopsom can you crackle popsom?

Popple excuse me popsom jopsom?

Iranian Days (continued)

Can you hear me?

Excuse me, sir, can you hear me?

Padishah Shahrban al-Marwazi, can you hear me?

Shahrban opens his eyes to find himself hanging by his heels as if readied to be split in half by an executioner's chopper in the punishment of Shakk but snuffing instead a sponge of vinegar. He is being sprinkled with rosewater mingled with musk and civet by a swarthy man in a white gown whose breath smells of cloves.

'Thought for a time you were dead,' says the doc. 'No vital signs, blue in the face. Thought you'd been hitting the henbane.'

'Where am I? *What* am I? Where is my orangutan and with you be The Peace and the mercy of Allah and His benediction!'

'You are Padishah Shahrban al-Marwazi and there's a reward out so you must be important.'

'I don't feel important. But if so, I am certainly underappreciated.'

'It seems you fell over in the mosque and hit your head. Has this happened before? A touch of the sun, perhaps. We checked you out thoroughly. A bit of bleeding but you'll be okay. There is no harm in you and boon of health befall you. Are you feeling on top of things and upbeat?'

'Not really. I just had a terrible nightmare. There must be something wrong with me, surely, to be hanging by my heels. Where am I?'

'Cordoba mosque infirmary. We are trying to get your legs moving. You don't seem able to walk.'

'Was I, perhaps, sold in the market? Because the last thing I recall is a Viking beating me about the ears then putting a neck-loop round my neck and dragging me to a longboat in chains and what was worse, except for his moustachios, he had the face of my father-in-law.'

'You came down hard on the side of the head. It's lucky you're Persian.'

'Why has the mosque an infirmary?'

'We find the mosque arcades can have a strange effect on folk. It is not uncommon for True-Believers to pass out in them, even pass away.'

'What year is this?'

'Don't you worry your head about that. I conclude you have suffered a concussion. You have an enlarged heart, a pair of enlarged eyebrows and a much enlarged penis.'

'Oh, I am nothing out of the ordinary which is my entire problem. Yet here I am, a stranger in a strange land, who never felt so alone.'

'No one is truly alone, my friend. Seek refuge in Allah from Satan the Stoned!'

'Well said! If I were back in my palace I would order your mouth stuffed with jewels and pearls as you've given me hope. Why, I'm starting to feel myself again. What was your name?'

'Baruch. I'm a Jew. The Turks who stole your money have been caught and crucified then shot with shafts to resemble porcupines and your money will be returned, compliments of the Emir. I'm authorised to tell you that you will soon be on your way home.'

'I *must* speak with an oneiromant to expound me my dream!'

'We don't have that kind of thing in Cordoba. I suggest that on return to Merv ...'

'*Merv!* There's a name rings a bell. I must speak to the Pir in my lodge in Merv before my dream has faded.'

So the doc lets loose the chain. 'Nurse! Bring this man a sherbet. He is free to leave.'

It is a tedious journey home under constant threat of Berber assault, but it gives the Shah time to put his thoughts in order, though his brain is by no means the size of his heart or penis. By the time he is back in The Father of Safety he is a new man, even a modern one, having formulated, on the way home, an audacious provocation. He brusquely dismisses Abu Bakr – the man only wanting to tell him he has two new daughters off the groaning-stool and that the woman who sells the pigeon poults has found him a third cucurbit – and demands to speak at once with Shahrazad and Dinazad.

'Sabbah-ak' Allah bi'l khayr,' he says to them. 'Good morning, ladies. I have a dream. In this dream I see many women all but naked but don't get the wrong idea. They are unmolested and freed of the tyranny of kinsmen, working as Wazirs, Qadis and mirabs. I see them holding chairs in universities, becoming firemen, bishops and rabbis, dressing entirely to suit themselves, living alone if they so desire, divorcing their husbands if and when they choose. I see them in command of their own destinies, drinking alcohol, eating bhang, smoking opium and ephedra, walking the streets at night unaccompanied, conversing with young men never before seen while laying about stark naked in the sun, indulging in each and every sexual peccadillo assured of universal respect – and all thanks to two tablets a day of *dong quai* and *gancao*, washed down with pregnant mare's piss. You go, girls! I'm setting you free. You may, if you wish, leave Merv today, but for the time being, as free women, please don't show your faces in public, which might suggest to a man that you thought of him as boy, eunuch or Nazarene. These things take time. Such is the case as regards you. As concerning me, there is no help but that I must don white woollen-gear and become an ecstatic, a Darwaysh, a recluse aloof from earthly things and dedicated to orison; I must become an howling Dervish in tall, sugar-loaf felt cap and earn my place in paradise, for the Fiat of Fate has driven me to the matter foredoomed to me from all Eternity. Prayer carries me halfway to Allah; fasting brings me to the door of His palace which alms-deeds cause me to enter. Good day to you both. May Allah bless you and your fathers, and have mercy on the wombs that bore you and the loins that begat you.'

Shahrazad, wincing, is clutching at her belly as though seized of a gripe.

Abu Bakr is very dirty. 'You can't just release your slaves like that! What are you thinking! They have no means of earning a living. They have never done a day's work. You are condemning them to prostitution or menial labour. It is the cruellest thing ever I heard of.'

'They are your daughters, the life-stuff of your liver, so you do with them as you see fit, Abuyah. Now don't forget to order in that *dong quai* and *gancao* and have it distributed freely. I want nothing more to do with women, as after waste comes knowledge of worth and they are all of one and the same taste and little of wit and must needs the intelligent consort with the intelligent. I have learned my lesson. And now must I see 'Ali Zindiq Ibn al-Waqt 'Abd al-Kimiya as I have a dream I need him to expound.'

'We found you another brass cucurbit, Sahib.'

'I want nothing to do with it. I take refuge in Allah from Satan the Stoned!'

'Your wives have borne you two lovely daughters, Shahrban, but you must father a son, for the sake of the Dynasty. You've two new daughters, navel strings all cut and tied and eyes kohl'd.'

'Why can't a daughter run the Dynasty? Poo to the Samanid Dynasty, say I! My life is a light matter to me, Abu Bakr, and when I am dead, let the world be ruined after me. I was, forsooth, in reprobation and sorely in danger of the Judgement till I set my trust in Almighty Allah and extolled be the Causer of causes and the Liberator of necks! Has Shahrazad's daughter ... has Shahrazad's daughter the ...'

'Perky boobs? Oh yes, I'm told she's on track for the perky boobs.'

Sons of the Rumour gather in the lodge to hear the Shah recount his dream and the Pir expound upon it. But before he can do so, the Wazir draws the Pir aside, for a quiet word. 'Shahrazad's in love with him. By the mighty inscription on the seal ring of Sulayman, in setting her free he's put her on the job. Could we not have someone set him straight? I was thinking perhaps ... Musa?'

'Musa wa Muzi's our man. And what about that third Jinni, the True-Believer in the kumkum?'

'We'll snaffle him for ourselves. We must rid this oasis of salt.'

The Shah now recounts his dream, complete to the flight, as it were, of Sulayman's green silk carpet (on whom be The Peace!).

The Pir, after listening, says, 'Hmm. It would seem you have been given a glimpse of a future existence, which is unusual. But contained within it was a vision of a past life, which is more customary.

'In the past life, it would seem you were an Irish monk, so that you wasted your time, which was pretty ordinary. But in the future life, it appears you attain, at some point, to Happiness, then lose it, which is rather avarage.'

'Ah yes,' says the Shah, 'but I see the problem and forewarned is forearmed! I turn back where one should never turn back. I turn back in pity and must pay the price. Well, I am prepared to pay it and why not in advance? As I told the Wazir, there is no help for it but that I must don woollen Fakir-gear – felt hat, short skirt and wide blue pantaloons – to become a Sayih, or howling Dervish, for whatso is decreed unto the creature, perforce he must fulfil. I am, as you would glean, a Saudawi, a melancholic, in whose temperament the black bile predominates, which makes me dull, sullen company.

'It seems to me as though I were suspended in a bottomless well by a thin rope at which a rodent gnaws, and all I can think to do is to amuse myself by licking at some honey left by bees on the revetment. In other words, worldy pleasures being illusory and tyranny having grown to me distasteful, I am resolved that henceforth I shall live in the Kaysariyah, the chief mart of the merchants close by the mosque, with Dervish gear – begging bowl and Darabukkah-drum. I shall pray all night and fast dawn till dark as Saim al-Dahr – except on the two feast days of 'Id when Mervis embark upon the river to divert themselves by gazing the one upon the other. I do this in the hope that folk may deal with me kindly and graciously. I may, as Sufic Salikan, occasionally follow my face to the cemetery and circumambulate the tombs, till my course lead me to that mausoleum wherein is the appointed term of my days. I shall certainly, at some point, undertake Hajj al-Sharif to earn the green turband and I shall, I suppose, have as pillow a spare suit of clothes for Friday prayers.'

'Ya Abu Kalansuwah, father of a tall, sugar-loaf felt Dervish-cap,' says Musa, 'you've gone too far.' Musa wa Muzi, Moses the Troublesome, ancient Khwaja facially tattooed in Lantsa script, continues, 'Kurban-at basham – may I be your sacrifice, O Shadow of Allah? Be charitable, by all means, and abstemious, yes. In the words of Rabban Hillel, "If I am not for myself, who will be? But if I am for myself only, what am I? And if not now, when? The more flesh the more worms; the more possessions the more anxiety; the more women the more sorcery; the more concubines the more lewdness; the more ghulams the more theft; the more Torah the more life; the more contemplation the more wisdom; the more counsel the more understanding; the more righteousness the more peace." The Talmud teaches that ten strong things were created in this world, Shahrban, and you were not one of them. The mountain is strong but iron cuts through it. The iron is strong but fire melts it. The fire is strong but water quenches it. The water is strong but clouds bear it. The clouds are strong but wind scatters them. The wind is strong but the body endures it. The body is strong but fear crushes the body. Fear is strong but wine dispels fear. Wine is strong but sleep defeats wine. Death is mightier than all things but charity for the Torah teaches us that deeds of charity save us even from death.

'A Shah, however, cannot become a Dervish. Emperor Wu three times abdicated to become an indigent bonze, forcing his ministers, on each occasion, to redeem him for a string of cash. Let me now speak of the Longest Journey, Shahrban, which you have yet to complete ...'

Blue Melons

I was born in a *kishlak* that no publican could find before we produced our world famous *buzkachi* player Abu Haqid. I've gone searching for thorny rosewood with him. There were men wearing quilts and skullcaps from every horde in that *kishlak*; Chitralis, Kanjutis, Dulanis, Badakhshis, Ladakhis, Khitans with wispy little beards. What made the place unbearable was not the frozen windblown sand that piled every day of the plurry year up against the door, but that everything came from somewhere else – the corals from Cordoba, the carpets from Balkh, the dogs from Maracanda. Nothing we produced ourselves was thought to have any merit so the rice we ate we imported from Pagan, the rambutans from Borneo, the dried fish from Kwang-chou and the figs from Afrodisias. We ate and drank to the strains of a Kuchean 'ud. We had stores of lapis lazuli.

'Great place this,' my father enthused without much conviction as he'd come from Shash and certainly anyone born in that *kishlak* left as soon as they could. My brothers became mercenaries but I was destined for a more adventurous life. Soldiers, from what I've seen of them, spend their lives hunting dead poplars.

Notice how certain toddlers, though they be barely able to walk, cannot pass by a berm without demanding to be lifted that they may walk it? Seen the smile on their dial as they do? Where I come from, this was considered the call of the caravan.

So I became a *Mukharrij,* a trade in which you start young, because by the time you've learned it you're too old to practise. And it's not just a matter of knowing your routes and learning all your songs – as I developed my deep bass voice I became most welcome – you need to be able to breathe without air, see in the dark and balance a load. You have to know your pastures and tell a bread-pasture from a fruit-pasture. Elderly Bactrian camels, *Bukhti,* are great sandstorm sensors and water diviners, but they cannot bear imbalance. Tie things right you can seat on a camel an eight-piece band with an acrobat troupe, but one loose knot, a yak rope chafing a hump on some snowblind beast, will bring the whole string – maybe ten to a string, worth fourteen bolts of silk apiece, not to mention the load – quicker undone than a Gypsy horse thief or a flash flood. You need to know your knots and your anatomy, given a camel's proneness to suppurating saddle sores. We took up to two hundred strings from Blazing Beacon to the Jade Gate Pass where, as my master used to remark, we were no more than a teardrop on an eyelash.

Cameleers are generally men from the Moving Sands or the Gobi so I was a bit unusual being a Jew from the Roof of the World. Well, I'm not a proper Jew as many a proper Jew has observed: mother was only a proselyte, a Caspian Khazar, while father was an Aza from the Koko-Nor, a Xianbi. Fierce devils, the Xianbi, always fighting the Chinese and Tibetans. He'd met mother in Shash where he worked as a chandler in lapis lazuli. Then he got into financial strife and had to disappear. He'd worked out the best place to do so is a *kishlak*, up with the brown bears and wild yaks and well beyond the ken of the publicans of Sarikol, Wakhan and Little Balur. We certainly paid no taxes before we gained fame through Abu Haqid.

I began my Longest Journey, to the Land of Happiness, outside Khotan, though some insist the journey has no end.

It has, as I attest, a turning point.

Summer caravans always travel by night through Altishahr. At the lowest point of Altishahr, Yar-khoto, you're below sea level but most of the time you're at four thousand feet, five if you're climbing a dune. The passes that take you out of the Altishahr Basin are fifteen thousand feet high but you see more ponies and yaks up there than what you might see camels.

Opening east on the Black Gobi, the Moving Sands in the middle of that Basin are a full six months from east to west – a month from Hami to Anxi, and herded in to the north, south and west by the world's highest mountains. It's a place you can get sunstroke and frostbite at the same time, doff your cap and slippers, unless of course you were snugly coated in human dung, of which more anon. At dusk, the temperature drops like a shooting star and cameleers don heavy coats – I'd a lovely wolfskin number given me by an old Kyrghyz took a shine to my singing.

Like to hear me sing?

Suit yourself. Two thousand camels with a bell on each string sound a tocsin but only to the silent, so at night there's always the chance of collision with an oncoming caravan. In the event of such a tangle we'd stop for a yak, however much our merchants grumbled. Boil up a brew of the old yak butter tea, you know, toss some bhang on the fire?

Wasn't expecting company, not that night, on the southern route.

No one much takes the southern route unless they've an interest in jade or idols – twice the northern rate for camel hire and acrobats. Khotan, though, is the centre of the world jade trade and always was, and Buddhist monks come up from Taksasila over the Baroghil pass to Yarkhand. We had a cargo of scrap – swordless hilts and bells without tongues – while them oncoming, according to their inventory, had unmatched horseshoes and keys with no locks. As to tales of contraband rhubarb paid for in opium – could be something to it. Only three or four strings, no bells, no acrobats, no lights, low profile. I was hunting round for a bit of dung to light a fire when a Turk from the other caravan comes up and says, 'We're down a man.'

Thinking he wanted our medicine camel, which happened to be in my string, I asked what seemed to be the problem; whether the man concerned was lame or feverish or incontinent. In the case of a constipation (opium) I had a remedy: rhubarb, and not just any old rhubarb, *mountain* rhubarb with the gold flowers from Kwan-Kian and Siningfu. Rhubarb, would you believe, features in the cosmogony of Fire worship? The Mazdayasnian Adam and Eve sprang from the earth as rhubarb plants. Most of our potions, as you'd expect, were sherbets and leeches, but we carried herbs for breathlessness and headache, which we'd bought from a corps in the Tibetan Army.

'No,' he says, 'he's not lame or feverish or incontinent. He found his *home*. He's a Bon-po.'

Bon-po if you don't know is the old religion of Tibet.

'What do you mean "found his home"?'

'Sittin' up in yonder cave.'

'Want me to fetch him?'

'If ya like.'

'Hold me coat.'

☾

Left Khotan at midnight hoping for fifteen miles by dawn, but the gravel under our felt slippers has pushed out seventy miles from the scarp all along the Kunlun Shan and camels are soft-footed. Wouldn't be so bad if there were a drop of water there wasn't full of salt. Hard country, except in spring when glaciers melt and floods flash. Grey soil, where you see a bit of soil and the Kunlun massif always shrouded in dust. Dusty from Charkhlik to Karghalik on that southern road; always dusty. Here and there you'll find an oasis featuring a dusty poplar, but both Jade rivers were dry and the oncoming cameleers spitting blood. After a scramble I found your man in a cave and he wasn't a young man – Tibetan; face of brown leather, slits for eyes, never seen a bath – hasn't the double-lidded eyes of a camel and cannot close his nostrils.

Back in the time of which I speak Tibetans were moving on the Basin. They had the Tang on the run. They had occupied Kucha and Miran striking north from Koko-nor, that big sea at ten thousand feet, the world's highest ocean, home to the Aza who live along its shores in their black yak-hair tents. My father spoke of a time when thousands of Aza were killed by hail. Kucha to the north of the Sands has walls only six miles round, but its territory, like that of many Nanlu kingdoms, extends for several days, while Miran is just a tiny kingdom – oddly enough it has a tiny king – where the road to Lhasa meets the road to Khotan. What with Tibetans effectively blocking both roads through Altishahr, Chang'an silk and Dragon Well tea was paying taxes to the Uighurs, heading by Peilu through the Onion Range then down from the Warm Lake through Fergana to Shash then on to Merv.

There's a plant grows up by that Warm Lake has a dark blue flower which if you make an infusion from the root and soak a shirtcoat in it then give it to a man to wear after he's just taken a bath, he'll sicken and die within a few months in a very natural manner. Cameleers are always looking for this plant as we could never satisfy demand and you wonder why we don't marry or bathe.

'Home!' says your man in dog-Sogdian. We all spoke a bit of dog-Sogdian. He seemed happy but then we cameleers are gloomy men. Some say it's because the songs we sing are meant to frighten hungry ghosts. Hungry ghosts from those mummified corpses in the Black Gobi give some folk the heebie-jeebies. Not me, mate! I was only ever superstitious once, perhaps twice.

'Here I am,' says your man in the cave. 'I'm home or at least I'm close.'

'I doubt you was born up here,' I observed, with which he at once agreed.

'I'm from the Southern Bamboo where this cave would be full of bats,' he says, 'but did *you* feel at home where *you* was born? If so, why then so restless? Can't sit still we cameleers, we're like Sakyamuni or Jesus – indeed, I'm told this Tajik prophet, what's his name, he *was* a cameleer – as was Zarathushtra, judging by the fact that *ushtra* means "camel" in Gathi and like those lads, always on the lookout, and what is it we're looking for? In a word, Home. We can't find it and most of us, well, we don't even know we're looking. Sakyamuni found his under a Bo tree while mine is somewhere here. It could be this spot or could be that. You have to find the right *spot*. But I've narrowed it down.'

'Oh, of all the superstitious crap,' I said, squatting next to him. 'How can you be sure?'

'I'm sure,' he says, 'because I'm *looking* for it. Did you never enter some strange oasis only to find it familiar?'

'They all look pretty much the same to me,' I says, 'so I likes to move on. My *yaylak* is the road and the solace of care is in one of these three things: that a man should see what he never before saw, or hear what he never before heard, or tread a road that he never before trod.'

'Where you're looking for your life before this,' he explained, 'or, strictly speaking, the exit. You didn't know that. You think you're admiring the scenery while happily earning a living. Wrong. We travel not for trafficking alone: we search for *clues*. All our past lives create this life but the last leaves the strongest impression. You didn't know that, but even so, you could sense it. Indeed, you're driven to seek it out if you're the kind of man can't sit still, which you certainly are – sit still! Every time I pass this cave I feel a longing to stop. To me, this is the most beautiful place in the world, the destination of all travel. You ask was I *born* here? Ask, rather, whether I once *died* in this cave.'

'Oh, enough of your superstitious crap,' I said. 'But supposing I were superstitious – I wonder if I could find *my* home. Trouble is, I'm Jewish.'

'Where's your problem? Took you for Aza. Been to Egypt? That's where Jews are from. They're Gypos.'

'Never been west o' Shash, mate, and as to Aza …'

'Well, at least you now know what you're looking for. Only at *Home* will you be Happy and able to stay out of mischief. At least you now know what you're looking for.'

I thought of what I'd been up to in Khotan. I was mischief-prone. 'Won't be bored up here?' I inquired.

'*Bored?* You must be *joking*!'

'All right then, I'll leave you to it, good luck.' And I starts to clamber down. See, I knew he wouldn't be amenable to reason. They seldom are, the Bon. I've heard that in their religion to abstain from wickedness is unlawful.

'Wait,' he says when I'm halfway down.

'What now?'

'You're right, I may get bored. But if you was to wall me in so I couldn't get out, do you see?'

'Oh, I dunno,' I said. 'It'd be a lot of work and what's in it for me?'

'I will pray to my gods *bstanpag Shen-rabs, Kun-tu-bzang-po,* the black goddess *Dreuma* and the *Great Uncarved Block* that you may learn the purpose of your life.'

'As if we can know the purpose of our lives!'

'I know the purpose of *my* life. It's just I can't put it into words.'

'Oh, come come,' I says, trying to draw the man out. 'My breast is the grave of secrets.'

But he said no more.

I'd never walled anyone into a cave. It takes about a week. The canyon was littered with suitable stones but getting them up was a chore. Not only would he not assist, he insisted I use mortar, which meant I had to walk all the way back to Khotan just for lime. Khotan, full of Buddhist monasteries, has the tallest walls in Altishahr so it's a hard place to miss.

The Tibetan told me Tibetans had just built their first Royal lamasery, but Bon demons kept knocking down the walls so the king had had to send for this yogin from Swat, Lotus-Born, to sort them. And what with Uighurs filling the north of the Basin with their Manichee monasteries, there were that many homeless demons on the road was another reason to be quitting it.

I didn't have to quit the road. They'd taken my coat – can't work without a coat.

In a soak scratched by a wild camel I found the wet sand I needed and when I'd finished building that wall I knew the Bon-Po wouldn't knock it down. He'd never get out of that cave. Water sufficient to quench his thirst had moistened the rear rock face and I'd gathered him a few reeds and weeds and tamarisk leaves to chew.

These, he said, would keep him going until he found the right spot and once he had found the right spot he was bent on some serious meditation. He meant to spend the rest of his life staring at a wall, like Bodhidharma.

He spoke of the power that accrues when you die in the same place over and again.

He spoke of having encountered the same cameleer in three different bodies.

'Ever we meet again,' he said, 'I'll make this *mudra*.' And he made a certain gesture. 'Well, thanks for your help,' he said as I left or I hope that's what he said as I couldn't properly hear.

Taking one last look at my handicraft I departed for Khotan.

That wall looked *rough*. I was still considering whether to go back and tuckpoint when I passed the beacon fort. Now, I'd assumed it was empty and I think it had been the last time I passed, but two huge fires at once blazed up from two of the three fire brackets and five of the six Tibetans on duty came running out to apprehend me. Satisfied I was alone, they shouted to their colleague to give the all-clear – which meant suffocating one fire – and having declared they served the cause of *Khri Ide gtsug btsan* – the same king who'd commissioned Lotus-Born to drive out the demons – they marched me back, tattooed my face and threw me in the slot where they disposed of sewage. Tibetans hate Aza worse than they hate the Uighur or the Chinese.

I couldn't stand up or lie down. Soldiers on duty in beacon towers are generally there to be punished and grumpy and vicious because they get bored on alert with nothing to do but hunt wood.

So now I have '*Om Mani Padme Hum*' tattooed across my forehead and 'Property *Khri Ide gtsug btsan*' from ear to ear like a chinstrap and not even delicately done and Jews are forbidden tattoos.

Om Mani Padme Hum – tattooed, as you see, in Lantsa. It means Om! The Jewel in the Lotus! Hum! Being the *mantra* of *Bodhisattva Avalokiteshvara* (Sanskrit), *Chenrazee* (Tibetan), *Kwan-shih-yin* (Chinese), all these wretched languages, patron god of Tibet, repetition of which in this world and immediately upon dying is efficacious in bringing to a close the cycle of rebirth in the six worlds, the '*om*' serving to close the door of rebirth to the god world, the '*ma*' to the titan world, the '*ni*' to the human world, the '*pad*' to the brute world, the '*me*' to the world of the hungry ghosts and '*hum*' to the worlds of the various devils in all their various hells.

I don't know how long I was held there. It was too dark to see. They used the slot for a latrine so I got to speak to them from time to time. One of them spoke a little Sogdian. I told him my brother Israil served in his army but he had it in his head I was a spy and intended to have me tortured, he said, to vindicate his lighting of the beacon. I mentioned I'd seen a big dead juniper tree in a gorge, which I had done, but when it came to locating the gorge I made it the gorge where my wall stood – this to give me an estimate of how long he'd be away. Sure enough, the five big men went off to fetch the wood leaving only the smallest, youngest boy to guard the fort. I knew his movements. When he came to use the slot I pulled him in. He couldn't put up much of a fight with his trowsers round his ankles. I gave him a right thrashing then set off stinking for Khotan. They'd only dried meat to eat in that fort and I couldn't find water. Tibetans don't believe in washing and suffocate fires with their fists.

Near where Khotan was saved from the Huns by the Rat King chewing through their bridles, a mud-brick wall in the north-western corner bears a sign in thirty-six languages. Probably says 'Keep out' but I'm only guessing as I can't read. In any event I climbed that wall hoping to find some clothes. I wasn't worried to be naked as being covered in dung gives protection from the sun, but I didn't want to be taken for a Sky Clad Jain, not in Khotan.

Inside the wall I found a *karez* as they call the qanat in Altishahr, an underground channel irrigating melons. I'd never in my life seen a blue melon and here was a field fairly full of them – hundreds of these bright blue melons doing well within the four clay walls. The *karez,* which might have been fifty foot deep where it took the mountain melt, was here only just below the surface of the loess as the water ran off into the desert to the north through a gap which I could see in the mud brick.

I was making towards the central hut of tamarisk stalk and daub in the shade of a big heap of melon fruits, all sliced up and drying in the sun, when out jumps this one-eyed cameleer I knew as Tson, shouting, 'Melon thief!'

'Shut your stupid face,' I said, 'as if I'd want your stupid melons.' But being hungry I'd grabbed me a few strips of dried melon and was chewing them.

A duke emerged from the hut on one of those horses that sweat blood and he had an eagle chained to his arm and a goitred footman with a parasol. A good many Khotanese have goitres, even the young girls.

'Caught in the act,' says Tson to this duke. 'It's Miso, the villainous Aza.'

'Ugly Sky Clad Jain,' says the duke. 'Can he read? No, I guess not. The Khotanese blue melon must never leave the Kingdom of Khotan. Only a Khotanese *bodhisattva* is fit to partake of a blue melon. What shall we do with him now then, Tson? He's eaten half that melon.'

Given, like many cameleers, to self-cautery and covered in burns, Tson wanted to gouge out my eyes then wipe the blade of his knife on my beard. I recalled he blamed me for starting that brawl in the brothel in which he lost an eye. When I say 'brothel', cameleers marry girls on arrival in a caravanserai. As we leave we say to them, 'Be thou to me as my mother's back,' and we're divorced. It's a convenient institution.

'Word of warning, sir,' I says. 'Tibetans are close by.'

'*Poo!*' says the duke. 'The smell of you, in here, desecrating holy melons. How *dare* you come here naked, you filthy Jain, you dirty *Digambara*. You are not worth the paring of a nail. Probably looking for seed.' He turns to his footman. 'Drive him off as is. See the *elegance* of it, the wit? Off with him into the Moving Sands. Let him take his seed into the desert. Let's see how he copes with the ghuls and the phantoms and the bells and the drums and the singing of the revellers. It's men like this have caused every problem we have in this world of the six.'

Inflamed by the rhetoric, Tson and the footman drove me back over the wall. The eagle then drove me into the desert and so began my Longest Journey.

Once in the desert I wept for it didn't seem to me to be fair. Eighteen years old, as good as dead and all because a man can't read. Tibetans would know from my ugly tattoo that I was an escapee, while Khotanese would be sure to execute me on the duke's order. The Khotanese have an idol of the northern Heavenly King in their gate; they have that wooden *Sakyamuni* that flew over the Himalayas by itself; they have their carts that creak under idols – *Buddhas, Bodhisattvas, Devatas, Dharmapalas* – they sweep the streets and hang the gates in silk and burn frankincense, but if you're not there on one of their fourteen feast days expect no mercy.

And all because a man can't read and helped himself to some dried melon.

Recall I was naked. The duke, were he observant, would have noticed I was circumcised, but not every duke wants to be seen staring at a young man's shit-encrusted cock. Filthy hair in matted dreadlocks, covered from head to toe in shit – Sky Clad Jain to all appearance. Sky Clad monks are not permitted to bathe or to light fires. This is the path of *Mahavira* 'Great Hero' once followed by the *Buddha* as well, but Sky Clad Jains are unwelcome in Khotan because *Sakyamuni* couldn't stick the hard yards, according to the Sky Clad Jain..

No cameleer ever heard of a solitary south–north crossing of the Moving Sands or at least I never did. There is supposedly a north–south road between the Bedal Pass and Khotan but I never met anyone who travelled it and you wouldn't travel it except in winter as you'd want to be laden up with blocks of ice for drinking water. You'd never find a road.

Air temperature in that Basin drops to minus forty in winter. In summer it reaches forty plus. Even so, I accomplished a solitary traverse in forty days, travelling at two miles an hour, camel speed. When I say 'I' did it, I was assisted. Indeed, I was never less alone.

Now why is this so easy to forget? So easy to forget and yet so hard.

Seventy miles of glacial gravel then disintegrated rock where a grain of 'sand' can be the size of a mare's teat grape, then smaller grains all the way down to dust mounted into thousand-foot dunes and these dunes, while never intermingling, are always creeping back and forth, always blowing to and fro – 'a desert where is none save He'. Hundreds of miles of gravel and loess, quite fertile where it gets a bit of water, but nothing growing in those dry river channels, the rivers always changing their courses – only desert tamarisk and sarakaul. In an attempt to sleep by day I would burrow, marmot-like, into a dune; trying to follow the stars by night I'd shiver in the freezing wind. An experienced cameleer, I could ignore the ghuls and the phantoms and the bells and the drums and the singing of the revellers, but I didn't get any sleep and at first I couldn't find provender yet I'd had my first-ever bath and was snugly dressed by the time I reached Aksu, city-state under the Mountains of Heaven with apricots drying on the roofs.

For days I floated around that oasis as though bathing in cold water, through green wavy fields of grain, diving in verdure of gardens and grasses, splashing through pastures fresh and plentiful, quenching my hot, rubicund eyes in the bountiful shade of the apricot trees.

And as you'd expect they showered me with gifts, as the first man ever to have entered from the south and in summer and all the way from Khotan. Free wine, entertainment, you name it. Over the grit of a flood-cleared channel through the grounds of a Manichee monastery I came, dressed in plaid and belching melon gas – blue melon gas – blue, yellow and red plaid. My voice had become a high tenor. My tattooed face wore an unthreatening smile. I'd become superstitious, even penitential, but it didn't long last. See, it never does. Not in this world of the six.

Two streams, the Black and White Jade, irrigate Khotan's cereals and fruits and provide water for the paper mills while washing lumps and sometimes boulders of jade down from the Kunlun. Khotan is the home of jade but the jade comes from Tibet. In summer those streams – the Karakash and Yurungkash – run north ninety miles to form the Khotan River which eventually disappears into the Moving Sands, just as the mighty Murghab River here disappears into the Black Sands and the Goldbearer River beyond Bukhara disappears into the Red Sands. Only the Oxus has that riparian mile-deep jungle of nosebreaker vines, all full of tigers and pheasants and swine, to protect it from the Black Sands and the Red, the Karakum and Kyzylkum deserts. The Oxus, unlike most desert rivers, doesn't wander round like a drunk.

Black and White Jade rivers when I set out were dry. They meet, oftimes, on the edge of the oasis. Nanlu rivers only flow in spring and unpredictably, from glacial melt. Landslides and earthquakes up on the high plateau can take effect. Sometimes an ice causeway will block a river to produce a lake. I once took a string of camels over a causeway on the high plateau. When I returned the causeway had gone, so too a village downstream.

On this occasion, I think there must have been an avalanche, because one minute I'm trudging along a bed of the dry Khotan River, repenting, from the bottom of my heart, in perfect renunciation of past vice, all the sins I ever committed through the infinite eras of my past lives, through sympathy, antipathy or apathy, by means of body or mouth or will, motivated, I guess, by the prospect of my certain, imminent death – the next I'm fighting off blue melons and struggling to breathe in a spate. I was long gone from Khotan by this, too, right out among the dunes. The water, freezing, left me clean but now quite prone to sunburn, so I gathered me as many blue melons as I could to eat and to wear around my neck.

I reckon they taste better dry, but fresh they give more moisture.

Years later I heard the Black Jade River had washed away Khotan west.

Cameleers still speak of a time when Altishahr was riddled with great rivers, when the salt lakes were seas, when the ranges that rim the Basin were buried under ice. Over the years this ice has melted till now only glaciers remain and most of the rivers have disappeared as well.

They say there are cities under the dunes.

'Taklamakan', which Turks call the Sands, means, 'If you go in, don't expect to come out'. I wasn't looking for a city, I was just trying to keep my balance under a heap of blue melons when I stumbled over a mummy, the kind you meet with in the Black Gobi. He was a man about my own height with red hair under a witch's hat and warmly dressed in wool no less, while his eye sockets, rounder than a Frank's, told me that he was Tokharian – a Yuezhi. He wore a pair of deerskin leggings and a robe of tartan plaid with socks to match. Over the time it takes to eat a meal I found another red-haired mummy by a wall. This wall moreover was six foot thick so it had to be a city wall. Both these men wore tartan plaid so now I was clean, now I had clothes, and thanks to those blue melons, I had food and drink. I suppose I'd discovered a lost city but I wouldn't be able to find it today.

I went back and fetched me a few more melons as the wool I didn't need to wear could serve me as a rope. I guess I had about forty all up – half of which I dragged and half I wore.

I never felt so *Happy*! I'd become completely superstitious. I'd stumbled over more than just mummies and melons out there. I was *Home*.

I polished off the last blue melon before entering Aksu. I didn't want any trouble. So all I have now to remind me of what I endured is a respect for superstition.

I partied at Aksu until they began to tire of me and started asking whether I wouldn't prefer to pay for my mare's teat grape wine. Come sunset each evening you'd find me down by the Manichee monastery staring out at the Sands, bottle of wine in hand. One afternoon a girl I'd married – those were the days when bare-faced women could walk the streets unaccompanied – came upon me in that place and said, 'What's wrong with you?'

'How do you mean?' I replied, speaking slowly and carefully the way a drunk does. 'How could anything be wrong? I haven't worked in over a month and I've all the wine I can drink.'

'Think I don't know when a man's unhappy? Spit it out, Miso!'

I burst into tears. Pointing at the dunes I said, 'I belong out there. There's a road among those dunes goes down south to Khotan. I was never so Happy as on it. I'm able to ignore the ghuls and the phantoms and the bells and the drums and the singing of the revellers as I'm an experienced cameleer and the desert is my penitentiary.'

Just then we noticed a Manichee monk in his white silk tunic and turband, so we got up and left. Whenever I saw this particular monk I'd always up and leave. He was looking for me I thought and I fancied he wanted to lecture me. They're not supposed to walk, let alone drink wine, as it hurts the soil. By the same token, Sky Clad Jains are not allowed to fan themselves.

The things people believe!

'I have to go back out,' I says to the wife, 'as you've clarified matters. This time though, I'll take camels, I'll be more professional. Be thou to me as my mother's back! Hey, could you lend me some cash? No wait, I got that back to front. Lend me the cash first.'

She couldn't deny me the cash, she said, as I'd been a generous husband. Even so, she was sorry to see me bent on my drunken proposal, but by next morning I'd left Aksu with three young female camels. They were *Rahil,* small dromedaries with noses soft to kiss, not really fit for burden but able to cover a hundred miles in a day. They can go without water for sixteen days in cold weather but all camels do better with a weekly drink.

The first died not far out of Aksu. I don't know what happened there. Her death deprived me of my tent, my fur coat and my blanket, because when I tried to load these items on the other two, having first given them the *nakh* to kneel – 'Ikh! Ikh! Ikh!' – they had nothing to say. You can only load a camel to the point where she don't complain. If all's well, she'll complain.

The second disappeared in a sandstorm. I think the peg through her nose fell out but her loss deprived me of half my water and half my remaining provender.

The third died on her feet within sight of the Kunlun Shan. She broke, hock-deep, through the crust of a salt lake and hadn't the strength to climb out and I couldn't pull her. By this stage I'd been eating her blood – you can't kill a camel by cutting the throat, you have to stab it in that part of the throat where camels are stabbed, *al-labbah* – and drinking her piss which had made me so sick I couldn't bear the stench of myself. So again I had to strip off my clothes and I lost my fine witch's hat and rare Tocharian kilt and came in as I went out, naked and melting – save for a ruby I'd buried in my shoulder – this time crawling on the gravel.

Was I capable of Happiness? I was incapable of *fear*. As matters went from bad to worse – I never did find that riverbed – I felt nothing but indifference and so detached from all that was happening to me it was like a dream; only it wasn't a meaningful dream and it didn't seem to be *mine*. I felt as if I had stumbled into someone else's meaningless dream.

'Go on,' I croaked at last through my blood-cracked lips. 'You know who You are. I've no water to appease my thirst and I want to die as I've had enough here, but being a Jew I require a sign.'

She gave me one. The instant I uttered my prayer I saw a little water-wagtail and followed it half a mile to a pool of soda water, yellow with tamarisk. When you're at home you can't be fussed, so I drank my fill of that water.

And so there I sat, lost in one world, found in the Pure Land a second time, only this time I knew it wouldn't last and it didn't, but I meant to enjoy it.

When night fell I got to my feet and headed to the hills. I don't recall crossing a road – surely I'd have seen wheel ruts? No matter, I started to sing and dance as I headed up some dusty canyon. I might have been anywhere at all between Charkhlik and Karghalik but making for the Tsaidam, that great grazing land west of Koko-nor, the Aza heartland.

You never should drink stagnant soda water as it gives you blisters.

A few nights in – fasting, weary and more Unhappy than Happy – I started to smell Tibetans. A bit further in I knew it had to be more than just a couple. They were either very old or very young or had cholera because they were incontinent. I followed the stench and in due course staggered, in moonlight, on a frightful scene. I'd stumbled over *Shalmari*. Tibetan cameleers are always joking of Shalmari but I hadn't taken them seriously.

On a bare hill above a saltpan stood a dozen stakes of green poplar, each *khazuk* about the thickness of a man's arm and roughly trimmed to a point with an adze. Each had been driven into the ground to a height of about six foot. Most were bare, a few draped in bones, with six freshly impaled bodies wrapped around the rest in the punishment known to the Arab as *Salb*. Three of these miserable creatures had their feet upon the ground, one moving as if walking, one with her knees bent as if sitting, one with his bloody, befouled backside right flush on the stony earth.

Three were actually up in the air, their bodies writhing as they inched down on the stake, while one actually had the stake that entered his anus projecting from his throat. He wore the garb of a Bon-po lama – black witch's hat, surmounted by a peacock's feather and human skull. To my surprise he was still alive, his hands groping for his mouth, but always detaching themselves again when they secured a purchase on the stake. When this happened, his legs, in periodic contact with the ground, would seek to uplift his body, but the stake would then redden and the legs relax. Ooh, it was a shocking sight. As you may imagine it transfixed me. Indeed, I was so appalled by what I saw I scarcely noticed Tson until he came right up and punched me in the arm.

'Miso!' he says. 'Ya Rakib! We'd thought we'd seen the last of you till we heard you sing. That's Miso, we says, best basso in the Basin. You're not a ghost? I dare say not. You want to get yourself some clothing, mate. Don't get caught up here, Miso. You wouldn't want to join our friends up on the hill. Care for a cuppa?'

'Love one.'

'Lonely here at times,' says Tson, stoking up the fire. 'Still, I guess it's work.'

'What kind?'

Tson had his black hands mixing up the salt and rancid butter. 'Ghafir – pretty much a ghafir these days, mate. Melon guard, villain guard. Miss the camels though, don't you?'

'No. Why do you need to guard this lot? They're not going anywhere.'

'Just to ensure that no one tries to give them water which would put them out of their misery. Not that anyone has. Slack job. Oh, they scream for their mother something shocking at first, but they often speak the truth, once they see all hope is gone. I've learned some interesting things about my haircut. There you go.'

'Ta. What else do you do?'

'Help impale, cut fresh stakes as required – Assistant Royal Impaler.'

'How long do they last?'

'Hard to say. At first I had a notion that if they were still moving they were still alive? And if they weren't then they were dead? But that doesn't seem to be the case. Now I just wait till the buzzards and wolves have eaten their fill, then I take down the bones, crush them to tsampa and stick them on that rock over there.'

'And how long has *he* been up? My breast is the grave of secrets.'

'One with the stake right through? Did that, might have been ... last week? Lose track of time out here. Om! That's a tidy piece of work. Hum! Masterful impalement, that. You're not a ghost, are you, Miso?'

'No.'

'Didn't think so. Perhaps you've seen one. In any event, I'm glad you're here to see that impalement. I was hoping someone might. How'd you find the place?'

'Stumbled over it.'

'My word, you're a great stumbler. I tell you what, you grab that tea, we'll go take a closer look. Get the pale right through like that, you have to adjust the body many times and they don't always want to cooperate. Once up, a drink of water would kill them through haemorrhage. As in crucifixion, they die of cramp.'

'What did she do, that girl?'

'Prostitute.'

'Him?'

'Schismatic.'

Drinking tea we strolled *Shalmari*, viewing all impalements.

'Everyone here,' says Tson, 'is heading for one of the various hells, so *Khri Ide gtsug btsan* is trying to ease their passage. He's a compassionate king.'

'What has she done?'

'Sorceress. Her husband died of no apparent cause.'

'Him?'

'Lama skipped a passage reading a sacred text, no wait; he might be that mystic failed in his tantric vows. Hey, you've gone pale.'

'Been drinking soda water, Tson. Need to lie down.'

'Wait till you've taken a closer look at the one with the pale right through. He's a *kafir*! A kafir in Tibet! Denies the very existence of gods! Laughs at the notion. That, of course, is the one sin for which there can be no forgiveness. Him and that lama are off to Avitchi hell, which is the worst hell of all. Nothing we can organise here prepares a man for that; still, we do our best. There are eight hot hells and eight cold hells as well as Avitchi hell, and then you have your Doorless Iron House and the Hill of Spikes, which we've tried here to replicate. Mind you, it's not up to *Khri Ide gtsug btsan* to judge who goes where; that's a job for *Gshin-rje-gshed-po*, wrathful aspect of *Avalokiteshvara*, whose mantra you have tattooed on your forehead – well done! That should stand you in good stead when you meet with *Dharma-Raja*.'

'I don't understand a word you say.'

'Oh, yes you do.'

'Oh, no I don't and I want to go home!'

'Not yet. Shame to visit the Hill of Spikes, not study the perfect impalement. I tell you what, I'll donate his quilt. How's that? You must be cold. The tea in your mug is frozen solid and there you are stark naked. You're not a Sky Clad Jain?'

Tson reenacted the twisting and pulling of the torso and the limbs involved, all the time laughing at how the man had insulted the Royal Impaler, calling his mother a whore with the morals of an alley cat. And then the man's head lolled a bit on the stake and I fancied his eyes met mine and he made a *mudra*. He made a certain gesture.

So I took that quilt, the pair of slippers and skullcap and went back to the road.

Nightfall, a few days later, I stumbled on the gravel where my journey had begun. And then it started raining and it never rains in the Kunlun Shan.

What I'd seen and heard on that Hill had effaced my sense of achievement. I was never so Unhappy. If, as a failed mystic, I, too, was headed for Avitchi hell, I had to implore *Avalokiteshvara*, whose mantra I wear on my brow – for all the world as if my face were a *spyang-pu* on a funeral effigy – implore his pardon and forgiveness for my sins, over all prior existences, but I hadn't the energy. I couldn't do it from the bottom of my heart. You need both heat and timing.

Have I mentioned that, while in a superstitious state, I discovered myself immortal? Oh yes. This was after I'd begged forgiveness for my sins from *Bodhisattva Avalokiteshvara*, who transports to the *Pure Land* of *Amitabha Buddha* all who repent and no longer desire to live in drunkenness and die in dreaming. This was out in the Moving Sands on my first-ever south–north venture before I was spared, by means of Khotanese blue melons, from certain death.

I have a feeling I was heard and helped by *Avalokiteshvara*'s consort, *Kuan-shi-yin*, Compassionate Listener, invoked, as so often I'd heard, in the form of *Sgrolma*, Divine Mother, *Shakti* of *Amogha-Siddhi*, the goddess who listens to Tibetan cameleers who are Ready to Repent from the Bottom of their Hearts. I'd heard quite a few of them do that. You wouldn't have thought them religious till you saw them in a bit of strife. Then it was bring in the Lamas, mate.

I must have dozed off. When I opened my eyes, the usual parching desert wind was blowing off the Sands, but the rain had precipitated the dust so myriad pools of muddy water lay dimpling on the gravel. I looked up, dazzled by a blaze of golden light which proved to be the leaves of a nearby poplar, looking and sounding like prayer flags. All the dust having washed away, the leaves were sparkling brightly until, as the wind intensified, they were gradually torn from the boughs.

I never saw anything so beautiful. I don't think I'd ever really *scrutinised* a tree. I watched that poplar till the leaves had gone.

Later in the day, still sitting where I sat, I saw a caravan approaching from the east.

Summer was over and the eight-month winter in the Nanlu Basin had begun.

Thereafter followed my wasted years, spent hanging round the Kashgar market, a wild fellow dressed in rags whose face would terrify the children. A bit younger than your average dervish, I had my pick of rotten fruit. Did you know the word 'dervish' means 'beggar' in Dari? I prefer 'kalander'.

One day, as I was holding the nose-peg on a camel, getting her sores packed with pepper, having hobbled her near foreleg with her halter just above the knee, a man came by in a heavy fur coat, though the day was hot and the flies thick. He wore a hat of green chintz bordered with black lambskin but his hair, which fell to his waist, was thick, long, rank and *green*. He stopped to stare at me and I noticed that he wore phylacteries. These are the boxes filled with scraps of paper on which are written sacred words in square Hebrew, which Jews wear as they pray. He had one on his forehead and another on his arm, next to a hooded falcon. Dismounting his bullock and squatting in his high-heeled boots, he continued to stare at me till eventually, the camel was finished her treatment and I received a dirham for my pains.

'And what's your fookin' problem?' I said to this man when the camel had gone. See, I thought he wanted a fight.

'*You're* the one with the problem,' he said. 'Care to get it off your chest?'

'Why would I talk to a *Yid*,' I sneered.

'Because you are one.' Then he said something, speaking in Xianbi, gave me a little *hope*. Not much hope, but before night fell, I'd given that dirham the flick. Just flicked it away, with finger and thumb, not looking to see where it landed.

I asked him his name.

'*Makhdum-i-Azam*,' he said and smiled. '*Rumouroghli. Rumourzada. Ibn Rumour*.'

Then I recounted my life story even as I've told it you, beginning, 'I was born in a *kishlak* that no publican could find' right down to, 'summer was over and the eight-month winter in the Nanlu Basin had begun'.

He listened patiently. When I'd finished, he paused, then said, '*Shekinah* has shown Her face to you, Musa. That much I saw from your eyes, riding by, but you mustn't think of yourself as a mystic who failed in his tantric vows. *Gautama Buddha* was a bitter Stoic; I should say no more than that. I want you to think of yourself as a soul still *making* the Longest Journey and I tell you the saint who *fails* to abandon his bliss is lost in *both* worlds!'

Oh, the comfort of these words!

He clambered back on his bullock which lifted its tail, like a he-camel in rut, and moved off.

'Wait!' I shouted after him. 'I still don't know the purpose of my life!'

'The answer awaits you in Aksu,' he said. Then he vanished and I haven't seen him since.

I know now it was the Presence Khidr, *as-salamu 'alaykum*.

It was the Jew they call the Green One.

I left Kashgar that same day meaning to travel straight to Aksu, a journey up the northern road of maybe two to three months, but I got caught up in Tumchuq and had to overwinter there so I didn't arrive in Aksu until the following spring. I found work in a caravan tending newborn camel calves, which have to travel in a *maksar*, a cradle on their mother's back for the first few weeks, and loading half-grown youngsters who cannot carry a full load but have to carry something, generally tent poles and iron pots, which they do in a *haudaj*, a rude pack saddle girt with a single cord, mostly made of mimosa wood on a pad of old tent cloth stuffed with grass.

Seeing Aksu, desert iris rimming the sprouting corn, I jumped ship, hoping to reacquire, by entering from the south, a sense of purpose.

I retraced my steps from my glorious adventure to where I'd tossed my last blue rind.

Passing again through the Manichee monastery, I noticed there was a feast on – that's if you call a feed of vegetables and fruit with no wine a feast. I asked a passing layman what it was and he said it was the Feast of Bema that commemorates the crucifixion and flaying alive of Mani, on whom be Peace.

'Why not join us?' said the Sart. 'Make friends with the Kingdom of Light as revealed to us by the Pure One, *Mar Ammo*, blessings on his name.'

These Pure Ones, *al-Dinawariyyah*, I learned, are schismatic Manichees who broke from the Church in Ctesiphon fully five hundred years ago. Their prophet Mar Ammo is buried near Balkh, in what is purportedly the Tomb of Caliph 'Ali.

I declined as politely as I could. Then I noticed a platter of fruit go by and among the cucurbits on this platter were melons – *blue* melons.

'Where'd you get those?' I asked the man who was holding the platter of fruit. He wore, as they all do, Sogdian garb – white raiments – Phrygian cap, belted silken overjacket, silken trowsers and boots of silk brocade.

'Wouldn't you like to know,' he said. 'My breast is the grave of secrets but this much I will divulge. The Elect have established that these melons, upon being belched, release more light than any other fruit or vegetable, for which reason they are kept exclusively for the Feast of Bema.'

Just then, that same old monk came up who used to pester me before, scampering like a fakir over hot coals and heading straight for me.

'Friend and benefactor!' he shouted.

I suppose I wasn't hard to recognise.

He took me by the arm and dragged me down to the vegetable patch where I saw a row of melons with only cotyledons up.

'There!' he said, pointing at a stake which stood in a corner of the potager. 'X marks the spot where you gave this monastery the most precious gift any Auditor could give. Remember you took that massive dump when you come in out of the desert?'

'Not the kind of thing I'd recall,' I said, backing away. 'Now, if you don't mind, I'm off to discover the purpose of my life, which awaits me here in Aksu.'

'Ah,' he said, 'but you just discovered it! The morsel of meat in your mother's womb had an arsehole before it had a mouth and in your compassion you have done for us what no other Auditor could have. You stored and fertilised to perfection a seed in your own human dung and from that precious seedling we now have blue melons – all thanks to you.'

So, unlike other Hearers at that Feast I'd achieved, it seemed, my life purpose. The stake in the garden marked, according to the Presence Khidr, my halfway point.

I got well and truly drunk that night. To think it was all over.

My death will come in due course. I am the son of a century now but it ill-behoves me to show impatience, time being an illusion. By God's Grace, I think I know what to hope for as I die – a further bout of superstition.

I remarried the wife from Aksu – luckily, as required by *surah al-Baqarah* she'd been remarried and redivorced – and I still had that ruby I buried in my shoulder to pay for the reception. We settled in Merv where we raised our family and I found work in the orchards. I eat a bit of meat, which serves to enrich my dung, and drink a bit of wine, which serves to dull my *huzn*, the grief that follows the Mystical Divorce.

Iranian Days (concluded)

And after this, the final tale, is preached the final sermon.

'The Talmud, in a comment on Torah, Deuteronomy VI, 5, teaches that the heart of man contains two impulses – the *yezer tov*, or good impulse; and the *yezer ra*, or evil impulse. In a comment on Torah, Genesis 1, 13, "And God saw everything which He had made and behold it was very good", the Talmud insists that "very good" here applies to both these impulses. But, it is asked, is *yezer ra*, the evil impulse, then very good? And the answer is given, "Were it not for *yezer ra*, a man would not build a house, marry a wife, beget children or conduct his business affairs".

'I think I understand your problem, Shahrban; again from the Talmud: for everything there is a substitute, except for the wife of one's youth.

'Man is a kind of ape, a creature who thinks of himself as important, while, in fact, the role of animals, especially apes, including Man, is to assist plants. Because they can process the light from the sun, plants are higher beings than we are. All life depends on the vegetable world's capacity to process light, and animals need plants for food, but plants require animals as well; in particular, they need assistance in rotting when they die and help in spreading out.

'Why did God create Man? Was it that he might glorify his Maker through the cultivation of virtue? I have learned that Man's true purpose is found in his dung, that thing he most despises and least values, yet often enough he refuses grain and fruit, preferring to gorge himself on milk and flesh. How foolish! Creatures such as the orangutan can anyway disseminate and fertilise. Man, who prefers to configure himself as the Centrepiece of God's Creation is, in fact, at best a superfluity, at worst a menace, the Ape who has Forgot.

'The first half of his Longest Journey sees him penitential in the face of certain death, strips him of vainglory and deposits him in Paradise, a Garden watered by a Running Stream. He is not alone there because he is now married to the Shakti who dwells within him. This we call the Rumour. At the same time, the Shakti of Yahweh, Shekinah the Protector, enfolds him in Her Tender Wings. She is the myrinominous Darling Whose Wisdom is better than Law, Whose Comfort is sweeter than wine. No man, having enjoyed Her Favours, can ever be content again without them. She is Happiness. She manifests in the Ark of the Covenant over the Mercyseat. When Jews ceased to be nomads and occupied Jerusalem, She moved from the Ark of the Covenant to the Holy of Holies. When the veil of the Temple was rent in twain as Jesus gave up the Ghost, She left the Holy of Holies, moving out into this world. As the Pillar of Fire by night, She leads the Children out of Exile. Until She becomes a Bride, no man may speak with God face to face. Resting peacefully in Paradise, the traveller sees himself immortal.'

'Well, thanks for your tale,' says the Shah, backing off from this ancient, tattooed Khwaja.

'Wait!' says Musa. 'I've not finished yet, though dear God, would that I had. To his surprise, the man is not content. Why not? He has achieved the Magisterium. And yet, being animal, not yet vegetable, he moves, for movement is his Nature. He has no *desire* to move, well knowing that movement must take him from his bliss, and yet he finds himself rising to his feet, but how to act? He is beyond good and evil.'

'That being so,' says the Shah, 'he were better off dead. He should kill himself.'

'He can't. He's immortal, remember? He just learned he lives in Life Eternal.'

'Ah well, if he has climbed the peak of a mountain I guess he has to redescend. Or if, as I suspect, he has plumbed a crevasse he should certainly reemerge. Having reached the outermost point of his transit, he must retrace his steps. That should be easy.'

'Yes, he returns but no, it is the hardest part of the Longest Journey. Why? Because to a man who has achieved the Magisterium, all that remains is Women's Work and Child's Play. Amen.'

And so they reunited, Shahrban and Shahrazad, in order to procreate and do their duty, drowned in the sea of their love and dazed in the desert of their passion, though never meeting as husband and wife but always and forever as strangers, confecting, through audacious provocation, a thousand variations and a variation on their first and one encounter; two principals in a grim passion play in which ancient scars were forever being reopened; co-conspirators in compaction of time, performing for each other's benefit, until – interrupted by child-birth feasts, conscious that nothing carnal endures and exhausted by ludic exploration – growing old, with Shahrban now on the coat and Shahrazad a respected scholar, expert in all the principles of law and religion, and the canons of medicine and the prolegomena of science, her own woman with her own income – the merest of mere lovers, bound in ritual of retribution superintended by The Great Pander, still quietly confident of irrenuncibility so long as there persists in this Ape that has Forgot the pomp of genetic immortality; whereby he proposes to become, not just the first and the only man in all this world, but also the best; till finally, old and separately domiciled, observing the piety of silence, meeting only at weddings and funerals and sixtieth birthday parties – all hope of understanding absconding but abiding in all good cheer and pleasures – there came to them at last the Destroyer of delights and the Sunderer of societies, the Plunderer of palaces and the Caterer to cemeteries, the Garnerer of graves and the Orphaner of children, the Peopler of the mausolea; to wit, the Cup of Death, the Murderer of great and small, and Praise be to She who Comforteth Man and Blessings on Her Sinless Sons, but Glory be to He who Hath for Partner None and in whose Hand are the Keys to the Seen and the Unseen!

Wassalaam

Tammat

Salaam Chishti Khwaja Hazrat Nizamuddin Awliya

Salaam Finan Wali Allah

Salaam Colman Wali Allah

AUTHOR'S NOTE

Prompted by the Cronulla riot of 2005 at which I was present, this novel elaborates the frame tale of the *Arabian Nights* ('purely Persian perfunctorily Arabised' – Burton). There is no consensus on the transliteration of Arabic: a degree of textual inconsistency (Azan, adhan? Omar, 'Umar? Qadi, Kadi?), perhaps not inappropriate to a yarn set at the turn of the second century of the Hijrah, will be apparent to an expert. I have introduced coffee (mentioned twelve times in *The Nights*, the oldest tales of which appear to date from the eighth century AD, but which assumed present *form* only in the thirteenth) though coffee did not replace wine in Al-Islam before AD circa 1550.

Especially helpful to me as secondary sources were non-fictional works by Leo Wieger, Arnold Toynbee, Cyril Glasse, Henry Corbin, Svat Soucek, Maulana Mohammed Ali, George St George, Marco Polo/Rustichello (Yule-Cordier), Jean Guitton, Colin Thubron, Susan Whitfield, Frances Wood, Roger Collins, Gerald Brenan, Charles E. Hill, W. Y. Evans-Wentz, S. A. Nigosian, R. C. C. Fynes, N. J. Dawood,

Uinseann O Maidin, Tim Gordon, Ben Zion Bokser, Michael Flecker, Fred Pearce and Jason Elliot.

Thanks to the National Library of Australia for a 2008 Harold White Fellowship, funded from the Ray Mathew and Eva Kollsman Trust, that made possible a perlection of Sir Richard Burton's seventeen-volume *magnum opus, Alf Laylah Wa Laylah: The Book of the Thousand Nights and a Night, being a plain and literal translation of the Arabian Nights Entertainments, with introduction, explanatory notes on the manners and customs of Moslem men and a terminal essay on the history of The Nights* (illustrated Benares edition 1885–8, printed by 'the Burton Club' – aka Oliver Nutcott, Farleigh Road, Stoke Newington – for private subscribers only, limited to a thousand sets and including *Supplemental Nights, with notes anthropological and explanatory*), held in the National Library of Australia rare book collection; and to the Literature Board of the Australia Council, the Australian Government's Arts Funding and Advisory Body, for a New Work grant during which this elaboration of the frame tale was commenced. The illustration of the Jinni (artist unknown) is taken from Burton's *Alf Laylah Wa Laylah*. Particular thanks, for extraction and reproduction, to National Library of Australia staff Loui Seselja, Margy Burn, Marie-Louise Ayres and Dereta Lennon.

My premise is that a major flashpoint now exists between (fundamentalist) Islamic man and (anti-Christian) secular Western woman. In 1885 Burton could observe (*Alf Laylah Wa Laylah*, IX, 304, footnote):

> 'Practically throughout the civilised world there are only two ways of treating women. Moslems keep them close, defend them from all kinds of temptations and if they go wrong kill them. Christians place them upon a pedestal, the observed of all

> observers, expose them to every danger and if they fall, accuse and abuse them instead of themselves ... I shall have more to say upon this curious subject, the treatment of women who can be thoroughly guarded only by two things, firstly their hearts and secondly by the "Spanish Padlock".'

Burton, though a Qadiri Sufi, could scarcely have envisaged Cronulla 2005.

Jean Guitton might have. Writing in *Great Heresies and Church Councils* (1963) he observes:

> 'The Arabs have been able to avoid all forms of rapprochement with Christian humanism and industrial technology, with this Christian and lay society where the Church is separate from the State and woman about to emancipate herself; so full of ambiguities in conduct, and in the variety of meaning it gives to such words as "liberty" "equality" or "love" ... Islam could guard itself against the practicing atheism of the West only by opposing everything that came from the West: all contacts with the Occident were considered deadly. Christianity, which opposed the summary and cruel faith of Islam, was deadly. And deadly also was the anti-Christianism of the West, which, had it triumphed, would have forced Islam to stop worshipping God. This resistance in two directions compelled Islam to reject *en bloc* this ambiguous West which is both Christian and anti-Christian and blind to its internal contradiction. If Islam is as hostile to one as to the other, it is yet more hostile, and rightly so, to the admixture.'

LEGEND

Shahrban (Farsi): City-defender – used in the Breslau edition
Shahrazad: City-freer. Scheherazade in older editions
Dinazad: Religion-freer – Richardson edition

Jacket calligraphy from a ghazal by Hafiz